Draconda and Others

John Martin Leahy

DRACONDA AND OTHERS

The Complete Weird Stories, Volume 1

Edited by S. T. Joshi

Sarnath Press • Seattle

Cover art by Allen Koszowski.

Copyright © 2024 by Sarnath Press

Published by Sarnath Press, Seattle, WA.

All rights reserved.

Contents

Introduction 7
Draconda 13
The Voices from the Cliff 234
The Voice of Bills 248
In Amundsen's Tent 265
The Isle of the Fairy Morgana 282
Bibliography 303

Introduction

Very little is known of the life of John Martin Leahy (1886–1967), although some facts that may shed light on his work have recently emerged.[1] Leahy was born on 16 May 1886 in Newcastle, King County, Washington State, the son of Michael Joseph Leahy and Elizabeth Ann "Lizzie" Martin Leahy. John's father was the son of Irish immigrants; his mother's family was from Kentucky; John's middle name Martin was taken from his mother's maiden name. He was the eldest son, and three sisters (Katie, Mary, and Margaret) and two brothers (Irvin and Jim) followed him.

Census data show Leahy as living in Newcastle as a toddler in 1890; by 1910 he is found in Seattle, where he lived with his family; his father was employed at the Northern Pacific Railroad at this time. Curiously, Leahy's own occupation was listed as basket maker. The 1920 census lists his occupation as stenographer; in the 1940 and 1950 censuses his occupation is given as either "writer fiction" [sic] or "freelance writer," although by this time Leahy was in fact writing—or, at any rate, publishing—nothing. In 1942 his World War II registration card gives his place of employment as Puget Basket & Package Company in Seattle. Leahy never married. An undated newspaper article by Doug Margerson states that "John became an eccentric and a recluse, living out his life in a cabin on Lake Sammamish, surrounded by books and the watercolors he taught himself to paint."

Leahy published four short stories and three serialized novels, all in *Weird Tales* except for one of the novels. His skills as an artist paid dividends in one instance, as he was the cover artist on the Fantasy Publishing Company's reprint of *Drome* (1952). But this modest body of work—included in its entirety in this volume—is far above the level of routine pulp fiction.

It may well be the case that Leahy's three novels—*Draconda* (*Weird Tales,* November 1923–May/June/July 1924), *The Living Death* (*Science and Invention,* October 1924–May 1925), and *Drome* (*Weird Tales,* January–May 1927)—are

---

1. For many of these details I am deeply indebted to the research of Sunni K Brock.

variations on the same basic idea: the notion of a lost race of human or quasi-human beings, either on this planet or on Venus. *Draconda* is in many ways the most interesting of these, at least from a philosophical perspective. Here, the scientist Henry Quainfan has found a way to get to Venus. He is convinced that Venus is inhabited and believes that the surface of the planet is "cool and equable." This was not, at the time, as preposterous as it now sounds. There was much speculation as to the surface conditions of the planet, some astronomers believing that Venus was steamy and swampy like our own Palaeozoic age, others believing that it was a barren desert blown by dust storms; still others thought that the planet was covered with huge oceans of carbonated water or even with hot oil. It was only in 1956 that radio waves showed the surface temperature to be a minimum of 570□ Fahrenheit, while in 1968 radar and radio observations at last confirmed the temperature to be 900□ Fahrenheit and the surface atmospheric pressure to be at least ninety times that of the earth.

In any event, Quainfan and his friends Rider Farnermain and Morgan St. Cloud undertake the voyage in a vessel called the *Hornet*. Landing on Venus, they find evidence of creatures they are accustomed to seeing on Earth, including the footprints of "a naked human foot." Eventually they come upon an entire civilization of human creatures, led by a beautiful queen named Draconda. Incredibly, she speaks English. How can this be?

Throughout the early parts of the novel, Leahy's characters conduct a philosophical/religious debate over the implications of the existence of an intelligent species on another planet. Farnermain is apparently an orthodox Christian—indeed, one who is somewhat old-fashioned in his views. Quainfan accuses him of believing that "the Universe was made for man." Quainfan himself is a "materialist." The existence of humans (and other creatures known on Earth) on Venus triggers a discussion of the validity of the theory of evolution. Farnermain throws down a gauntlet: "Where now is your evolution? Where now is your Darwinian pipe-dream?" Quainfan is, indeed, initially taken aback; when he sees what appears to be a lion, he bluntly states, "All my evolutionary beliefs are shattered." Later he acknowledges that the "Almighty" placed human beings on both Earth and Venus for some unknown purpose. But this discussion is rendered null and void, and the truth of evolution vindicated, when Draconda ultimately explains (not entirely plausibly) how she did come from Earth, and also how she could be both only twenty-five years old on Venus but a hundred and twenty-five years old on Earth. (Whether her explanation sufficiently accounts for the presence on Venus of the other members of her civilization is not at all clear.)

Religion in Draconda's realm also plays a factor in the novel. When the terrestrial explorers first come upon the people of Venus, they are conducting a barbaric religious rite involving human sacrifice. The explorers break up the ceremony and save a young woman, Mynine, who was about to be killed. But her love for Quainfan turns to hate when he falls in love with Draconda; and Mynine thereafter leads a campaign to overthrow Draconda. The final segments of the novel present an exciting account of the conflict between Draconda's forces and Mynine's (aided by a high-priest, Sallysherib, who also harbors hostility toward the queen). Leahy repeatedly cites the battle of Cannae (in which the Carthaginian general Hannibal, in 216 B.C.E., defeated the Roman army by a pincer movement), as Draconda's forces triumph in the same manner. *Draconda* is the longest of Leahy's three novels and probably the richest in its intellectual underpinnings and dramatic pacing.

The Living Death appeared in Hugo Gernsback's *Science and Invention,* a proto-science fiction magazine that began publication in 1913 under the title *The Electric Experimenter;* in 1920 the title changed to *Science and Invention* (this had previously been the subtitle of the magazine), and it ran under this title until it ceased publication in 1931. It was in fact predominantly a nonfiction magazine, and what fiction it published more focused on scientific gadgetry than Gernsback's *Amazing Stories* (1926f.). *The Living Death* has a quasi-scientific premise in the scientist Darwin Frontenac's invention of a means of restoring life to creatures who are in a state of suspended animation. Whether this can be done with human beings is an untested assumption, but Frontenac has a chance to conduct such an experiment when a colleague, Stanley Livingstone, reports on an expedition to the Antarctic that was undertaken on the belief that "there may be an unknown race somewhere in the heart of Antarctica." Livingstone is well aware that the climate of the Antarctic continent was once tropical, but he is nonetheless astonished when he and his expedition come upon a realm they call the Gardens of Paradise. But the exploration of this unknown land turns ominous when Livingstone finds one of his party killed—his head severed, and his body nowhere to be seen. Later Livingstone comes upon the body of a beautiful young woman encased in ice. She must be at least 300,000 years old. Can she be alive? Livingstone comes back and, when he hears of Frontenac's invention, implores him to go back to the Antarctic and rescue the ice-encased woman.

Frontenac, along with his colleague Bond McQuestion, do exactly that. Early in the expedition Livingstone himself succumbs to a killer whale. The explorers also encounter hideous harpy-like entities as well as a "huge bear-man."

But of course they are successful in bringing back the young woman (whom they dub Sleeping Beauty) and bringing her to life.

Drome takes place, somewhat implausibly, at—or, rather, *under*—Mt. Rainier, where again an entire unknown civilization is found. The scenario is largely identical to that of *Draconda*. In 1858, an expedition to the mountain—the tallest in the continental United States, at more than 14,000 feet—had found evidence of human beings, as well as of some hideous shapeless monster, underneath the mountain. Now, Milton Rhodes recreates the journey, as he learns that a recent death on the mountain appears to confirm the accounts of the earlier expedition. Rhodes and his companion, Bill Carter, find both a lovely young woman and a batlike monster, whom they dub "the angel and the demon." The "angel" proves to be Drorathusa, a priestess of the underground civilization. She and others of her clan lead Rhodes and Carter to their city, Lellolando, which has a population of 15,000 (!). Later they come to the capital, called the Golden City, where they meet Queen Lepraylya. Further adventures ensue, somewhat along the lines of *Draconda*.

By the time *Drome* appeared, Leahy had established a foothold in *Weird Tales* with the short stories "The Voices in the Cliff" (May 1925) and "The Voice of Bills" (October 1926). After *Drome,* Leahy placed "In Amundsen's Tent" (January 1928) and "The Isle of the Fairy Morgana" (February 1928) in the magazine. Like his novels, these stories share some salient characteristics. "The Voices in the Cliff" features a know-it-all detective, Guy Oxford, who manages to explain how he saw the murder of a woman by her husband, who threw her off a cliff, even though Oxford was on a ship 80 miles out at sea. Oxford is insistent that there is nothing supernatural in the overall scenario. Oxford returns in "The Isle of the Fairy Morgana" to pressure another murderer to confess to his crime by an approximately similar means. "The Voice of Bills" is yet another murder tale that suggests the supernatural only to explain it away at the end.

Leahy's most striking short story—and most celebrated work overall—is "In Amundsen's Tent." Again set in the Antarctic, the tale is in essence a warning not to explore the Antarctic any further, lest subsequent explorers meet the fate of Robert Drumgold, whose diary forms the bulk of the text. Drumgold's account tells of an encounter with a nameless and tantalizingly undescribed entity that is suggested to have emerged from outer space; at one point the human protagonists even speculate that the entity is "hibernating." Dogs react with terror and loathing at the entity. Early in the tale Drumgold engages in a kind of cosmic speculation, wondering whether the earth or the universe is really "made for man": "May not there be other beings—yes, even on this very earth of ours—more wonderful—yes, and more terrible too—than he?"

It should be evident from this synopsis that "In Amundsen's Tent" was at least a partial influence upon Lovecraft's short novel *At the Mountains of Madness*, written in 1931. The premise of both stories is the warning against exploring a realm that harbors unthinkable horrors. The notion of some hibernating alien species is strikingly similar to that of Lovecraft's Old Ones, who are found by human explorers in a state of cryogenic suspended animation in a cave in Antarctica. Lovecraft commented on the story in a letter to August Derleth (December 13, 1927—the issue had appeared about a month before its cover date), remarking: "'In Amundsen's Tent' was *the* story of the issue, though the style is poor—as always with Leahy." That last comment makes clear that Lovecraft read Leahy's previous work in *Weird Tales*, although it is not clear that he read *The Living Death*, also set in Antarctica.

Certain crudities or deficiencies in Leahy's narrative might have inspired Lovecraft to see if he could do better. In particular, Leahy's story ends up being something of a tease, in that he refuses to describe the entity in the tent in any way aside from suggesting its extraterrestrial origin. Lovecraft, in the early stages of his quasi-science fiction phase, made sure to depict the Old Ones with meticulous precision. He avoids any sense of anticlimax in this clinical description because he withholds the true horror of the story—the protoplasmic shoggoth—until the end. And of course Lovecraft vastly expands on the cosmic implications of his narrative, supplying a detailed account of the origin of the Old Ones in the remotest reaches of the galaxy, their advent to earth, and their battles with other alien races, such as the "Cthulhu spawn" and the fungi from Yuggoth (from "The Whisperer in Darkness").

After his story in the February 1928 issue of *Weird Tales*, Leahy fell silent literarily. Why this was the case—he was only in his early forties at this time—is unknown. He did do the cover art for *Drome* when it was published in book form in 1952 by the Fantasy Publishing Co., but that is the last we hear of him. His two other serialized novels have not been reissued in print; aside from "In Amundsen's Tent," which has been reprinted on numerous occasions, his short stories are also little-known.

Leahy was certainly above average as a writer for the pulp magazines, in spite of certain annoying stylistic tics (most notably his use of such affected archaisms as "'twas," "forsooth," and so on) and a generally hysterical and flamboyant style that seeks to wring as much tension out of a given situation or episode as possible.

But there is no question that his novels and tales are entertaining and even at times thought-provoking, and that is enough to justify their reprinting in this omnibus.

—S. T. JOSHI

Draconda

> "We cannot for a moment suppose that our own little planet is the only one throughout the whole universe on which may be found the fruits of civilization, warm firesides, friendships, the desire to penetrate the mysteries of creation."
> —Simon Newcomb.

CHAPTER 1
HER PICTURE

There was a smile in those cool grey eyes of his.

"But that is sheer nonsense!" I exclaimed.

Henry Quainfan laughed.

"You think so, Rider?" he said.

"I *know* so!"

"You are so often sure! But you are wrong, old *tillicum;* you are wrong!"

"Now, look here," said I, "let's get this thing straight. Though competent authorities (among whom, it seems, you are to be numbered) assure me that it is possible, yet this love-at-first-sight business seems to me—"

"There you go!" he smiled. "That isn't what I meant."

I stared at him.

"Elucidate," said I.

"That there is such a thing as love at first sight is, I believe, indisputable. But that isn't what I made reference to; it was to the vision—the mind photograph, as it were—that the man and the woman in this romance had of each other."

"But everybody has a *dream* mate," said I, who was becoming more mystified than ever.

"Yes," Henry Quainfan nodded; "but that mate is vague—as the novelist says. That mate cannot be described at all. Yes, everyone has a dream mate. But this is the point, Rider; can everyone tell the color of that dream one's eyes and hair, for instance? I should say not."

"So should I," I told him.

"But to return to this man and woman. They were different; each knew the color of the dream lover's eyes and hair; each had a picture such as you and I have of some person we have known well; it was, indeed, as if they had known each other—had known and loved each other ere they came into this world."

"That is all very well," said I. "It was. But there's something that you forget."

"What?" he asked.

"This: it's only a story."

"Rider," he laughed, "do you know what you are?"

I told him I didn't.

"Pachycephalic."

"I'm glad it's nothing worse. But," said I, "proceed with this erotic—I mean tommyrotic—business."

"Very well. These *dream lovers* were different; the woman for long believed that she would one day meet the man whose picture had, in some mysterious way, been stamped upon her mind, stamped so plainly that she could even tell the color of his hair and eyes, and the man believed that he would one day meet his picture woman as a real flesh and blood woman.

"But, as she grew older, the woman slowly, reluctantly (and never quite fully) came to believe that he whose likeness was stamped upon her mind did not exist at all. Mind you, Rider, she never fully believed this. She tried to make herself believe it, but in her heart of hearts there was always a doubt."

"I remember," said I. "But *that* is, I believe, more or less true of every woman—and every man."

"Maybe it is," he nodded. "But as for *this* man, he never doubted; he was true to his dream woman to the end. But she married, they met, and of course the moment they saw each other they loved—and she fainted, and all those things happened."

"But confound it!" I exclaimed.

"Well?" he queried sweetly.

"What's the idea? Surely you don't take this piece of fiction—this moonshine in the mustard-pot—seriously?"

"Seriously? No," said he. "And yet—"

He was looking at me with an odd expression in his eyes. What in the world was he driving at?

"But let me tell you something, Rider," he said. "To no one have I ever told it, and I know that it will not go farther. It is this:

"I am like the two persons in this romance!"

"What?" I cried.

"It is a fact; I am like them," he told me. "Upon my mind is stamped a woman's picture, stamped just as those pictures were stamped upon theirs. Rider, it is as if I had known her, had loved her in some other world."

I stared at him. Where on earth had he got it?

"Do you think," I asked him, "that you will ever meet the lady?"

He shook his head.

"No," he smiled. "Being a Darwinian, how can I believe that the woman whose likeness is stamped upon my mind is a real flesh and blood woman? She is nothing. And yet that picture, Rider! As I have said, it is just as if I had known her, had loved her in a preterrestrial life. I see her now."

He shut his eyes. A brief silence ensued.

"I see her now just as you can see your father and mother, your brothers and sister. Her hair is black, black as the raven's plumage; her eyes are black, too, and her complexion olive; and she is beautiful, inexpressibly beautiful. Never have I seen a woman with beauty such as hers. It alone would prove that this mysterious picture of mine is of no real woman; her beauty transcends that of the daughters of men."

He opened his eyes, looked at me and laughed softly.

"Perhaps you think that I am a fool, Rider; but what I have just told you is the truth, the whole truth and nothing but the truth. It is even so. If I were not *scientific*, I could believe that we lived and loved in some other world and that somewhere, some time we would meet in this—or some other. But it can never be."

"The explanation?" I queried.

"I have none. Whence came her picture, I do not know. Something abnormal stamped it upon my cerebrine cells, that is all; and it is nothing, and it signifies nothing. And now note the paradox, Rider—of a truth I am ashamed to say it; in my mind I am *sure* that this woman of mine is nothing, as sure as I am that certain of our progenitors were apes and that others were slimy things that had crawled up out of the slime of the sea—"

"Then you are not very sure," said I.

He smiled a little.

"Though in my mind I am sure of this," he went on, "yet in my heart of hearts at times I *am not sure*. At such times it seems that there come to me faint memories of another and far more beautiful world—come as faint strains of music come when one does not know whether he is awake or asleep. These times are when I hear certain pieces of music and sometimes when I look upon grand scenery.

"But hah! This is foolishness. Coming as it does from an evolutionist, it is worse than foolishness, and so now there is an end of it."

He turned his look toward the fireplace and sat gazing into the flames, a strange, shadowy expression in his eyes.

For a long time there was silence.

Shadows swayed and flickered in the dim light of the great room as though swung and shook by spirit hands; and the Cartesian devil there on the table stared at me with that glassy, mocking smile.

But that devil was not alone. There was an angel beside him. The angel, though, was not looking at me; her eyes were on Henry Quainfan.

And as I gazed, a strange thing happened.

It was as though I was in that abysmal darkness which lies beyond the farthest star, that awful night which hides the answer to all man's doubts and questionings; and of a sudden I saw a vision there—a vision angelic, ineffable, blinding.

I came to earth with a start.

My fancy had transformed that creature in her glass prison into a vision wondrous beyond all speech.

I smiled at this momentary phantasm of mine.

And yet—it was as though I had caught a glimpse of the Ultimate Mystery.

CHAPTER 2
"I'VE GOT AN IDEA!"

Of a sudden Henry Quainfan broke the silence.

"By the way, Rider, I didn't tell you of that accident (if I may so call it) which I had the other day in the laboratory, did I?"

I shook my head.

"It was a strange thing," he went on, "the strangest thing in many a long day! You know, I was carrying on some experiments with—"

He ended suddenly and sat staring into the flames.

Now, I knew that he had been experimenting, but what those experiments were, I had not the slightest idea. That he was deep in radio-activity and much interested in certain problems of astronomy (a science in which, strange to say, I had never taken any interest) I well knew; but I had no means of telling in what direction his experiments might tend.

Only a day or two before, he had explained to me that marvelous discovery, "negative gravity," or radiation pressure—mathematically deducted by Clerk Maxwell and proved by the Russian Lebedew and the Americans Nichols and Hull.

It was this, Henry had explained, which drives the tail of a comet away from the sun—a phenomenon which had always been a mystery to astronomers and physicists. Fictionists had airily (and mysteriously) overcome gravitation in order to land the super-inventor hero on the Moon or Mars, and readers had accepted their wild fancies with a smile; and yet here was the sun's terrific gravitational pull overcome before their very eyes.

Whereas gravitation acts on the mass, radiation pressure acts on the surface area. If a body—the earth, for instance—was reduced to a cloud of dust, the surface of the earth-stuff would, it is obvious, be incalculably increased; but the mass of it would not be changed at all. If the particles fell below a certain size, the light-pressure would overcome the pull of gravitation, and that which had been the earth would be blown away into space.

All this I understood perfectly well. But when he launched into a little lecture on molecules, atoms and corpuscles; energy corpuscular, atomic and molecular; to say nothing of cathode, ultra-violet and infra-red rays, alpha, beta and gamma rays, mysterious somethings called ions, negative and positive charges and goodness only knows what else besides—well, it all was very strange and wonderful, but I could not make head or tail of it.

And then he went on to explain that the atom itself—instead of being, as scientists had supposed, the smallest particle of matter—is in reality *a solar system*. In this space so inconceivably tiny, the planets (the corpuscles or electrons) are flying around and around the atomic sun, and with prodigious velocities. This orbital movement of the electrons it is which sets going the ether disturbances which are called radiant energy. Those electrons, said Henry Quainfan, that propagate the ether waves which, on striking matter, produce violent light, make about 800,000,000,000,000 revolutions in a *single second* of time!

And right there I called a halt.

"That will do!" I told him. "That's got Alice in Wonderland done to a frazzle!"

"Of course it has," said he. "The wonders of science—"

"Is that science?" I wanted to know.

Henry Quainfan said that it was.

"But eight hundred trillion times in a second?" I exclaimed. "Nobody ever saw that!"

"Of course nobody ever *saw* it," he smiled. "Nobody ever saw a molecule even."

"Poor Alice!" I murmured.

"It is in these molecules, atoms and corpuscles, however," went on Henry, "that the great discoveries of the future will be made. Somewhere in them lies the key to gravitation, to the mystery of matter itself, space and the stars, and—who knows?—maybe of the mind and death."

"Man will never unlock that door!" said I.

"There are other ways of opening doors," smiled Henry Quainfan: "he may pick the lock. Don't be too sure, Rider. For instance, Comte declared that the constitution of the stars must forever remain unknown, and then came spectrum analysis, which has made visible stars that man has never seen with the eye, and in all probability never will see, and told us of what the stars are made and even the rate of approach or recession. Lord Kelvin too, proved—with mathematics—that man could never fly, and yet today he is doing that very thing.

"So don't be too sure, Rider. The scientist has eyes besides those in his head. Leverrier and Adams couldn't see Neptune, but they told the astronomers where to point the telescope, and there was a new world gleaming in the field."

"But that," put in Morgan St. Cloud, "instead of being, as is often stated, the greatest triumph of mathematical astronomy, was in reality a happy accident. Bode's law breaks down with Neptune; the elements of the planet's orbit which Leverrier and Adams had deduced were away off."

"Certainly," nodded Henry. "It was a half billion miles nearer the sun than it should have been, and its mass was only about half of that predicted—and yet the planet was found within less than a degree of the spot indicated by Leverrier."

But St. Cloud shook his head.

"How many things that scientists trumpet as triumphs," said he, "are in reality happy accidents, how often that which is stated as a fact is nothing but surmise! Why, our old friend Captain Lemuel Gulliver, of romantic memory, scored a greater triumph than did Adams and Leverrier!"[1]

---

1. "They have likewise discovered," Gulliver tells us in the Voyage to Laputa, "two lesser stars, or satellites, which revolve about Mars; whereof the innermost is distant from the centre of the primary planet exactly three of his diameters, and the outermost five; the former revolves in the space of ten hours, and the latter in twenty-one and a half."

This bit of Gulliver's is the most astonishing thing of its kind on record. For the moons of Mars were not discovered until the opposition of 1877 (celebrated, also, by Schiaparelli's discovery of the famous and mysterious canali) when Professor Asaph Hall found them with the great twenty-six-inch telescope of the Washington Observatory.—R. F.

That, by the way, was like St. Cloud.

But to return to that fire-lit library.

Of a sudden Henry Quainfan straightened up in his chair. He made an odd exclamation and stared at me across the table.

"Good heavens!" he exclaimed.

"What is it now?" I asked him.

"Why didn't I think of *that* before?"

Certainly I couldn't tell him.

"Blockhead, mole!" he cried.

"I know I am, but this is—"

"Me!" he cried, bringing his clenched hand down on the table.

The angel and the devil danced a little, the latter moving so that the curvature of the glass distorted his grin into one strangely grotesque, and more mocking than ever. And still his look was upon me.

"But I see it now!" Henry Quainfan cried. "Rider—"

"Yes?" I suggested.

"I've got an idea!" he exclaimed.

"As though you and ideas were strangers!" I smiled.

He remained silent, plunged in thought, and I fell to wondering what discovery was going to be added now to that amazing list of his, little dreaming how momentous that discovery was to be to him, Morgan St. Cloud and myself—of that awful, unimaginable thing it was to bring to St. Cloud.

CHAPTER 3
ST. CLOUD

With Henry Quainfan lived Morgan St. Cloud, his assistant. There were, by the way, two servants—Buttermore, the cook, and Blimper, who was everything from a sort of *valet de chambre* to helper in the workshop when that was necessary.

And now that I come to Morgan St. Cloud, I find my pen hesitant. How can I, with marks on paper—or in any other way for that matter—paint a portrait of Morgan St. Cloud. I despair of conveying, in any adequate manner, that picture of this dark, courtly, magnetic and mysterious man which haunts my memory in so terrible a manner, and will haunt it to my dying hour.

Mysterious I have called him, and he was. And yet here again I grope in vain for words. I cannot give you an idea of that strange quality in his manner, in his dark eyes, in that dark smile of his even, which was always so puzzling —mysterious.

I give it up.

He was about fifty years of age, and strikingly handsome. He drew women's eyes as a flame draws moths. Of his past we knew virtually nothing. On that he had chosen to maintain an almost utter silence, and Henry Quainfan had not pushed inquiries.

That he was a son of Fortune fallen on evil days was obvious; but more than that we did not know.

Of his misfortune I never heard him complain. His philosophy in this seemed to be that it is better to have a bare foot than no foot at all. And this was remarkable in that he was apt to kick up a rumpus over nothing. There are men who can be heard a half block if they cannot find a cuff-button, but would await the end of the world with equanimity. St. Cloud was something like that—a man of remarkable strength in some ways and in others of lamentable and strange weaknesses.

I have often wondered at that mystery of chance which brought these two, Henry Quainfan and Morgan St. Cloud, together—these two of all men!

And yet *was* it chance? Who can say? Perhaps after all it was Fate. For my part, I cannot help thinking that as I look back on the awful drama.

At any rate, Fate must have chuckled, and long too, at the terrible joke. Fate makes no jokes, and laughs at none, that are not terrible.

"If the Almighty had not made her so," as I once heard Draconda say, "she would go mad."

For a time I sat there looking into the flames and thinking. When my eyes turned again to Henry Quainfan it was to find him engrossed in calculations of some sort, computing in that long red notebook which he had with him always.

It was then that the purr of a motor reached my ears. The sound grew swiftly louder. Glancing through one of the windows, I saw the bushes and driveway lighted up, and knew that St. Cloud had come.

In a few minutes he entered. So engrossed, however, was Henry Quainfan in his problem that he remained utterly unaware of St. Cloud's presence in the room.

"Ah, Rider," said St. Cloud, "I thought I'd find you here."

He drew a chair up towards the fire a little and seated himself, his dark look lingering for a few moments on the golden-haired man there in the great rocker, utterly unconscious of St. Cloud, myself—everything save his great problem.

"Dropped in on my way back," went on St. Cloud, "and your man told me you had gone out. Hadn't taken the auto, though, he said, so I knew that you hadn't gone far."

For a time he chatted on, then of a sudden paused and for a little space watched Henry Quainfan.

"In deep," observed St. Cloud.

I nodded.

"Doesn't even know I've arrived," said St. Cloud. "He'll soon be as bad as old Sir Isaac chasing the falling moon. Wonder what it is now?"

I shrugged my shoulders.

"Heaven knows. Seems to be *some* idea, but what it is about is more than I can even guess at."

"Maybe, now," smiled St. Cloud, "he's figuring out how to separate the positive sphere—funny thing that, Rider, that positive sphere—from the atom. He'll probably do it—with mathematics. You can prove anything with mathematics, Rider; but the validity of your assumptions—ah, there's the rub."

"But what's that?" I asked.

"What?"

"That thing called a positive sphere."

"No one knows," St. Cloud told me airily, waving a hand. "Henry was coming to it the other day when you interrupted the lecture."

"But eight hundred trillion times in a *second!*" I exclaimed.

"Well, it's so, Rider," St. Cloud declared. "And some go even faster. Now, you know me: you know that, when it comes to theories, assumptions, hypotheses, and so on, that I'm from Missouri—and yet Science has got Romance knocked into a cocked hat."

"But so much of it, if I may presume to judge, must be sheer guess-work!" I objected.

"It is. And worse than that even. But so much of it isn't. Yes, Keats was wrong, all wrong, Rider, poetasters to the contrary notwithstanding."

"Was he?" said I, wondering how.

"He was," nodded St. Cloud. "He declared that Science would kill Fancy, Romance, Imagination—I've forgotten the exact word; but he was wrong, Rider, all wrong, was Keats. Imagination! Good heavens, there is so much imagination that the scientist has a time of it to keep his feet firmly planted on the earth."

"That's precisely what I thought."

"But you don't think it in the right way," he declared.

"If Mr. Scientist would only stay on the earth!" I told him. "But that's just it. He is never satisfied, indeed doesn't seem to be a scientist, until he is mounted on some mathematical or some-other-kind-of Rocinante, galloping down the Milky Way and tilting with cosmic windmills!"

St. Cloud smiled.

"Come back to earth, Rider."

Henry Quainfan, by the way, was still engrossed in his calculations.

"There is something in that, though," St. Cloud admitted. "But all the same, Rider, you are wrong, as wrong as Keats, and—I know you'll pardon me—for the same reason."

"But all this theory!" I said. "However, you mentioned a mysterious something called a positive sphere?"

"That too is theory," said St. Cloud. "It isn't that even, but only an hypothesis. How shall I put it, though? Well, when we went to school, we learned in physics that matter was found in three conditions—solid, liquid and gaseous. Didn't we?"

I said we did.

"Well, it isn't. There are *four*."

"Four!" I exclaimed.

"Four," nodded St. Cloud. "The fourth is found in the cathode stream—but not only there. The cathode stream doesn't consist of ordinary light, but of particles of matter that are neither solid, liquid nor gaseous."

"Then what on earth are they?"

"Nothing but charges of negative electricity. Those are the electrons or corpuscles. But the problem is simply this: that mysterious sphere which holds the electrons in their orbits is *positive* electricity, and *that* has never been separated from atoms of matter. As we have seen, the negative has."

"But why on earth should anybody want to separate it?" said I.

"Rider," smiled St. Cloud, "you are as bad as Keats! Why, for one thing, to see what would happen. As Henry remarked the other day, it is there that the great discoveries of the future lie. The Crookes tube was only a plaything, and yet it gave humanity the X-ray. Much of this wondering and investigating may strike one as being idle, and yet it may unlock many and—who knows?—terrible secrets."

At this moment Henry Quainfan looked up. His eyes lingered on St. Cloud with a curious, questioning and yet far-away look in them.

"Back, Morgan?" said he, and it was as though his thoughts were far away.

"Back," smiled the dark man. "Back for some time."

"For some time? I'm becoming infernally absent-minded!" exclaimed Henry Quainfan.

"I was telling Rider you'd soon be as bad as old Newton."

St. Cloud turned to me.

"Do you know what he did the other day?"

I didn't.

"He thought that the mustard-pot was the sugar-bowl!"

St. Cloud laughed.

"You should have seen Buttermore! That's not so bad, though—is it?—as that time he went out in the downpour holding a golf club up in the air! Ha, ha, he thought he'd get hold of an umbrella!"

"Laugh away," smiled Henry Quainfan. "But I have an idea that Morgan St. Cloud may do worse than mistake a golf club for an umbrella before we are done with this."

"This?" St Cloud queried.

Henry Quainfan nodded.

"For I've got an idea—if I may say so, the most wonderful of ideas. We've got some stiff work ahead of us now, Morgan, I fancy. If I hadn't been a blockhead, I'd have seen it before!"

"*Fifth* state of matter—maybe," proffered St. Cloud.

"Perhaps," smiled Henry Quainfan. "And how would you like it in the fourth dimension?"

"Lead on, Macduff!" exclaimed the other, smiling that dark St. Cloudian smile.

CHAPTER 4
DONE

"Simply had to break away!"

Thus spoke St. Cloud as he took a seat before my fireplace. And indeed his dark features bore the impress of that intense application which had followed (for these many days now) the inception of Quainfan's idea.

Night had just closed in, black and stormy. The wind was growling and roaring and flinging the rain angrily against the windows.

"Great Jupiter Ammon!" St. Cloud exclaimed. "This thing will bowl me over yet. How on earth does he stand it?"

I wondered that myself.

"How is it coming on?" I asked.

His hand made a cabalistic sweep.

"Oh, it's coming on! It's coming!" said St. Cloud. "The only thing is this: where is it going to end?"

He turned his dark look upon me.

"This is a mysterious business, Rider," said he gravely. "Henry has done things over there to make a fellow's hair stand on end!"

"It's like *that?*" I exclaimed.

"Worse!" declared St. Cloud. "It's uncanny—some of it. Creepy! You wouldn't believe me if I told you some of the things I've seen over there."

I made an interrogative exclamation.

"I know you wouldn't, Rider," St. Cloud declared. "You'd think I was losing my wits."

A strange expression settled on his face, and for a time he sat brooding in silence.

Of a sudden he made a wild gesture.

"But it's all Greek to me, Rider! I'm in the dark—Cimmerian darkness. I'm there, I see it done, I even help do things; but I know no more about it, or to what it tends, than I know about the way the ladies on Venus do up their hair."

The touch of levity in his manner vanished, vanished as suddenly as it had come.

"At times, Rider," said he, "I am afraid."

"Afraid?"

"Afraid," he nodded. "And I say it without shame."

"Of what?" I asked him quickly.

"That's it. I don't know of what. But I've seen him do it."

I looked at him inquiringly, but he only gazed at me with a curious expression in his dark eyes.

What was it, I wondered, that he wanted to tell me?

"The mystery in your words," I observed, "would incline one to the belief that there is, after all, something in these wild tales that are going around, and have even got into the press."

"And there is," said St. Cloud. "Of course, the most of it is sheer nonsense, but there is foundation for some of it just the same. For instance, there's that gull story."

I nodded.

"I was going to ask if there was anything in that."

"There is. That's one of the stories there is something in."

"Brooks was telling me about it the day before yesterday," said I. "You know, there was something rather curious in his manner when he mentioned Henry Quainfan; he seems to think that Henry is a danger to the community—indeed, that he has leagued himself with some of the powers of darkness. He was amusedly indignant, was Brooks, about these mysterious happenings. He said something about tax-payers and dangers to the community concomitant to the presence in it of scientific investigators—though I'm afraid Brooks didn't use quite so flattering a term as that."

"And the gulls?" queried St. Cloud.

"It was like this. His wife, Brooks said, had her eyes on them at the very instant that it happened—though I must say that Mrs. Brooks in the role of a gullologist is itself something of a mystery—but the birds had attracted her attention by the peculiar sharpness and rapid sequence of their cries. There were two of them, and they were wheeling swiftly in sharp circles, about two hundred feet up, and—Brooks laid great stress on this—they were directly over the laboratory."

"Only partly correct," remarked St. Cloud. "For I saw *that* episode myself. The gulls were by no means directly over the laboratory, and there were *three* of them, not two. But then what?"

"Of a sudden a greenish flame, dazzling with darting tongues of phosphorescence—that's the way Brooks described it—shot up out of the laboratory. It did not reach the gulls, however, but something as terrible did: where each gull was appeared a sudden puff of flame—"

"*Green,* I suppose," smiled St. Cloud.

"Brooks didn't say as to that. But there came two puffs of flame, and presto! the gulls had vanished—not even a feather remained!"

"Much moonshine," smiled St. Cloud. "As I said, there were three gulls; one of them, though, wasn't touched at all. However, the two others did vanish, but not precisely in the way that Brooks describes. There weren't any puffs of flame. Also, no flame shot up out of the laboratory, though naturally Mrs. Brooks thought that it was a flame. It was a stream of light—a *sword* of fluorescence."

"But the gulls?"

"Oh, they disappeared all right—vanished from before your very eyes!"

"But where to?"

"I don't know, Rider. Where the flame goes, I fancy, when it disappears."

"Since things like that happen, it's no wonder that people are beginning to talk."

"It's no wonder at all, Rider, And I haven't seen all the things that Henry has done. Then there's Nettleton's fantastic yarn, and that falling eagle, and the—"

"I saw that eagle," I said.

"Dead as a door nail when he came down, wasn't he?"

"As Archaeopteryx."

"And marks on him that were a puzzle to the wisest head?"

"I heard at least twenty explanations, and there wasn't a one of them that would do."

"You know," said St. Cloud, "it's no wonder people are beginning to imagine things and to feel uneasy."

"What," I asked, "does Henry think about that? Or does he know?"

"Oh, he knows. Somebody put the matter to him—more strongly it seems than Brooks did to you. Only last night Henry remarked that he would cart the laboratory far into some desert in the West or some mountain fastness—some place where he could at least watch a cathode stream without giving people the nightmare—only—"

"Only what?"

"Only he had something else in mind—a remarkable journey of some kind, he said."

"A journey," said I. "This is becoming interesting."

"Henry's words implied that it would be interesting," said St. Cloud, "mighty interesting. But as to how, where, why, when or what—well, I haven't the slightest idea when it comes to that."

"It seems to me that there is something odd there," I remarked.

"Where, Rider?" St. Cloud wanted to know.

"Why, planning a journey when he is so deep in this business of throwing people into hysterics."

"That's just the way it struck me," said St. Cloud. "And that's why I couldn't help thinking, though the idea seems utterly fantastic, that it—this mysterious journey he so vaguely speaks about—is somehow connected with this."

"This?"

"Precisely," nodded St. Cloud; "this terrible research of his, Rider, for it is that—terrible and more than terrible."

"But good heavens!"

I stared at him.

"Well?" he queried.

"How can this have anything to do with that?"

"I wish I knew, Rider. However, in all likelihood it is only a wild fancy of mine; but it persists. All I know is this; if it's so, it is a journey in which I for one certainly have no desire to accompany him."

"I should say so! Not with *swords* of green light, with something that makes eagles fall down out of the sky and gulls vanish into nothingness—and Heaven only knows what else. Excuse me!"

St. Cloud smiled and sat gazing into the flames.

And then of a sudden out of the storm he came—Henry Quainfan, bareheaded, out of breath, in that long yellow work coat, just as he had quitted the laboratory, his cheeks flushed, his eyes shining in a way that made me feel queer.

Thus he burst in upon us—the water running from him in streams.

To say that I was surprised would be putting it rather mildly; this was not like Henry Quainfan.

"Good heavens!" I exclaimed, foolishly enough, "what's happened?"

"Happened?"

Henry Quainfan laughed, and that laugh of his, I thought, was tinged with something hysterical; but that might have been only a fancy.

"It's finished, Rider!" he exclaimed. "It's solved; I've done it—done it at last!"

I thrust forth my hand in congratulation, and the force with which he gripped it made me wince. St. Cloud's slender fingers, it was patent, were seized in a grip equally crushing.

"So you've got it?" said I, wondering what on earth it was that he had got.

"Padlocked, as it were," Henry Quainfan smiled. "I've solved the whole business, and everything's worked out, too—decided!"

"Decided!" I echoed. "Everything?"

"Just so," he nodded. "But *that* will be my little secret for the present."

He sank into the chair I had drawn up.

"Heavens," said he, "but I'm tired—damnably tired!"

The golden head sank forward, and he covered his eyes with his hand.

Of a sudden he uttered an exclamation and straightened up.

"Great guns!" he said. "Here I am tearing around like a wild man!"

He stood up.

"Bareheaded!" he exclaimed. "And I've ruined your carpet, Rider. But, now that I have made a fool of myself, I'm going home."

I protested.

"No," said he. "Why, I'll be asleep in two minutes."

"Sleep here," I told him.

But he shook his head.

"Sit down!" I commanded. "I'm going to get something to warm you up."

He smiled his thanks, but said:

"No, Rider; I'm going home."

"But, man, it's coming down in torrents, and—"

"Let her come!" said Henry Quainfan.

And out he went into the rain and storm.

And out with him went Morgan St. Cloud and Rider Farnermain, the former (with arm linked in his) on his left, the latter (ditto) on his right—as if to protect this indomitable one from the puny elements.

CHAPTER 5
"QUO VADIS?"

"That's all right, too!" said Morgan St. Cloud. "I can't explain it, though that doesn't mean that I haven't got an explanation. But there the riddle is—and none the less a riddle, I admit, because it's a fact. Whether by accident or design, here we are—in the very center of the Universe!"

I may remark that (besides being in the center of the Universe) we were in Henry Quainfan's library. This, too, was the second night after that in which he burst in upon us out of the storm. However, he had as yet thrown no light whatever on that achievement the consummation of which had sent him to St. Cloud and me, bareheaded and excited, through the wind and the rain—or on that "little secret" of his.

"There you are!" said I to Henry. "Why are we here—in the very center of the starry stage?"

"Why," he smiled, "aren't we in the constellation Sagittarius, or Draco, or Canis Major, or the Big Dipper?"

"I find it hard," I persisted, "to believe that this anomalous position of our sun and his planets is simply a fortuitous one."

"And I find it more than hard, impossible," said Henry Quainfan, "to believe that the Universe was made for man."

"Oh, I don't say *that*," St. Cloud explained. "But I don't believe that man is as the beasts that perish. And as for this central position of our solar system, I can't help fancying that—that it does mean something."

"It is true that our sun seems to be in the center of that vast space ringed round by the Milky Way," said Henry, "but in reality he may not be. For instance, we find Professor Newcomb himself expressing a doubt that these things are as they seem. After instancing Ptolemy's *proof* that the earth was fixed in the center of the Universe, Newcomb says:

"'May we not be the victims of some fallacy, as he was?'

"But granting that we are in the very center of Creation?" Henry went on. "What then? What does it prove? That the heavens were made for man? Why, how often does that noble creature even look at them? Does it prove that we must look at a human being—a thing a brother to the tiger and the ape, and like as not more beastly than either—if we would behold the noblest work of the Almighty God!"

"I don't know," answered Morgan St. Cloud. "I wouldn't go so far as that. All I say is this: that the greatest mystery which ever confronts a human being is—humanity."

"But Rider goes that far."

"I do," I told him. "I believe, with Dr. Wallace, that this position of our earth in the center of the Universe (along with a thousand other things) goes to prove just that."

"But it doesn't prove anything at all," Henry Quainfan said, "Dr. Wallace and Rider Farnermain to the contrary notwithstanding. For our sun wasn't always here. He too is on his way. Every morning of our lives finds him over a million miles farther on that journey of his towards the glorious star in the northern heavens known to men as Alpha Lyrae."

"That our sun is making a journey through space, and a stupendous one, no one can doubt," said St. Cloud. "But one can doubt that the apex of the sun's way is Alpha Lyrae—indeed, that there is any apex or anti-apex at all. That's all assumption. That our sun is traveling in a straight line may be a fact, but as a matter of fact it's only an assumption. Maybe, for all we know, his journey is a circle, or an ellipse, or a parabola—"

"Or a corkscrew," smiled Henry Quainfan.

"Or a fishhook," said St. Cloud.

"Pigs," Henry Quainfan told him, "fly through the air with their tails forward."

"If my aunt," said St. Cloud, "had been a man, she'd be my uncle."

"You simps," I put in, "remind me of Simpkins."

"Who was who?" Henry asked.

"The farmer who had half a sectionful of noise but a thimbleful of wool."

"That," St. Cloud told him, "was when Simpkins sheared his pig."

Henry Quainfan laughed.

"And the same day he put a hat on a hen. But we agree famously; it's something."

"But that it's from Canopus to Vega—nothing but assumption!" St. Cloud persisted.

"Have it your way!" Henry Quainfan laughed. "When it comes to the teachings of science, Morgan St. Cloud is sometimes as hopeless as Rider Farnermain on man's place in the Universe. As to the voyage that our sun with his planets is making through space, I admit that we are not absolutely sure that the course is a straight one. But the evidence we have teaches us that it is so. But straight or crooked, ellipse, parabola, corkscrew or fishhook—there is the terrible mystery of it all! Where was the sun when the first life stirred and moved on this planet of ours; to what part of the Universe will he have flown when that last miserable human awaits the end of humanity and all of humanity's hopes and dreams?"

Said I:

"And in this epic of the worlds—terrible, I admit, and in the light of science more terrible even than it ever was in the imaginations of the ancients—but amidst all this play and interplay of forces stupendous and cosmic, amidst all this mysterious power and starry beauty, yet man, man with his godlike intellect, which is even unlocking the mysteries of star and nebula—yet man, you say, dies as the beasts that perish, is no more to the Almighty Creator than is the ape or the wolf?"

"Of course he is not," said Henry Quainfan. "Or the sparrow that falls—or the kangaroo that hops."

"Then why are we here? Why do we love and suffer and dream and die, if eternal blackness is the end of it all? What is it all about?"

"That," returned Henry Quainfan, "is the very thing I want you anthropocentricists to tell me. But I know you won't, and for a good reason; you can't. You can talk about dreams, and you ask what it's all about if man hasn't got a soul that lives when he dies; but that is not an answer to anything.

"And as for that mysterious power and starry beauty you make so much of, how often does your noble man—this being with the godlike intellect—how often does he even think of that? He (and he's male and female) is thinking of other things—as your wolf or ape thinks of other things; of bottles asparkle with booze, for instance, of the belly and the loins."

I winced (mentally) as that blow struck. That is the way with your materialist; he rains upon you stones fished out of the muck of the physical puddle, while you (for of course the flower's perfume and beauty are lost on him) can only fling at him the rose petals of faith and the spirit.

"We could talk about man's place in the Universe for the rest of our lives!" I told him. "But we shall never know the answer till we die."

"But I don't want to wait till I die; I think I can get *an* answer now," said Henry Quainfan. "At any rate, I purpose to try. And that brings me to the little journey I hinted about to you, Morgan."

"Lord!" exclaimed St. Cloud. "Must be some journey if it is going to solve the mystery of life and death!"

"Oh, not *that!*" Henry Quainfan said. "But I believe that it will shed a dazzling light on man's place in Creation. If Rider will come along, I think he will find man—man, that noble creature with the godlike intellect—I think, Rider, that you will find him tumbled into the dust from his throne."

"Has it got anything to do with this gull and eagle business?" I asked him.

Henry Quainfan laughed.

"That was nothing," he said. "There will be danger of course, maybe death—and perhaps worse than death even. But there will be nothing to fear from that."

"*Quo vadis?*" asked St. Cloud.

"Venus!" said Henry Quainfan.

With a sudden movement Morgan St. Cloud straightened up in his chair.

"What's that?"

"Venus," Henry Quainfan told him.

"You mean Venus the planet?"

"Foolish question number one!" smiled Henry Quainfan.

"What other Venus is there?"

Morgan St. Cloud laughed.

"What's the idea, Henry?" he wanted to know.

"But I'm speaking in all seriousness," Henry told him. "I said Venus, and I didn't mean Timbuctoo—Venus the planet, probably the loveliest of all the worlds that go round our sun. Yes, even more wonderful, perhaps, than our own wonderful world—which Rider thinks is the king-pin of Creation."

"Do you mean to tell me," I asked him, "that you have conquered gravitation?"

"Just that. I've discovered a negative gravity. And not only that: I can turn it off and on, so to speak—the same as you do the water in your tap."

I stared at him.

"It will have to soak in, I suppose," said I. "For this is coming big."

"You know, I marvel now," said Morgan St. Cloud, "that I didn't know it. Once I was blind, but now I can see. It's always like that. I thought of this, too, but of course it was only to dismiss it from my mind as one of the wildest of fancies—something like that fourth dimension stuff. Gravitation conquered, interplanetary travel—great Jupiter Jerusalem, how could I imagine that that was possible?"

"Physicists—that is, some of them—have known that it was possible," Henry Quainfan said, "possible if man could only find out *how*. To the layman, however, it has always been a wild dream—wilder even than his wildest fiction, which after all is pretty tame stuff. The talking-machine, the X-ray, the submarine and the airplane—all those things were dreams until men found out how. They were never *impossible*."

He turned to me, and there was a smile in those gray eyes of his.

"So don't be too sure. Rider, don't be too sure that the great mystery will never be solved—the mystery, that is, of life and death."

"But—"

"Well?" he queried.

"How on earth can this mad journey shed any light on those things—on the mystery of life and death and our place in God's Creation?"

"What we find at the end of it," returned Henry Quainfan, "will answer that."

CHAPTER 6
THE GREAT ENIGMA AND MYSTERY

"But—" began St. Cloud.

Henry looked at him inquiringly.

"But again, Morgan," he suggested.

"You talk as though the whole thing were settled."

"And it is. Everything's worked out. It's only a matter of detail now. That's what I meant when I said everything was decided."

That dubious expression on St. Cloud's features did not lift.

"But won't there have to be experiments, trial trips, or something?"

"Experiments? Great guns, haven't I been doing that? Of course, problems will come up, but, unless I'm greatly mistaken, by no means hard ones. Those are all solved. I can send a piece of Quainfanity—which in common parlance would be negative gravity—I can send a piece of Quainfanity out into space. I've done it of course—more than once. The thing now is to go out with it. I tell your Morgan, I've got this thing down to a T."

"I'm glad of that," returned St. Cloud, "because it is going to take you a long way up. But what's it to be like—this Quainfanomobile thing you are going to make the journey in?"

"Imagine a lemon—"

"That," put in St. Cloud, "is just what I have been imagining."

"A big steel lemon with windows in it. I've even got it named, too; it's the *Hornet*. And inside I see Morgan St. Cloud, Rider Farnermain and yours truly."

"Oh, no you don't!" I told him. "You don't see Rider Farnermain inside that steel lemon!"

"Nor me," St Cloud told him. "That's what I meant when I spoke of the whole business being settled."

"But I think I do see you," Henry smiled, "Rider and Morgan. However, if you won't come along, then I'll go it alone. You will have plenty of time to make up your minds. None of us has near kith or kin, so that if disaster overtakes us, there will be no one to deluge the earth with tears, or to say thank God as he (or she) hastens to put on mourning. And one thing: not a word of this must get out. You will remember that neither Blimper nor Buttermore is in the house. I saw to that, and I instance it so that each of you will be very careful."

"So it's Cytherea?" said Morgan St. Cloud.

"Aphrodite," nodded Henry Quainfan.

"From something I read somewhere," I remarked, "I got the idea that this planet is in a fix that is simply awful. Why did you choose her?"

"Because she is after all probably the most wonderful planet in our solar system. As for the superior planets, it is extremely probable that not one of them is habitable save Mars; the others, it seems, are nothing but gas. And as to Mars, its rarefied air would cause a Terrestrial much inconvenience, even if it would not render his sojourn there utterly impossible. So there remain only Venus and Mars; Mercury is like the moon, dead. Of course Venus resembles the earth much more than does Mars; indeed, Venus is Terra's twin sister."

"Sometimes, though," St. Cloud observed, "twin sisters don't resemble each other very closely."

"Tell me something about Venus," I asked Henry. "You know that my astronomical attainments are not great."

"In the first place, she is well named; she is to us the most beautiful of the planets, the loveliest and the most mysterious—and the only one, by the way, mentioned by Homer. Though, with the exception of the moon and the asteroid Eros (or some comet), she of all the heavenly bodies comes the nearest to us, yet is Venus one of the great enigmas and mysteries of astronomy."

"One would think," said I, "since she approaches us the most nearly, that she would be known the best."

"But you forget, Rider," Henry smiled, "that she is Venus! She has a hundred moods and a thousand veils, and a time for each of them all. Galileo, with his little spy-glass, discovered that 'The Mother of Loves imitates the shapes of Cynthia;'[2] but since his day men, albeit armed with the most powerful telescopes, have learned but little more—that is, about Venus herself; her orbit of course (the most nearly circular in the solar system) is known, and her volume and mass, with a high degree of certainty. But Venus herself still refuses to unveil—or, rather, wears one guise for one man and a different for the next.

"For instance, to See she is in all the loveliness of youth, a veritable twin sister to the earth; while to Lowell she is wrinkled and lined, stamped with the marks of an age terrible beyond all words.

"Her distance from the sun is sixty-seven millions of miles, her diameter is about seven thousand eight hundred, and her sidereal revolution is made in two hundred and twenty-five days—two hundred and twenty-four days and seventeen hours, very nearly."

"Then," said I, "if we were to set foot on Venus—good heavens, I'd be *forty* years old!"

"That's what you would."

"That settles it," I told him. "I stay here on the earth. I'm not looking for the Fountain of Age. Now, if it was the Fountain of Youth—"

"You'll find that on Jupiter," put in St. Cloud; "you'd be about two years old on Jupiter."

"Better still; take Neptune, Rider," smiled Henry Quainfan, "you'd be not quite two *months* old there!"

"Oh, this science!" I exclaimed. "No wonder Newton—it was Newton, wasn't it?—when he had made a hole for the big chickens, decided it would be a

---

2. *Cynthiae figures aemulatur Mater Amorum.*

shame to keep the little chickens from following after, and so made a little hole, too, for them! I can understand it."

"Now," Henry went on, "Venus is certainly Terra's twin sister if she have a succession of day and night on her surface such as we know here, and if the inclination of her axis is at all like that of the earth's. Unfortunately, however, what with the glare of the planet's atmosphere, nothing is certainly known on these points."

"It seems," I observed, "that this planet is indeed something of a mystery."

"Didn't I tell you that she is well named? Those men of ancient times, Rider, were wiser than the men of today—who are forever blowing their own trumpets and pounding their own drums—will give them credit for."

"Yes," nodded St. Cloud. "And after all the loudest drum has nothing in it but wind. But you said a true word there. For instance, there's that figure of Nisroch which Layard found in the ruins of Nineveh."

Henry nodded.

"Who," I asked, "was this fellow Nisroch?"

"Saturn," St. Cloud told me. "And—in this figure, that is—he had a ring around him."

"Suppose it had been a pump-handle or a handsaw."

"Handsaws," St. Cloud said, "are good things, but not to shave with."

"You'll remember, Rider," said Henry Quainfan, "that the planet Saturn is ringed. How did those old boys know that?"

"But—do you think they really did know it?"

"I wish I knew! There's the ring, though."

"But—"

"Well?" he queried.

"They would have had to have telescopes to know that."

"Precisely. And that's just what Proctor thought this discovery of Layard's indicated."[3]

"How old, it seems, the world is, and man is!"

"And how young! But to return to Aphrodite.

"As for her axial period, the elder Cassini was the first to make a determination, and he set it down as twenty-three hours and fifteen minutes. Bianchini, in

---

3. "Was there once a now forgotten age when men were as learned as we are today, and did a little of this knowledge descend to their degenerate successors in the form of uncomprehended traditions?"—Garrett P. Serviss.

1726, gave it as twenty-four *days* and eight hours; but J. Cassini pointed out that there could be deduced, also, from the observations of Bianchini an axial period of twenty-three hours and twenty minutes. That given by Schroeter, in 1789, was twenty-three hours, twenty-one minutes and nineteen seconds, which he afterwards corrected and made twenty-three hours, twenty minutes and 7.977 seconds, From over ten thousand observations, De Vico, of Rome, deduced a diurnal rotation of twenty-three hours, twenty-one minutes and 21.956 seconds—a conclusive deduction, one would think.

"However, in 1890, Schiaparelli made the startling announcement that Venus rotates very slowly, that her axial rotation is probably isochronous with her orbital revolution; in other words, that she always keeps one face turned toward the sun, just as the moon does toward the earth.

"Lowell's observations led him to the same conclusion. Her sky—which others declare is densely cloud-laden—he finds invariably clear (the great brilliancy of her atmosphere, indeed, he explains by this very clearness) and he also finds certain faint spoke-like markings, which do not move across the planet's disk, as they would do did Venus rotate like the earth.

"Then Belopolsky sought to solve the problem with the spectroscope; the displacement of the lines showed a rotation period of about twenty-three hours. This would seem to conclude the question; but Lowell followed suit; and the Flagstaff spectrograms, taken by Slipher, gave no evidence whatever of a rapid rotation.

"'They yielded, indeed,' Lowell tells us, 'testimony to a negative rotation of three months, which, interpreted, means that so slow a spin as this was beyond their power to precise.'

"On the other hand, Professor See—who claims that Venus is an inhabited world—is convinced that the rapid rotation is the true one; indeed, he declares that 'a period of about twenty-four hours is shown to be the only one possible.'

"So there you are. Judge for yourself."

"I find a lot of leaves," I told him, "but very few grapes. However, what do you believe?"

"That the evidence is preponderantly in favor of the short period of rotation."

"Let us hope 'tis the true one," said I. "Heaven pity the poor planet if one side is an oven and the other an ice-box."

"In point of fact," Henry went on, "I am convinced that the planet's axial spin is a rapid one. For, as Arrhenius has pointed out, if one side of the planet was in eternal darkness she would not have any atmosphere to speak of; the temperature on that night side would be near minus two hundred and seventy-three degrees Centigrade—the absolute zero—and all the atmospheric gases would be there, and frozen liquid or solid.[4]

"But we find no such thing on Venus; her atmosphere, as both visual and spectroscopic observations show, is a dense one, probably even denser than our own, and contains a considerable amount of water-vapor.

"So much, though, for her diurnal spin. When it comes to her axis, there is a like uncertainty. Some observers believe that it is nearly perpendicular to the plane of her orbit. If this is so, then she has no appreciable succession of seasons, but the seasons (if we may so call them) lie in zones and are perennial, and day and night, everywhere on the planet, are of equal length.

"Others, however, assure us that the inclination is in reality about the same as that of Terra's axis; while still others picture a world as terrible, almost, as that Venus of Schiaparelli and Lowell.

"According to these observers in question, her axis is far from the perpendicular, is inclined to the plane of her orbit at an angle of probably no more than fifteen degrees. That of the earth's is sixty-six and one-half degrees. Venus' equator, therefore, is, roughly, where the earth's *axis* is and her axis is in about the same place as Terra's equator. If this is so, the torrid and temperate zones overlap each other, and the boreal and austral regions have, at one solstice, a frigid temperature and a torrid heat at the other, which would make things mighty uncomfortable for Terrestrials.

"However, for my part, I believe that we have nothing to fear from this remarkable inclination—that in this respect, as in so many others, Venus closely resembles the earth.

"The difference between the gravities of the respective orbs is not noteworthy.

"The planet has no moon.

"And now what more? Venus must be inhabited. Her physical habitudes must closely resemble those of this planet. Of course, because of her greater proximity to the sun, the amount of light and heat that is poured upon Venus greatly exceeds that which this planet of our receives; but the heavy cloud-envelope is a good protection, reflecting much of it and rendering the surface of the planet cool and equable.

"But even if there is no cloud-envelope, even if the Venusian skies are as

---

4. Except the helium and the hydrogen.—H. Q.

clear as our skies, one could live in the temperate, subarctic and arctic zones, though no Terrestrial could endure the heat poured down upon her equatorial regions.

"Then there are the mountain and the plateau heights; one could find any kind of climate.

"So men could surely live on her surface, cloud-envelope or no cloud-envelope—that is, so far as the rigors of climate are concerned. Whether the Cythereans, or Venusians—or whatever we choose to call her inhabitants—would permit one to live in comfort remains to be seen; and I am going to see.

"It is obvious that it would be idle to speculate on the manner of inhabitants that people her solitudes or swarming cities. Perhaps there are creatures of high intelligence there, but there may be nothing of the kind. Who can say? But one thing is certain."

"And that is——" I suggested.

"There are no human beings!"

"I knew it was that."

"If we believed that each kind of living things was created by a direct fiat of the Creator—if we believed this, then the belief that Venus may be inhabited by human beings would be tenable; but, since evolution is an incontestable fact, this belief is an utter absurdity: evolution cannot progress along parallel, identical lines on two planets."

"I can see as far into a millstone as another man," I told him.

"That was true once, Rider, but not now: the other fellow may have an X-ray."

Said St. Cloud:

> "'In that star of the west, by whose shadowy splendor,
>   At twilight so often we've roamed thro' the dew,
> There are maidens, perhaps, who have bosoms as tender,
>   And look, in their twilights, as lovely as you.'"

CHAPTER 7
THE HORNET

"By the way," said I, "where is Venus now?"

"Approaching superior conjunction," returned Henry; "she is lost in the sun's rays."

"From there whither?" I asked.

"Over east of the sun, and evening star."

"Going or coming then?"

"Coming, until inferior conjunction—that's when she is between the earth and the sun—when she passes back to the west of him and is morning star once more."

"Then," said I, "I suppose your plan of campaign will be something like this: you will meet the lady when she is in this inferior conjunction, as you call it—which, if I understand it aright, is when she is nearest the earth."

"Precisely," he nodded.

"Otherwise, you would be going out of your way to meet her, or would be chasing her around."

"Just so. And she goes twenty-two miles a second."

"Whew! At that rate, it shouldn't take her long to come round to this point where you are to meet her."

"About nine months and a half: she has to catch up with the earth, you know."

"Nine months and a half at twenty-two miles a second! Great Jupiter Ammon! Well, anyway, that will give you time enough for the *Hornet*, won't it?"

"And to spare," nodded Henry, "or I'm a billy-goat."

As it turned out, Henry was no billy-goat; before the Queen of Beauty had reached what astronomers call her greatest elongation (a queer jargon these star-gazers have) the *Hornet* was finished.

What was the *Hornet* like? Imagine a lemon—a big steel lemon, twenty feet long and ten feet through the middle. That is just what the *Hornet* was like in shape, save that the ends had been snipped off, as it were. And in each end was a thick but perfectly transparent glass, looking like a ship's port. Indeed, one of these gleaming disks was imbedded in a heavy steel frame which swung inward on hinges—for all the world like a port. This, of course, was to permit our ingress and egress; when the door was closed, the *Hornet* was as air-tight as a pop-bottle.

It must not be supposed, however, that these were the only windows; there were six of them all told in this marvelous thing that was to be our world—so tiny a world, dashing on and on through the deeps of space, on toward utter destruction.

As I have said, Venus had not yet reached her greatest elongation, which means that there remained about two months before the start: it was Henry's belief that the *Hornet* would travel across that terrible abyss with at least the speed of the earth in her orbit; in other words, fifteen days or so after quitting our world, if all went well we should be on the Planet of Love.

"But maybe we'll run into a meteor," said St. Cloud—who, by the way, had said this thing a hundred times if he had said it once.

"Of course," nodded Henry Quainfan. "But maybe we sha'n't. Space, I believe, is rather spacious, Morgan."

"And meteors, I believe, are rather multitudinous."

"Oh, well," Henry said, "Fortune can take from us nothing but what she gave."

"But Miss Fortune can."

"He that sitteth on the ground can't tumble, Morgan."

"As well sit still as rise up and fall."

"Hope," Henry told him, "is as cheap as despair."

"He may hope for the best that's prepared for the worst."

"He that always fears danger," said Henry, "always feels it."

"And he that passes a judgment as he runs overtakes repentance."

"Experience, we all know, keeps a dear school—"

"And fools like us," said St. Cloud, "will learn in no other."

"He that fears not the future may enjoy the present."

"In Golgotha," said Morgan St. Cloud, "are skulls of all sizes."

"And in Hell," Henry told him, "they now have fans."

St. Cloud smiled his dark smile and turned to me.

"Why didn't you come to my help, Rider?"

"Silence," I explained, "is wisdom when speaking is folly."

"Right," said he. "But sometimes 'tis wisdom to seem a fool."

Though the *Hornet* was done, we were by no means, in the days that followed, twiddling our thumbs; on the contrary, I positively believe that we were the busiest mortals in the whole state.

Two trial ascents were made, though not to a great height. The first Henry Quainfan insisted on making alone.

"Not that I doubt my absolute control of the *Hornet*," said he; "experiments have made me confident of that. Just caution, you know."

In neither instance was the height attained more than twenty miles. Though this was a record-smasher, in view of what followed it was in reality nothing.

Then we had to decide upon and procure (not so easy an office as may be fancied) those things necessary for our undertaking—firearms, medicines, food, and so on.

Venus reached her greatest elongation—a dazzling half moon of silver in Henry's little telescope, a four-inch refractor. She now began rapidly to approach the sun and swing into the crescent.

Then at last came the day.

CHAPTER 8
INTO THE DEPTHS

In the *Hornet* was a goodly supply of solidified air. There was also (among other things) a water apparatus, an apparatus to remove carbonic anhydrid from the atmosphere, and one to supply oxygen.

"We have nothing," Henry Quainfan made asseveration, "to fear for our respiratory or alimentary machinery."

Also, there was an apparatus with which he hoped to send electromagnetic waves from Venus to the earth; but this, alas, was never attempted.

He had given a code to an ill-starred inventor named Homer L. Wood—a code that, if communication across that awful gap proved possible, none of the uninitiated would be apt to decipher. He had not explained things to Wood, had merely given him the code and the information that some time he might receive something which would bring him fame and fortune.

Poor Wood! I fear he shall have to wait many a long day for that unknown something.

What would be the use of dwelling on those last hours on the planet of our birth? I could not describe them. If I tried to put down on paper the sensations that came thronging into my breast and the thoughts which came thronging into my mind, I should only fail miserably.

So I shall hasten on.

That last night passed slowly. I slept but little, and, when I did sleep, it was only to dream the most terrible dreams.

And the day passed slowly. We did not talk much and moved about restlessly.

At one time, indeed, I felt like backing out, but the feeling soon passed away.

"I wonder," Henry smiled, "what Blimper and Buttermore will think. I would like to hear some of the explanations!"

"There will be some wild stories now," I said.

"But none I imagine, Rider, so wild as the truth itself."

"I don't think there will," said St. Cloud.

And now, as I look back, I don't think that there was.

Once or twice I heard Henry Quainfan singing, in a low voice. I remember the following:

> "I love a maid, a mystic maid,
>   Whose form no eyes but mine can see;
> She comes in light, she comes in shade,
>   And beautiful in both is she."

Then there were those two lines which have become imbedded in my memory, though at the time I thought nothing of them. Here they are:

> "When thou wert given we were as one,
>   Who now are two and widely sundered."

At last night came down on the world, black and threatening. Thus the weather favored us, for with a clear sky, somebody might see the *Hornet* go heavenward; and that was just what Henry Quainfan did not want anybody to do.

On the whole world not a single soul knew that three men were going to launch out into the ether deeps this night.

About an hour after the coming of darkness, a strong wind came up, and a little later a heavy rain began to descend, bolting out, over there in the west, the city's light-spangled hills.

Well, we three took our last look at the world and entered the *Hornet*.

The little chamber was lighted by an electric bulb. Blinds were drawn over the windows.

My heart was going *Thumpety-thump,* my face I knew was pale, and there was a sickening sensation in, to use a phrase of Henry's, my "scrobiculus cordis."

With a face upon which there was not the slightest tinge of pallor and with heads that were perfectly steady, Henry closed the door and made it fast.

For a time he moved about—busy and yet in reality doing nothing.

"All ready now!" he said.

There succeeded a short silence. St. Cloud and I stood expectant, moveless.

Henry, however, seemed to have plunged into thought.

I breathed a silent prayer to the dread Being who created the innumerable hosts of stars and the awful wastes of space, and notes when sparrows fall.

Of a sudden Henry Quainfan roused himself.

"Now we go!" he said.

The next moment there was a slight jerk. We were off. Our little world was rushing away from the earth with the speed of a bullet. And down below people would pass the night as was their wont, would get up in the morning and proceed with their little earthly affairs as usual, would see, day after day, the sun rise, pursue his way through the heavens and sink, as they always had—while we three should never see the great luminary in the terrestrial heavens again, had left the earth forever and were rushing up and out into the icy and bottomless deeps of space.

CHAPTER 9
THE ABYSS

It would be difficult to say why, but in my mind this has always seemed the point where the astounding, and in some ways awful, drama of Draconda really began.

And this is perhaps remarkable in that what was to follow—I mean that drop sunward for the matter of something like thirty millions of miles—had (and has) the seeming of some wondrous and terrible dream.

Of a sudden my mind became a panic—a mad riot. What an utter fool, what a colossal ass I had been to come on this mad journey! If I could only get out! But it was too late; I couldn't do that now. The earth must already, I knew, be at a terrific distance below us, and the *Hornet*—this tiny thing that was now our world—was rushing up and out with appalling speed. Get out, indeed! We were committed, and committed with a vengeance.

St. Cloud was, I believe, as scared as myself; but Henry Quainfan appeared to be utterly unaffected. Those nerves of his were nerves of steel.

At length he smiled at us and said:

"Well, we're on our way!"

A remark that struck me as positively idiotic.

St. Cloud made an exclamation.

I said:

"How far are we up?"

Henry Quainfan turned his eyes to a thing that looked something like an auto speedometer.

"Just about ten miles now," he said airily.

"I didn't think it was more than half that," I told him. "We are certainly going some."

"Not yet, Rider," he smiled. "It's the atmosphere, you know. As soon as we get out of it, we'll pick up speed."

"If it wasn't for that hissing or whistling sound," said Morgan St. Cloud, "I could swear that the *Hornet* was at rest. There is no swaying, nothing to show that we are moving."

"That's so," I said. "Why, Henry, these darkened windows?"

Henry Quainfan nodded.

"And it will take but one look to destroy that illusion of rest.

"You see," he added, his finger poised over a button, "I didn't want any of those gullologists to see us go up. Also, it probably was good for our nerves. And in all likelihood, we'll need all the nerves we've got before very long. This thing is going to be—well, decidedly *unearthly*."

"It's our minds we've got to watch," put in Morgan.

"Precisely."

Henry's finger pressed down, and the blind shot away from the window (ingeniously protected) in the floor of the *Hornet*. Then he rapidly released all the other blinds and turned off the light.

The sky was of the intensest black, and the stars shone as they never do in the depths of that aerial ocean in which men have their being.

I dropped on my knees and peered earthward. The sight was stupendous, appalling even, and yet after all I beheld but a vast expanse of world involved in the uncertainty and mystery of night.

"It's still *hollow*," I said.

"Of course," returned Henry. "But after a time it will be a sphere."

I referred, of course, to the seeming concavity of the earth—that most strange phenomenon, and well known to aeronauts.

It was some minutes afterwards—how many I don't know—that it came. I had just straightened up and was looking out one of the windows. St. Cloud was beside me looking too. He gave a sharp exclamation. At that instant across that star-powdered blackness shot a sword of fire, and as the eye leaped to follow, that plunging point of it was shattered into a thousand incandescent fragments.

"What now?" came Henry's voice.

"A meteor," returned St. Cloud. "And it was infernally close. If that thing had hit the *Hornet*! Bullets are snails compared with those boys."

"Yes," said Henry Quainfan; "it was probably going something like twenty or thirty miles a second—that is, when it came plunging into the atmosphere. Those waifs of space do constitute a danger, a danger by no means insignificant—

the only real danger, though, I believe, that confronts us in this our drop sunward."

"Some consolation, that," St. Cloud told him.

"Oh, well," he added, "a good hope is better than a bad possession."

"And death," Henry said, "has nothing terrible in it save what life has made so."

"I am not so sure of that," said Morgan St. Cloud.

"You're a cheerful couple!" I interposed. "Is Venus the Planet of Death?"

"She may be that, Rider," muttered St. Cloud, "and something even worse. At any rate, she is the Planet of Love: isn't that bad enough?"

"Maybe," Henry Quainfan said. "For what is Love but Death's Dawn?"

"For Goodness' sake," I exclaimed, "give over this cabalistic stuff and talk sense!"

"I thought we were doing that, Rider," Henry laughed. "We might as well talk the sheerest nonsense, though, as stand chewing our thoughts. Confound it, I wish we were out of this!"

"What's that?" I asked him.

He laughed.

"I don't mean out of the *Hornet*, Rider. I wouldn't wish that for the world and all the kingdoms of the world. Had that feeling been possible, I would have remained there below. What I mean is this: out of the atmosphere."

"Of course," I said.

"Don't get impatient," growled Morgan St. Cloud. "You'll probably wish yourself back in it before we are done."

"Icarus, eh?" queried Henry Quainfan.

"Great guns, *no!*" St. Cloud replied.

"The air," I remarked, somewhat irrelevantly, "must be deucedly rarefied at this height."

"It is," Henry returned. "But it goes up a long way, how far nobody knows: the highest meteors are about eighty miles up.

"The atmosphere at that altitude, and upward, must be nothing but hydrogen. Dr. Wegener, however, has postulated a substance above the hydrogen even. He assumes that the green line in the spectrum of the auroral arches is due to this unknown gas of remarkable tenuity, to which he has given the name geocoronium.

"You will remember, Rider," he added, "that helium was seen in the sun long before it was discovered, by Ramsay, on the earth."

"I remember," I said. "And I remember, too, that the great Herschel believed in the *sun's habitability*."

"Rider," Henry laughed, "do you think you will ever get over it?"

"And above this geocoronium, I suppose," put in St. Cloud, "lies that other gas of remarkable tenuity (and ubiquity) called perhapsium."

"And above your perhapsium," said Henry, "you'll probably find it-may-be-there-ium."

"Science in a nutshell!" I observed. "Coronium itself is hypothetical stuff, and yet here we find another postulated substance named after it. I am beginning to believe that Keats *was* wrong."

"Of course he was, Rider," said St, Cloud. "All you've got to do is look out one of these windows to see that."

"You score," I told him.

And he did indeed.

In stranger places we were to find ourselves, and things unimaginable we were to see and hear; but never before had men (save in wild fancy) beheld such a thing as this.

We were, of course, now far above the altitude reached by the highest clouds, the cirrus, though the so-called "luminous night clouds" were observed in some instances at a height of fifty miles above the earth; but these anomalous phenomena were not clouds in the usual meaning of that term.

Also, we were in that mysterious region called the stratosphere, the discovery of which (by Teisserenc de Bort and Assman) demolished the belief entertained by scientists that there was a steady decrease in temperature with increase of altitude, until at last the absolute zero of space itself was reached—for in the stratosphere the temperature is constant. Furthermore, there is a decrease in the rotational velocity of the stratospheric lamellae as one goes upward, with the result that the outermost parts of the earth's atmosphere do not rotate at all!

Steadily upward the *Hornet* sped, past that point reached by the highest "night clouds," past that region in which the highest meteors are seen, up till the moon (in her third quarter) came swimming into view from behind the bulge of the earth, hurling through the windows a light that was blinding in its white intensity.

And up and up and out!

Up till the sunlight smote through the windows, burning and blinding—and blinding—and soon of a strange bluish color. We had issued from the earth's shadow; we were now in endless day. And yet, paradoxical though it be, those ether deeps are pitch black.

"We'll give her the gas!" said Henry Quainfan.

Now it was that our drop sunward to the Queen of Beauty really began. And it was now that something happened which at first was simply horrible.

I had been standing perfectly still for some time; I started to step past St. Cloud—and then it happened.

I don't know how to describe it. My brain and body seemed suddenly to become disassociated. I felt like one entering some horrible nightmare.

Uttering a wild exclamation, I thrust forth a hand to the wall, and then came another mystery: on the instant I found myself up in the air and doing an amazing acrobatic stunt, for I was in the act of turning upside down. Contact with the opposite wall, however, put an end to this unaccountable bouleversement of mine.

"What on earth is the matter?" I cried.

"Easy, Rider," Henry laughed. "Stay still! Let yourself relax."

"But in Heaven's name what is it?"

"You've forgotten. It's the loss of weight. Your muscles, though, have lost none of their strength."

"Good Lord!" I said. "And this thing's only begun."

"Of course. Keep a grip on your movements until you get used to it. We are now eight thousand miles from the earth, and so your weight has been reduced to about eighteen pounds."

"Eighteen pounds! Man's size and no heavier than a baby!"

"And worse is coming," smiled St. Cloud. "From now on, ethereal's the word."

"Doll baby's the word," said Henry. "For after a time, when we shall have passed out of the region in which the earth's gravity is stronger than the sun's our combined weight will be less than half a pound!"

"Good heavens!" I said. "It's unearthly now; what will it be like then, when we each weigh no more than an ounce or two?"

"We'll get used to it," he told me.

However, I never did succeed in entirely ridding myself of that terrible feeling of disembodiment.

To weigh no more than a little doll baby and yet possess the full stature and strength of a man—well, *perhaps* you can imagine the unearthliness of it.

The swing of the *Hornet* soon brought the edge of the earth's illuminated hemisphere into view. Oh, the wonder of that sight! There are other things (and perhaps—who knows?—there will be more) to dim, in a measure, the awful beauty of it; but, in my dying hour, one of the visions on which memory will linger is that tremendous sickle of light.

The crescent broadened, in what seemed a time incredibly short—though my chronometric sense had, as it were, been knocked into a cocked hat—there was no longer a crescent earth but a *half earth* hanging there below us, the terminator stretching across the vast and lonely wastes of the Pacific.

It would be difficult to decide what was the most salient thing in that stupendous view of our earth; but certainly nothing was more striking, at any rate to me, than its dominant color—a blue that was almost an azure.

Nor did this beautiful color fade away with distance. For it is a strange fact (as a study made at the Lowell Observatory on the earth-light sent to the moon had shown) that our earth shines among the starry hosts with a bluish light. And yet, when you think of it, it is not a strange thing, either; the planets have each its distinctive—its jewel—color; for instance, Venus is a dazzling white, Mars is red, while Uranus is sea-green.

The earth, as the *Hornet* swung between it and the sun, became gibbous and waxed to the full.

There, unmistakable as though laid down on map or library globe—though not, by the way, on the confounded Mercator projection, which distorts the earth's features out of all likeness to the reality—was visible that hemisphere from about midway the Pacific Ocean to Africa and Europe. There, in the west, the dawn was shaking its soft light over the calm solitudes of nature and the proud and troubled cities of mankind.

It was some little time after this that St. Cloud made his discovery, a discovery which will possess great interest for earth's astronomers—that is, if they ever hear of it. Perhaps, however, this St. Cloudian discovery will have to await "confirmation elsewhere" before incorporation with the body of astronomic fact.

"By Jo!" St. Cloud suddenly exclaimed. "Look at that!"

"What now?" asked Henry Quainfan, moving to St. Cloud's window.

"Look at the moon—look at that lunar corona."

Henry made an exclamation.

"So she's got an atmosphere after all!"

"Seems to be the nearest thing to an airy nothing possible, though—more attenuated, it looks, than a comet's caudal appendage."

"Yes," said Henry. "Things, though, are not always what they seem. But look at those stars shining through it."

As he spoke I saw it; the stars, as I soon made out, were shining through that faint nebulosity with no diminution whatever of brightness—unless, indeed, it was those stars at the satellite's limb.

A photograph of the solar corona (that beautiful mystery of which virtually no more is known by scientists today than in the time of Philostratus and Plutarch) will give a good idea of what we saw—a phenomenon rendered forever invisible to the inhabitants of the earth by the earth's luminous atmosphere. Allowance, however, must be made for the exceeding faintness of the lunar glory.

Then, when the *Hornet* had sped some thousands of miles farther on its journey, came another discovery, made by Henry Quainfan; the earth too has its corona. As seen from space, it is not surrounded by a thin atmospheric shell, but by a mystic pearly glory extending for thousands of miles out into space.

The coronal extension is greatest at the equator, and at the poles are faint rifts (like those in the solar halo) for all the world like magnetic lines of force.

The light I have called pearly, and yet I don't know whether that is really the right word or not. It is a thing of strange, ghostly beauty, fading away so imperceptibly that the eye endeavors in vain to trace its boundary. Also, unaccountable changes in form and extension, some of them incredibly rapid, are seen in it.

At length I turned my eyes from Terra and gazed out into the starry deeps. For here where there is no night (or day either for that matter) the stars are visible forever. There, separated from my hand only by the thickness of that diaphanous disk, was space itself—space, of which the wisest scientist (with his hypothetical ether and other postulates remarkable) knows nothing, save this: though it looks like nothing, yet it must be something.

For my part, at no time during our long journey could I bring myself to see that space was anything—though, forsooth, I knew that it couldn't be nothing. Just the same, however, it *was* nothing—how in the Universe could it be anything? And those awful velvety deeps of nothing crushed my soul into infinitesimalness with their placid, unchanging terribleness. One cannot, I believe, imagine the terrible thing that is in that abyss of space; one must see it to know. And no man on earth ever has seen it.

On and on dashed this mysterious thing that was now our world, and ever the earth with her attendant orb (which, too, at length became full) showed a diminution of magnitude and surface detail.

Came the time when they were no longer to be looked for below but overhead; the earth (at the distance of one hundred and sixty thousand miles) had lost her hold on us, the sun's pull was now the dominant one, and the floor of the *Hornet* was sunward.

St. Cloud was the first to succumb to sleep, and I followed. At that time the earth was about a million miles distant—presenting a disk about the size of the moon's as seen in the terrestrial heavens.

To my surprise, as I disposed myself for sleep, there were no troubling fears. Unearthly the thing was, with the seeming of a dream, and yet it was—so safe!

Henry, as he monkeyed away with some apparatus, was singing in a low voice, once the following pessimistic lines of Swinburne's:

> "He weaves, and is clothed with derision;
> Sows, and he shall not reap;
> His life is a watch or a vision
> Between a sleep and a sleep."

And then, just before unconsciousness settled upon me, as if from far away through dreamy silence came the following beautiful lines of Moore's, though the singer was not uttering them with that feeling which would have been concomitant to their utterance; perhaps I fancy, he did not even know what he was singing:

> "As down in the sunless retreats of the Ocean,
> Sweet flowers are springing no mortal can see,
> So, deep in my soul the still prayer of devotion,
> Unheard by the world, rises silent to Thee,
> My God! silent to Thee—
> Pure, warm, silent, to Thee.
>
> "As still to the star of its worship, tho' clouded,
> The needle points faithfully o'er the dim sea,
> So, dark as I roam, in this wintry world shrouded,
> The hope of my spirit turns trembling to Thee,
> My God! trembling, to Thee."

Then came silence.

CHAPTER 10
THE TWELFTH DAY

In my sleep I was haunted, tortured by dreams that are simply indescribable. I had thought I knew what horrible dreams were, but I never knew until then.

Their origin was, of course, to be found in the strange physical changes existent in our little world—in which my senses had slipped their moorings, as it were.

My waking was a slow affair, and reality and dream were inextricably tangled. That strange blue quality of the sunlight produced the wildest and most horrible effects upon my bewildered senses. It became a legion of ghostly monsters, from whom I madly fled for what seemed centuries of time. From this horror I was at last rescued by returning consciousness, but, indeed, it was only to find myself in another—in that indescribable feeling of disembodiment of which I have spoken.

"Morning, Rider," greeted Henry. "How did you sleep?"

"Like Dante," I told him.

"Ditto," said Morgan St. Cloud.

"And you?" I asked Henry.

"Like a top."

"Good heavens! Is there anything you're not immune to?"

"I suppose I'll become Rider Farnermain again some time, somewhere," I added; "but certainly I am somebody—*something* else now. Probably if I had shrunk as I lost weight, I'd feel natural!"

"What a nightmare!" he laughed.

"But I weigh less than two ounces! Isn't that what you said?"

"That's what you do. But wait till you stand on Venus; you'll weigh about one hundred and thirty-five pounds, as against your hundred and sixty on Terra."

"Oh, happy day!"

"Wait till you see!" admonished St. Cloud.

Henry raised a finger and shook it at Morgan.

"Doubting Thomas!" he said. "That man needs much whom nothing will content."

St. Cloud smiled his dark smile.

"Let's have breakfast," he said.

At first the strangeness of the thing kept me highly keyed up, but everything palls, even (so I've heard) a sweetheart's kisses. But if the sweetheart was a Draconda, this could never be. But then, where was there ever a woman like Draconda?

Henry had brought about five dozen books—for which wise provision I became profoundly thankful. At the time, though, I had thought it absurd. To suppose that we should want to read!

But we did, for here we were imprisoned in this steel shell with absolutely nothing to do but look; and we couldn't always be looking—even though the whole Universe, from the Pole Star to the Octant, was at all times visible.

There, within a vast circle described about the southern celestial pole, were those stars which my eye had never seen on the earth. There blazed the great sun Canopus, second only to Sirius in brightness, though of a magnitude so vast that some have imagined that it must be the center of the sidereal system itself. (Another scientific pipe-dream.) There, too, by that mysterious void called the Coal Sack, shone the world-famous Southern Cross.

In my mind, however, this constellation (which, by the way, in ancient times belonged to Centaurus and was visible in the middle latitudes of the north) is surpassed in beauty by the Northern Cross, in the constellation Cygnus—which glitters overhead in our late summer skies.

But here is a strange thing, though what meaning it may have or whether it has any, I do not presume to say: the Southern Cross—the mystic beauty of which has caught the imagination of Christendom—disappeared from the skies of the Holy City about the time Christ died on Calvary.

I have mentioned the change in the color of the sunlight—which, here in the ether deeps, was a pale, unearthly blue. And yet it really was not blue, either; it was—what shall I say?—only *bluish*.

Here enters, again, the earth's atmosphere, which scatters and destroys the blue rays from the sun, thus giving it (as seen from the earth) its yellow color. But with no atmosphere between, the great luminary is a pale blue. Towards the edge of the disk, however—because the light there comes through the solar atmosphere at an oblique angle—the blue changes to the loveliest lilac upon which the eye ever lingered. And above this lilac were seen those scarlet flames, eruptive and quiescent, upon which scientists have bestowed the meaningless name "prominences" or "protuberances,"[5] and enveloping all the glorious corona itself.

On the earth the prominences can be seen only during the totality of a solar eclipse—though, of course, the scientist now can study them at any time by means of the spectroscope. However, all his attempts to render the corona perceptible have failed utterly, so that this radiant stellate mystery can be seen only when the moon hides the face of the sun—a phenomenon which never lasts more than a few minutes, and cannot possibly last more than eight.

But here (with the eye properly protected, of course) all this solar mystery

---

5. "It is unfortunate that no more appropriate and graphic name has yet been found for objects of such wonderful beauty and interest."—Young.

and beauty was at all times visible.

Hour after hour Henry spent in studying the corona, setting down his observations with great care and fullness. This coronal nebulosity in which our sun is immersed is a thing of greater wonder and mystery than any scientist ever has dreamed, and of it some strange things could be told. But this is not the place, nor is this the pen, to set them down.

The days slowly passed, the reality (and the memory) involved in the eerie seeming of a dream—if the word day can be used in speaking of a time in which there was no day. For here in this appalling abyss, through which the *Hornet* was rushing on its way with a speed greater than that with which the earth bowls along in its orbit, there is only the profoundest night.

Outside, there was no such thing as sunshine, nothing but the intensest blackness, only pulsations (hypothetical) in the (hypothetical) ether—no such thing, Henry Quainfan said, as *temperature* even—and yet there was the sunshine flooding through our windows!

It was some considerable time before I could get this strange physical paradox through my head.

Poor Keats! He was wrong after all!

The halfway point was passed on the eighth day. On the twelfth, three-fourths of the journey lay behind us, and we began to feel that we were getting somewhere.

CHAPTER 11
DE PROFUNDIS

Venus was rapidly approaching the sun—a tiny new moon against the pearly radiance of the corona.

It was on the fifteenth day, in the "forenoon" that she moved onto the sun's disk, and Henry, so to speak, held her there. The planet was now the size of our satellite—encircled by that blazing ring of sun.

"Only a million miles more!" said Henry airily.

And now that the landing was imminent, I began to imagine—well, some of the wildest, most fantastic things that it ever entered the mind to conceive. What of mystery and horror was there, under our eyes but hidden from their searching?

Of this world on which we would soon move inhabitants, we knew no more than when we had quitted our own, save only—Henry had discovered this, with his powerful field glasses—that the rapid rotation was the true one, though just how rapid it had not been possible to determine.

That black ball ever grew in magnitude, at length, when we were something like a half million miles distant, completely hiding from sight the disk of the great sun—twice the size of that sun which Terrestrials see.

A beautiful phenomenon now presented itself; the atmosphere was seen encircling the planet like a ring of luminescent silver. And beyond this effulgence, out in all directions, swept the coronal rays and streamers.

The planet, which had been black, or rather, the darkest of purples, slowly, as its disk encroached on the coronal radiance, turned to an ashen grey. But it was not all grey, for there, a thing of mystic beauty, was that "phosphorescence" which is visible even from the earth—explained by some observers as intense auroras (which it is) and by Lowell as the reflection of starshine from vast ice-sheets.

In all my memory there is not a single hour analogous to any of those that succeeded. I have spoken of wild things imagined, for that we were drawing to the end of our journey; but I greatly fear (and I confess it is not without shame) that now my confounded imagination went completely mad in limning, on the canvas of my brain, the things that might be waiting.

At length Henry Quainfan exclaimed cheerily:

"Only a quarter of a million miles farther!"

Venus now presented a disk as large as a dozen moons.

The increase in magnitude was extraordinary, and it took place with ever accelerated rapidity; in two hours' time—we then were distant about one hundred and fifty thousand miles—the area covered by the planet was equal to that of *fifty* moons.

In a half hour or so, we had entered Venus' gravitational domain—the region in which her gravity is dominant over the sun's.

"There's not the slightest sensible increase in weight, though," I remarked when Henry told me this.

"That will come later—or, rather, it will be something else."

"What do you mean?"

"I mean—"

But he was studying the Venusian world again.

"I can see dark things," he said. "Shadowy, indefinite, however. Whether continents, or what, I can't make out."

I had been wondering about something—and waiting for Henry to mention it. That he had not done so was, however, not surprising. So I asked:

"Are we going to land on this night side?"

"The business is apt to be dark enough," interposed St. Cloud, "without landing in darkness."

"No," Henry returned. "What we are going to do is this: hold straight on until very near—say, ten thousand or eight thousand miles—then swing out of the planet's shadow and over to the sunlit hemisphere."

"Before or behind?" queried St. Cloud.

"Behind," said Henry.

"Why not in the zone of morning?"

"I think," said Henry, "that by the time it comes, darkness will not be unwelcome."

"I wonder!" Morgan said.

When the distance mentioned was attained, the planet presented that same aspect of mystery and darkness—save for the darting, flickering and swaying of the auroras, a phenomenon of extraordinary beauty. But we had other things to think about.

"Venus guards her mysteries to the last," observed Henry. "But—now for the world of sunlight! We ought to see something there."

"I wonder what," said St. Cloud.

"You'll soon see," Henry told him.

And we did.

The *Hornet*—her velocity greatly diminished—swung out into the sunlight, as she went round drawing in slowly towards the planet.

And now comes a curious thing. It had been bothering me for some time. At first I had thought nothing of it. Then it had increased until I could dismiss it from my mind only by an effort. Now even that was impossible, and I held silence no longer.

"I don't know what it is," I said, "but there's something queer coming over me—a feeling of extreme weakness."

"Where do you feel weak, Rider?" Henry wanted to know.

"All over, it seems."

"That's funny."

"But especially in the knees," I added, "and accompanied by dizziness."

"That's the first time I ever heard of a fellow getting dizzy in the knees!"

"If you had it," I exclaimed, "you wouldn't stand there grinning about it!"

"I've got it."

"What on earth—?"

I stared at him. He was keeping a sharp lookout, however, and did not answer for some moments.

"Your knees are all right, Rider. It's Venus that's doing it. She's restoring your weight, you know."

"Blockhead!" I exclaimed at myself. "Of course!"

"We're only four thousand miles from her surface," he said, "and so—just think of it!—you weigh about thirty-five pounds! For two weeks your weight has been virtually *nil,* so can you blame your knees for feeling dizzy?"

"Great Jupiter Ammon," I exclaimed, "what will it be like when we stand on Venusian soil? Why, I won't be able to stand; I'll have to sit."

"Ditto," said St. Cloud.

"It will pass away quickly," Henry smiled.

A moment afterwards he drew back from the window, a hand over his eyes.

"We can't stand that," he said. "Lord, what an albedo!"

"Those dark glasses, Morgan," he added.

St. Cloud was already fetching them.

"What do you make of it?" I asked after a short pause.

"Not much—yet," he returned. "Wait till we get over farther."

St. Cloud and I waited in silence.

"There is a vast expanse of sunlit world now," Henry said at length, "but the glare of the atmosphere—by the goddess Urania, it's no wonder that Venus has always been a mystery to astronomers."

"Cloud-wrapped?" queried St. Cloud, bending over to look, and almost instantly drawing back, blinking and half blinded.

"Protect your eyes," Henry told him. "They can't stand that."

"No," reverting to St. Cloud's query, "she is not cloud-wrapped—that is, in the sense that her surface is completely hidden from view. There are many—countless openings. I can see land, great reaches of it, and water too. But that confounded glare—whence comes its intensity? But—"

"Yes?" said St. Cloud.

"The thing to do is to find *the* place and land!"

"March on, Macduff!" said Morgan.

As regards the high albedo of Venus, by the way, it can, in a large measure, be explained by the hygrometric state of her atmosphere; but it is a certainty that this will not account for it all.

Though a great mass of water vapor is held in suspension, yet Venus is by no means, as most observers believe, encased in an unbroken shell of cloud—a condition that would have to exist to produce (by means of water vapor) her remarkable albedo—placed by Muller at ninety-two per cent!

The X in the phenomenon, there can be little doubt, must lie hidden in some peculiar composition, or perhaps unknown constituent, of the atmosphere.

But an end to speculation, or this (awful thought) will read like a scientific treatise, instead of what it is—a narrative of unparalleled but *sober* fact.

The *Hornet* continued on, drawing northward as well as in toward the surface. At length—we were then but a thousand miles or so up—the midday point was attained, and then it was that our descent into the Venusian world began.

We had issued at last from the terrible depths of space; but what awaited us in these other deeps—these deeps into which we were now descending?

CHAPTER 12
THE SCREAM

We dropped swiftly. Down we went through that attenuated atmosphere which shares but slightly in the planet's axial spin; down into those strata which, with depth, move ever more swiftly to the eastward, and yet from below are *east winds;* and at last into that region of cloud.

"Looks like home," smiled Henry Quainfan.

"Home!" ejaculated St. Cloud. "Good Lord!"

"Well, it's a world—a terrestrial world. Land and water, hills and valleys, forests and mountains—and sun and cloud.

"What's wrong with it, Morgan?" he added.

"Oh, it looks all right," returned St. Cloud. "But—"

He stared down in silence.

"You were butting, Morgan," suggested Henry.

"Yes," said St. Cloud; "I thought of something—but we'll soon be there to see."

The world below had indeed an earth-like aspect, and I wondered if there were any intelligent creatures down there looking up at the *Hornet,* which was descending toward a lake coruscant in the rays of the great Venusian sun. In the east there was a stupendous mountain wall. The height of it was awful. But the point toward which we were descending claimed my attention, and this point was a little island, separated from the mainland by a narrow ribbon of water.

Lower and lower the *Hornet* sank, as gently as a snowflake falling; and at last, with an agitation of tiny trees and of foliage, it came to rest on the landward shore of the island.

Our long journey was at an end. We had traversed that awful and ever-changing gap which lies between Terra and Venus, and were safe and sound—with Heaven only knew what of adventure, discovery (and perhaps horror) before us.

In awe we pressed to the thick glass and looked out upon this alien world. It was indeed as if we had landed in some tellurian intertropical region. Here earth-like trees rose up; the sunlight glittered on the brilliant, luxuriant foliage; clouds dotted the blue immensity above; and the placid sheet of water glimmered in the sunlight.

"Water—trees—beauty—*life!*" murmured Morgan St. Cloud. "God moves in mysterious ways. Perhaps—who knows?—*souls!*"

"Of course," I said.

"See 'em yet, Rider?" Henry Quainfan asked.

"Grin away," I told him. "But would the Creator have made all this," and I waved a hand toward that sunlit beauty outside, "for nothing?"

"If anything is made for nothing, then nothing is made for anything," said he. "But that doesn't prove that that world must be the abode of human beings."

"You'll see."

"Of course I'll see," he smiled.

"By Jo," came St. Cloud's exclamation, "look at that!"

"What?" we asked, moving to his window.

"Look at that Gargantuan Cypripedium!"

"Oh," said Henry, a note of disappointment, I thought, in his voice.

For my part, I wondered what in the world this Cypripedium thing was. I don't know what I expected to see, but what I did see, thirty or forty feet distant in the gloom of the forest, was the largest and most gorgeous orchid that any eye ever saw.

"What a beauty!" exclaimed Morgan.

"Planted by the goddess Flora herself," Henry nodded. "But what I would like to see is animal life—something that moves!"

"Of course," concurred St. Cloud. "Haven't seen even a mosquito, though."

"Here's hoping we don't! But what are we staying in here for, bottled up like so many Cartesian imps?"

"What do you think of this Venusian air?" queried St. Cloud. "As dense as some have supposed? If it is, it may knock us flat."

"Nothing like that," Henry told him, "though it may render our breathing more or less difficult. But we'll soon find that out; there's the valve, you know."

Henry moved toward it forthwith.

"Suppose," said St. Cloud, "that we can't live in this world after all, even though it is so much like our own. You know, it is possible that there may be some—"

"Possible but highly improbable," Henry said. "Here goes to see!"

Came a faint hissing sound—which, however, died away almost instantly—and a strange feeling of suffocation in throat and lungs.

"How much more?" said St. Cloud, a little anxiously.

And I caught at that curious change in his voice.

"We've got it all now," Henry returned after a brief pause.

That change was in his voice, too—due, of course, to the density of the Venusian atmosphere.

This change, however, was not one of volume; it was merely a curious reverberating quality, and by no means one pronounced. Indeed, it was faint, elusive as curious; in a time surprisingly short we were unaware of any difference.

Also, that difficulty we experienced in breathing gradually passed away, though this took place much more slowly than the other; indeed, it was some days before respiration became normal.

"Now to issue!" exclaimed Henry Quainfan, leaving the valve and moving towards the door.

St. Cloud and I pressed after him—crowded so close that I fancy we impeded his movements as he proceeded to unloosen the fastenings.

He worked swiftly; that steel-rimmed glass disk moved inward on its hinges—and (romantic vision) Henry Quainfan stuck his head out.

"Hello!" he called out, and for the first time in my life, I believe, I heard awe in his voice.

He looked back at us and smiled.

"Nobody answers!"

"Silent as the grave," Morgan said.

"Well, out we go!" exclaimed Henry.

Even as he spoke, he was on his way; but St. Cloud grabbed him a little wildly and pulled him back.

"Not like that," St. Cloud told him.

"Like what?"

"Good heavens, there's no telling what kind of a world this is. You want a gun."

"That's right," Henry nodded. "I do, though the chances are that there is nothing dangerous here on this island."

"You can't tell anything about it," said Morgan. "Remember this is not the earth but a world of which we know nothing. There may be boa-constrictors in there," jerking a finger toward the gloomy depths of the forest; "or tigers or arboreal devil-fishes or something. Heavens, who knows what! Wait till I get you a rifle."

"That's right," I said. "For my part, you won't see me out there unarmed."

"I should say not!"

"Of course," Henry nodded.

A few moments, and St. Cloud handed him a Winchester and ammunition.

"I forgot all about weapons," Henry said, clicking in the cartridges.

He waited until St. Cloud and I had loaded our rifles, too, then moved again to the door.

And out he went, while I stood holding his weapon in readiness. Even as I heard his feet touch the ground, his fingers closed on the piece. Wonderful that feeling of security which the touch of a rifle imparts!

He stepped away a few paces. Of a sudden his body came into a slightly crouching attitude, and his eyes leaped hither and yon—over every visible object, it seemed. But as suddenly he drew his fine, powerful form erect, and his lips moved, though no words reached the ear—moved in prayer I should have thought, only Henry Quainfan never prayed.

But this was only for a few seconds. "Come on," he called softly.

I moved back a little from the manhole.

"*Seniores priores,* Morgan," I said.

"I thank you, Rider," he returned in that courtly way of his.

And so the second earth-man set foot on Venusian soil.

I followed forthwith, and as soon as my feet touched the ground I—*danced!*

"I wonder," said Morgan, "if there *is* anything in there."

As he spoke he made a motion with his rifle toward those gloomy and silent depths of the forest.

Henry, who had been standing silent and moveless, as if his thoughts were mingled with others far away, turned his eyes, though with a somewhat vacuous expression, in the direction indicated, and then, without speaking, he gazed away towards the terrific and cloud-involved heights of that mountain wall there in the east.

If it had not been for this wall, I could have imagined ourselves on the earth.

"Well, we're armed," I told St. Cloud. "Oh, we're armed, but—"

He left the thought unfinished.

"By Jo!" he exclaimed.

And to my surprise he went stalking off into that gloom which he seemed to dread so much.

For a moment I couldn't imagine what had got into him; then I saw; he was going for that Cypripedium.

"Look out for those boas and tree-octopuses, Morgan," Henry smiled after him.

"I am!"

And he was. But nothing happened. In a brief space St. Cloud was back with that great flower in his hands.

"Did you ever see anything like it?" he exclaimed.

Certainly we never had—nor had any one ever seen its like on the earth. For a little time we stood gazing at its strange beauty. Then Morgan and I began poking around. Henry Quainfan, however, remained standing in the same spot—silent, abstracted.

St. Cloud and I picked leaves, crushing some of them between thumb and finger; we broke twigs, picked up stones, some of which we sent flying out into the water; and we went down to the edge and splashed in the liquid with our hands.

And at last we fell on our knees, and I offered up thanks for our safe journey through the deeps and petitioned a continuance of that Divine protection which had brought us to Aphrodite unharmed, the while Henry Quainfan (to whom this praying was but so much superstition) stood attentive and respectful.

Then I fetched from the *Hornet* the national colors; Henry hastened to cut a pole, and in a few minutes the stars and stripes was raised to the Venusian breeze.

I had just straightened up after making the staff solid when, from out the forest across that narrow sheet of water, there rose an awful and lingering scream, in which there was an elusive throbbing and, it seemed, a ring that was feminine—though I felt certain, what with its awful intenseness, that it could not come from a woman's lips—and which cut and slashed the silence like a knife and pierced to the inmost recesses of our souls.

CHAPTER 13
LIFE THAT MOVES

The terrible scream sank—died away. A half minute or so passed, and still all was silent.

"I wonder—" began St. Cloud.

I glanced at him, inquiringly.

"It sounded like a woman's scream," he said.

I nodded.

"But it couldn't have been," I told him.

I looked at Henry. His lips severed for speech, but the words that he was about to utter became strange sounds in his throat, for that same sudden and awful scream came again out of the depths of the slumbering forest.

Upward it rushed and up and up, in it that same elusive throbbing which we had detected before. Also, it seemed nearer this time, but I knew that that might be only fancy.

Then suddenly it ceased, as suddenly as it had come, and all was still once more.

"Good heavens," exclaimed St, Cloud, "can that really be a human being in there—a woman? What do you make of it, Henry?"

Henry, who was leaning on his Winchester, shook his head slowly, still gazing in the direction whence had come that awful scream.

"It's no woman," he said. "An animal gave that. Woman!" he ejaculated. "Now, how on earth could evolution—"

He was interrupted by a sharp exclamation from the lips of St. Cloud.

"Look!" St. Cloud cried out. "Look there!"

Before my eyes had leaped to the spot toward which he was pointing, a dull splash came to our ears. Something had leaped into the lake from a wall of rock which, several hundred feet off to the right, rose straight up from the water's edge to a height of twelve or fifteen feet.

The water was deep there, for the thing had disappeared. In an instant, however, it broke the surface and at that same instant another shot out into the air and vanished near the first, which was striking out for our island. Up came the second one, to follow along in the wake of the other.

The water rose in front of them in little waves, which made broken streams that fleshed like streams of silver. And upon the heads of these Venusian creatures were the ramified horns of the deer!

I gave a cry of delight and turned in triumph to Henry.

"Deer!" he exclaimed, staring at the things like a man doubting the reality of the images thrown upon his retina.

"Where now is your evolution?" I asked jubilantly. "Where now is your Darwinian pipe-dream?"

Henry looked at me, his face thought absent, but said nothing.

"Not so fast, Rider," cautioned St. Cloud. "They look just like our common deer, but remember we see nothing but their heads. And as for those horns—well, that doesn't necessitate a direct creative fiat."

"Of course not, Rider," said Henry Quainfan. "You might as well say that the rhinoceros is descended from Triceratops."

A few moments later the animals issued from the water, and in an instant they had vanished into the depths of the forest.

No pursuer had emerged from the trees whence had come that awful scream.

Henry Quainfan turned to me, a smile in his eyes.

"Where, Rider," he asked, "did you see that animal on the earth?"

"Grin away. But they're deer!"

"So they are. And—"

He pointed upward.

"That's sky."

"Just wait," I told him. "Before very long, your evolutionary theories and hypotheses will look like the walls of Jericho."

"One thing's certain," said Morgan, "the scream didn't come from that kind of animal."

"Of course not," Henry said.

"And another thing," added St. Cloud, "why didn't we bowl one over? Venison steak for supper, and we just stood looking!"

"I never thought of that," I told him.

"Same here," said Henry. "But we can get them."

The ripples made by the passage of the animals slowly died away, the water resumed its dimpled smoothness, and a great silence settled down on the wild and lonely spot.

For a time we did not speak; each was lost in his thoughts.

I found it hard to realize that this was not our own world; that the orb of my birth floated through space millions and millions of miles away. I wondered if I should ever return to the earth, and, though it seems very strange, it somehow did not seem to matter much whether I should or not.

And what awaited us here in this unknown land? What denizens dwelt in the gloom of these mighty trees? Were there on this planet also two-legged animals like ourselves? If so, would we fall in love, take and give in marriage? Go out to battle, slay and be slain? Would a day find us again on our own natal planet, honored of men as the greatest discoverers of the ages? Or would we meet death here, far from our own—water roar or slumber over our bones, or blood-dripping fangs tear them asunder?

These thoughts came to me, and many more—thoughts that I could not catch and imprison in words, that seemed the more terrible or beautiful because they were faint and elusive.

What thoughts came to my companions, I do not know. I looked at Henry Quainfan. He stood in the same spot, in the same attitude of profound meditation. And as I looked there welled up in me a mighty admiration and love for this silent and strange friend of mine—the only real friend I had ever had in all my life.

There he stood, silent and leaning on his Winchester, the greatest discoverer of all time. What must have been his thoughts as he stood there? What he must have felt? But he gave no sign. He just stood here, calm and unreadable, leaning on the rifle and gazing with eyes that did not see.

I did not see it coming, nor did St. Cloud, or he would have said something.

My look was on the desolate and awful beauty of that stupendous mountain wall. Oh, the height of it! It seemed it must touch the very stars. In a way, it is the most awful and beautiful thing that I have ever seen—except Draconda.

Suddenly my heart was in my throat, and I nearly jumped straight up into the air. Swinging round, I saw Henry lowering the Winchester from his shoulder and something brilliantly colored, and fifty or sixty feet distant, falling to the ground, where it lay struggling feebly.

We hurried to it.

"By the great Nimrod," exclaimed St. Cloud, "if that isn't a Chinese pheasant's uncle, what is it?"

"Chinese pheasant, my eye!" Henry Quainfan ejaculated.

The bird, which had ceased its struggles, lay breathing heavily and in great pain.

"The poor devil," said Henry, looking at the dying creature ruefully. "We must put an end to its suffering."

Kneeling down, with a quick movement he broke the bird's neck.

This was the first thing I had seen him kill since his boyhood days. In his beliefs, he was a materialist, utter and terrible, and yet he would never go hunting or even fishing, holding it a crime needlessly to destroy any creature. If necessary for food, it was a different matter entirely; but just to satiate that beast which is in every human being—you should have heard Henry express his feelings on that subject.

Never shall I forget the quarrel—a pyrotechnical one indeed—which he once had with a preacher on seeing the man of God setting out with shotgun and hounds for a day's shooting.

"Feathers!" Henry exclaimed, looking down at the dead bird with a curious expression of surprise and bepuzzlement. "What a remarkable coincidence! What a coincidence that evolution has progressed along parallel, identical lines on two planets!"

"Coincidence, my thumb!" I told him. "That evolution business—what is it but moonshine? Before long you'll see that it's so. Just look about you. Look at these trees. There is nothing in them to tell us that we are not on the earth. There are no familiar ones, 'tis true, but we have seen only this one spot. The chances are we'll find them; indeed, I feel sure of that."

"You are so often sure, Rider," he observed with a glint of amusement in his eyes.

"We'll find humans too!" I declared.

Henry laughed.

"You think there is nothing in the Universe greater than man."

And he laughed again.

"That's just what I do."

"No, you go still farther, Rider; you believe that the Universe was made for man. Anthropocentricism! It's funny you don't believe that the world is flat! I tell you what, Rider, man is no more than a butterfly or a canary-bird—except to himself. Remember that: except to himself. He is no more to the Universe."

"That's right," said I; "put the cart before the horse. It's what the Universe is to man."

"Poppycock!" said Henry Quainfan. "The Universe could get along very well without him. Indeed, when he goes down into darkness, the Universe will never know it. Without him—this being with the godlike intellect, which he uses for purposes anything but godlike—without him, the sun would still shine, the planets swing on in their orbits, and the Galaxy would not then go crumbling away to nothing.

"Man just happened to be, that is all; and he happened to be because some ancestor of his—with an intellect only animal—climbed up into the trees, climbed back down and walked upright, and because this was thus and that was otherwise. Ontogeny, geological succession and homological structure, Rider—those are the things that one can't get away from. If each species was separately created by a direct fiat of the Creator, why, Rider my boy, why in the world in a certain stage of their ontogenetic development do all—but we have threshed this out before and threshed in vain. Still, in your mind, man remains the kingpin of the Cosmos."

"Of course. I believe that the soul of one human being is more to the Creator than all His worlds."

"Pickled moonshine!" Henry ejaculated.

"As for your evolution," I said, "you can't even pickle that."

"At any rate, Rider," he answered, "Science sees with her eyes and her brains, while Faith—"

"I know what you're going to say," I interposed.

"While Faith sees with her ears."

I turned to St. Cloud.

"Hopeless, Morgan," I observed.

"Yes," said the dark man, smiling that dark smile of his: "both of you."

CHAPTER 14
THE DISCOVERY

"I think it would be a good idea," said Henry Quainfan shortly afterward, "to explore our island."

"It would," concurred Morgan. "You know—"

He sent a glance into that silent gloom of the forest.

"There may be something in there," he added, "watching every move we make."

Henry Quainfan slowly turned his look toward that sylvan darkness.

"It's possible," he nodded.

This possibility, though, didn't seem to worry Henry any.

"However," I remarked, "before this exploration of ours begins, we want to get one of those deer animals."

"That's what we do," said Morgan. "I wonder, now, if this Chinese pheasant is good to eat."

"Looks like it," I said.

Henry nodded.

"We can try it, anyway. As for those deer, we'll need only one of them; I'd let the other escape."

"We haven't got 'em yet," St. Cloud reminded him.

"The first thing," said I, "is a knife. Anything you fellows want?"

"Nothing, I guess," answered St. Cloud, "unless you bring me one, too."

"My binoculars, Rider," Henry said. "You know, I may be able to spot one of those tree-octopi in time."

"You may spot something worse than an octopus up a tree," St. Cloud told him.

"I don't doubt that, Morgan. But not here."

"Here's hoping," said St. Cloud.

I entered the *Hornet* and handed out Henry's glasses and a knife (sheathed) for St. Cloud.

Then we started.

We soon found our quarry. We had proceeded as noiselessly as possible, but the animals had heard us, and little wonder; the forest was so thick. There they stood at the water's edge (on the lakeward side), heads up and ready to fly.

I happened to be to the fore as we attained the opening which brought them into view, and taking swift aim, I fired.

"Hit!" I cried.

Bang! went Morgan's rifle in my ear.

"Missed!" he ejaculated, throwing in another cartridge.

His animal was leaping away into the lake.

"Let him go, Morgan," came Henry's voice. "Let the poor devil go. One of them's enough."

St. Cloud muttered something; turning, however, I saw him slowly lowering the rifle.

We pushed forward rapidly, in a few moments breaking from the undergrowth out upon the shingle.

"What a beautiful creature!" said Henry Quainfan, as we hovered about the victim.

"How like," remarked St. Cloud, "and yet how unlike."

He drew his big knife. Bending over, he slashed open the buck's throat, the blood twisting itself this way and that among the stones, like a live thing, to diffuse its crimson in the crystal water—still agitated by the mad dash of that escaping deer, which was headed straight across the lake.

"Venison steak for supper!" said St. Cloud, smacking his lips.

I laid my rifle down carefully (for that weapon was a thing to be carefully guarded now) and began rolling up my sleeves.

"Now to dress our kill," I said. "Then we'll take him in and begin explorations—though I have an idea that there's not much to explore on this island."

"Of course," nodded Henry Quainfan. "And so, while you fellows are busy, I'll look it over."

St. Cloud turned to Henry. He made a couple of passes with his bloody knife in the direction of the trees.

"Don't you go in there, Henry," he said earnestly. "Wait for us. We won't be long. It may be all right, of course, and then it may be infernally otherwise. Good heavens, this isn't the earth!"

"Ta-ta!" said Henry Quainfan, turning. "See you later."

We watched him moving away into the gloom. He stopped, smiled as he waved a hand to us and the next instant had vanished from sight.

"Confound him!" said St. Cloud. "What did he do that for?"

"He could have waited," I returned. "Still—what can there be?"

"This world of Venus, Rider, is as mysterious now—even though we know what it is—as it was when we quitted the earth."

"Hardly that."

"Probably more so, Rider. Heaven only knows what we are going to see."

We set to work, and in a short time we were on our way back to the *Hornet*, I with the dressed deer on my back.

Arrived there, we looked and listened; but the eye caught no sign of Henry Quainfan, and not the faintest sound came from out the forest, save the sad, gentle whispering of the wind.

St. Cloud made a megaphone of his hands and called out:

"*Yo-ho-o-o-o!*"

The sound rolled away into silence; but from the dark recesses of those trees before us, came no voice in answer.

We waited a little while. The silence seemed to grow heavier—oppressive.

Then St. Cloud raised his voice again:

"Oh, Henry! *Yo-ho-o-o-o-o!*"

Still no answer.

"Good heavens!" burst out Morgan.

"I wonder——" I began.

But I didn't know what it was that I wondered.

"Something's happened, Rider."

"Come," said I, starting toward the trees. "This must be looked into."

We moved forward rapidly, but we had taken scarcely twenty steps when a sharp voice came, stopping us in our tracks.

"Hello!" said the voice.

And the next moment Henry Quainfan's face moved into view from behind a tree-trunk.

"Of all the fool things!" burst out St. Cloud—though (I regret to say) with embellishments most forcible. "Why didn't you sing out?"

"Just a fancy of mine."

"Don't have any more fancies like that," I told him. "I thought something had got you."

"No—but I got something."

As he spoke, he raised his left hand.

"What do you think of this?"

St. Cloud gave an exclamation.

"*The* proof!" I cried. "Only a human being could have made it!"

"I knew you'd say that," smiled Henry Quainfan.

CHAPTER 15
DARKNESS FALLS

I stared at him and then at that thing which he was holding up for our inspection—a small ax or tomahawk, incased in rust and handle worm-eaten and decayed.

"Do you mean to tell me," I burst out, "that you still believe——?"

"This weapon, Rider," he interrupted, "for I suppose it was a weapon, proves that this wild Venusian world is the abode of intelligent beings. But that is all that it does prove. As to what those beings are, it tells us nothing."

"Indeed!" I exclaimed, turning the ax over and over in my hands. "It tells me! This is man's handiwork. Look at it! Great Jupiter Ammon, when you see your first Venusian man, I suppose you'll say he's only an hallucination or something."

"If what I see is a *homo sapiens* (or *stupidus*) I suppose I will."

"How about it, Morgan?" I asked.

St. Cloud reached forth a hand for the weapon, which he examined minutely and in silence.

"Strange," he said finally. "And yet not strange, after all. Where, Henry, did you find this?"

Henry Quainfan stuck his thumb over his shoulder.

"In there, over near the other shore. Nearly stepped right over it."

"Maybe," suggested St. Cloud, "there is something else."

But Henry Quainfan shook his head.

"Not in that spot."

"I thought the owner's skeleton might be lying somewhere nearby."

"I thought that, too, and so looked carefully all around. But nothing was there, save what you have got in your hand."

"It's been lying in there for years," observed St. Cloud.

"Of course."

"And its owner?" I queried. "*What* left it there?"

St. Cloud shrugged his shoulders.

"Who knows, Rider? Maybe you are right; indeed, I'm inclined to that belief myself; at the same time, though, I don't blink the possibility that its owner might have been something very different."

"Smoke that in your pipe, Rider," smiled Henry. "But come, and I'll show you the spot."

Accordingly we went. But we did not find anything new. We searched the gloomy recesses of that island from one end to the other, but discovered nothing.

When we returned to the *Hornet,* the great sun was sinking behind the tree-tops in the west, the departing rays softening the brilliant green of the foliage and drawing over distant objects a subtle veil of the tenderest violet, rendering them uncertain and lovely as visions seen in a dream.

"Great guns," exclaimed St. Cloud, "evening already! Where has the time gone?"

"How long have we been here?" I asked Henry.

"Don't know, Rider. I forgot to look. It was just about midday when we landed, but we don't know how long it takes Venus to make her diurnal spin—to say nothing of the inclination of her axis. All I know is that the rotation is swift, like the earth's, and that the axis isn't upright to the orbital plane, which gives the planet days and nights of variable length, and seasons."

"As for the seasonal part of the business," I ventured, "wouldn't the compass shed light on that, by showing how far to the north or south of the west point the sun is going down?"

"Hello, Keats!" St. Cloud grinned.

"Rider," said Henry, "remember what Morgan has been pounding into my ear; this isn't the earth. It is the stars that will make everything clear. And on the earth man doesn't get his direction from the compass; if he did, sometimes he would be traveling south when headed north. He gets his orientation from the stars. He can't trust his compass until they have shown him how untrustworthy it is."

"What care we about seasons and stars?" exclaimed St. Cloud. "What-ho for a fire and the sizzle of venison steak!"

"I second the motion," I told him.

"For my part," said Henry Quainfan, "I am going down to the point and scrutinize the shores, like the bear that went over the hill to see what I can see— signs of *men*, perhaps."

And he grinned at me.

Accordingly St. Cloud and I set about to light our fire, while Henry, Winchester in hand, walked to the farther end of the island to sweep the margin of the lake with his powerful glasses.

The fire was going brightly, enhancing the gloom of the trees, when Henry returned.

"See anything?" I asked him.

He nodded, but remained looking at me in silence.

"Anything unusual?" I queried. "You're about as communicative, at times, as the Sphinx."

"I don'' know for sure what it is. Let's go out on that rock, and you can see it for yourself."

He turned as he ceased speaking; St. Cloud and I followed.

"There it is," said Henry Quainfan when we had clambered up beside him. "What is that?"

He pointed toward a spot nearly two miles away on the farther shore.

"What is what?" I wanted to know.

For not a sign of anything unusual could I descry.

"There!" said St. Cloud. "I see it—but 'tis gone."

I had been straining my eyes, but not a thing had I seen; and my eyesight is supposed to be excellent. I had just opened my mouth to speak, however, when, above that distant wall of trees, a nebulous something appeared and in a moment had vanished.

"What is it?" Henry asked.

"Smoke!" I declared.

"What, Morgan?"

"Wait a minute," returned St. Cloud, "until it comes again."

"There it is," Henry told him.

There was that nebulous thing again. This time, however, it hovered above the tree-tops for a little space and then slowly drifted away into nothingness.

"It *does* look like smoke," said St. Cloud.

"Of course it is," I declared. "And only intelligent things make fires."

"Funny we didn't notice it before," mused Henry.

"Maybe it wasn't there," I remarked.

"A little while ago," he added, "it was a thin and straight column."

"Let's see the glasses," Morgan said.

"They won't throw any light on the matter, though," returned Henry, reaching the glasses over to St. Cloud. "Probably if it wasn't for this haze—which renders everything so dreamily beautiful—we could come to a positive conclusion."

"If that isn't smoke," I wanted to know, "what is it?"

"I think it's water vapor, Rider, arising probably from a hot spring."

"Hot spring, my ear! Look at that bluish tinge."

"It does seem to have a bluish tinge, all right," observed St. Cloud, handing the glasses to me; "but, you know, that may be due to the haze."

"Doubting Tom," said I, "meet Doubting Thomas."

I brought the glasses to a focus and for some time studied the phenomenon closely.

"You were right," I observed, returning the binoculars to Henry: "they don't solve the problem."

"So you think there are human beings over there behind that wall of trees?" he queried, examining a spot about four miles distant with the glasses.

"I think the vapor indicates that, for I don't believe that it is the vapor of water. But an answer to the question easily can be had."

"Yes," he nodded. "And in the morning we'll get it."

"Maybe we will," put in Morgan.

"I thought I saw something move down on that point," Henry added, pointing with his finger; "but I couldn't tell for sure because of the fading light."

We soon returned to the fire. When we finished the first meal eaten by terrestrial men on the Planet of Love, darkness was falling. The sky, though dotted with fleecy clouds, was clear, and the brighter stars already were twinkling down at us.

For a time St. Cloud and I carried on a rambling conversation, but Henry Quainfan was silent. He sat with his back against a small tree and, with his head slightly bowed, gazed across the water into the blackness whence had come that awful scream.

St. Cloud and I talked on, but Henry said never a word. I do not believe he heard us. And at last, we too, were silent, and then could be heard only the lazy crackling of the fire, which cast a lurid light for a little distance out upon the glassy water.

I wondered if Henry was thinking of that awful scream, which, now when I thought of it, rang again in my ears. It was unlikely, I thought, that his mind was dwelling on that. It was the death cry of some animal, that was all, and now it was all over; never again would that unknown thing know joy or sorrow, fear or the throes of death. It was gone, was in the nothing into which the beasts go, into which all sentient things go save men and women and the men-children and women-children of men and women. It was gone and would be no more forever. And into that terrible blackness (awful thought) Henry Quainfan believed that he would be lowered by the hands of Death.

Ere long, however, Henry came out of that fit of abstraction, to devote his attention to the stars.

"What do you make of it?" St. Cloud asked him after a time.

"Wait a while," Henry returned.

And it was a while, during which he continued his watch of the heavens.

"Well, what do you know about that!" he sang out at last.

"What?" St. Cloud asked, rising and directing his steps toward Henry Quainfan.

I followed.

"What star is that?" Henry said, indicating a blazing diamond in the northern heavens and halfway up to the zenith, in which direction auroral beams were shooting up—giving one the idea of swords in the hands of hidden cosmic giants—quivered and vanished.

"Alpha of the Lyre," returned Cloud.

"Our pole star," Henry told him: "the apex of the sun's way."

"What a coincidence!" murmured St. Cloud.

"Co—what?"

"Incidence."

"How so, Morgan?"

"Why, she was the earth's pole star once and will be again, in the distant future—eleven thousand years, isn't it?"

"It seems," I observed, "that Terra and Venus are indeed twin sisters. How strange that their axis should be tilted at the same angle!"

"Approximately," said Henry. "In point of fact, though, Rider, nothing is strange. But see here—here's the whole business in a nutshell:

"There's the pole of the ecliptic, between those faint stars, Delta and Zeta Draconis astronomers call them—though this constellation is no longer a dragon but only a serpent, for (cruel ginks!) they lopped off its wings to make the asterism called the Little Bear. But that isn't the Venusian ecliptic pole; owing to the inclination of the planet's orbit, it lies off here the distance of six lunar diameters. That spot there would be our pole if the axis of Venus was perpendicular to the orbital plane."

"But it isn't," was my sage observation.

"It isn't," said Henry Quainfan, "though how far Vega may be from the pole itself remains to be determined, for the chances are that (like Polaris) it does not mark the precise spot where there is no diurnal motion.

"The height of the pole," he added, "gives the latitude directly (there is no longitude) and the season can be—"

"Look!" cried St. Cloud.

There in the east, above one of the peaks of that awful cordillera, were the earth and the moon—the former shining with a splendor that was truly wonderful, her bluish light, however, less pronounced here in the deeps of this aerial ocean.

In silence, and with indescribable feelings, we three stood gazing. One was silent and dead, a floating cinder, the other teeming with life and the sound and stirring of life; but none of those sounds that we knew so well came to our ears, and naught could we see but starshine, for the earth was as any of the stars that swing in the unutterable immensity of God's ether sea—a thing unutterably infinitesimal.

Then came (and with a rush) a sight so strangely, weirdly beautiful that it beggars description. No pen could convey an adequate picture of what we saw—the Venusian aurora in all its terrific intensity and awesome beauty.

But at last we tore ourselves away from the sight and entered the *Hornet*.

Henry was asleep almost instantly. How I envied him that faculty of dropping off, apparently under any circumstances, almost the moment his head touched the pillow!

St. Cloud and I exchanged a number of speculations, some of them curious and wild enough, and then of a sudden he fell silent.

For some time I lay watching the flaming of the aurora overhead, wondering about the morrow and about things which the mind never should conjure up; wondering and wondering—and wondering on in my dreams.

CHAPTER 16
DESTROYED

When I awoke, the sunlight, pale and yellowish, was slanting in through the windows. St. Cloud was still sleeping, but Henry was gone.

I rose, went to the manhole and stuck my head out; a fire was going, and seated by it, his rifle beside him, was Henry Quainfan—shaving.

The sun had just shoved his great disk above the cordillera, which loomed up dim and evanescent as a Turnerian vision in that curious haze of morning.

The air was cool and sweet. A great silence pressed down on the place, disturbed only by the crackling of the fire, and the flag hung motionless against its staff.

"Hello, Beau Brummel!" I sang out—and heard St. Cloud stir and mutter behind me.

"Morning, Rider," returned Henry. "How did you sleep?"

"Fine, only I had some queer dreams."

"Your imagination," Henry explained. "You let it have free rein."

"No dream, I'll wager, like mine!" muttered St. Cloud.

I turned, to see him sitting up with an expression on his dark features that often comes to me now—though at the time I thought but little of it, save that his dream must have been one truly terrible.

"About this world?" I queried.

"And another, Rider. But—"

He made a wild gesture and stared at me with a strange look in his eyes.

"I wish I couldn't think about it," he said; "to talk about it—that's out of the question."

I think I know now what St. Cloud dreamed, and so perhaps will you ere I am done.

I went out, soon followed by Morgan.

"Great explorers you two!" observed Henry Quainfan. "Slumbering the morning away as though you were at home, instead of on an alien planet with

Heaven only knows what things at hand awaiting discovery!"

Rather to my surprise, St. Cloud remained silent, staring moodily about him.

"As for you," I observed to Henry, "you seem to anticipate a meeting with Aphrodite herself."

He stroked his chin with placid satisfaction.

"Better follow suit, Rider, you look like the devil."

"Thanks—but I'll wait till we meet the lady."

"Then you're in for a beard to your feet."

"Indeed!" I said. "But—is that smoke still rising?"

"I don't know, Rider; never looked."

"Great explorer you are!" I told him. "A Venusian could be creeping up behind each tree, and you be none the wiser."

"We'll soon solve the mystery," he returned. "For as soon as we have had breakfast—"

"Breakfast!" interrupted St. Cloud, giving the place a periscopic examination. "A man could break his neck here sooner than his fast."

"Hope," said Henry Quainfan, "makes a good breakfast."

"But, oh," Morgan told him, "what a supper!"

"Where nothing is," I observed, "a little would ease."

"Every time the sheep bleateth, Rider," Henry said, "he loseth a mouthful."

"Which, translated, means that we must get our own breakfast. And after breakfast? You started to tell us that."

"After breakfast, we'll build a raft."

"A what?" I exclaimed.

"A raft. A canoe's grandfather. A thing that floats and on which you can go gliding over the bounding billows."

"Great Jupiter Ammon!" said Morgan. "Are we going to explore this place on a—darn it, on a catamaran?"

"That's the idea," Henry nodded.

"Why not in the *Hornet?*"

"We've been corked up in that steel bottle for two weeks; here we are in this Cytherean beauty and mystery—and you want to be a pickled explorer, as it were! Come, Morgan; if we are going to see this world, we want to live in it, walk about in it, fight in it if it need be—not merely peek at it from the oculi of the *Hornet*. And not only that, but the outing is just the thing we need."

"Outing!" echoed Morgan. "Good heavens!"

"Of course, we'll have to be careful," said Henry; "for who knows what terrible denizens may be prowling about in this wilderness?"

He turned his look to me.

"What do you think of it, Rider?"

"I think it capital," I told him. "You are right: those steel walls are very fine, but we didn't come here to remain like so many bees in a bottle."

"Sail on, Palinurus," Morgan said to Henry; "but I tell you this: I don't like the voyage before us."

Then, as though addressing himself to some figure standing there behind Henry Quainfan:

"Welcome, Mischief, if thou comest alone!"

Accordingly, as soon as breakfast was done, we set to work on the raft, using the boles of small trees. It was soon made, was about twenty feet long by four in width and pointed at each end.

Little did we dream, as we looked upon our completed craft, how long that journey we were destined to make upon it.

We immediately got ready to embark.

And now comes a curious thing. Morgan St. Cloud I may call the Cautious, Henry Quainfan the Nonchalant. And yet when it came to this excursion, which would take us to we knew not what, it was Henry Quainfan who armed himself to the teeth, while St. Cloud regarded his Winchester, cartridge-belt and hunting knife as sufficient for any emergency likely to confront us. At Henry's importunity, however, he added a revolver—in a holster attached to a belt beaded with cartridges.

Indeed, for my part, I thought such an armament (including the revolver, that is) sufficient, and took virtually the same as St. Cloud. But how was I to know? Heaven only knows how many times I have wished that Morgan and myself had loaded ourselves down like Henry Quainfan.

He *was* armed. To begin with, there was, of course, his Winchester; at each hip, pendent from a loaded cartridge-belt, was a .44 Colt's revolver; over his left shoulder, and passing under his right arm, were two belts filled with rifle cartridges; and at his right hip, in a sheath, almost hidden by the holster there, was a big hunting-knife—to say nothing of the cartridges he had stuffed into his pockets.

"Great Jupiter!" exclaimed St. Cloud. "Do you intend to kill all the Venusians on the globe?"

"It looks like it, all right!" I laughed.

"He who laughs last laughs best," said Henry Quainfan, "though here's truly hoping that I won't have any occasion to indulge in cachinnation."

"Cachinnation is right," St. Cloud observed, "for in that case, there'll be no mirth in your laugh."

Everything was soon ready, and we pushed off—with the flag at the masthead. We had provided ourselves with long poles and with paddles. Of course, the raft would be an awkward thing to paddle, but by going straight across we would save six or eight miles that appeared uninteresting—if such a word can be used in speaking of anything in this place.

It was with keen anticipation on my part that we started on this voyage of ours—longer than any of us dreamed. We poled around the nearer end of the island, the one where Henry had swept the lake and the shores with his glasses, and headed across.

That mysterious vapor, I have forgotten to say, was still rising.

As we were going round that point, I turned and looked back at the *Hornet*, obeying an impulse that I can almost believe was prescient. Something else claimed the attention of Morgan and Henry, and so mine were the eyes to see the *Hornet* for the last time.

St. Cloud soon produced a fishing line and a fly-hook, which he had chanced upon that morning in one of his pockets—St. Cloud was nothing if not a disciple of old Izaak Walton—attached the line to his pole, which made a ludicrous rod, and cast.

Henry and I had ceased to paddle and were watching expectantly. Hardly had the treacherous fly struck the water when there came a streak of silver out of the greenish depths. There was a splash, and the fish came inboard, wiggling violently.

"Aha!" exclaimed Morgan, "what do you think of that?"

He held the fish up for us to see.

"Gentlemen," he said, *"Mr. Salmo Purpuratus!"*

"Cutthroat!" I exclaimed.

Henry Quainfan took off his hat and ran his fingers through his curls.

"What the deuce," said he, "is that fellow doing here?"

"It is quite a coincidence, all right," remarked Morgan. "I've caught hundreds of trout just like him on the earth."

"It does make a fellow's Darwinism feel a little groggy," Henry admitted.

We reached the shore (it was very warm now) and poled along toward that point behind which the vapor was rising into the still sir.

"By Jo!" exclaimed St. Cloud. "Look there! It is smoke!"

"It is," Henry Quainfan nodded, "and aqueous vapor, too. See, the smoke is a little to one side now; from the island, the two were in the line of sight."

"And that means intelligent life," I said.

"It looks like it," returned Henry earnestly. "We'll soon see."

St. Cloud ran his eye, with apparent apprehension, along the margin of the forest.

"Maybe," he said, "we are *seen*."

We proceeded with senses on the qui vive, expectancy it seemed in the very air about us. Minute succeeded minute, however, and nothing happened. We reached the point, doubled it, and there at last our objective was before our eyes.

"We were both correct, Rider," Henry observed, speaking in guarded tones: "there is my thermal spring, all right, and there your fire—or rather, smoke, for I do not see any flame."

"Nor," said Morgan, "do I see any signs of *men*. How on earth, now, do you explain that fire?"

"I can't," Henry returned. "Wait till we get there and see."

Slowly, with sight and hearing at the quintessence of keenness, we drew nearer to the shore. At last the raft grounded; after a few moments of scrutiny, Henry stepped off.

"Nobody at home!" he observed.

St. Cloud and I followed at his heels.

Of a sudden Henry gave a sharp exclamation.

"There you are!" he said, pointing with his rifle. "That explains it!"

And it did. There, fifteen feet or so before us, were the charred sticks and dead ashes of a camp-fire.

"Great heavens!" said St. Cloud, glancing (a little nervously, I thought) into the gloom of the trees. "Men!"

"Men have been here," nodded Henry Quainfan. "But that doesn't mean *human* men."

We moved forward slowly, with feelings that I shall not attempt to describe.

"The flames," observed St. Cloud, "traveled from the abandoned fire over into that log, which has been smoldering away ever since."

"Just so," nodded Henry. "But—let's be careful now; what we want to find is footprints."

"I have my doubts," I remarked. "Evidently some days have elapsed since those Venusians kindled their fire in this spot."

"And it has rained since," said Henry.

"How," I asked, "do you know that?"

"It is plain; look at the ashes."

"And look at those charred bones," said Morgan. "Alas, people have to eat even on Venus!"

"I suppose we'll have to page Robinson Crusoe," mused Henry Quainfan at last; "I don't see the ghost of a footprint."

"Here's hoping," I said, "that we don't have to wait so long as Crusoe did."

"Don't worry," St. Cloud told me; "you won't."

But not a footprint, nor anything like one, could we find in that spot, though we scrutinized every inch of ground.

"Well," Henry said, "here is another proof that Venus is the abode of intelligent creatures. However, they seem to have deserted these solitudes, but surely they cannot have gone far."

"Maybe," came the typical St. Cloudian observation, "before this business is done, we'll wish that they had gone farther."

"If the devil was a hog," said Henry Quinlan, "everybody would have plenty of bacon."

This first day of ours on the planet Venus, it is quite needless to say, was full of interest and wonder, but I cannot pen that interest and wonder—must leave it to the reader's imagination.

We encountered no danger, discovered no further sign of intelligent life.

When the shades of evening were falling, we were about ten miles from the *Hornet,* and we then ran the raft ashore, lighted a fire, pitched the tent and took our evening's repast.

We had seen several streams entering the lake, but had found no outlet.

The night passed uneventfully. We kept the fire burning brightly, and each took a turn at watching, while the others slept.

During my watch, about midnight, there came through the still air a sudden and distant screaming—a terrible sound; but it soon ceased, without awakening my companions. Save for a pair of green eyes that peered at me now and again in the blackness of the trees, that was all.

I have forgotten to mention the length of the Venusian day. The Venusian day is almost the same as the terrestrial one. There is a difference of but eight minutes, the day here being eight minutes shorter than the day on Terra. The Venusian mean solar day is twenty-three hours and fifty-two minutes, as against the terrestrial mean solar day of twenty-four hours. Venus turns on her axis nearly two hundred and twenty-seven times during her journey round the sun, and so her year (since one rotation, so far as day and night are concerned, is lost) contains very nearly two hundred and twenty-six days—two hundred and twenty-five days, twenty-two hours, forty-nine minutes and (I believe) seven seconds.

On the succeeding day, about noon, we discovered the outlet—about fifty feet wide, swift and deep.

And as darkness was coming down on the lonely place, came the thing that destroyed.

We were returning to the island—Farnermain Island, by the way, it had been named by Henry and St. Cloud. We were but a half mile or so distant. St. Cloud saw it first—above the trees, high in the sky behind us, a fiery thing that shot through the atmosphere with a hissing sound, leaving behind it a greenish train, which lingered for hours, swaying about in the air-currents like some monstrous serpent.

But right over our heads it came and down to earth, burying itself in Farnermain Island and utterly destroying the *Hornet*. Not a vestige remained of the thing in which we had made our long journey through space to the Planet of Love, to this wild Venusian solitude, upon which the eyes of terrestrial men had never lighted before ours had.

CHAPTER 17
WHAT?

"Gone!" said Henry Quainfan. "It's good-bye to the earth now!"

The huge meteorite had ignited some bushes and trees, and by the light of the fire, which was spreading rapidly, we saw at a glance that Henry's words were only too true.

There we stood on the raft, a hundred yards or so away, and just looked. I remember that an aquatic bird sent its raucous cry across the water and that once, from the deeps of the forest behind us, came a great savage roar.

"Yes!" burst out St. Cloud, "and a beautiful fix we are in now, I must say! It's Venus for the rest of our days—though the chances are those days will not be many. That's what we've got for going exploring on an infernal antediluvian catamaran! If we had gone in the *Hornet,* as we should have done—"

"If's are very fine things, Morgan," Henry interrupted, "but they don't help the toothache."

I saw St. Cloud's dark eyes flash in the dusky light and thought an outburst imminent; but a swift change passed over the man.

"Forgive me, old top," he said. "But, you know, this thing hit me hard."

"If we had been there in the *Hornet*," was my sage remark, "it would have hit us harder."

"What chance of chances!" murmured Henry Quainfan. "That of all spots!"

"Probably it wasn't chance after all," Morgan said.

Henry turned and looked at him.

"What do you mean?" he asked.

"I mean," returned St. Cloud boldly, "that I see in this the hand of God raised in warning against man's proud presumption!"

Henry Quainfan gave him a look of sheer amazement.

"What in the world are you talking about?"

"We have broken one of the Creator's laws, so to say, and—"

"Say how!" Henry Quainfan broke in sharply.

"The Almighty never intended (to use such an expression for want of a better one) that man should leave the earth and go to another world."

"Fiddlesticks!" said Henry. "Your fancy, Morgan, is riding a merry-go-round."

And I confess that I thought something like that myself. That St. Cloud, in spite of his strong scientific beliefs, was a good bit of a mystic, I well knew; but I had never expected to find him entertaining a belief so bizarre as this.

Sometimes, though, I find myself wondering if it was so bizarre after all.

And as for mysticism and science, who can draw the boundary between them? Indeed, is there a boundary at all to draw? Are they not, in truth, one and the same thing—known to men by different names simply because those seeking the key which will unlock the Mystery-of-It-All do not follow one clue? Though a man travels toward the east, he will come to the west.

Henry Quainfan dipped his paddle.

"Let's land and—look," he said.

"I don't think we'll do much looking," I observed; "for see how that fire is spreading. Did you notice how dry things were in those trees! The whole island will soon be a furnace."

"At any rate," Henry returned, "we can go in close."

We started.

"It strikes me as curious," he added, "that there is no steam; that thing landed close to the water's edge."

"But," I remarked, "look how it flung the gravel up, in all directions; that keeps the water out."

"Does it?" exclaimed St. Cloud. "Look at that!"

I was already looking. Steam had broken out as though from a burst boiler pipe. And the next instant came a terrific explosion. A great cloud of steam shot into the air, and stones came plunking into the water thick as hail, some of them passing within dangerous proximity.

"Excuse me!" I said, beginning to wield my paddle with great diligence—though in the opposite direction. "I'd rather look from a distance."

"Ditto," said St. Cloud, following my example.

"That's probably the only blow-out," protested Henry Quainfan.

But we kept on going.

"You can examine this miniature Vesuvius," I told him, "in the morning."

"I guess you're right," he said, dipping his own blade.

The fire, which, as I have said, was spreading rapidly, was flooding the water (rippling merrily) with a ghostly day. The light played upon the tree trunks along that shore which we were approaching, struggled into the dense forest and became lost in the darkness.

A steady wind was blowing, carrying the sparks lakeward and thus saving the forest from the conflagration.

The bow of the raft grounded on the pebbly shore, and Henry and I stepped off. St. Cloud did not follow. There he sat on the *Nancy Lee* (for so Henry had christened our catamaran) staring across at the fiery grave of the *Hornet* with an air of utter and gloomy abstraction.

"Well," said Henry after a time, "I see no reason why we should starve to death just because the *Hornet* has been destroyed. I move that we get something to eat."

"Yes," I nodded.

I must confess, however, that I was not the possessor of a hearty appetite just then—though I had been a short time before.

"Morgan takes it hard," observed Henry as we were breaking the firewood. "You can't blame him any, though. And yet—maybe all this is a fortunate misfortune, so to speak."

I made an interrogative noise.

"Just so, Rider," he went on. "Why, now, should we weep and gnash our teeth when, for all we know to the contrary, this catastrophe which has befallen us may be the precursor of some wondrous fortune? Probably on a day Morgan will render up thanks to the Omnipotence for the destruction of the *Hornet*."

"But—" I began.

"But what?" he queried, smiling.

"It is so frightfully unlikely."

"What, Rider?" he laughed. "Unlikely? And you believe in anthropocentricism!"

"What on earth has anthropocentricism got to do with it?"

"Everything. For look you! You believe that man is the greatest thing in all Creation, that all things were made for him, that there are men and women on this world that Tellurians call Venus. Unlikely, when you believe that? Why, Rider, perhaps you and Morgan will marry queens!"

And he grinned.

"Couldn't we have gone to them in the *Hornet?*"

"Not these ladies I have in mind, Rider."

My belief that there is nothing in the Universe greater than man, that a grand and beautiful world would be a useless thing unless peopled with men and women (or in some way subservient to the existence of human creatures on other orbs) was the source of much amusement to Henry Quainfan—was Ptolemaic, antediluvian.

"Of course I believe that," I told him, "leaving out those queens, that is. It seems plain to me that the earth was prepared, and in all likelihood created, for this very purpose—to be an abode for man. One has but to look about him to see proofs of that express purpose. They are everywhere, anybody can see them—'proofs of special forethought and adaptation,' as, I remember, it is put in the only text-book on astronomy into which I ever poked my nose. And here are the very words with which the writer clinches the matter:

"'Coal and oil in the earth for fuel and light, forests for timber, metals in the mountains for machinery, rivers for navigation, and level plains for corn.'"

"As for the rivers, Rider," queried Henry, "how did he explain rapids and quicksands? It seems he forgot a few things, as those who think they have discovered the creative purposes so often do. The poppy, for instance? Created that man might have opium? He might have told us, too, about cobras, earthquakes, tornadoes, sunken rocks (for navigation), tigers, typhoons and rattlesnakes. Why do we find these things? To enable man to remember at times the uncertainty of life—that the sunlight in which he has his laughter is shadowed by the wings of Death? And as for those metals in the mountains? Might they not have been put there so man—this being with the godlike intellect—could make himself a corkscrew?"

"Hopeless!" I exclaimed. "Utterly hopeless! When you look at a rose, do you see nothing but thorns?"

"When I look at a prickly-pear, I don't see a cucumber."

"You don't see a pear, either."

"He's blind enough, Rider, who can't see the holes in a sieve."

"To change the subject," I said. "What are we going to do now? Go down that river?"

"Of course. What else can we do?"

"Heavens," I queried, "when our ammunition is gone?"

"We'll be Pithecanthropi then, Rider—unless these Venusians take a hand in the matter."

"I fancy that's just what they are going to do."

"Of course," he nodded. "It's only a question of time."

Not long afterwards, I heard him singing away to himself in a very low voice, once the following lines from Kipling's *To the True Romance*:

> "As thou didst teach all lovers' speech,
>   And Life all mystery,
> So shalt Thou rule by every school
>   Till love and longing die,
> Who wast or yet the lights were set,
>   A whisper in the Void,
> Who shalt be sung through planets young
>   When this is clean destroyed."

I slept but little that night, but enough to have many horrible dreams.

In the morning, first thing, we went across to smoldering Farnermain Island to see the grave of the *Hornet*. All to be seen, however, was the huge meteorite (the dull radiation of which was still sufficient to keep us at a little distance) and the upflung earth and gravel: not a vestige of the *Hornet* was anywhere to be found.

Breakfast eaten, preparations were begun immediately for our journey down the river. We gathered a goodly supply of vegetables something like the carrot and the turnip, and I was fortunate enough to get another deer.

At last we stepped aboard the *Nancy Lee* and shoved off.

We went across to the island again, but this time we did not go ashore—stood there for some minutes in silence, just looking.

Then Henry Quainfan dipped his pole and started the raft, St. Cloud and I followed suit, and thus began our long journey into the Unknown.

We swung the raft back to the shore and skirted it, arriving at the river in about two hours' time.

"And now—what?" said St. Cloud as its densely-wooded banks began to slip past us.

Henry smiled his slow smile but said nothing.

"Yes," I said, "—what?"

CHAPTER 18
THE THING IN THE NIGHT

All we had to do was steer the *Nancy Lee*. Our progress we estimated at two miles an hour. Though in the shade nearly all the time, we found it very warm. And the heat and light would have been powerful indeed if it had not been for that curious flocculence drawn over the sky like a curtain.

I have yet, by the way, to see the Venusian firmament cloudless from horizon to horizon. You must not get the idea, though, that this is a gloomy place—in any way analogous to the earth (as pictured) in Carboniferous times. Quite the contrary, this world of Venus. For despite the ever-present clouds, it is a world of intense light, brilliant foliage, of colors wonderful beyond all description.

At times came the songs of birds and the drone of insects. The water whispered dreamily. Occasionally came the splash of a leaping fish. But all these sounds seemed but the voice, as it were, of the great silence which reigned over this vast wilderness through which we were floating.

Dense and dark that forest rose up (with here and there a dash of brilliant color) and sometimes I wondered if some savage cormorant of those gloomy depths had greedy eyes fixed upon us.

At length we went ashore to cook our noonday meal. As we were shoving the raft out into the stream, a great roar swept through the forest.

"Lion?" queried St. Cloud.

We listened intently for a space, but the sound did not come again.

On and on we floated, hour after hour; and when twilight came creeping over the world, the topography of the valley had not changed at all.

We selected an open spot wherein to pass the night and ran the *Nancy Lee* ashore.

Henry stepped off first, Winchester in hand. I saw him go up the bank, stand and peer about him into that thickening gloom.

I had stepped ashore and was drawing the raft up farther when a sharp exclamation burst from the lips of St. Cloud, who, standing at the stern of the raft, was staring over my head with horror-wide eyes.

I straightened up, swinging round as I did so, to see a great tawny thing spring into the air straight toward Henry Quainfan.

I cried out in horror and closed my eyes. A shot rang out. I looked and saw that terrible beast turn a complete somersault and strike the ground. Henry had not had time to throw the rifle to his shoulder; he had fired from the hip. Came a horrible, indescribable noise from the animal, which was thrashing wildly about. Another shot rang out, and that thrashing ceased suddenly.

Grabbing my rifle, I rushed up the bank, followed by Morgan. There, in the death quiver, lay a lion—just like the caged lions we so often had seen on the earth, save for its mane, larger than the mane of any terrestrial lion I ever heard of.

"A close call, Henry!" St. Cloud cried excitedly. "I thought you were a goner that time."

Henry Quainfan smiled—as though he had killed a lion every morning before breakfast.

"Lucky my back wasn't turned," he said. "And has it occurred to you that this fellow may have a mate close at hand?"

I jumped, and St. Cloud flung forth a startled oath. We had not thought of that. But the lion had been alone, or, if he had one, his companion did not put in an appearance.

When the excitement produced by this sudden and almost fatal incident had somewhat subsided, St. Cloud and I fell to making a fire, though not without casting many a glance at the deepening gloom that was drawing a thick veil over the deeps of the slumbering forest.

The fire was soon blazing brightly, enhancing the encircling gloom.

It was quite dark when we sat down to eat; and this night we ate what remained of the food we had brought from the *Hornet*, the last of our terrestrial food, some beef. And very good it tasted, too.

It was obvious that that lion was something of a mystery to Henry Quainfan. Here was presented another of those very remarkable "coincidences." His belief in Darwinism, I thought, was surely shattered now. He did not acquaint us with his thoughts, however, but sat brooding in silence (his eyes now and again resting on the body of the lion) and for my part, I never even mentioned evolution.

The night passed uneventfully. During my watch, I heard no sounds, save the low, melancholy whisperings of the river.

At dawn we shoved the *Nancy Lee* out into the stream and floated on.

The river soon became sluggish, and so we plied our peddles: the depth of the stream made poling impossible.

That day passed uneventfully. Likewise did the night. And on the succeeding day, about three hours after sunrise, we entered the great swamp.

And that swamp! A muddy, slimy, dismal wilderness, a gloomy place of reeds, of rotting vegetation, filamentiferous trees, strange water birds and great alligator-like reptiles.

On and on, hour after hour, we paddled down the sluggish stream, which often split into many streams; and when twilight was deepening to darkness, still on every hand stretched the swamp, miasmal and dismal.

We ran the raft up to a big moss-festooned tree, lighted a fire on its great roots and, standing on the raft, cooked our venison. When we had eaten, we made on the raft a hearth of water-soaked roots, upon which we lighted a little fire. Having secured a goodly supply of chips, we shoved the *Nancy Lee* out into the slough and moored it there by putting a couple of the poles between the logs and sinking them deep into the mud.

We felt safer out there.

Suddenly there came from out the darkness a blood-curdling wail. Icy shivers ran up and down my spine. It was not strong, was a throbbing wail—with a plaintive note that was simply awful. A strange thing was that we could form no opinion as to its distance, nor could we even tell precisely the direction whence it came through the darkness.

For five minutes or so it rose and fell, and then we heard it no more. I have never heard anything like it in all my life; I have never heard anything so ghostly, so burdened with—oh, I do not know what.

Lost souls must wail like that.

"It sounds," said Henry, "like the wail of a thing that is dead and that wails because it is dead and cannot die."

That was a miserable night. We lay with the rope passed over our bodies in order that we might not roll off the raft in our sleep. I was afraid of those alligator-things, though Henry (for what reason I could not imagine) said he thought that there was nothing to fear from them. And in dreams I fled wildly through that soggy wilderness, sinking into the mud and slime up to my knees, and floundering and screaming, with a half dozen or so of the hideous saurians in swift pursuit.

Of course, each of us took a turn at watching. Several times, during my vigil, there was a stirring (which I connected with the alligators) in the water near us. Once, for a little space, a pair of red eyes gleamed in that inky blackness beyond the ring of feeble light cast by our fire: and once, too, from a distance, there came a great splashing.

At last the blessed light came creeping through that awful place, and directly we resumed our paddling.

Hour after hour passed, the sun reached its zenith, and still there was no change.

Sometimes snakes swam across the water, swiftly and silently, and long-legged water birds hied themselves to concealment as we approached. Now an alligator went into the water with a loud splash, now as silently as a shadow. Here and there flowed streams of sunshine; now and again insects came and passed. Though it was ever changing, ever slipping past, still the view was always the same.

And when the sun went down, there was no change.

Another miserable night came and went. Mile on mile we paddled, hour after hour, and still that dismal, terrible view. I saw pictures of ourselves toiling on and on, day after day, ever growing weaker and weaker, ever paddling in an endless, steaming swamp, until at last . . .

As often as I flung them away, the horrible pictures of our end would come floating back across a background of hateful and gloomy forest.

But the swamp was not interminable: this day we issued from its sickly deeps.

As the sun was setting, suddenly we came to a great hill, through which a remarkable canyon had been cut by the emerging river: and a shout went up as the welcome and lovely sight met our eyes.

We landed just below the canyon, where was discovered the spoor of deer; and the next morning, an hour or two after sunrise, we proceeded on our voyage, a goodly supply of vegetables, berries and venison aboard the *Nancy Lee*.

A stubby beard clothed St. Cloud's face and mine, but the face of Henry Quainfan was as smooth as A. Belvedere's. He had, since the landing—yes, even in that infernal swamp—shaved every day.

We had proceeded five or six miles, and St. Cloud and I were engaged in languid conversation, when an exclamation suddenly burst from the lips of Henry, who was at the bow.

Instinctively St. Cloud and I made a movement toward our rifles.

"Look!" Henry cried, pointing ahead. "Look at that!"

We were rounding a sharp bend, and before us, about two hundred yards away, was the ruin of a bridge which in some far time had arched the stream.

"Another proof of intelligent life," said Henry. "But it appears that this place is not the abode of intelligent beings now. However, such creatures must be somewhere near, and we have but to go till we find them."

"Or till they find us," said Morgan. "And maybe, for all we know, some of them have got guns."

"Well," Henry smiled back at him, "haven't we?"

We landed just above the ruin. On the opposite side of the river, all trace of the bridge had been swept away.

But one arch remained, which was of the kind called extradosed, its span about thirty feet. The archstones, massive blocks of sandstone, were beautifully carved—even the intrados. One of the springers was half covered, the other completely so, with earth, for the river—which, by the way, we had named the Quainfan, that is, St. Cloud and I—had not only deserted its old channel but had filled it up.

We passed through the arch, proceeded up the bank and out upon this relic of a departed civilization.

The ruins of the departed are always invested with a peculiar air of deep sadness and mockery. A sense of loneliness and ineffable insignificance takes possession of one as he gazes upon them, and it strikes him as a mockery that works of men endure and frown on and on, from age to age, through sunshine, and destructive inclemencies of the weather and the vicissitudes of centuries, when the noble beings that built them are as the dust that is blown hither and yon by the desert wind.

At least so it has always been to me, and so it was as I stood there on that relic of an unknown people, wondering what joy and sorrow had passed over those stones on which we alien creatures now stood, what laughter and tears, what love and hate, hope and fear and blasted hope.

At last Henry wandered off into the forest, leaving St. Cloud and me musing there on the ruin.

"Hey!" his voice came suddenly. "Come and see this!"

"What now, I wonder?" exclaimed Morgan as we turned to answer the call.

"We'll soon see."

We pushed on rapidly through the dense undergrowth, broke through a thorny tangle and stood beside Henry Quainfan.

"What do you think of that?" he said, waving his hand. "There is another sad memento of a vanished people."

"Human people?" I couldn't help querying.

"I fancy," he returned, "that we'll soon have the answer to that question."

We stood before a frowning, creeper-veiled stone structure, which had well withstood the ravages of time. It was of but a single story, was richly carved and possessed features which reminded us most forcibly of the Egyptian style of architecture. There was the same solidity, the same flat roof, the same converging of the exterior surfaces of the walls. The resemblance, to say the least, was a very striking one.

The building, we found, was about forty feet wide and about twice that in length.

We hoped to find among the numerous sculptures the likeness of the beings that had builded this solitary edifice, but in this we met with disappointment.

And, as I stood there in that gloomy building, I wondered how many hundreds of years had rolled across the globe since those massive blocks of stone were put in place, with what revels, and agony perhaps, those massive walls had rung, what manner of beings had reared them up, and why those ancient denizens had departed this place, now the home of wild beasts and silence.

About a hundred yards from this building, we discovered a shaft of stone some eighty feet in height. There were some curious hieroglyphics sculptured on this huge monolith, but, of course, we could make nothing of these. None of the many characters represented was human.

And, though we searched that forest roundabout for hours, we found nothing more. This was something of a surprise to us, for why should only this one building have been erected here?

When the shades of evening were coming down, we repaired to the raft, pitched the tent on the bank by the bridge, lighted a fire and took our saltless, unsavory repast.

When awakened that night by Henry to take my turn at guarding, I thought there was something out of the ordinary in his manner; as I issued from the tent, his words told me this had been no mere fancy on my part.

'You're apt to find your watch enlivened, Rider."

"By what?" I asked quickly.

"I wish I knew. There's something down there."

And he pointed with his rifle into the darkness.

"I saw it," he added, "just as it was gliding into the bushes."

"When was this, and what was it?"

"About five minutes ago. I have been straining my eyes and ears ever since, but I haven't seen or heard a thing. As for what I saw—listen!"

The sharp snapping of a twig, which was succeeded by the faint rustling of leaves, came to our ears.

A few moments of breathless expectation followed, but not the faintest sound came to our strained organs of hearing.

"I suppose it's an animal," I said, "and doubtless it will not approach because of the fire."

Henry, who had placed himself before the fire, so that he might see the better, and who now stood staring into the darkness with a look of absent-mindedness on his face, vouchsafed no reply.

A minute or so passed, and, at the expiration of that period, he turned suddenly and spoke.

"Of course," he said, "it was in almost total darkness, and I didn't see it till it was entering the bushes; all the same I think I saw a biped."

"Biped?"

"Just so. Furthermore, I think this biped was——"

He looked at me with a curious expression in his eyes.

"Well?" I queried.

"You must remember that I got but a glimpse of it, and that——"

And again he looked at me.

"Go on," I said, not a little puzzled.

He peered again at the spot where the thing had disappeared and stood musing awhile in silence.

"Rider," he said suddenly, "remember what I said concerning the imperfect——"

"I remember that," I interrupted him. "What on earth do you think you saw?"

"I believe," he made answer, "that I saw—a man!"

"What?" I exclaimed. "A human?"

"Just so. A man—or a quasi-human animal. But remember——"

He was interrupted by a loud splash, coming from downstream. We peered into the darkness, listening intently.

"It sounded like——" I began, to be interrupted by another splash, more distant, it seemed, than the first.

"Hush!" Henry whispered. "There! Look!"

Suddenly he gripped my arm.

"See!" he exclaimed. "See that!"

At the edge of that faint stream of starshine which flowed along the center of the river, was a moving black thing, a thing that glided swiftly down the stream. It had no distinct outline, was simply a piece of moving blackness, and, almost that instant my eyes lighted upon it, it vanished into darkness.

CHAPTER 19
THE FOOTPRINT

"Probably a canoe," I said, peering down the river, the either margin of which was in blackness cast by the wall of trees.

Henry dropped the butt of his rifle to the earth and stood musing awhile in silence—his senses, however, on the alert for any lurking danger.

"I suppose so," he nodded. "The infernal thing was visible but for a moment; I couldn't make out any shape, to say nothing of the being, or beings, that propelled it. Could you?"

I shook my head.

"Couldn't see anything but a piece of blackness that moved."

"All I could make out, too," said Henry. "But I believe 'twas a man I saw."

"We'll soon know," I said, "for undoubtedly, before long, we shall have a host of them upon us."

"Oh, we'll learn soon, all right.

"I didn't expect," he went on, "to see a single living thing on this planet at all like any terrestrial creature; and it is unnecessary to dwell upon the egregious coincidences that we have seen."

"Coincidences, my eye!"

"All my evolutionary beliefs are shattered, Rider. I don't know what to think now. I am prepared for anything. I am beyond surprise. It would not astonish me at all to see, at any moment, a man stalk into the firelight and say in English, or any other terrestrial tongue:

"'How do you do! Welcome, strangers. Welcome. Whence come you?'"

"If we were only sure of that welcome part of the business," I remarked, "it would be very fine."

"You're catching it from Morgan," he smiled.

"Confound it," I said, "this is enough to make a fellow imagine things—all manner of things."

"I can't understand it, Rider," he told me. "It is a mystery—everything. I can't believe in Darwinism now; and how in the world can I believe in the other?"

"How," I demanded, "can you not believe in the other?"

"But you don't understand it, Rider. How can I believe that the species were created separately, were brought into existence by a direct fiat—or, rather, fiats—of the Creator? How can I believe that—knowing what I know?

"But, on the other hand—well, take that lion, for instance: it was just like a terrestrial lion, save for the heavier mane, but, then, the manes of terrestrial lions differ. The Venusian lion and the earthly lion must have been placed upon their respective orbs by direct creative fiats of the Almighty—and are not the result of countless slight modifications produced by the incessant and pitiless struggle for existence and preserved by Natural Selection. Of course, evolution has always seemed to you a thing absurd: but you never took the trouble to learn anything at all about it."

"And so," I observed, "saved myself a lot of profitless trouble. For I was sure, all the time, that evolution was nothing but a pipe-dream."

"You so often are sure," he smiled. "Now, the data—"

"But I was right!" I cried triumphantly. "I was right. You yourself have said it."

"Now," he went on, "the data advanced by the evolutionists are unanswerable. To an impartial mind, a mind divested of preconceived opinions and bent on attaining the truth, evolution, when examined even cursorily, is an obvious thing. It is plain—plain as the sun and the moon are plain."

"Certainly," I said; "it is not the only error that is plain as day. That's a way errors have."

"Furthermore," Henry continued, "Darwinism adds sublimity to life, robs death of its terrors and gives a beautiful and orderly Universe instead of the capricious old one."

"Indeed!" I broke in. "That is just what it does not do. For it leaves the Cosmos the victim of blind, awful Chance."

"Haven't I told you a thousand times that there is no such thing as chance? That is only a name man has coined for something he doesn't understand."

"I can't see that."

"As I said, Rider, the evolutionary data are unanswerable. There is geological succession, homological structure and embryonic development, for instance. At a certain stage in their embryonic development, all vertebrates possess gill-arches. Why, if each species was separately created, is this thing so?"

"I might ask that superannuated question: Why is a hen?"

"If all the species can be traced back to a common ancestor, however, then this ontogenetic fact is easily explained; but, if each species is the result of a direct creative fiat, then this embryonic fact is a deep mystery, a mystery unsolvable."

"Well," I demanded, "what isn't a mystery—a mystery deep, unsolvable? You and I are mysteries, light and darkness, love and hate, life and death—everything."

"Granted. Ultimate knowledge never can be attained. And now, to come back, take homological structure. If the species are the results of special and independent creations, why is there such a thing as homological structure? Please tell me that. You can't."

"Of course I can't."

"If we accept Darwinism, however, the reason for its existence is at once plain. The hand of man, of Ornithorhynchus, the flipper of a seal, the paddle of a mole and the wing of a bat—different as these things and creatures are one to another—all arise from the same fundamental form. If evolution is, as you call it, a pipe-dream, why is this thing so? If each species was brought into the world by a special act of creation, why, Rider, are there structures so nearly identical in creatures so diverse?"

"Again, Professor," I said, "behold the hen!"

"Yes—why all this talk? For Venus has given us an answer—one as unmistakable as it is puzzling.

"One thing is certain," he went on in a changed voice: "we soon shall learn what these Venusian men are like. Perhaps, too—"

He broke off with an exclamation. "Well?" I queried.

"There may be spoor down there."

"Why didn't you think of that before?"

"I return the question, Rider," he smiled. "Let's go see."

He took a brand from the fire, and, with this as a torch, we went down the bank.

We examined the ground at the spot where that unknown creature had glided into the bushes, but we found nothing there.

A little farther on, we came to stones that had been disturbed. I was examining one of these (it had been turned upside down) and the earth roundabout it when Henry, who had proceeded a few steps, suddenly exclaimed:

"Here it is!"

"What?" I asked, stepping forward.

He did not answer but pointed with his Winchester to the ground a couple of feet before him.

And there, in the soft earth contiguous to a little spring that welled up out of the sand, was a footprint—*the print of a naked human foot!*

CHAPTER 20
PLUTO'S CAVE

"*Homo* after all!" said Henry Quainfan. "*Stupidus,* though, I fancy. See, there are other footprints."

Staring at this one, I had not seen the others, but, on looking, I saw them at once. There were found three perfect ones in all and two imperfect impressions.

"It's my idea," Henry remarked, "that there was only one man here."

"Probably a lucky thing for us," I told him.

"Let us," he said a few moments later, "see if we can find the spot where our Venusian ran the canoe ashore—or whatever that thing was we saw."

Accordingly we proceeded along the water's edge, and a hundred feet or so beyond the footprints, we discovered the spot.

"Maybe this is dangerous," said I, glancing apprehensively into that inky darkness. "They easily could steal near unseen, spear us or fill us full of arrows."

"I think, Rider, this fellow was alone," Henry returned, "and he is gone."

"But he may not have far to go."

"That is true. But, on the other hand, he may have a long, long way. However, the torch is dying down, it seems we have found all there is to be seen, so let's go back."

We returned to the tent forthwith and awoke St. Cloud, to whom I gave a succinct account of what we had seen, the while Henry stood gazing down the river and musing in silence.

Of course, Morgan had to have a look at the footprints and the spot where the canoe (as we thought it) had been grounded. Henry and I accompanied him, and he prosecuted his examination with many exclamations and uneasy glances into the surrounding darkness.

Indeed, by the way, all things considered, this proceeding on our part (and the previous one) was a risky business, not to use a stronger adjective.

"Maybe," said St. Cloud, directing apprehensive looks into that Cimmerian darkness, "there's a score of them creeping upon us this very minute. If only they haven't got guns!"

"We'd be safer," Henry told him, "if they had."

"Great Jupiter, what do you mean?"

"Why, beings with the civilization that implies would not be apt to shoot us Terrestrials down in cold blood."

"I'd hate to wager my soul on that," said Morgan. "This is a ticklish business any way you look at it."

"It's plain," Henry said, "that the man who left these footprints is a savage, and savages don't have guns."

"Some savages do," said Morgan. "But how do you know that the Venusian is a savage?"

"Why, look at his footprint."

Morgan looked, but it was patent he saw nothing but a footprint.

"I'm not Natty Bumppo," he said, straightening up.

"Unless I am greatly mistaken," Harry explained, "the gentleman never has had a shoe on his foot, and you know that, if he were civilized at all, he would in all likelihood have his feet encased in some sort of footgear."

"Cannibals, maybe," proffered St. Cloud.

"Perhaps these Venusians," said Henry, "these savages, are dwellers on the outskirts of a great civilization. Perhaps somewhere down there are great cities, mighty kings and queens—kings with their men-servants and women-servants, their wives and concubines. Probably, Morgan, there are things down there more wonderful than anything ever seen on the earth."

"But here are these savages," said St. Cloud: "they are between us and the maybe civilization of yours—those wonderful kings and queens. And perhaps, for all we know, down there are things more terrible than anything ever seen on the earth."

"Morgan," Henry laughed, "you're as optimistic as an owl."

"Let's get out of this," returned the other, "though, great guns, going into the light of that fire is only offering ourselves as targets!"

"But, if we put it out," I interposed, "hens—or something more terrible—may come in and gobble us up."

"Precisely," nodded Henry Quainfan. "We're between the devil and the deep darkness. But, as for these Venusians, Morgan, why not give them the benefit of the doubt?"

"Just so," said I, "they may prove to be pretty fine fellows after all."

"I'm from Missouri," St. Cloud told us.

As soon as we returned to the tent, Henry lay down and in a few moments was fast asleep. As has been said, it was now my watch. St. Cloud, though, chose to share it instead of sleeping. The latter, however, he probably would have found impossible. At any rate, when my time was up, such was my experience, and so I watched the night out with Morgan.

We kept the fire burning brightly and continually swept the surrounding darkness with eyes drawn to the utmost. Nothing was seen, however, though more than once some sound in the forest seemed to betray the lurking of danger.

Once, too, a faint and distant roar, which we thought that of a lion, drifted through that terrible silence.

When day broke, we examined the shore again, but we discovered nothing and, when we shoved the *Nancy Lee* out into the stream and resumed our journey, I could not banish that strange feeling of foreboding which had come to me.

Always were our eyes employed in a keen scrutiny, now of the dark and silent margin of trees on either side, now of the river ahead. Hour after hour passed, though nothing happened, we maintained an undiminished vigilance.

We ate our midday meal (consisting of some venison cooked that morning, some berries and vegetables) without landing. On and on we floated down the stream, and no sign of men met our eyes.

But the hour was drawing near.

Before the sun had marked mid-afternoon, the river swung sharply to the left and soon ran along the base of a low range of mountains. The current here was very swift, so swift, indeed, that we became uneasy. And soon we came to the largest tributary we had yet seen, which merged its waters with the Quainfan just above a deep and evil-looking canyon and which issued lazily from a big-mouthed cavern.

We ran the raft ashore at this yawning hole, which Henry afterwards named Pluto's Cave, and stood looking in.

A dull and distant roar was borne to our ears on the quiet air, and, on the slow-moving surface of the emerging water, there were little streams and eddies of foam.

And, somewhere up there on the mountain, borne along toward us on the black bosom of this hypogeal river, was "the jeweled woman."

CHAPTER 21
THE JEWELED WOMAN—THE FIRST MAN

And now I come to what may prove not the strangest one by any means but the most—how shall I put it?—the most outré chapter of all.

Indeed, one phase of the matter is something of a puzzle to me to this very day.

As I have said, we ran the raft ashore just above a deep and evil-looking canyon. Its walls were precipitous, and we feared that it might contain rapids. There was none so far as we could see, but this was only for several hundred yards, owing to a bend, and we had no way of knowing how long that sinister-looking canyon was.

The valley here is very narrow and hemmed in on the other side by another range of mountains.

"Hope we aren't held up here by rapids," said Henry. "For, you know, I would hate like the dickens to have to abandon the *Nancy Lee*."

"So would I," nodded Morgan. "She's a good little craft, bless her, and has brought us many a long mile in safety—though, like the true feminine she is, she's darned hard to steer."

"Funny thing," mused Henry Quainfan.

"Funny thing what?" demanded St. Cloud.

"Why here we are on an alien world, and yet here are women."

He paused and looked at us thoughtfully, then added:

"And only Heaven knows what will come to each of us through the love or hate of a woman."

In days that followed often I had occasion to remember those words of his at Pluto's Cave.

"Well," said Morgan airily, "one thing is certain—"

He was interrupted by a curious exclamation from Henry Quainfan.

I, who had been looking down the river, swung round on the instant, to see Henry staring into the cavern.

"What is it?" asked Morgan.

Henry gave no answer. I followed his gaze and saw something floating toward us on that subterrane darkness.

A moment or two later, my eyes growing accustomed to the deep obscurity, I made out a human form on a raft.

"By Heaven," exclaimed Henry suddenly, "it's a woman!"

Even as he spoke, I saw that it was so.

And slowly the woman floated toward us out of the darkness. Soon she was in the powerful sunlight. And now a strange thing happened: that rude raft swung toward us, swung in and grounded at our very feet.

Henry and Morgan swore. I became suddenly weak and sat down. I remember noting as I did so that her hair was black, that most of it was in the water, moving slowly in the gentle current, and shivering as my eyes fell upon her breast.

"Ye gods!" exclaimed Henry Quainfan in horror. "Look at that!"

I looked and shivered again. Her dripping breast was quite naked, and it was covered with great welts—horribly slashed and torn. She was dead. We cut the strips of hide that bound her to the raft and laid her on the land. Hands and feet were bound, the hands behind her back, and upon her face, one of great beauty, was stamped a look of unutterable horror.

"God!" said Henry, shuddering. "What a hellish piece of work! And see how beautiful she is—even with that awful, unutterable horror on her face. What a fiend is this thing with the godlike intellect, the biggest monster that ever met a shadow in the sun and he lifts his hands in horror at blood-dripping claws and fangs! I wonder, now, why they did this."

He stretched out a hand, brushed the wet hair from her cheek, leaned over and kissed the dead woman on the forehead, and it seemed to me a proper and beautiful thing to do.

I have called her beautiful; she was, indeed, one of the most beautiful women I have ever seen. Her skin was olive, her hair raven, and her age I thought was about twenty-five—that is terrestrial years. Her eyes were closed—I was glad they were—and her lips slightly severed. Her dress was of skins with the hair removed, richly colored and reached just below the knee. The bodice had been torn off, though not from the skirt, so that the lash might strike the naked flesh. Then were no marks beyond those welts and lacerations. Evidently she had been lashed ere tied to the raft, and I shuddered to think of her horrible end in that subterranean cavern.

But there were the jewels. I have called her the jeweled woman, and, of a truth, she was the jeweled woman. From each ear was pendent a rough diamond of the first water and weighing, Henry thought, about eighty carats; about her neck were two strings of rubies, most of them spinel, though some were those wondrous gems that lapidaries call pigeon's blood, and about her waist a multi-calerous zone thickly studded with sapphires.

"There's a fortune there," observed St. Cloud.

Henry Quainfan looked it him quickly, and his eyes were hard.

"Is that what you see?" he asked.

The dark eyes of St. Cloud flashed, his lips parted for speech, but of a sudden he changed his mind and stood silent.

Henry drew his hunting-knife and cut the thongs which bound her wrists and ankles. Then he covered up her breast and folded her hands. Her dress and wealth of hair now were streaming in the powerful sunlight. Henry arose and stood looking down at her face, his own a little pale, his lips slightly parted.

St. Cloud, I believe, was looking at the sapphires.

"I wish," said Henry, lifting his gaze up to the mountain through which the woman had come down to us, "that I could get a chance to speak with my Winchester to the fellows that did this."

"Maybe after all," St. Cloud said, "she deserved what she got!"

Henry looked at him fixedly for a few moments, his eyes cold as steel, then turned away with something like disgust.

"What I can't understand," Morgan added, "is why they turned her adrift with all those jewels."

Neither of us made any response to this. The silence that followed had something strange about it.

"Well," said Henry at last, "let's bury her. We can dig the grave with one of the axes and with the paddles. We'll pile stones on her so the beasts cannot tear asunder her bones.

"'Lay her i' th' earth: And from her fair and unpolluted flesh may violets spring!'"

I felt like crying; and suddenly, from somewhere in the forest across the river, came a strong and prolonged cry of agony, then silence—heavy, awful.

"Yes, let's inter this girl," said Henry, "and get away from the cursed spot."

A short silence ensued, to be broken by Morgan.

"Are you going to bury her with all those stones on?" he asked.

What happened was a surprising thing.

Henry Quainfan turned on him fiercely, his gray eyes seeming to emit points of steel.

"Of course!" he told St. Cloud vehemently. "That is just what we are going to do: bury her with all her jewels."

"The infernal foolishness!" said Morgan. 'Think of it: those stones are—"

Haley broke in upon his speech like a thunderclap.

"Think of it—ghouls!" he cried.

"I tell you—" began St. Cloud.

But Henry Quainfan lashed in with curses—stinging, terrible. The words leapt from his lips. They swung and cracked like the lash of a whip. I was amazed. St. Cloud had taken a step backward in his surprise at this sudden and totally unexpected outburst, and there he stood with blazing eyes, waiting for Henry to cease.

He soon did, and then St. Cloud lashed back. They flung curses back and forth. I became uneasy. Things were looking serious. What was this madness which had entered my companions? It was as if I could hear the rustle of Tragedy's wings, and in the forest the wind whispered and birds sang.

And then the mystery of Henry Quainfan rushed upon me. He was a materialist (or, rather, he had been). He hoped for no future reward. To him there was no future existence even. After this life came death indeed—nothing. When dead, he would be nothing and dwell for all eternity in the darkness of nothing, as I so often had heard him put it.

And such a man, fearing no Heavenly judgment, one would think, easily could commit any crime which he knows would bring no retribution from man, and of such crimes there are many. Yet there he was cursing a man who would take diamonds and rubies from a dead woman; and the man whom he cursed, and who hurled his curses back, believed in Heavenly retribution, that every act done in the flesh we are to find weighed in the balance.

"This will never do," said I to myself.

And at that instant I noticed that St. Cloud's right hand had strayed to his revolver.

"I must put a stop to this crazy business."

I opened my month to speak, but no words left my lips: Morgan's revolver, blue and cold looking, was glittering in the sunlight.

Henry laughed.

"Why don't you shoot?" he taunted.

But St. Cloud did not shoot. His arm fell inertly to his side; for a moment I thought the weapon was going to fall from his grasp, and he stood looking not at Henry Quainfan but at the jeweled woman.

"Here, here!" said I, at last finding speech. "This will never do! Put away that revolver, Morgan. And now shake hands, you two fools, and let all this disagreeable nonsense be forgotten."

St. Cloud slowly returned the revolver to its holster. But neither offered to take the other's hand. For my part, glad that Tragedy had departed, I said nothing more, but left it to them to settle as they saw fit.

Morgan sat down and stared across the river. Henry looked at him coldly for a while, then of a sudden turned and went out upon the raft, where he got an axe and a paddle. On stepping ashore, however, he suddenly dropped these tools and returned to get his blanket, which he laid over the dead woman.

"We'll wrap her in it," he said. "Rider, will you go down and reconnoiter the canyon? Morgan and I will dig the grave. Keep your eyes open, now."

The canyon I found about three-quarters of a mile in length and free of rapids. At length I ascended to a coign of vantage, where were caught, through openings in the trees, glimpses of the river several miles away.

Suddenly there was a sound behind me, the sound of bushes being pushed asunder cautiously but swiftly.

I swung round, heard a sharp exclamation and found myself face to face with a Venusian.

CHAPTER 22
STRAIGHT TOWARD US

Surprise was mutual. In a flash my rifle was up, and the man (almost as white as myself and naked save for a leopard-skin about the middle) raised his spear as though to hurl it at me with all his might.

How it happened that he did not let fly—who can tell that? But he did not. The weapon remained there poised above his head, my finger caressed the trigger, and thus we stood staring at each other.

We were separated by the distance of only five or six yards. Had he made the least threatening movement, I should have fired.

I smiled. The savage did not smile back, but he hesitatingly lowered his weapon, uttering as he did so this expressive exclamation:

"*Umk!*"

At that moment came the discovery that my Venusian was not alone. There was a faint rustling in the bushes from which he had just issued; soon the foliage was pushed asunder, and the head and shoulders of the second man were thrust into view.

Face instinct with surprise, he stared across at me.

He said something in a sharp voice, never moving his heady look for a single instant. The answer his companion gave was short—monosyllabic, in fact. In a few moments, with extreme caution (he had an arrow fitted to his bowstring) the newcomer emerged and took his stand beside the first.

He, too, was naked save for a skin about the waist. He had no spear. A quiver full of arrows was at his back, the feathered ends sticking up above his right shoulder. Each man carried a tomahawk, steel bitted, and the first had a bow and quiver as well as that vicious-looking spear of his. His eyes were black, the other's blue, their black hair long and unkept, beards scanty. Each had a metal band encircling his left wrist, a string of claws round his neck and on his breast a bird tattooed in vivid scarlet.

It was patent that they did not know what to make of me and plain, too, I thought, that they recognized the rifle as a weapon.

They talked earnestly together for a few moments, never taking their keen eyes off me for the fraction of a second even.

Directly they neared, I smiled once more and started to move toward them but stopped instanter when they raised their weapons with sudden menace.

Again they spoke earnestly, their language sounding soft and musical, very much like the Spanish.

Then of a sudden they half turned and began to move back, watching me as they went; a few moments, they had vanished into the foliage and I was alone once more.

When I reached the cavern, Henry and Morgan were already filling in the shallow grave.

"Any rapids, Rider?" Henry asked, leaning on his paddle, which served as a spade.

"None," I told him. "The river is pretty swift in a few places, but we can make it through all right."

"Good. You know, I was afraid of that canyon."

"No, there are no rapids there, but I found—or, rather, the find found me—but guess what I saw."

"Venusians?" he asked.

I nodded, and St. Cloud gave a quick glance behind him, then this way and that into the gloom of the forest.

"Venusians," I nodded. "Two."

"Tell us about it," Henry said quickly.

I did.

"So they are white, too," said Morgan.

"White as ourselves—allowing for their Venusian tan, that is."

"Well, what do you know about that!"

"Did you think to find them green?" Henry queried. "Have you forgotten our Lady of the Jewels?"

"After all what a remarkable thing," said Morgan—"these people just like ourselves!"

"That," said Henry, "to use St. Cloudian phraseology, remains to be seen."

"It won't remain long," the other returned. "Unless I'm mightily mistaken, we are in for something now."

Henry Quainfan made no response. He resumed his labor with a sobriety of demeanor that showed his thoughts suddenly had gone to other things.

The last spade of earth cast, we stood thus for some moments in silence.

"We can do no more," said Henry Quainfan, "so let's get away from this cursed place. You know, the sight of that woman his affected me strangely I do not understand. That was why I flew at Morgan suddenly and vehemently. I am sorry, Morgan, as I told you—though not for the stand I took."

"All the same," returned St. Cloud, "it was blanked foolishness."

"The sun is getting low," I put in, for I wanted to change the subject, "we had better be on our way."

"We had," Henry nodded.

We retraced our steps to the raft forthwith. I was about to step aboard when a strong liquid song filled the air. Turning, I saw a yellow, canary-like bird singing on the grave of the jeweled woman.

"Look," I said.

They already had seen.

"She could not have a sweeter or a sadder requiem," said Henry.

For a little while we stood looking.

"Well, Rider," came Henry's voice, "come aboard, and let's shove off."

A few moments, and we were gliding down the stream; a few minutes, and in the swift waters of the canyon—which we ran without mishap.

Suddenly objects were involved in a curious darkness. The sky was turning black and threatening; a strong wind was springing up.

"Going to rain," I observed.

"Pour, you mean," said St. Cloud.

"And typhoon," said Henry.

At length, as twilight was creeping over the wild place, we ran the *Nancy Lee* ashore.

To our surprise, we had seen no Venusians.

"Must be very sparsely populated," said Henry, "or—"

"Look at that sky," observed Morgan. "It's going to come down in sheets. And hear the wind."

The wind was now a growing gale. The branches were tossing wildly, the boles bending before it.

"Dangerous place, this," said St. Cloud, looking up at those tossing branches.

"Some of these trees are liable to be uprooted—or snapped off. Maybe we'll find one of them crashing down on us."

This was a peradventure only too obvious. But we had to take our chances; there was nothing else we could do.

We pitched the tent in what we deemed the safest spot. Just as we were adding the finishing touches, it began to rain. Rain! It did rain. Rain! It came down in streams. Hour after hour it came down in streams. The night, of inky blackness, now and again was shivered by lightning. And there we stood huddled in the tent, listening to the thunder, the rain and the roaring of the wind overhead. Now and then we heard a tree come crashing to the earth. One came down near us, shaking the ground beneath our feet.

"The river will be swollen," Henry said suddenly; "the raft will be carried away unless we draw it up farther."

"Out we go," I returned.

"Where the deuce is that rope?" said he, and I heard him groping about in the darkness. "Ah, here it is. For we'd better tie it, too."

So out we went; it was pitch black. We felt our way to the raft, drew it up and made it fast to a tree. When we again stood huddled in the tent, we were wet to the skin.

And rain! Hour after hour it came down—a veritable flood. Now and again St. Cloud would fling forth a smothered oath. Henry seldom spoke. At last, about two hours before daybreak, there was a sudden diminution in that fury of the gale, when the dark twilight came stealing over the flooded place, the rain was falling straight down, the air being absolutely motionless.

Not a single wink of sleep did any one of us get that night.

And then Venus smiled, in that sudden way she has: blue spots appeared overhead, a little while, and the rays of the sun were flashing on tree trunk and foliage.

We remained in this spot that day and night, resuming our voyage ere it was yet full light.

We had kept a sharp lookout for Venusians, but never a vestige of one had been seen—a circumstance which called forth some little speculation on our part.

It was a beautiful day, though very hot. We all were frightfully sunburnt, none of us having been used to an extra-foraneous life, as Henry saw fit to dub it. And, when noon came, not a single Venusian had been seen.

"Strange," said Henry.

"Maybe we're being watched this very moment," remarked St. Cloud, glancing into the dark depths of the forest.

"Possible," Henry nodded.

"And see that alligator thing over there," I said, "at the mouth of that slough, just gliding into the water."

This, by the way, was the first one we had seen since our issuance from the great swamp.

"And by Heaven!" exclaimed St. Cloud the next moment, "there's a Venusian!"

We looked in the direction in which he was pointing and beheld a man, about a hundred yards ahead, standing on the shore and watching us closely.

"Hello, there!" hallooed Henry Quainfan, who was at the stern of the raft, dipping his paddle and swinging the bow toward the spot where the Venusian stood.

The man made no reply, gave no sign that he had heard. He just stood there and looked at us.

"There may be more of them in the trees," said Morgan, reaching for his Winchester.

When we were about a hundred feet from him, the Venusian turned suddenly, and, looking back at us over his shoulder, he glided swiftly away into the forest, and we saw him no more.

"Pleasant cuss," said Henry.

About the middle of the afternoon we came to a village, but it was deserted. It consisted of a dozen huts made of branches and long leaves, and it was evident that it had been deserted for some considerable time.

After a brief examination of the place, we returned to the *Nancy Lee* and floated on down the stream—with Expectancy sitting at the helm, so to speak.

The sun swung lower and lower. At last he sank behind the world, and the forest gloom begin to deepen about us.

Of a sudden St. Cloud exclaimed that he saw a Venusian. We looked in the direction he indicated, but neither Henry nor I saw a Venusian. However, we saw some bushes moving. Soon they were still.

The man, we were told, was disappearing when Morgan's eyes lighted upon him.

"We're in too close," said Morgan, his finger on the trigger of his rifle. "We're too near this shore."

"That's right," observed Henry as I picked up my weapon. "There may be a lot of them here, and they may attack at any instant. And we are in too close to this shore."

He placed his Winchester in a spot where he could reach it easily and quickly, then urged the craft toward the center of the stream.

Our eyes swept the wall of trees from which we slowly were drawing away, but we saw no movement of the foliage, heard not the faintest sound.

A few minutes passed. We were nearing a bend. At the moment, we all were looking ahead. Suddenly, with a swish, an arrow shot past my head and into the river with a vicious *thug*.

We swung round. The Winchester flew to my shoulder. I saw bushes moving; no Venusian, however, was to be seen.

"Don't shoot until you see him," said Henry. "Don't throw away a single bullet even. There—there he is!"

The Venusian's head and shoulders had appeared. He had another arrow fitted to the string—indeed, was in the act of drawing it to its head.

I took swift aim—but did not fire. St. Cloud saved that Venusian's life. A sharp cry burst from his lips just as I was going to press the trigger, causing my eyes to leap from the Venusian to him.

We were rounding the bend now, and St. Cloud was pointing ahead, a little wildly, looking back at us over his shoulder.

That instant my eyes fell on what had caused Morgan to cry out, the arrow from the bow of the Venusian whose life he had saved struck with a sharp rap, pinning my right trouser leg to the raft, just below the knee.

And this is what St. Cloud had seen: a big war-canoe, filled with Venusians, just come into view from behind a wall of trees, gliding out into the stream and heading straight toward us.

CHAPTER 23
"LEENAM DRACONDA"

The Venusians' paddles rose and fell swiftly and in unison. A half dozen or so of the warriors were standing, and in the fading light I noted that all of these had bows.

"Hold on, Morgan," said Henry. "Better wait a little—till they're closer."

The last word scarcely had left his lips when the air was filled with whoops and shrieks horrible beyond all words—threatening, for an instant, to arrest the coursing blood in our veins.

Came a feeble echo from that Venusian behind us.

I kicked back. Henry, his eyes fixed ahead, had laid aside the paddle and taken up his Winchester. The Venusian had drawn another arrow to its head; even as my eyes struck him, the arrow left the bow, but it fell short. I raised the rifle and drew a bead on the savage, and this time it was Henry who saved that Venusian's life.

"Don't waste a bullet on him," he said. "We're out of range, I think. Keep your eyes on those fellows ahead, but don't shoot till you have to."

"There, see!" exclaimed St. Cloud. "They're going to let us have it!"

"Don't miss," said Henry Quainfan earnestly.

Then to me:

"Wait, Rider. I think one bullet will be enough."

The two foremost Venusians—the canyon was something over a hundred feet from us now—were drawing their bows. Came another burst of those horrible whoops and shrieks—cut short by the crack of Morgan's rifle.

The foremost warrior went down like a sack of lead, his right arm hanging over the side of the canoe, the fingers splashing the glancing element.

Henry had been right. The paddles became still, the Venusians like statues, apparently stupefied by this strange manner of slaying, and the wonted silence settled down again upon the darkling world.

"I thought so," said Henry.

Morgan was drawing a bead on another warrior.

"Wait," said Henry. "I think that shot did it—that we are safe from attack."

St. Cloud slowly lowered the weapon, keeping his finger on the trigger.

The Venusians were gesticulating wildly now, suddenly the paddles were dipped, and the canoe shot ahead, the bow swinging away from us.

As the canoe shot across, about thirty feet away, one of the warriors started to draw his bow. Morgan's rifle flew to his shoulder, the weapon barked, and the unfortunate Venusian, after clutching wildly at the empty air for a few seconds, fell into the water with a loud splash, his body writhing and turning and arms and legs moving spasmodically as he sank from sight.

There was, to my deep thankfulness, no further sign of hostility. The canoe described a swift arc and fled toward the place whence it had come.

We followed, and soon, on rounding the wall of trees, the ruined city met our eyes.

The canoe raced toward the shore, upon which several fires were burning, and we crawled along after it. A murmur from the watching Venusians ran along the strand. It must have aroused them, to say the least, to see their score of warriors in the big canoe fleeing so wildly from three men on a raft. The murmur was answered by a many-throated cry from warriors. There were several small canoes in the stream, and thereat they darted shoreward. Pandemonium reigned before us. The place was deserted when the big war-canoe struck the shore, the warriors leaped out, fled up the bank, and soon they, too, had vanished into the evening shadows.

"The best thing to do," said Henry Quinlan, "is to go right on, make believe that we are afraid of nothing."

When we were nearing the shore, however, St. Cloud's paddle suddenly became still.

"Keep right on," said Henry earnestly. "We've made a good impression."

"I should say we have," I said.

"So, whatever we do," Henry added, "we must not appear hesitant."

"I suppose so," said Morgan, dipping his blade. "Circumstance seems to be master here. All the same we may be going right into an ambush."

We ran the *Nancy Lee* ashore near the big canoe. Before us rose stone steps, upon which the hand of Ruin had long ago fallen. These we ascended and found ourselves before an arch in the crumbling city wall. Through it we passed, and now a broad street stretched away between ruined buildings of stone, in which lived these savage Venusians. But not a single Venusian was anywhere to be seen.

"We did make an impression!" said I.

"Phenomenal," Henry said. "But let's stroll up the boulevard. I suppose some of them will put in an appearance before long."

We had proceeded but a hundred feet, however, when he stopped suddenly.

"Listen," he said.

The next moment he had disappeared cautiously through a huge doorway, from which came the flickering of firelight.

"Papoose," said Morgan.

Henry soon issued with the baby in his arms. It had yellow hair and blue eyes and no more clothes than a papoose baboon.

For a space it stared at him, as if saying to itself:

"Well, who the dickens are you?"

Then it smiled through its tears and babbled something in baby talk. Babies always did like Henry.

"These poor Venusians must have got an awful scare," said Henry, "when the mother of this tot ran away and left it."

He leaned his rifle against the wall, seated himself in the doorway and began playing with the baby.

"You've certainly got a fine daddy and mama, you little son of a gun," he said. "You ought to—"

"What the deuce is on the programme now?" put in St. Cloud, looking about for Venusians.

"Wait till they come back, I suppose," returned Henry. "What else can we do?"

"Nothing, it seems," said Morgan. "But they may make an attack."

"I hardly think so."

Twilight now was deepening to darkness. A number of fires lighted up the street, one of them burning near the spot where we had halted.

At last we saw some Venusians coming down the street toward us. They came slowly, often hesitating. There were about twenty. The deputation was headed by two men, one of them an old man with a long white beard and long white hair. His attire was scanty but richly decorated, and a plethora of bone and metal ornaments decked his person. We rightly conjectured that he was a priest. As for his companion, he was middle-aged, powerfully built and evil of visage—evidently a chief as powerful in influence as he was in person.

"You're the leader," said I to Henry. "You handle this diplomatic business."

St. Cloud and I stepped back a little to show that Henry was our pendragon, as St. Cloud put it. Henry was still holding the baby. Now this tribe, called the Oham, has a peculiar custom. Incredible though it may seem, no man in it ever touches a baby. No man would think of touching one. To the men babies are taboo. If he touches one, even if it is a matter of life and death, an Oham man's wife divorces him instanter, and he is doomed to a state of celibacy. Wherefore the Oham men do not touch babies. No Oham man touches son or daughter till he or she is full grown.

All this, by the way, we learned from Draconda.

At length the deputation came to a halt, bowing low. Then succeeded an awkward silence. Neither side, of course, could speak a word intelligible to the other. The old man said something in the tongue at the Ohams. Henry smiled in answer, then, by means of signs, endeavored to express that amity which we so cordially hoped would prevail. Whereupon the old Venusian, with pantomime, told us that the city was ours and expressed the hope that our lordships would not harm his people. Henry answered, as best he could, that nothing was farther from our thoughts. And now it was that we heard Draconda's name for the first time. After exchanging a few words with the chief[6] the old Venusian pointed into the northwest and said:

"Leenam Draconda."

These words he repeated several times—as if their very utterance had something potent, talismanic.

Henry nodded.

"Leenam Draconda," he said loftily.

Then to us:

"Wonder who—or what—the Leenam Draconda is."

"King, maybe," I returned.

"Queen, I fancy," said Morgan.

Came a halt in the proceedings, when suddenly the old Venusian spoke in a language there was no possibility of misconstruing: he opened his mouth and pointed down his throat.

Henry said we would, whereupon the old man gave a command, and one of the men (none of them, by the way, carried a weapon) saluted and sped away up the street.

"The royal poison-preparer," said St. Cloud.

Whereat Henry Quainfan laughed outright to the evident astonishment of our savage hosts.

Henry put the baby back where he had found it, and we started, the old man and the evil-visaged chief in the lead, their followers strung out behind us.

"I don't like this formation," muttered St. Cloud, looking straight before him and endeavoring to hide his apprehension. "They could rush us now."

"They could," Henry said, "but they can't."

When we had proceeded a short distance, perhaps two hundred yards, we turned to the right, entering another street. A hundred yards or so, and we halted before an imposing edifice, the home of the priest.

Here again was that Egyptian-like style of architecture, and the building was in pretty good condition. We entered and found ourselves in a large room, down which ran two rows of massive columns and in the center of which a little fire was burning lazily, flooding the great room with a lurid light and casting great shadows upon the floor, the columns and the walls.

On the floor, surrounding the fire, were a few furs and a goodly number of

---

6. The old man, as we afterward learned, was the head chief as well as head priest.— R. F.

multicolorous mats, upon which the Venusians and ourselves took seat; a silence fell, disturbed only by the crackling of the fire.

CHAPTER 24
"BLANCHE!"

My eyes ran along the walls, which were richly sculptured with war, hunting and love scenes.

And where now were the warriors, the hunters, the lovers? Where the dripping of blood and the trembling lips? Where now the men who had raised up these great buildings in some lost age of the planet, loved and taken maids to wife? The dazzling beauties who had made men's heads to swim, their laughter and their tears? Where now were the masters and the slaves, the poets and the fools, the kings and the beggars, the queens and the hetaeras? Gone, utterly gone—gone and lost forever. The glory of those men and women of old time had utterly perished, their great palaces fallen into ruin, now the habitation of the savage Ohams.

And yet gone was not perished! That was true only of their flesh, gone to the earth whence it came; their spirits lived on even now—who knew where?

These gloomy meditations were brought to an end by Henry Quainfan—for which you'll perhaps be thankful.

"Funny thing," he said: "the architecture is Egyptian, but the sculpturing is Greek."

"Not the only thing that's Greek," put in Morgan.

"And this Leenam Draconda?" Henry added. "What will happen when we meet?"

"If we ever do!" said St. Cloud.

"Draconda! A man's name, that, or a woman's?"

"Woman's, I think," I told him.

"Sounds like it to me," said Morgan.

Henry Quainfan nodded.

"When I come to think of it, I believe it is. I'm going to find out."

"How?" I wanted to know.

"It will be easy."

He came to his feet and was about to make a sign to the old Venusian when a woman entered with an armful of wood. She was about fifty years of age and unutterably ugly—the ugliest female of the species, I believe, that I have ever set eyes on.

When she had gone, Henry walked over to the nearest wall and laid his left hand on a canephore.

"Draconda?" he asked. "Leenam Draconda?"

The old priest and the chief shook their heads. The former pointed into the northwest.

"Draconda," he said. "Leenam Draconda."

Henry pointed to himself.

"Draconda?" he asked.

Then he pointed to the canephore again.

"Draconda? Leenam Draconda?"

The Venusians looked at him with bepuzzlement depicted on their swarthy lineaments. Then suddenly a smile of comprehension lighted up the old man's face; he nodded his white head vigorously.

"Leenam Draconda," he said, pointing to the sculptured woman. "Leenam Draconda."

He pointed to Henry and shook his head, then to the canephore and nodded, saying:

"Leenam Draconda."

Henry nodded and returned to his seat.

"Must be the queen," he said.

"It seems strange to me," I remarked, "that savages such as these are ruled by a woman."

"But perhaps there is civilization over there in the northwest," Henry returned. "Probably we are now in a mighty empire and this is merely a border people. You know, there may be—"

I followed the direction of his look, to see a young woman entering the room, bearing in each jeweled hand a steaming bowl. She was not beautiful, was not even pretty; but, as I soon saw, she possessed in an unusual degree that fascinating something possessed by so many women whom Venus has slighted.

She wore a coarsely woven dress of vegetable fiber, reaching just below the knee. It was cut low at her jeweled, sun-browned neck; on her little feet were sandals. She was, as we afterward learned, the old priest's daughter. Also, she was beloved by that evil-visaged giant beside him.

And now comes a curious thing, a custom that, strangely enough, prevails throughout Draconda's kingdom: the prerogative of love-making belongs to the woman, never, under any circumstances, is to be exercised by mere man.

When the eyes of this maid met Henry's, I saw the blood creep up to her olive skin, and I thought a greater trembling seized her hands. Swiftly I glanced at the chief and the priest.

The old man was looking straight at the girl. His face was expressionless. But the giant's face was not so; and I did not like that look which I saw upon it. On the instant I knew that he was frightfully jealous. My eyes went back to Henry Quainfan, to find him as impassive as that column of steam behind him.

One of the bowls she placed before Henry, the other before me. It was, as we afterward learned, a great honor to be waited upon by the old priest's daughter, an honor accorded to very few—in this instance, only her father and the chief in addition to ourselves, the rest of the company being waited upon by another maiden. It was a good meal, consisting of meat, a kind of bread, vegetables and fruit.

I noted that the princess—for princess she was—glanced often at Henry, glanced in a bold yet tremulous way. I could not mistake the meaning of those glances. No one could. Her boldness gave me a curiously uncomfortable feeling. But she was doing only what any other Oham maid would have done. We were not on Terra but on Venus, in the land of the Ohams; and there the women make love as it should be made in the land of the Ohams—and in no namby-pamby fashion do they make it, either.

At length the old Venusian (in pantomime, of course) asked us whence we had come. Henry arose and pointed to that doorway through which we had entered. We all issued. In the street stood little groups of Venusians, like troubled sprites.

Above the great cordillera, there in the east, blazed our wondrous earth with its attendant star. Henry pointed to it—explained to them that we had come from that world in the sky.

"Oh!" exclaimed the girl, her eyes wide.

The old man, however, the light of the torch flickering on his swarthy features, nodded is if he had expected something like that.

Again he pointed into the northwest.

"Leenam Draconda," he said.

Our eyes came back to that glorious star in the east, strange emotions—poignant, now tender—hovering about us as we gazed.

There were very few clouds this night, the heavens arching over us in all their cosmic mystery and beauty.

Though a great mass of water vapor is held in suspension, the condition of the Venusian atmosphere, by the way, is not at all like that which is believed to exist by Terra's astronomers.

Terrestrial observers believe that the planet is hidden by dense masses of the vapor of water, so vapor-wrapped that it is virtually impossible to see any markings on the globe. When it comes to the determinations of the planet's albedo, however, one finds a discrepancy that accords very ill with the boasted precision of science, but it is usually given as about that of cloud or fresh-fallen snow. The great brilliancy of the planet, therefore, proves it to be surrounded by dense cloud-masses. So the Venusians (if there are any) have a sky in which there are seldom any openings, nights of appalling darkness and a difficult time making astronomical observations. Perhaps, indeed, there never are any openings through which the inhabitants can view the stars; perhaps the faint markings seen on the Venusian disk are shadows cast upon lower cloud-strata.

Of course, all observers are not in concordance when it comes to this—for instance, Lowell found the disk of Venus cloudless—but there is no doubt that our astronomers can make but very unsatisfactory observations tending to throw light upon the physical habitudes of this most beautiful planet, that they can see no markings worthy of very serious consideration save the indisputable indentation in the southern horn, made, it is believed, by great mountains or by clouds forced to a high altitude by the striking of wind against a mountain chain. But this, of course, is not because of a dense cloud-envelope. Why it is that terrestrial observers cannot see the surface of Venus, I do not know. As yet it is a mystery that, it is not too much to say, baffles hypothesis even.

To return:

We reentered the place and took seat again. Whenever we spoke, the Venusians were as silent, as attentive, as though oracles fell from our lips.

Now and again I heard the name of Draconda spoken, and, at such times, I thought that something very like fear came into the girl's eyes.

The night wore along. That scene often comes to me—the dark forms of the Venusians on either hand; the playing of the firelight on the grim, earnest faces; the huge shadows, as the flames flickered or leaped, quivering or swaying on the columns and walls.

At length our desire for repose was indicated, whereupon the old Venusian arose and, bearing an earthen lamp, conducted us to our sleeping-chamber, a place about twenty feet wide and twenty-five in length. It had one window, over which a mat curtain was hung, gently swaying in the night breeze, as though touched by the hands of hovering spirits.

"A strange business," I observed as the footfall of our host died away on the ear, "strange from beginning to end."

"Keep in the present, Rider," St. Cloud said: "the future is as dark as the visage of that chief—and the end of this business is there."

"One thing," said Henry: "we must keep a sharp lookout this night. Though we seem to have tumbled into clover, there may be treachery afoot."

"Just what I was going to say," Morgan told him. "I have an idea, though, that no harm will come to you if that young lady can prevent it."

Henry frowned; he stood silent.

"I'll keep first watch," I volunteered.

"And I the second," said Henry.

He sat down and stared at a love scene on the wall.

"Make X rays of your oculi, Rider," admonished St. Cloud as he disposed himself for slumber. "No telling what those gentleman have planned. I wouldn't put anything past that confounded chief."

A silence fell, to be broken suddenly by Morgan.

"Wonder if I'll ever get to sleep!" he exclaimed. "Every time I shut my eyes, I see that fellow going down, the poor devil, and the one with his arm hanging over the side of the canoe. What did they attack us like that for? Not a nice thing, I tell you, to kill a man! But—I suppose you'll soon know what it is like."

It was some time ere he fell asleep. Suddenly he began to mutter in fearful tones, tossing himself about as though struggling to escape some terrifying thing in his dreams.

"The killing haunts his sleep," said Henry.

But St. Cloud was not dreaming of that.

"Blanche! Blanche!"

The words broke from his lips in tones tense with horror.

And it is a fact that, for an instant, I thought some hidden presence there in the room flung the name back at the sleeper in savage mockery. But that, of course, was only the echo.

There he was sleeping in this ruined city, and his dreams took him back across that awful intermundane abyss to some lost or forsaken terrestrial maid—to whom I did not know. I had never heard of Blanche, and little did I dream—but that will be set down in its proper place.

The name Blanche was not heard again.

For some time Henry sat there in silence, staring at the wall with eyes that I knew did not see.

"If you're going to hold the second watch," I told him at last, "you'd better be pounding your ear."

"Quite so," he returned.

He looked at me with a curious expression in his eyes.

"By the way, Rider," he began, "that girl—"

I waited, but he did not finish—lay down without saying anything more and soon was fast asleep.

And I fell to pondering on the strangeness of love as I sat there, the Winchester across my knees, senses on the alert—wondering what this girl's love would bring to her and to us.

As Haggard's Nyleptha says, "Passion is like the lightning, it is beautiful, and it links the earth to heaven, but, alas, it blinds!"

Also, alas, it links the earth to hell.

CHAPTER 25
CYNOCENE

Minute after minute passed, bringing no sign or sound of treachery. The soft whispering of the breeze stole into the rooms; once or twice the distant, mournful howl of a dog or wolf was borne to the ear; but, otherwise, a profound silence brooded over this place of ruin and darkness, a silence deep as though never broken by the footfall of man or beast.

At the expiration of the appointed time, I awoke Henry.

"A quiet watch, Rider?" he asked.

"It may be nothing but fancy," I told him, "but it seems too quiet."

"How so?"

"I can't say; but the place is as silent as a tomb."

"In a way it is. And, indeed, what isn't a tomb? Life feeds on Death: hideous, isn't it, when you think of it that way?"

"I don't," I told him.

"Sleep, Rider," he said, "sleep. The time is not ours to choose, so make the best of it."

"That lamp," I observed, "will soon burn itself out. Did that old potentate figure on that?"

"It won't matter," he returned. "I've got the flash-light, you know. Sweet dreams, Rider."

As doubtless has been noticed, Henry Quainfan was at times, and sometimes in the most unlikely times, confounded absent-minded, but (lest doubts be entertained as to his watchfulness) it should be remarked that he was a veritable

Argus when the occasion demanded.

As for my dreams, they were anything but sweet. First came that war-canoe driving across the waters, and struggles and horrors that I thought never would end. Then the dark face of that chief appeared, malignant and gibbering, and blood and torture our portion. Horror succeeded horror, and at last I stood in the presence of Draconda herself, when suddenly a cowled thing stalked out of those deep shadows behind her—the sight of it flinging me into shuddering consciousness.

The light of morning was in the place.

"Just going to wake you, Rider," came Henry's voice. "Word was brought a minute ago that breakfast only awaits our presence."

"See a ghost?" St. Cloud smiled at me.

I shivered, in spite of myself.

"I hope it was that," I told him.

It was about three hours before midday when we set out to see the city. In addition to ourselves there were six persons in our little party. They were: Fagnam, the old priest, who was the head chief also, indeed king; that giant of the evil visage, Molimnos; the girl whose name was Cynocene, and three others—the last men of no mean importance in the Oham councils but to play no part in what I am to tell.

The city had been surrounded by a strong and lofty wall, now a crumbled ruin, though places were seen which had well withstood the assaults of the ages. Most of the buildings were in ruins, but some, thanks to their Egyptian-like massiveness, were in really excellent condition.

Through this scene of battered grandeur, flowed a small, swift river, the waters of which in past centuries had been confined between embankments of stone. In one place, indeed, it still flowed there; but, smashing its way through the feeble barrier raised by man, it had long ago chosen a course of its own, strewing the place with destruction and ruin.

Undermined by its waters, two-thirds of it fallen, we found what undoubtedly had been the grandest edifice of all—a temple. In this melancholy ruin, were found several fine statues and some wonderful sculptures in basso and alto-relievo.

We ate our lunch by the stream, under the shade of some noble trees. After a little rest we resumed our exploration.

An hour passed, another; and then it was that we entered that naos in which I was destined to spill the blood of man for the first time—a massive, gloomy thing, utterly unlike anything we had seen.

Entering, we found ourselves in a long, narrow room, down the center of which ran a row of twenty square pillars. There were few windows in this place; the walls bore no decoration of any kind.

At the farther end of this room, was a doorway, small and dark. Pointing toward this, old Fagnam started on. He was followed by Morgan; the rest of us were strung out behind.

I glanced back, to see Cynocene slip her right hand into Henry's left. It was patent that the girl was agitated not a little; indeed, none of the Venusians seemed to be enjoying himself. I saw Henry's hand close hesitatingly over hers, and what I saw on the face of the chief—well, it caused me to drop back a step or two, so that I might keep an eye on the fellow.

"Now for the chamber of mystery," said Henry.

And his voice sounded strange, ghostly in the gloomy place.

"Lucifer's sanctum," muttered St. Cloud.

"The old priest," I observed, "is the only one that appears unperturbed. Cynocene is trembling."

At the sound of her name, Cynocene looked at us quickly.

"She's frightened not a little," I said.

Henry looked at her smiling, and she looked up him with eyes, soft, and clinging, that made something rise up in my throat and a wave of pity surge over me.

That dark doorway I have mentioned was low, so low, indeed, that the old priest had to stoop to enter.

"Fumy thing, that," said Henry Quainfan.

Morgan, at the doorway, stopped and looked back at us.

"Now what on earth is in there?" he said.

"Go on," Henry returned, "and you'll get the answer."

Old Fagnam had turned and was motioning for Morgan to follow.

"Infernally dark in here," muttered St. Cloud as he stooped to enter.

For a second or two there was silence, when his voice came reverberating from the chamber in awful tones.

"Great heavens!" he cried out. "Look at that!"

"What is it?" I asked.

No answer came.

"Go on, Rider!" said Henry, giving me a shove.

And in I went—because I couldn't do anything else. Henry and Cynocene were at my heels; I could hear the others following.

As I stooped to go through that thick doorway, the thought occurred to me:

"Have they brought us here to make an end of us? Why didn't Morgan answer?"

And, as I went through, I shifted the Winchester to my left hand and my right closed on the butt of the Colt's.

But Morgan was safe. He was standing right in front of me. That was why I didn't see it. The priest had vanished.

"Look!" cried Morgan, stepping to one side. "Look there!"

I looked. At that moment Henry and the girl stepped to my side. There before us, about twenty-five feet away, dimly seen in the light that struggled in through a tiny window on either side, was a face grinning at us—a face, it seemed, suspended in the empty air—huge, horrible, quasi-human, white and stamped with an expression of unutterable cruelty and fiendish mockery. The thing made me shiver from head to foot. The girl gave a sharp cry and flung her arms around Henry's neck, looking back over her shoulder at that thing which grinned. Came a muttering from the floor, discovering the whereness of old Fagnam. There the old boy was, flat on his stomach. Down went the others, all save Cynocene, and she too would have prostrated herself before that thing of horror if Henry had not stopped her.

"Doré or Poe never visioned a thing like that," said Henry. "Did you ever see such cruelty and mockery?"

In a little while, our eyes growing accustomed to the darkness, we could make out, though indistinctly, the body of the statue.

"Let's go up," said Henry, "and get a good look."

At this proposal the girl manifested surprise and alarm, endeavored to dissuade us from it. Seeing, however, that her dehortation would be futile, she suddenly announced (with signs, of course) that she would go back and await our return in the other room.

Accordingly Cynocene left the place, and we stepped forward, to the manifest horror of the Venusians, who perhaps expected to see us blasted for this sacrilegious proceeding.

The body, naked above the waist, was that of a woman; in her hands, which rested on the right knee, she held a real human skull. With only the head visible, suspended, as it were, in the empty air, the sight had been an uncanny one; but, now that all was visible, it was simply a very horrible thing in stone.

I happened to glance back at the doorway; there I saw a dark form, which vanished suddenly.

I thought of Molimnos and Cynocene. So imperfect had been that glimpse, however, that I could not tell whether it was the chief or not.

I thought it well to make sure.

"One of the Venusians just went out," I told Henry as I started back. "I think it was Molimnos."

We retraced out steps swiftly, myself in the lead. Just as we were passing those prostrate Venusians, came a shriek, sudden, piercing, horrible.

One leap took me into the doorway.

About halfway down the room, were the chief and Cynocene. The girl was on her knees, one hand on the floor, the other in his iron grip, her eyes, wide with horror, fixed on the knife raised high above the giant's head. A stream of sunshine flowed in upon them, lighting up the chief from the elbow of his upraised arm to his waist and lighting up Cynocene's whole person. There were faint shadows on her upturned face. Her lips were parted, but voiceless as the lips of the dead.

I threw the rifle to my shoulder and fired. If I had been a second longer, or Chance had not directed the bullet to his heart—for my aim, I fear, had little enough to do with it—that blade would have been buried in Cynocene's heaving breast. The report thundered round the rocky walls, and, spinning round twice, Molimnos crashed down dead.

We rushed to the girl and found her unhurt.

But I have often thought that it would have been a kind stroke of Fate had the love-mad Molimnos plunged his weapon into Cynocene's heart, for then would not have occurred that terrible thing it is now my task to relate.

The third day after this terrible business in the temple of gloom was the one decided upon for our departure.

The first part of our journey to Draconda, old Fagnam had explained, would be by canoe. It would take two days to reach that point down the river whence the road ran away to Loom, the name of the city when Draconda lived, and he himself was going to accompany us that far. That second part of our journey, considerably the longer, would be by horse.

On this day in question, we were up with the dawn. As soon as I saw her, I knew that Cynocene had had a bad night of it. I wished heartily that we were gone.

Our breakfast that morning was gloomy affair. At last came that time so welcomed and yet dreaded so much—the time for departure. Then, however, to my surprise, we learned that Cynocene was not going down to the shore to see us off.

St. Cloud and I pressed her hand in farewell and started; but scarcely a half dozen steps had been taken when a low, sudden cry brought us to a stop and turned us round in our tracks.

Cynocene had flung her arms round Henry's neck and was weeping in a way that was simply terrible. He put his arm about the girl and held her close, and she pressed her cheek against his—beginning to weep more terribly than ever in that embrace in which she knew there was no love.

Of a sudden Henry tore himself free and started away; the next instant the girl drew a hidden dagger, raised it high above her breast and struck.

With a wild cry, Henry sprang to her side and caught her in his arms. He knelt down on the stone floor, holding her head gently against his shoulder.

A single look showed that the girl could not live, that death might come at any moment. Old Fagnam was beside himself with grief. Cynocene raised her arms and tried to put them around Henry's neck, but her strength was ebbing away too swiftly. Then she raised her face for him to kiss her. He bent his head, kissed her on the lips; the next moment she gave a painful sigh, her head sank forward, and Henry Quainfan held a corpse in his arms.

He came to his feet, his eyes swimming in tears.

"Take me away, Rider," he said weakly, reeling like a drunken man. "Take me away."

CHAPTER 26
THE SACRIFICE

The words spoken by Henry Quainfan in the concluding sentences of the preceding chapter convey a far better idea of the effect upon him than possible by any I could set down; so I shall hasten on.

We did not go forth on our journey to Draconda that day, nor the next or the one following that, for we stayed for the poor girl's funeral—the interment being on this last day mentioned, as is the Oham custom.

On this day, some two hours after the sun had passed the meridian, about four score persons, of both sexes, and of evident rank, as rank goes in this barbaric place, came gliding into that great room in which we had first seen Cynocene—in the gloom of which she now lay a corpse. Silent as shadows they came (indeed, almost as silently) and took seat on the flagging, from which every covering had been removed save that rug of fur on which Cynocene herself lay. Beside her sat old Fagnam, not an ornament of any kind on his person now, silent, moveless, his gray locks shorn.

The old man's gaze seemed fixed in vacancy itself. There was not the slightest change in it, not a lineament moved, while the people were entering.

Came a long, painful silence. Once to our ears drifted the far howl of a dog.

Then one of the priests arose and began to speak. For many minutes his low voice was heard, echoing mournfully from the rocky walls. At last he stood silent, then suddenly started a song, low, wailing, a thing terrible to hear. The others joined in, men and women, everyone save old Fagnam, and for many minutes that awful epicedium rose and fell on the cold ears of the dead.

The song was followed by a silence which lasted for several minutes, when the bereaved old man stood up and began to speak. Once we knew that he was speaking of ourselves—or perhaps of Henry only, for it was upon him that all eyes were suddenly turned. In the stillness that succeeded, two priests arose and, after Fagnam had taken the last, lingering look at his daughter, concealed the face of Cynocene forever from mortal eyes.

The bier on which she lay was now lifted up by young women, who walked slowly from the place with measured tread. Behind them moved Fagnam, his white head bowed. As the old man was passing us, the priest who had spoken requested, with signs, that we step in beside him, which we did.

The street was crowded. Every Oham, I believe, was there. Down the lane formed by the hundreds of savages, we walked, the people falling in behind us. There was no sound of voices. Could be heard only the low sound of those hundreds of feet on the stones.

In something like twenty minutes, we reached the grave, near a flower-burdened tree. Here Cynocene was laid on a bed of white roses. Four priests now stepped forward and wrapped the body in tough bark, when it was lowered into the earth amidst an utter silence. Then eight maidens, four on either side of the grave, moved to the edge and covered Cynocene with flowers.

As they stepped back, the officiating priest took up a handful of earth and, uttering a few words in tones deep and solemn, let it fall from his fingers into the grave. Then a low sound, something like the wail of weary waves on the beach, erupted through the still air. Slowly it increased in volume, slowly died away, and this dirge was sung by the women only. As it fell on the ear, a half dozen men began filling in the grave. I saw tears trickling down old Fagnam's cheeks; and this bereaved old barbarian and the man from another world who stood the innocent cause of his bereavement stood side by side and watched.

The next day we bade good-bye to the Ohams and the *Nancy Lee*, just as the great sun was rising above the cordillera, starting on our journey to Draconda in that very war-canoe in which the score of Venusians had set out to attack us.

Old Fagnam, sorrowful and silent, commanded the party. It rained all that afternoon but not heavily. For two days we journeyed down the river, passing through a country very sparsely populated, and some ruins that I wish I could stop to describe; and, just as the sun was setting, going down in a blood-dripping sky, we came to another ruined city, more interesting even than the first. This place of ruin is about three times as large as that in which dwell the Ohams and is inhabited by about five thousand savages—or, strictly, barbarians—who are called Cumnees. Its ruins, many and colossal, were found very interesting, but I shall not pause to describe even the most wonderful.

The next morning, early, at the first blush of twilight, a courier mounted on a horse left to bear for the first stage of its journey the message that would give Queen Draconda intelligence of the arrival in her kingdom of "the men from the stars."

The day following, we said good-bye to old Fagnam, who had fallen ill, though not seriously, and, with his *kamnos,* or chief of the Cumnees, and an escort of fifty warriors, we set out for Loom, which we were told was about ten days distant. I have often thought of old Fagnam, and I wonder if he has yet gone to meet his Cynocene and them who went before her, for he was full of years.[7]

---

7. Since the above was written, old Fagnam has been killed. The Ohams, who live on the frontier, were attacked early one morning by a Wilcom Lincom or army—the jeweled woman was a Wilcom—and for several hours the battle raged furiously and the issue was doubtful. The surprise was not complete, but, before they could rally, many Ohams were slain. The Wilcoms, though greatly outnumbering the attacked, were finally repulsed, but not before they had slain half or more of the Oham warriors.

Among these was old Fagnam, who directed his warriors almost to the last, old man though he was. The head priest of the Ohams, though not his subordinates of the sacerdotal order, must be a warrior as well as a priest, and all the chiefs are subject to his mandates. Through the cowardice of some of his warriors or through a misunderstanding—most think it was the latter—Fagnam was cut off with only half a dozen followers; and the grim old priest and warrior fought gallantly, singing his wild war-song, until he was brained from behind.

Two men remained fighting when he went down. Thus passed old Fagnam. About two scores of Oham women were carried away captive by the defeated Wilcoms, five scores or so were slain and about the same number of children. It was a dark day for the Ohams. Even as I write this, an army of Ohams and Cumnees is preparing to march into and (it is hoped) subdue the land of the hated Wilcoms.—R. F.

We were mounted on wiry little horses and followed what remained of an ancient road, running close to an affluent of the Quainfan—and through a forest so dense that we did not see a ray of sunshine all that day, weirdly silent, too, save for the occasional cries of parrot-like birds. Several imposing ruins were passed, almost hidden by clinging forest growth. On stopping before one of them, there came to my mind these words of the prophet Jeremiah:

"I beheld, and, lo, the fruitful place was a wilderness, and all the cities thereof were broken down."

About an hour before the falling of darkness, we entered a large town, composed of strong huts and inhabited by a people a little farther advanced than the Ohams or the Cumnees. We were now at the foot of a jagged mountain range, and the next morning we began the ascent of its airy defiles; but this range is a dwarf compared with that great wall in the east. On the succeeding day, when the shades of evening came down on the world, we were shivering in a wind-swept pass, wherein we spent one of the most miserable nights I have ever known.

The descent, begun about the middle of the afternoon and ended near midday of the day following, was very difficult and left us, we judged, five or six thousand feet higher than the valley of the Quainfan.

We now found ourselves in a thickly-populated region, our eyes greeted by signs of civilization, a rude civilization, it is true, but one which was good to look upon nevertheless.

About two hours before sundown, we rode into a beautiful little city, a modern one, and here the next day we said good-bye to our Cumnee friends.

We journeyed on steadily, with a new escort, following the aforementioned road, the ruins of which had threaded the dizzy defiles of the jagged range behind us and which was here, well taken care of, one of the finest highways I have ever seen; and everywhere were vestiges, mournful and eloquent, of that great civilization which had reigned over this land in some far time, in some age deep in the shadows of departed days.

We found the climate delightful and the civilization, as we advanced steadily into the northwest, gradually becoming of a higher order and consequently more pleasing.

Word of our arrival had spread with the swiftness of the wind, giving us the most fantastic characters; and, at our approach to a city, the whole population turned out to look with awe upon men from the stars, who "slew with thunder."

The intelligence that we slew with thunder gave Draconda much concern,

She did not believe that we had come from the Blue Star but that we were the harbingers of some mighty Venusian people. She knew from this thunder story that we possessed firearms, and so the queen greatly feared for the safety of her kingdom—or, strictly, empire—fearing that after us would come armies of conquest, before the onset of which her warriors with their swords, bows and spears would be destroyed incontinently, that even now she could feel her throne trembling, that in the near future it would be hurled into the dust.

But she sent forth word that every honor be accorded these mysterious strangers, sent an envoy to meet us and awaited our coming into her presence with impatience and foreboding. The reader can easily imagine how troubled, how filled with fear even, was the mind of the queen, upon whose horizon our coming had massed great storm-clouds that might send sudden and frightful destruction down upon her nation.

It was about two hours after nightfall, and soon after passing some great ruins over in the southwest black against the serene starlit sky, when we rode into the city of Polom. There we met the queen's embassy, headed by a very handsome (and, as we subsequently learned, very powerful) young lord named Ta Antom, which means The Wolf—a man who will play an important part in what follows.

Also, as will be seen forthwith, we met this night, in a most remarkable manner, another person destined to play an important role in the awful drama, a woman—Mynine. And, as it soon proved, evil was that hour in which we set eyes on her.

The queen had given word, as has been said, that every honor be accorded us—and The Wolf, who had been awaiting our arrival, accorded us an honor by conducting us to that terrible place of meeting.

The city of Polom we found almost deserted, a circumstance which we were at a loss to account. However, it soon was made clear. The people had gone to the great temple of Teenemtos, where was to be offered this night the horrible sacrifice of two beautiful virgins. This sacrifice (Teenemtos is the god of fecundity) has taken place every seven years for centuries. To this terrible place we rode forthwith, conducted by The Wolf, who was accompanied by a number of men of inferior, though evidently very high, rank.

The temple, which is a colossal naos and the work of that vanished people, rather plain but replete with frowning majesty, and in excellent condition, about a mile from the city and stands alone.

A great multitude of kneeling men, women and children ringed the temple around; there must have been thirty thousand souls there. At the edge at the crowd, and before the temple, we dismounted, then proceeded to that great flight of steps which led up to the place of sacrifice—where a lurid fire was burning, where were seated the persons of the highest rank and whither we were being conducted by The Wolf.

Now, we had reached the very foot of those steps without having discovered what was taking place up there by that lurid fire. Of course, it was obvious that this vast assemblage was a religious one, but it had not entered our heads that we might be approaching the temple of an anthropophagous god.

I was lifting one of my feet up to the first step when a horrible shriek drove through the air. Then was falling the moment of the first sacrifice to Teenemtos. That awful shriek was succeeded by an exclamation of horror from the lips of Henry Quainfan; and I, on looking up, saw a purple-robed, white-bearded man, in the full light of that lurid fire, drive a long knife into the left side of a woman, who had been stripped naked and placed upon a raised stone slab, where she was held down by four men, likewise dressed in purple.

This sudden horror made my vision to become blurry; but, through the blur, I saw another woman, a little to one side and farther away, *in puris naturalibus,* the second victim for the sacrifice, whose slender white body was wilting in the arms of the two men, young and robed in purple, that supported her.

CHAPTER 27
MYNINE

From above instantly arose a diabolical chant, in which that kneeling multitude on the ground joined and which rushed up and smote the star-studded sky. It was as if the voices of so many devils filled the air.

We looked at one another, but no words left our lips. We were struck speechless. There we stood, as if chained to the spot, until the slain woman was removed from the slab and the two men who held the second sacrificial victim began dragging her toward the sacred stone.

I looked at Henry, whose face was ghastly pale in the lurid light, his lips slightly parted. On his handsome face was stamped the most awful look of horror. He was staring at the scene above (The Wolf, who had ascended a half dozen steps or so, was looking back curiously and interrogatively) and suddenly, with an exclamation, he threw the Winchester to his shoulder.

"You pay for that, you old devil!" he muttered.

As the fatal weapon settled into aim, the people near us ceased to chant, and a murmur of surprise and awe welled up. Those above, apparently, had not noticed us, that which was taking place up there engrossing their attention. The old man who had slain the woman was standing with his back to us, his head turned to one side, looking at the victim that was being dragged toward his dripping knife.

"Don't miss!" I told Henry.

"I won't!" he muttered.

The sharp report rang out, and the old priest dropped. He would never make another sacrificial kill. The chanting above and the chanting and murmur by us ceased on the instant. A heavy silence fell upon the temple and the surrounding multitude, disturbed only by the crackling of the ghostly fires and that movement of surprise which agitated the kneeling people.

"Come on!" cried Henry, starting up the steps.

I sprang after him. As I started, St. Cloud's Winchester barked, and one of those men that were holding the girl went down a corpse.

A murmur swept over the crowd and waxed and waned. Up the great flight of steps sprang we three Terrestrials. Soon above and below us pandemonium broke out. Those who had been officiating at the immolation turned and fled, all save one. He was a stalwart, middle-aged man, and he stood up there staring at us in a state of seeming stupefaction until Henry was nearly to the top, when the man suddenly seemed possessed of a paroxysm of maddening rage: his right arm shot back, and, lips drawn in a wolfish snarl, facial muscles twitching horribly, he hurled a big knife with terrific force straight at Henry's head.

The weapon just missed its mark, went flashing on through the air and buried itself, as we afterwards learned, to the hilt in the breast of a woman below.

The next instant I, who had halted at the first sign of hostility, pressed the trigger, and the priest pitched forward and came rolling down the steps to Henry Quainfan's feet. His right arm was under his body, the fingers of the left hand twitching as his spirit ebbed away.

A few leaps more took Henry to the top; a moment, and I was beside him.

The place we found tenanted only by the dead woman and the second virgin, whose life our timely and (as we were to learn) evil arrival had saved from the consuming flames of sacrifice.

The girl, golden-haired and strikingly beautiful, had sunk down on the floor and was looking at us with fear-filled eyes—they were blue eyes—in which tiny waves of hope surged and broke.

Henry took up a garment—perhaps her own, perhaps the dead virgin's there—and threw it over the maiden, who raised herself into a sitting position and began to draw its white folds about her.

Before us was the great entrance, through which had fled the priests, their attendants and even some of the spectators. On either side sat these privileged ones, in seats running in rows, as in an amphitheater, and they stared at us beings from another world—men from the stars, who slew with such crushing mystery—with fearful eyes.

A heavy silence had fallen on the spot, and it seemed to my heated imagination that this stillness was replete with portentousness, that, in the dark of unborn minutes, soon to fall upon this cursed place, moved and stirred struggle and blood and destruction.

"No danger in sight," observed Henry, glancing keenly this way and that.

"Not yet," I said. "Not in sight but maybe in darkness."

"Yes," said Morgan, "Only Heaven knows what is going on in there."

As he spoke, he made a motion with his rifle toward the great entrance. Henry and I looked, but nothing was to be seen there, no sound issued from out that cavernous darkness.

"Bet we are in for it now," St. Cloud added, his eyes sweeping over that great crowd below. "I have a presentiment that we shall never leave this place alive."

He shuddered the next moment as his eyes fell on the immolated maiden, her naked body white as a sheet on that dark floor of stone.

"What a piece of work is man!" he muttered.

Taking his eyes from the awful sight, Henry Quainfan looked into mine for a moment ere he opened his mouth to speak; but he did not speak, suddenly turning away and shaking his head bitterly, railing perhaps at that mystery of Providence which had permitted this thing of horror.

His look went to the young woman whose life we had saved. She was still there on the floor. Save for a few glances at St. Cloud and me, by the way, she had kept her look riveted on Henry.

St. Cloud made an exclamation. Turning, I saw that he too was looking at the girl.

"Venus herself!" said Morgan.

I turned quickly, for I thought a faint, murmurous sound had come from that yawning entrance behind us. However, nothing was to be seen or heard. Thinking that my fevered organs of hearing had deceived me, I brought my look back to the place of sacrifice.

"What a trap we're in!" St. Cloud exclaimed.

"Trap's the word," returned Henry.

It was indeed.

He picked up a sheet, like silk, stepped to the dead woman and covered up the form.

"Damnable!" he muttered. "Why didn't we arrive a few minutes sooner? Why didn't we notice what was going on up here?"

"What's happened is bad enough, but I fancy what's coming is worse," returned St. Cloud, looking down at the multitude, over which was sweeping a great excitement. "It looks like those fellows down there mean business."

"It does," said Henry.

"We didn't save this girl's life, after all," Morgan said.

"I know what you mean," I told him.

"Only from the knife of this old devil," and he kicked the white-bearded dead man, whose blade had been plunged to the victim's heart; "they'll get her yet and us men from the stars into the bargain."

"These gentlemen up here," I remarked, "don't look dangerous. Not a one of them seems to be armed."

"Darn poor consolation, that," muttered St. Cloud. "These boys here don't know what to do. The way they just stare! Damn 'em, I half wish they would try something! Now, why did that infernal fool bring us to this place?"

Henry Quainfan laughed.

"Go ask him, Morgan."

St. Cloud was peering down the steps.

"Like bees!" he muttered. "Bees!"

He turned his dark look to us.

"Their god is going to have a bigger sacrifice this night than they dreamed."

"Seems so," nodded Henry. "The first move is theirs, though, not ours. And as for this girl, she'll never be thrown on that slab: if death proves inevitable, I will shoot her."

He threw the barrel of his rifle into the hollow of his left arm and stood musing in silence, the while the girl gazed up at him and my eyes roved quickly on every hand.

"See down there!" exclaimed St. Cloud at last, pointing. "There's a fellow making an harangue."

"Yes," said I, "I've been watching him."

Harry's eyes slowly turned in the direction in which St. Cloud was pointing and rested vacuously on the Venusian, who was addressing the crowd in a loud voice.

"Urging them to attack," said Morgan. "One of those purple-robed devils, most likely. If they come, we shall be destroyed. They will attack from both the front and the rear—unless they are fools."

"Of course," I said.

"And don't stand there, Henry," Morgan broke out, "as though dreaming love dreams! We've got to get busy. We must sell our lives dearly. A few minutes, and we shall be even as she is."

He glanced at the dead woman.

"But they may not attack us," Henry returned, "though—"

"Look down there and see!" St. Cloud interrupted.

"It does look mighty like it. If they do—well, there'll be more than one weeping mother, widow and sweetheart when the morning's sun wings up. Many an unsung wanderer of our mighty race has gone down fighting in a far land—but none in a land so far as this! And we too shall be unsung. But listen to that fellow. His voice—"

He was interrupted by a yell from below.

"That's the forerunner of an attack," he went on, surveying the wild scene below with calm eyes. "It belongs to brute language, and we understand that language even as our savage progenitors of the Pleistocene understood."

Came another yell, louder than the first, and the Venusians near us gazed down whence it came.

"Yell, you hell-hounds!" muttered St. Cloud, throwing his rifle forward. "Yell, you sons of Satan, you spawn of Ahriman! That gentleman is speaking his last spoke."

On finishing this outburst, Morgan dropped on one knee, and his rifle settled his aim. The girl shrank back a little, and the eyes of every man and woman on either side of the place of sacrifice were fixed upon him. The doomed Venusian stood a little above his fellows and in the flare of several torches, which cast a little circle of light over the crowd that ringed him around. The rifle barked, and the man, turning half round, fell forward and disappeared. We saw another Venusian, who was standing just beyond him in a direct line with the Winchester, throw up his hands and pitch forward.

A silence rushed down, soon broken by a yell as wild and horrible as religious fervor and hatred for the beings who had desecrated the holy temple of Teenemtos could make it. A great commotion began below. Everywhere were dark figures hurrying. It seemed that the utmost confusion prevailed, but there was order down there, for soon a bunch of armed men was standing at the foot of the steps; and the sight made my heart sink.

Henry looked at St. Cloud, and a smile was hovering round his lips.

"Now you've done it!" he said.

St. Cloud made an exclamation and began to look about him anxiously.

"We've got to get into a better place than this!" he exclaimed suddenly. "See! They're getting ready to charge us now!"

Henry turned quickly and stepped to the girl. She was trembling violently, her wondrous eyes swimming in tears. In a moment he had assisted her to her feet; supporting the lovely creature with his left arm, he turned and looked at the crowd below, which had became silent. But the silence which had fallen upon it was the silence that presages a storm.

"Our only choice," said Henry, "is one of these raised places at the head of the steps. I propose we take the one on our left."

"Good!" I told him. "They're both alike, save this on the left is the nearer, and let's make it snappy!"

"Ditto!" said Morgan. "Great place, though, to put up a fight! One thing: if they miss us, they may hit their friends here behind."

Henry was already moving toward this place of vantage, half carrying the maiden—whose name was Mynine. And, under the light of subsequent events, terrible and bloody, it will be seen how sadly Destiny blundered in not delaying our arrival at this place of sacrifice—how horrible this thing which had stayed the immolation of Mynine.

But this seems to be a way Destiny has. How often I have wished we had been a few moments later in reaching that cursed temple of Teenemtos—God only knows how many times I have wished that!

But then, as we moved swiftly toward that chosen place, the events to spring from this lovely woman's dark soul were unknown to me—as (I believe) the events of the future usually are.

Henry lifted the girl to the ledge, the next instant was beside her. It was a place about six feet higher than the floor, perhaps twenty long but only six in width, flanking those seats where the worshipers sat, which was very fine; but a circumstance not so fine was that drop in front, sheer to the ground—a distance of perhaps fifty feet. A steeple-jack, of course, would have thought nothing of it, but all the same it was a spot with some unpleasant possibilities—its obvious advantages, though, precluding even a moment's hesitation.

St. Cloud was the second man up. Almost instantaneously, as I was catching a grip on the stone to follow, his cry rang out:

"Here they come!"

It was followed, almost accompanied, by the crack of his rifle, and up to the cloud-flecked, starlit sky rose a wild and lingering yell—from the throat of the Venusian his bullet had hit—and succeeded by the dull sound of many rushing feet.

CHAPTER 28
THE ATTACK

I lost no time in getting up on the ledge.

"I'll keep an eye on the entrance," said Henry, "and these fellows behind us. You two give all your attention to the steps."

And we did, or, rather, to the men charging up those steps—which, I have forgotten to say, were broken by two landing-places. No sound came from the watching multitude below or those watchers near us, and from the charging Venusians no cries, no sound of voices even, only those sounds made by their rapid movements.

Some were armed with spears, others with swords, the weapons flashing in that lurid light as though with imprisoned fire. Why they did not use bows and arrows, in the use of which they are proficient, has always been something of a mystery to me. Perhaps, though, there were no bows and arrows at hand, or it might have been for fear of killing some of those Venusians behind us.

And into that anadromous mass we poured our deadly fire. The men had started up with a rush, but, ere a quarter of the ascent even, that rush had abated not a little. Yet on they came, grim and silent as Fate.

"When your rifles are empty," said Henry, "I'll reload them—use your revolvers."

Hardly had he spoken when St. Cloud, who had kept up a rapid and deadly fire, sent his rifle toward him, drawing his revolver as he did so.

I glanced back at the entrance, dark and yawning as the mouth of a cavern. A charge, I thought, would come from there at any instant. But, as I glanced, the place was empty and (it seemed) silent.

The charging Venusians were near the top now. I fired the last bullet in my rifle, dropped that weapon and drew my revolver.

A few seconds, and Death would come leaping to our ledge.

I shot a look at Henry, who had emptied his own rifle and was now reloading St. Cloud's. I say reloading, but at that instant he was looking at the girl. I knew full well what was in his mind. With a yell that must have sounded more like a demon's than a man's, I turned and emptied my revolver into the crowd. To my amazement, it was beginning to waver now—waver when, with awful toll, it had attained the top.

"Give it to 'em—they're losing heart!" shouted Henry.

He dropped the rifle and drew his revolvers.

"They're beginning—*look out!*" he yelled.

The Venusians had halted confusedly, some, indeed, already were falling back, and from their midst came wild cries and yells and the groans of the wounded and the dying—a confused, terrible sound. But what had caused Henry to give his warning cry was the spears: the words were still in the air when they came, eight or ten of them—I don't know how many. Down went St. Cloud and I, flat on the stone, or as flat as the circumstances would permit—my sudden movement nearly precipitating me over the edge into that dark depth below.

And, at this very instant, through all that tumult and horror, came the sound, loud, unmistakable, of armed men behind—to be precise, behind and to the right.

The spears drove in all around us, the blade of one sending up a shower of sparks as it cut along the stone past my face. Every one of us, including the girl, was struck, though (it was nothing less than a miracle) not a one with point or blade.

Henry's revolvers barked. I came to my knees. The Venusians—who, had they pressed forward, would have destroyed us incontinently—of a sudden turned and started down the steps in the wildest confusion.

I looked behind. What had happened at the top of the steps had brought those Venusians in the entrance to a halt. I waited, hoping there would be no occasion for further spilling of blood; but St. Cloud began firing into their midst, whereupon they turned and vanished into the darkness whence they had come, leaving two wounded and one dead man there on the floor behind them.

"Praised be Nike!" cried Henry Quainfan. "I thought we were goners that time."

"Praised be Jehovah!" said I.

I turned and watched the men fleeing down the steps, several of whom were felled with bullets from St. Cloud's rifle.

"Hold on, Morgan!" exclaimed Henry. "Let the poor devils go!"

St. Cloud slowly lowered his Winchester, looking at Henry with disgust depicted on his handsome features.

"Yes—let 'em go!" he exclaimed angrily. "Every man that gets away means one more for the next attack."

"Good Lord!" Henry exclaimed.

Then in a changed voice:

"If you keep that up, you won't have a single bullet for the next attack—if there is another."

"If there is!" exclaimed St. Cloud. "Do you think they won't make us pay for this? Just wait till they recover their wits!"

He looked about him anxiously, a little wildly even.

"Here's where this mad journey of ours ends—in a heathenish, bloody place of sacrifice, in battle and madness."

"In battle perhaps," said Henry Quainfan, "but not in madness."

"It is mad!" exclaimed St. Cloud. "All this—and worse than madness! We should have known in that mad beginning: the Almighty—"

"Lord help us!" interrupted Henry.

"You're too late!" St. Cloud told him.

"Cheer up, Morgan," Henry smiled. "While there's life, there's hope, you know."

"Bosh!" said Morgan. "And we'd need it all if there was."

Of a sudden that smile of Henry's vanished, his face becoming hard and bleak. Not a little surprised, I wondered what had come to make this change, for I knew that his eyes had fallen on nothing to cause it. His gaze wandered over the steps, dotted with dead and wounded Venusians, over the multitude below and into the darkness and the mystery of night.

I broke the silence.

"What's the matter?" I asked him.

He looked at me quickly, then turned his eyes to the girl.

It was a little while ere he spoke:

"You remember, Rider, what I said I would do if death proved inevitable: I was on the point of doing it when they wavered. Another second—"

He shuddered, and Mynine, who knew that he had spoken of her, looked up at him with wondering (and wondrous) eyes.

"That," I told him, "should be left to God."

"Let 'em go!" came St. Cloud's voice.

He turned his look to Henry.

"I suppose," he said, "you're the fellow who wouldn't lend the devil a knife when he wanted to stab himself!"

Henry Quainfan laughed outright—the sound startling in that awful place.

St. Cloud muttered something unintelligible and turned his dark look back to the steps. One of the men there suddenly began screaming. He struggled into a sitting position, to his feet, clutched wildly at the empty air, collapsed and went rolling down to the landing-place, where he lay an inert and silent heap.

"O God," said St. Cloud, "why from heaven (or hell) to this prison and madness of the flesh?"

Followed a quarter of an hour or so of expectant waiting, when we saw a deputation with a big *white* flag coming toward the steps.

CHAPTER 29
THE TREACHERY OF THE WOLF

The little party came slowly up the steps, headed by The Wolf himself, the flag-bearer just behind him.

Henry descended from the place where we had made our stand and, with the barrel of the Winchester in the hollow of his left arm, stood awaiting the Venusians, none of whom was armed.

Near the top of the steps, they halted. For a few moments, there was an awkward pause. Then The Wolf opened negotiations—in pantomime.

The attack, he said, was deeply regretted; let there be peace—here he went through the motions of drawing a blade from the empty scabbard at his side and breaking the weapon across his knee, and pointed significantly to Henry's rifle—let there be peace, said Ta Antom, and accord him the pleasure of giving us safe conduct to the city of Loom, to Draconda, the queen.

A man of cunning was our handsome Ta Antom. He had no intention at all of conducting us safe to the queen. Already had he formed those plans with which he hoped to bring death upon us—more horrible than death here in battle—in that underground sepulcher of the ancient inhabitants of Loom.

Peace, Henry gave him answer, was our desire, and a speedy journey to Draconda; but, at the first sign of treachery, we would slay, slay, slay. Also, he made Ta Antom understand, no harm was to come to the girl.

This last, I noticed, displeased not a little the purple-robed men of the deputation—who, of course, were priests—but, after that momentary flash of displeasure, they gave no unacquiescent signs.

The maiden, Ta Antom assured him, would be as safe as ourselves.

In order to be brief, I will leave something to the imagination and merely say that the matter ended (or, rather, began) in our returning to the city, though, when leaving that terrible place, we feared greatly that the Venusians would put an end to us.

However, there was not the least sign of hostility: we didn't know The Wolf.

And now came a thing that gave us no little concern: with tears streaming down her cheeks, the girl made us understand that she dare not leave us—that to do so would mean instant and horrible death.

What on earth were we to do?

Henry Quainfan ran his fingers through his curls, a way he had when perplexed.

"We've got an armful now," he said.

We had indeed, and one that I feared was going to bring us trouble.

"We can't let them get their heathenish claws on her again," said Morgan.

"Of course not," Henry returned. "But a lady in the party, and one so lovely—heavens, I never figured on that!"

"I fancy," I told him, "that there are a few other things unfigured."

"Oh, well," he added, "it won't be long before we get to this wonderful queen of theirs. Heaven only knows what will happen then."

"I wonder," said Morgan, "if we will find Draconda as lovely as this young lady of ours. You know, I believe she is—with a single exception—the most beautiful woman I have ever seen."

"One thing I've noticed, though," Henry said: "her wonderful loveliness is marred by something—something elusive, mysterious. I don't know what it is, where it is; but I think it's in the eyes."

"I think you're seeing things," St. Cloud told him. "But how does this mysterious something strike you?"

"Our Mynine would make a terrible enemy."

St. Cloud gave his dark smile.

"She'll never be that—to us, I mean."

"Of course not," Henry smiled back.

Needless to say, we did not feel very safe this night, even though we had been permitted to return to the city unmolested. Something might happen at any moment. There was no telling what treachery might be afoot.

One of our rooms was occupied by our fair charge. Henry said he would take the first turn at watching and would awake me to relieve him in about two hours. St. Cloud and I lay down, though I feared I could not get to sleep, what with those terrible pictures of our fight at the temple that came and went in my closed eyes. So tired was I, however, that the pictures soon became blurry, then faded, and I sank into troubled sleep; and without was Henry keeping his vigil, eyes and ears keen for possible treachery.

But nothing happened this night.

By nine o'clock all was ready for the start.

Mynine's father and mother had come, evidently persons of wealth and position—though it was patent that they stood in no little awe of the head priest, dubbed by Henry the archbishop. And here I may as well give that diabolical plot which had brought about all this terrible business.

Of course, at that time we did not know it; what follows we learned from Draconda.

The victims for sacrifice were chosen *by lot:* to be by lot, however, a thing must be left to chance. Mynine was the only child, and the girl out of the way, at least half of the family wealth (on the extinction of the family, in which the priests could lend Atropos a hand) would go into the sacred coffers, the rest to the crown. In this lottery of death, however, the Loomian sovereign had no voice—unless, indeed, he (or she) had a victim in mind: what I mean is, no power resident in the crown could stay the doom pronounced.

However, the cavalcade started, with no little gratitude and apprehension on our part—the lamentation of mother and father filling the air, the maiden sobbing in a suppressed but terrible manner, as we rode away.

Hour after hour passed; nothing of import happened. A little after sunset, we rode into a small town, where we passed the night. The rising sun found our cavalcade in motion. We were still travelling on that great highway, which ran away to the city of Loom—and beyond.

Before us, extending from the east to the west, was a beautiful, though (comparatively speaking) low range of mountains.

It was about mid-afternoon when we came to it—that road leading off to the right and into which The Wolf turned.

We halted.

Didn't the great highway go on to Loom?

Oh, yes, The Wolf made answer, but this way was shorter.

I turned to Henry.

"What do you think of it?" I asked him.

"I think we may as well follow."

"The longest way round," said St. Cloud, "is sometimes the shortest way—I can't say home in this instance."

"Maybe it is, though," Henry smiled, as he started his horse.

As twilight was deepening toy darkness, we entered the little city of Wantos, where we passed the night.

We got under way about eight o'clock. It was two hours or so after midday when we rode into a place of ruins, a place silent and sad, behind which towered the mountains, at this point sheer for the last thousand feet.

The road became a street, and the street took us straight through to the mouth of a tunnel.

"An underground journey!" Henry exclaimed.

"I don't like this," said Morgan.

"I don't either," Henry returned. "There probably is nothing to fear, though. I don't think they have brought us here to make an end of us."

"It looks like it," interposed St. Cloud.

"They would have done that long since," Henry told him. "No—I think we'll be taken to Draconda now, who I hope will be kindly disposed toward us poor wanderers from an alien world."

Here we drew rein before the entrance. Some of the Venusians dismounted and got out metal lamps and jars filled with oil. We asked The Wolf how long this underground journey before us would last, and he answered, by indicating the position of the sun when we would issue, something less than an hour, as near as we could make out.

Out of the tunnel, the height and width of which we saw would permit two mounted persons to go side by side, flowed a little stream of sparkling water. On either side, was a caryatid, a cowled, terrible figure—a representation of Death.

"Good Lord!" exclaimed St. Cloud. "A tomb!"

"Looks like it," Henry nodded. "Queer place, this."

St. Cloud cast his dark look about him in an uneasy manner.

"I wish we had insisted on following that great highway."

"Too late now," Henry told him.

"Is it?" queried the other. "We could retrace our steps."

"Great guns!" Henry exclaimed. "Never! To these people, we are gods or demigods: do you want to destroy all that?"

"I guess you're right," St. Cloud admitted. "But I don't like it."

The Venusians stared in. Requesting with signs (and a magnificent smile) that we follow, Ta Antom touched spurs to his horse.

But we didn't move.

There were twenty armed men waiting to fall in behind us, and we made it plain to The Wolf that we wished these gentlemen to go before.

A slight smile, barely perceptible—which somehow I did not like—touched his mouth. What did Ta Antom have in mind? In that mind, were we even demigods? Henry's argument, I feared, was a weak one, after all. But what could we do? Exercising all caution possible, we must face it out.

Ta Antom waved his hand and spoke a word or two, whereupon the Venusians in question started. The prince swung in behind them, and we followed—Henry and I, each bearing a lamp, bringing up the rear.

When we had gone about an eighth of a mile, we came to two entrances, one on either side, about seven feet high and three in width, sculptured and richly lettered with characters that reminded me of the cuneiform characters of the ancient Mesopotamians and Persians.

"Tombs," said St. Cloud.

About sixty feet further on, we came to two more entrances; another sixty feet, and two more; and so on right along.

They all were about the same size, though some were much more striking than others, what with the nature or the abundance of the sculpturing.

Before one of them, Henry Quainfan suddenly drew rein.

"I'm going in," he said.

He reached his reins to me, dismounted and went in. Beyond the entrance, was a passage twenty feet or so in length, which conducted him into a large chamber. There he disappeared, but we could see the glow of his lamp as he moved about.

A few minutes, and he returned.

"Tomb," he said, taking the reins. "There are dozens of persons in there, men, women and children, all standing up in stone coffins in niches in the walls and as perfect as the day they died. The preservation is wonderful—uncanny. Better go in and look."

But I shook my head.

"These sepulchral surroundings give me the creeps," I told him. "I would like to see—but I won't."

"Ditto," said St. Cloud.

So we proceeded.

"Ancient dead?" I asked.

"I don't know, but I think they are. And I wonder what destroyed that great people, how many years have rolled across this planet since these great cities were made desolate, since this tunnel and these tomb caverns were hewn out of the living rock, how long those dead men and women have been staring and staring in the darkness—for their eyes are open."

I made an exclamation.

"Just so," he said: "there's a glass in each coffin. Some are dust-covered, some wiped clean."

He was silent for a little space.

"And I wonder why this life and death are, Rider. Surely there is some great purpose behind it all, else human beings would not have been placed on both Terra and Venus. But to me all is darkness. I don't know what to think any more."

"And immortality?" I asked.

He shook his head.

"It has been much in my thoughts, but I can't believe that the human soul is immortal. Of course, we are part of something that is immortal, but that does not make us immortal any more than does the fact that the rattlesnake is part of that same something make the rattlesnake immortal.

"What I mean is simply this: matter cannot be destroyed; it can be changed, but never destroyed."

"Only assumption!" I said.

"So a man," he went on, as though there had been no interruption, "when he kisses his sweetheart's lips, perhaps is thrilled by matter that was in some slimy and unknown Paleozoic creature, in a hideous dinosaur, an ichthyosaur, a gibbering Pithecanthropus, a bloody cannibal, a hideous snake that lurked in the jungle, or in a slimy thing that lived in the slimy deeps of the sea."

"What a strange, horrible way," I exclaimed, "you have of looking at things!"

"I don't blink," he said. "But—how can a thing that comes from the earth and the radiant energy of the sun be a thing immortal? And why on earth should any creature be immortal? Why should that purple-robed butcher who would have killed Mynine—how was he so much above this horse I am riding that he should have life everlasting, while this horse goes into the unending darkness of nothing?"

"Tell me," said I, "why the horse goes into the blackness eternal, and I will give answer."

"And yet," he went on, "this question comes: if this life is the *only one,* why were human beings placed on this planet that earth-men call Venus? That we find them on the two orbs proves that the Almighty placed them there, and it logically follows that He had some end in view (to use such inadequate phraseology because we have none better) when He created them Tellurians and Venusians. But what that end is—who can tell us that?

"And now, on the other hand, Rider, this question: why, if this life is *not* the only one, were human beings placed on the two planets—instead of that world into which they will enter when they die? You see, one gets nowhere. The fact that human beings were placed on both Terra and Venus does not go to prove that human beings are immortal, any more than does the fact that horses were placed on the two sister planets go to prove that horses are immortal."

"But you are no longer an aetiologist," I observed.

"No, I am not," he returned; "but I am a poor teleologist."

He looked at me and smiled curiously.

"I have seen that there is a purpose after all," he added, "or I think I have seen; but all is darkness."

He waved a hand despairingly.

"Oh, how infinitesimal is that which we poor humans can see and understand!" I said. "'Lo, these are parts of His ways; but how little a portion is heard of Him? but the thunder of His power who can understand?' When we seek, unaided by the teachings of the Almighty, to see the why and the wisdom of things, we are soon in darkness. 'He stretcheth out the north over the empty place, and hangeth the earth upon nothing.' We don't know why, or why He fills the worlds with life, human and beastly; but I can only believe that it is for some glorious purpose—perhaps to be revealed to us in the end."

"It may be so," he mused; "but wish I could catch at least adumbrations of that purpose."

Here silence fell.

A few minutes later, the Venusians came to a stop.

"Look at that!" said Henry as we drew rein. "It's different."

We were near an entrance that, unlike any of the others, had a door, a ponderous door of granite. This door was about eight feet in height, in width four or over. Near the top, were two openings, perhaps six by eighteen inches. In thickness, it was all of a foot.

Ta Antom dismounted and signed for one of the lamp-bearers to do likewise. Then he put a hand to the door and pressed lightly; that great stone swung in almost as easily as a house-door on its hinges.

"What a piece of work!" Henry exclaimed. "Did you ever see anything like it? I thought that such things were to be found only in romance."

"Wonder if he expects us to go in there."

Thus I voiced my apprehension.

"Looks like it," said Henry.

"Something interesting in here," The Wolf told us—with signs, of course.

He seemed to take it for granted that we would enter.

"Wonder what's the idea," said Henry.

"Trap," Morgan said.

"I hardly think so," Henry returned. "He would not have had to bring us here for that. All the same we'll keep an eye on the fellow."

He dismounted; I followed suit. St. Cloud sat hesitant. Mynine looked scared.

"I tell you," said Morgan, "I don't like this business. There may be treachery lurking about in this darkness. Heaven knows, these tombs are a good place for it."

"Well, if it is here treachery will come—whether we go in or whether we don't," Henry said. "Keep rifle or revolver ready for instant action."

St. Cloud muttered something, swung to the ground and helped his fair companion to dismount, who promptly placed herself at Henry's side.

"Bet they entomb us," said Morgan.

"If we keep an eye on this gentleman," Henry returned, "they can't do that without entombing him too."

"Why did he pass all the others," demanded St. Cloud, "and choose this one—which has a door—if he isn't up to something?"

"It does look suspicious," I put in.

"As I said," Henry told us, "if they harbor treachery, it will come—no matter what we do."

"But that," returned St. Cloud, "is no reason why we should walk right into a trap."

"We must be careful," Henry said. "Don't let him get out of your sight for a single instant."

"I won't," muttered St. Cloud. "Since it must be, in we go."

The Wolf was standing in the doorway waiting, the lamp-bearer in the passage beyond. We started in. What fools we were! Mynine clung to Henry's left arm. Morgan brushed past them and followed at the heels of The Wolf. I was in the rear.

Having proceeded through the passage, ten feet or so in length, we found ourselves in a great chamber—about forty feet in width and ten to the ceiling.

The silence hung heavy. Objects at the far end were visible, but so faint that we could not make an estimate of the length of the tomb. At the near end, and on either side, ran a stone bench, hewn out of living rock, about two feet high and three in width; and in the walls, leaning back in niches cut in the solid rock, were men, women and children, standing there in their stone coffins with hands folded on their breasts. These bodies were like those in that chamber which Henry had entered—apparently as perfect as the day life quitted them.

I shivered. A little cry burst from Mynine's lips, and she clung more tightly to Henry, who, holding his lamp with his left hand and his Winchester with his right, looked calmly about.

To me it was unutterably awful to look upon these earthly shells of spirits that had lived their earthly life in some remote age of the planet, and which stared at us as if yet tenanted by their departed souls, as if asking by whose leave we had entered this solemn place.

Why had Ta Antom wished us to enter this tomb chamber? I looked about carefully, scrutinizing every spot, but could see nothing that gave hint of lurking danger. It seemed that we were perfectly safe, but the fact that our Venusian had passed all those doorless chambers and chosen this one never left my mind.

We proceeded the length of the room, estimated as one hundred and forty feet; and there, at the end, it happened.

We must have become careless. I happened to look—I know not why—at that saturnine companion of The Wolf, and, the instant my eyes fell upon him, he extinguished his lamp with amazing, lightning-like swiftness. The movement of that stolid-looking being was so swift that the eye could scarcely follow it. I jerked my revolver out of the holster, on which weapon my right hand had been resting; but, ere it was out, almost in that same instant the light was extinguished by the lamp-bearer. The Wolf struck the lamp from Henry's hand in such a way that it, too, was extinguished, and the great chamber of the dead was plunged into blackness, pierced by a sharp scream, filled with unutterable terror, from the lips of Mynine.

That scream of hers was cut short by the report of my revolver, and we heard the lamp-bearer, who had started toward the entrance go down and groan feebly.

The Wolf was making, seemingly with great swiftness, toward the doorway, marked by a dim shaft of light. Again I fired into the darkness, hoping to hit the man by sheer luck, but The Wolf sped on. Then it was, while the thunder of my revolver filled the great room, that Henry's voice cut through the darkness:

"Don't shoot, Rider!"

And I heard him start in pursuit of The Wolf.

I started after him and fell over the wounded Venusian, the Winchester striking the floor with a crash. I came to my knees hurriedly and groped about for the weapon. As I found it, which I did in a second or two, flame leaped from Henry's rifle, and a great roar filled the tomb.

The next instant, that shaft of light vanished, the dull sound made by the closing of the door came to our ears, and then could be seen only those twin strips of light that marked the apertures in that entombing stone.

I stumbled on toward the dim light, in my ears the sounds made by the triumphant Venusians as they made the door fast without.

When I reached the mouth of the passage, they were moving away.

"Henry!" I called softly, my voice sounding strange in that awful place, like a weak and fear-burdened voice heard far away. "Oh, Henry!"

Came a mordant laugh from the tunnel—I think from the lips of The Wolf.

"Here!" came Henry's answer. "And all right. They've fixed us now, Rider."

I went on toward him, my heart pounding fiercely, the blood drumming in my ears.

"Yes—laugh, you hell-hounds!" said Henry to the departing Venusians. "Mock away—you spawn of Seth!"

Came a burst of laughter and cries in answer.

"All the same, Rider," he said, "the laugh is on us."

I was beside him now, and, leaning against the rock wall, I stood staring at that dying light struggling in through the apertures in the door and listening to the sounds of the horses' hoofs and the occasional voices and mocking laughter of the men.

The light became weaker and weaker, soon went out altogether: we were in utter blackness, in which it seemed must hover the spirits of those lifeless ones behind us in the great tomb cavern; and ere long the last sound from the triumphant Venusians had died away in the distance.

CHAPTER 30
THE GHOST

St. Cloud and Mynine had remained at the end of the room. No doubt it was owing to the Venusian's extreme weakness that one or both of them were not stabbed. The man was biding his time.

The effect this sudden and frightful treachery of The Wolf had upon me was at first something akin to stupefaction, then horror unutterable. In mercy, though, the former lasted for some time after we had returned to Mynine and St. Cloud.

I often have marveled that this was so, have often wondered why it was that indescribable horror soon to fall upon me did not come as I stood there by the door. I knew that we were entombed, but surely we should eventually discover some way of escape. My crushed, numb brain somehow would not admit that there might be none.

"Hey!" came St. Cloud's voice. "Henry—Rider!"

"Coming!" Henry returned. "Try to find one of those lamps."

So we went back to where St. Cloud and the fair Mynine were, and that wounded Venusian, feeling our way along the stone bench in the utter blackness.

As we drew near, we heard Morgan groping about.

"Haven't got a single match," he told us.

"Wonder if that Venusian is dead," said Henry.

"No," came St. Cloud's voice from the darkness.

There was an exclamation.

"Got it," he said.

"Hope none of the oil has run out," said Henry, opening his match-box. "Wish that flash-light hadn't got broken."

He struck a light. Mynine screamed, there was a flash of steel, and a sharp cry of pain rang through the tomb.

The Venusian had launched forward on one hand and with the other driven (and wrenched) a knife deep into Morgan's thigh.

The sudden movement of surprise that Henry gave extinguished the match, and the sepulchral blackness rushed back into the circle whence it had just been driven by the ghostly light, blotting out the faces and forms of my companions and the Venusian on the floor, and the blanched face and the white-robed form of Mynine.

"Cover him, Rider," said Henry, "the moment I strike. If he tries it again, shoot him."

I raised my Winchester in readiness. Henry struck the light. But there was no need to cover Draconda's warrior. He had sunk down as if utterly exhausted; apparently he had taxed his waning strength to the utmost to make the thrust.

I sprang to the side of St. Cloud, who I feared was about to fall. With drawn face and trembling hands, he drew the weapon. A fountain of blood came gushing forth. A savage oath burst from his throat. With all his might, he hurled the knife at the Venusian, but the weapon went wild, clattering its way into darkness along the floor.

Henry caught up the lamp and lighted it. Fortunately, not a drop of oil had escaped. Mynine and I helped St. Cloud to the bench, upon which he sank with a groan. I glanced at the Venusian, who was about fifteen feet from the spot, and saw a ghastly smile on his dark visage. He was near to death, and he must have known it, and yet there he was smiling away in triumph.

After satisfying himself that there was nothing to fear from the man, Henry reached the lamp to Mynine, and he and I began to bandage Morgan's wound, which was bleeding profusely, with the long strip of cloth that the lovely Venusian beside us had torn from her stola-like dress.

When we had done all that we could, the wound was still bleeding, though but slightly. Morgan had lost a deal of blood, and, as he had been somewhat ill for a day or two, I feared that he soon would be in a pretty bad way.

Somehow the fact that we were entombed hovered, as it were, in the background of my mind: the full horror of our situation had not come down upon me.

We had just finished the bandaging, however, when a sharp exclamation burst from St. Cloud—a sound strange and terrible to hear.

"What's the matter?" Henry asked.

Mynine was looking at Morgan with a curious expression in her wondrous eyes.

"Matter?" he ejaculated. "Matter's no name for it! What's the use of this bandaging, anyway? Tell me that! What's the good of anything now?"

He waved his hand in a gesture of awful despair.

"Entombed!" he burst out. "In Heaven's name, don't you know what this means? Buried alive!"

And then it was that the full horror of our situation came crashing down upon me. My heart gave a frightful leap, stood still, then went thumping madly. Things swam before my eyes, and there were streaks of vivid green and scarlet.

Mynine set the lamp down on the bench, and it was as though I saw her through a mist.

Suddenly Morgan's voice shattered the stillness, his words tense and harsh with an overmastering rage.

"You will grin, will you?" he yelled at the Venusian, whose ghastly grin of triumph waxed thereat. "The grin is on us, all right; but your bones will whiten here with ours! No, they'll come and fish you out—you'll be a hero!"

Morgan's right hand had gone to his revolver. The dying man flung forth a few words, which, from the expression that shot across Mynine's face, I knew were anything but a blessing.

St. Cloud jerked his revolver out. As he was raising it, however, Henry stepped in front of him and laid a hand on the weapon.

"That would be murder, Morgan," he said, his fingers closing on the cold steel.

"He helped to murder us!" cried St. Cloud, trying to free the revolver. "And—look at him grin!"

Henry took the weapon from him, gently though in a manner that showed plainly resistance would have been futile.

"The man is dying," he told St. Cloud. "What hurt can his grin do? He is going, and it is only a question of time before we follow. He has served his masters well and can grin at his work—or is it Draconda he has served?"

He spoke without bitterness, his voice quite natural. Mynine kept her lovely eyes on his face, and I saw tears gathering in their blue loveliness.

St. Cloud opened his mouth to speak, changed his mind and sat staring at the Venusian with an expression somewhat vacant.

"I'm going to see if I can find a way of escape," Henry said. "However, I'm not going to voice a hope that I don't entertain; in other words, I don't think there is any chance of our getting out of this place. Ta Antom, I believe, overlooked nothing when he made his plans. Real people in a real position like this, don't find hidden exits and things—as they do in novels and romances."

St. Cloud nor I made any response. We were watching the dying man, whose breathing now was quick and labored. Henry stepped toward him on some errand of mercy, but stopped when a ghastly, horrible grin appeared on the dark lineaments of the Venusian. That grin vanished, the man's head slowly rolled from side to side, there was a convulsive shudder, a long sigh escaped his drawn lips, and his spirit had quitted the flesh.

And mine the hand that had killed him.

"Well," said Henry Quainfan at length, "I'm going to see if I can find a way out of this hole."

He stepped over, picked up the dead man's lamp, from which half the oil had escaped, and, coming back, touched its wick to the flame of the other vessel.

"Only eight matches left," he told us.

St. Cloud nor I had a one!

"The prospect," said I, "is certainly not a bright one."

"No," smiled Henry; "but it might have been worse."

"Bunk!" St. Cloud exclaimed.

And I confess I thought he was about right.

With some facetious remark, Henry turned and walked away to begin his search for a way of escape from this terrible chamber.

He went into the passage and to the door. In a little while, Mynine arose, and, casting a shy glance at us, followed him. As she moved away into the darkness, her white dress gave her the seeming of a ghost.

St. Cloud raised himself up on an elbow and watched her for a space, then suddenly sank back and closed his eyes.

I got out my Bible. As I began to turn the pages of the sacred volume, Morgan opened his eyes.

"Yes—read something, Rider," he said. "I want to hear something from God's Book. I feel that I am very near to Him now, and my life in some ways— I'm afraid, Rider; I'm afraid!"

"Hush," said I. "Hush."

"Read. Read the first thing you come to."

What my eyes lighted upon was the fifty-fifth verse of the fifteenth chapter of Paul's First Epistle to the Corinthians.

"*'O death, where is thy sting?'*" I read. "*'O grave, where is thy victory?'*"

As I started the next verse, St. Cloud interrupted:

"The sting is there, Rider—I can only hope that it has no victory. But go on."

He closed his eyes wearily; I went on reading. He did not interrupt me any more. Now and again the sound of blows struck by Henry rolled round the tomb. And, as I read from the pages of the wonderful volume—and, indeed, was it owing solely to Chance that it was there in my hands?—but, as I read, strength came to me, strength to meet this horrible death that even now was watching.

At last I became aware that St. Cloud was breathing heavily; glancing at the pale face, I found him asleep.

Then I read to myself, and I prayed.

After a time, Henry and Mynine returned—and they came hand in hand. At first I was surprised, for I knew that Henry did not love the girl. Much had I marveled that she had not seen this. But, then, Love is blind—though that does not prevent the seeing of mirages most wondrous and strange.

I gave Henry an inquiring look, and he returned a look that was guilty and defiant.

And then of a sudden I saw why he had done this thing:

Death was certain; he would fill the girl's last hours with that happiness which he knew would be concomitant to the belief that she was loved.

And, judging from that rapt, yes, angelic look on her face, Mynine was happy now—even though she and the man she loved were entombed.

"No way of escape?" I asked, knowing full well that he had discovered none.

He shook his head; there was a short silence.

"No—at least, I didn't find any. I suppose we should examine every inch of the place, though."

"What would be the use?" I asked. "This is the end."

"I believe it is," he said soberly. "Phantasms of hope would avail us nothing here. Still, a fellow might as well be looking about the place as twiddling his thumbs."

"That treacherous Ta Antom!" I exclaimed. "Be sure, he knew what he was about!"

"He did. That's a wonderful door, Rider."

"I should say it is!"

He smiled a little.

"Oh, Morgan's asleep," he observed.

He and the girl moved past me and stood looking down on St. Cloud.

"Poor fellow!" Henry murmured and turned away.

"Come, Rider," he added, "let's make a thorough examination of this prison of ours."

Taking up the lamp, I arose, and we began our scrutiny of this dungeon of Erebus. But our examination, as systematic as it was minute, showed us nothing but the black hopelessness of our plight.

So we came back in silence and despair.

Morgan was still sleeping.

"I'll put out this light," Henry said, "for we mustn't waste any of the oil. And the wick in this other lamp can be lowered. Economy's the word now. When the oil is gone—darkness then, blackness unending."

So he extinguished his lamp, then took seat on the bench, where he instantly was joined by Mynine, and proceeded to lower the wick in the other vessel.

Of a verity, the stoutest heart that ever beat in human breast might well be appalled by this doom that impended.

The deep silence of the place closed in upon us. No words of mine could convey an adequate idea of that awful stillness—in which the ticking of our watches was like the clanging of gongs.

That scene often rises before my eyes: the coffins behind us; Morgan stretched out on the stone bench, lost in his troubled slumber; Henry and Mynine, his arm about the girl's shoulders, over which her golden hair fell in masses, her cheek pressed against his; and myself, brooding there with my face buried in my hands—the feeble illumination giving it all a weirdness that reminds me most forcibly of a terrible picture by Doré.

Minutes passed—hours.

Suddenly a scream filled the place—a sound so horrible that it brought me to my feet with a cry on my lips.

"Blanche! Blanche!"

St. Cloud was sitting up—staring down the room in the extremity of terror.

"Look!" he cried, pointing.

We looked, but nothing was there in the darkness.

"She's coming—her *ghost!*" he screamed.

We could do nothing. And slowly the ghost of Blanche came toward him out of the darkness. He thrust out his hands and screamed for us to keep her away.

"Don't laugh like that!" he implored, in a voice that sent shivers through me. "Why do you come to me thus as I die? I said things that weren't true! But—oh—oh!"

His eyes went shut, and he sank back in Henry's arms, merciful unconsciousness blotting out that ghost which had walked out of the sepulchral blackness and laughed at him.

CHAPTER 31
THE CRY IN THE DARKNESS

At length Henry Quainfan resumed his seat.

"I don't know what it's about," he said, "but, if this Blanche knew—"

His look completed the thought.

"Maybe she does know."

His expression was incredulous. "Do you believe *that?*"

"Oh, I don't say I believe it. Still—"

"Still—?" he queried.

"Who can say?"

"She would have to be dead, a ghost in truth. And how on earth could she get here?"

"If it was as easy to answer as it is to ask," I returned, "ultimate knowledge would have been man's long ago. A question as germane is: how did she, and every other human being, get to the earth, and whence? Tell me that, and I'll try to give you the answer to the other. *We* came here—and in the flesh."

"No," he smiled: "in the *Hornet*."

"And, when man, in his prison of the flesh, can do that, who can even imagine what powers are his when in the spirit?"

"It may strike you as paradoxical, Rider, and I say it in all humility of spirit, but only scientists can *imagine* that."

"Heaven save us from your scientists when it comes to things spiritual! With all their protoplasms and polysyllabic isms, what do they know about life save that it is something that lives? Whence came it? Spontaneous combustion—I mean, generation! Brought to the primordial earth in the icy heart of a fiery meteorite, suggests Lord Kelvin. Its seeds were, and are, driven through the abysms of space by the agency of radiation-pressure, Arrhenius tells us.

"I admit that the imagination is there, all right! And just remember the other wild fancies that scientists have given us.

"For instance:

"The surface of the sun is cold, that vast globe inhabited, according to the elder Herschel—while, according to Herschel the younger, fiery fishes go sporting about in the flaming solar ocean."[8]

"Your scientists should know what is in their own house before telling us what we shall, or shall not, find in the many mansions of the spirit."

"Spiritedly put," said Henry Quainfan. "But it amounts to simply this: 'Most that he knows I see, and all that he sees I know.'"

"After all," I said, "why talk about it—now?"

"I should think this the time of all times. Remember Socrates and the hemlock: shall a pagan show more fortitude than a follower of the Christ?"

Whether this was said with a fortifying purpose, or was only words of the moment, I do not know; but I doubt if he could have uttered anything that could more forcibly have produced that very effect.

---

8. In a letter to Nasmyth, Sir Jon Herschel wrote with respect to the famous "willow-leaves" of the sun:

"What can they be? Are they huge phosphorized fishes?"—R. F.

We should see!

All the same my heart shuddered and sank.

There was silence for a little while.

"You know," I said, "things come crowding into my mind—visions, memories, words spoken or written, some long forgotten. Among the words penned, induced no doubt by what has just been said, this haunting sentence of Poe's:

"'No thinking being lives who, at some luminous point of his life of thought, has not felt himself lost amid the surges of futile efforts at understanding or believing, that any thing exists *greater than his own soul.*'"

"So you waded through *Eureka*? What did you get out of it?"

"Not much: that and a few others. This, for instance:

"'We walk about, amid the destinies of our world-existence, encompassed by dim and ever present *Memories* of a Destiny more vast.'"

"Memories," echoed Henry Quainfan. "Long ago, when I told you of my dream woman, I spoke of memories."

"I remember. But you did not regard them as such."

"No, they just seemed so—whispering there was something in my brain that could never die, imprisoned there for a little span of years; something that remembered back to the gardens of Paradise and looked forward to a world as glorious as that of the dimly-remembered past."

I stared at him.

"That from a cold-blooded scientist!"

He smiled.

"Not cold-blooded. Only the intellect was cold—a cliff against which the waves of fancy beat in vain. The heart—how could I tell you that, Rider? of its sweet, foolish longings, the poignant ecstasy of dreams not of earth?"

"You have told me. And after all it is the heart, not the brain, that is the spirit's habitation."

"I understand, then," he said, "why so many people are heartless."

I said nothing to that.

"To show," he went on, "what utter moonshine these so-called soul memories are, since I have heard the name of Draconda—"

"Well?" I queried, wondering at his pause and the way he was looking at me.

"I have at times heard the name come echoing back from those memories of mine."

"Good heavens!" I exclaimed.

"Now who doubts?" he smiled.

"Well," said I, "if we get out of this, you will probably——"

"Wouldn't I be up against it?"

"I thought of that. But you needn't lose any sleep on that account."

"No. Ta Antom, of course, merely carried out Draconda's wishes, and this is the end—in the silence and blackness of a tomb."

"Not so," said I, "but the beginning of an adventure more wonderful than the one whose end draws near."

He made no response.

Again that awful stillness closed in upon the place.

And somehow the terrible hours crawled past.

"Rider," said Henry at length, "I'm going to sleep."

"Sweet dreams," I returned. "For my part, though, sleep is simply out of the question."

He looked at his chronometer.

"Midnight," he said.

He smiled, though a little wanly.

"Bedtime, Rider."

He lay down and in a few minutes was sound asleep. How I envied him! Mynine sat watching the sleeper, a white hand resting on his hair, on her face the most beautiful look of abandonment and love that I had ever seen in all my life. Never once did she look in my direction. It was a beautiful but pathetic sight—nay, the circumstances considered, a terrible one. Ere long she pillowed his head in her lap, leaning against the coffin behind her. Our eyes met; the girl blushed furiously. I sighed to myself; this wondrous creature's unrequited love was poignantly touching.

The light grew dimmer. I took the lamp which the dead Venusian had carried and poured its precious contents into the lighted one. When the flame sank again—darkness then, the utter blackness of death.

To my profound thankfulness, Morgan slept on. How I wished that slumber was mine! Then I could forget, or would I know even in my dreams? What wishes and thoughts Mynine had, I can only guess. There she sat, moveless, lovely and loving, with Henry's head in her lap.

At last, yielding to dire necessity, I extinguished the light.

A long time passed, how long I had no idea. I believe, too, that I dozed off; but, if so, it was only into the borderland of sleep. But this I do know: suddenly a cry came drifting into the place, faint and far—piercing to my heart like a sword of ice.

The movement made by the startled Mynine was strangely loud; from her lips broke a low though sharp exclamation:

"Oh!"

It must have been that sudden movement of hers which awakened Henry. I am sure the cry did not, and I do not think it was her exclamation.

He was wide awake in an instant; I could hear him raising himself up.

"Rider!" he said.

"Here I am."

"What's the matter? The girl is trembling terribly. What is it?"

"I don't know," was my stupid reply.

"Hear something?"

Before I could answer, that cry, faint and far, came drifting again through the darkness.

CHAPTER 32
DRACONDA

When The Wolf issued from the tunnel, elated by the success of his diabolical scheme, he left his company to follow at its leisure and with a single companion started with swiftness for Loom, with what he thought would be good tidings for the queen.

But, thank Heaven, Ta Antom was mistaken! The queen was greatly displeased—nay, was very angry.

It was about one hour before twelve when he reached the palace of Conderogan. There was a ball in the palace this night; on The Wolf's entering the great room, the dancing ceased directly. His coming was unexpected, and everybody naturally was surprised and eager to learn what the prince had to tell.

Going directly to her, he told Draconda what he had done. To his surprise, however, the queen, instead of commending his course of action, in anger interrupted his succinct account of the entombing of the men from the stars.

"I gave word," said Draconda, "that every honor was to be accorded these strange and mighty strangermen—and thus have you honored them, thus have you followed my wishes! How could I have honored them more than by asking you to be my envoy? Who knows what these men are? and whence they come? and what message they bring? You thought you were doing well to entomb these men, but, indeed, it was not so. The evil you have done must be undone—the men brought to me, as I said."

And thereat Queen Draconda gave word that a score of men, under a captain of her body-guard, go swiftly to the tombs, unprison us and see that we reached the palace of Conderogan safe and sound.

A ripple of surprise swept the room—and Draconda knew that her course would be rigorously condemned by the priesthood.

The little cavalcade set out immediately and reached the mouth of the tunnel at something like seven o'clock.

"By Heaven, Rider!" exclaimed Henry Quainfan.

"Yes?"

"They're coming to save us! Hear that?"

"Sounds like it!"

It seemed too good to be true; I found myself wondering if it wasn't a dream.

Ah, there were the sounds of the horses' hoofs on the rock floor. They grew distinct, loud and louder. There, a faint light—oh, so faint—came struggling in through the openings in the door. A few moments, and the Venusians were at the entrance.

Followed a short silence, broken by a peace-call, which Henry answered.

He struck a match and lighted the lamp. Mynine placed herself at his side, and we stood waiting.

The door swung open. For a moment the Venusians hesitated, then the commander boldly entered, followed by several of his men, and came on toward us, making peace-signs.

He was armed with a sword, the hilt flashing with jewels, his men with swords and long-handled spears. When within four or five yards, the captain halted, and he and his followers made obeisance. We bowed slightly in return; that is, Henry and myself—Mynine, a curious look in her eyes, standing moveless, her lovely and slender form drawn to its full and stately height.

As the captain prepared to say something in sign-language, a great voice thundered round the rocky walls. There was Morgan sitting up, his eyes fixed on the captain. Thus came the voice, making the Shakespearian quotation an interrogatory one:

> "'Be thou a spirit of health, or goblin damned,
> Bring with thee airs from heaven, or blasts from hell,
> Be thy intents wicked, or charitable?'

"Give answer, and quickly too, or I'll hurl you across the dreary steppes of

Tartary and bang your cocoa against the cedars of Lebanon!"

I went to St. Cloud at the beginning of this outburst, but I could not make him be still. One wild hallucination came swift at the heels of another. Imprecation after imprecation was hurled at the Venusians, come to save us from one of the most horrible deaths that a human being can die.

However, the captain, by making signs and speaking the queen's name, with difficulty, what with St. Cloud's gibberish, acquainted us with the purpose of his coming.

"May Heaven bless Draconda!" said Henry Quainfan.

Of course, St. Cloud could not ride. The Venusians made a stretcher for him, using two spears and as many saddle-blankets for that purpose, and all the while they worked at it, his gibberish and imprecations rained upon them.

When it was done, he vigorously protested against being placed on the stretcher, maintaining that the Venusians were goblins damned, emissaries of Mephistopheles, and goodness only knows what else, and that they intended throwing him into the Phlegethon, which, he declared, was not far distant.

At last, however, we prevailed upon him to lie still, and then we emerged from that dreadful place.

Fifteen minutes or so later, we were in the sunshine, having passed through the mountain.

For a space, with indescribable feelings, I sat looking back into the dark mouth of that tunnel. Then Mynine and I dismounted (Henry had walked beside St. Cloud), and we all, except poor Morgan, who would not touch a bite, ate breakfast—brought from a small town several miles distant by two of the captain's men, who, as he rode through on his way to the tombs, had been left there for that purpose. A thoughtful captain was he, and his name, by the way, was Sotom.

We were in a canyon about a mile wide at this point and probably a thousand feet deep. On every hand were beautiful forests, like that of the earth's tropics. Songs of birds and the drone of insects filled the air—a sharp contrast to that awful silence of the tomb. Everywhere were lovely flowers; strange insects, swift and iridescent, came and went; and great gorgeous butterflies, the like of which no man on earth ever saw, flitted hither and yon in the bright morning sunlight and the somber deeps of the forest.

Near the mouth of the tunnel were ten or twelve ruined buildings. They were very large, their walls and columns rising in massive and somber majesty, and Henry and I thought they had been used for some funeral purpose, in that far-gone time when those Venusians there in the mountain blackness lived and died. How many men and how many years had it taken to hew those great tomb chambers out of the living mountain rock? And what had destroyed that mighty ancient race, which had left monuments before which those of the ancient Tellurians sink almost into insignificance?

Ruins, ruins—everywhere were ruins. Scattered about this land were the skeletons of mighty cities, cities in which thousands upon thousands of men and women had lived and loved, taken and given in marriage, cities which had, certainly, rung with cheers for soldiers returning in triumph, with spoils and captives—and, perhaps, filled with cries of slaughtering invaders and all the manifold horrors of war.

In some of the ruins, dwelt barbarians (were they and these others descendants of that mighty people of old?) and, in others, the lion and the pard wandered unmolested of men. In that antiquity, what strange scenes had occurred at this place where we three Terrestrials now were? How many funeral processions had gone into that tunnel, how many the weeping men, women and children?

Well, they all were gone now, and long had they been gone; and, under that sky of theirs, the cosmic drama and mystery went on—and what was it all about?

As soon as breakfast—an excellent one—was finished, we went on, Henry walking beside St. Cloud, who thought himself the Inca Atahuallpa, borne along in a gorgeous sedan on the shoulders of Peruvian nobles to the city of Caxamalca to see Pizarro; and, in about an hour and a half, we entered that town I mentioned—not Caxamalca, by the way.

There a physician (he was a priest also) came, and he and Henry dressed Morgan's wound. The doctor would have given St. Cloud some medicine, but Henry, to the medico's chagrin, would not permit that, for he feared treachery.

I expressed the opinion that the man would not dare give St. Cloud anything nocuous, since Draconda had saved us from death; but Henry said he wouldn't take any chances.

"If he wanted to administer poison," I remarked, "he could put it into our food or drink."

"True," Henry returned; "but this is more tempting."

Presently Æsculapius quitted the room.

"Sleepy, Rider?" Henry queried.

"Rather."

"Then pound your ear. I'm going to follow suit."

"How about a guard?"

"There's Draconda's guard at the doors. I think we can risk it."

So I lay down, and (I almost said to my surprise) soon had sunk to sleep—if that dream-horror in which I found myself can be called sleep.

One dream was very strange—will haunt me to my dying hour.

Suddenly a white-robed veiled woman appeared before me in that sylvan gloom in which I was wandering. I was all alone. Where the woman came from, I could not tell. She seemed to take form in the air, but I was not sure: she appeared so suddenly. Throwing her veiled head forward, she raised a long cloth-swathed finger and said in measured and cavernous tones:

"I have come to warn you, O man! And take good heed, for I shall not repeat my words. And ask not who I am, but heed my warning and fly. You would not know if I told you. Turn back, O man, and never set foot in Loom—never let your eyes fall on Draconda. Flee—flee—flee, I say; for, if you meet this queen, then from that hour shall you be a man accursed!"

Then she vanished, as suddenly as she had come, and I awoke shuddering, to see that it was night and Henry in the light of the single burning lamp bending over St. Cloud, who was saying something that I could not catch, and to hear the soft tread of the sentry without, keeping watch over Mynine's door and ours.

For some time, I could not go to sleep, these words echoing and reechoing through the gloomy corridors of my brain:

"Flee—flee—flee, I say; for, if you meet this queen, then from that hour shall you be a man accursed."

When I came out of that dream-horror again, the dawn was blushing. St. Cloud was awake and happily in his right mind. He was in a poor way indeed, but Henry and I decided to proceed to Loom. The captain had secured a fine litter, and Morgan, we thought, would be comfortable during the journey to Draconda. However, had we not been so near to Loom, so near the end of our long and strange journey, and so anxious to learn what was in store for us, we would not have proceeded but would have waited till St. Cloud had somewhat recovered.

Shortly after the start, I told Henry about that dream of mine. Now, I did not believe in dreams, and I do not now; but somehow I could not keep that confounded thing out of my head.

"Funny," said Henry: "I, too, had a dream—one as strange as yours."

There was a short silence. His head was bowed in thought. Mynine was looking at him curiously, a troubled look, I thought, in her lovely eyes.

"Like mine—or pleasant?" I queried.

He did not answer for a space.

"No—not like yours, Rider: it hovers in my mind like a sweet memory that hurts."

I wished that he would go on, but he did not speak, and for a long time we rode in silence.

We traveled down the canyon for two hours or so, at the end of which time, we came to the great road again, which, descending the western wall, ran across the canyon floor and zigzagged its way up the eastern side. In a little while, we had climbed this latter, which is not very high at this place, and were riding through a level country. Everywhere were farmhouses and fields, and here and there little groups of Venusians waiting to see us pass.

At length the road begun to ascend a low and rugged range of hills—perhaps mountains would be the better word, for the outstanding heights rose to an altitude of probably three thousand feet. It was about three hours after midday when, on turning a sharp bend in a rugged defile, we came suddenly in view of the valley of Loom, and an exclamation of delight burst from my lips as the beautiful sight met my eyes.

We drew rein and gazed at the panorama spread out before us. Just below, clothing the steep sides of the range and a little of the valley, was noble forest—conserved by royal edict. Beyond were cultivated fields, diversified here and there with clumps of trees. Eight miles or so away lay a large lake, looking, as Henry said, like a piece of fallen sky. We could not see the southern extremity of this beautiful sheet of water, but, as we afterwards learned, the lake is about forty miles long. Its width averages about ten miles, and its name is Uava. To the northeast, the lake swept in a beautiful and even curve, and here was the city of Loom, and beyond it the ruins of ancient Loom.

The sky was almost cloudless, the air clear, there being no haziness at all, and so everything stood out distinct.

Floating on the placid surface of the Uava and separated from the modern Loom by a little piece of water, was an island. It was not large, and upon it was a great building, the queen's palace, the palace of Conderogan.

Beyond the lake, the country rose gently to the ramparts of rugged mountains; far in the east, faint and lovely as the cliffs of Paradise, rose the outstanding peaks of that awful cordillera.

Mynine pointed out that island resting on the untroubled breast of the Uava and said:

"Draconda. Leenam Draconda."

So that was Draconda's home, the home of the woman who had saved our lives! I stared at that island—wondering what awaited us three Terrestrials and the fair Mynine there.

"If certain Terrestrials could only see us now, Rider!" Henry Quainfan exclaimed with boyish enthusiasm, taking the glasses from his eyes. "If certain of those omnipercipient ginks could only see us now!"

"Wouldn't they stare!"

"No: they would proceed to tell us how it should have been done."

There ensued a short silence, which he broke, speaking in a changed voice:

"What awaits us down there, Rider? At last we come to the end of our journey—but is it the end? What is this Draconda like? She saved our lives—but what will she do with them in the end?"

"Any more questions?" I queried.

"A thousand; but I won't ask any more. And that dream woman of mine—somehow, I can't keep that dream out of my head."

"The dream—or the woman?"

"Both."

He smiled a little.

"Moonshine, Rider—moonshine."

He turned his eyes to the island of Conderogan, seemingly lost in a reverie; and I saw Mynine give him a troubled look under her long lashes.

I wondered if she feared that her queen would take her lover from her. I felt inexpressibly sorry for this lovely creature and wondered what the denouement of this affair would be like, knowing that partly civilized men and women cannot control themselves in erotic disaster as can their civilized brothers and sisters. Is this because, as civilization advances, love becomes more and more a matter of head than heart?

Also, I could not help thinking much of that vague something which had made Henry say, on the night we met her, that Mynine would make a terrible enemy. Now, love disaster for Mynine was, judging from the present aspect of things, which I was pretty sure would not change—love disaster for this girl was inevitable. When it came, would she become an enemy to Henry Quainfan? Would all her wondrous love, when she learned that he did not love her in return, metamorphose itself into a frightful hate? Would this happen, or would she take the blow, which I knew would be a terrible one indeed, quietly and endure her bitterness of heart as a sensible girl should?

These questions, and many others, came; but, it is needless to say, there came no answer.

Just before we started on, St. Cloud said wearily, gazing away at the island of Conderogan, on which we had told him was Draconda's home:

"I'll be glad when we are there. Then I can rest."

Poor St. Cloud! Ere long he was there on the island of Conderogan, and, in the palace of Conderogan, Death was waiting for him—waiting in a guise which, since time began, he had never worn before, in which, I believe, he will never be seen again.

We went on; about an hour afterwards, St. Cloud fell asleep.

The sun was setting when we entered the great city of Loom. The streets were crowded. We were much struck by the quietude that reigned in the vast crowds assembled to see us pass, the men from the stars, and by the great number of women who—to use Henry's phrase—had "pharmaceutical complexions."

We rode to the landing-place just opposite the island of Conderogan, where we dismounted.

Twilight had now fallen, and the island, whose sides rose straight up from the glassy surface of the water to the height of fifty feet or more, and the great palace upon it, in spite of the light that shone from the latter's windows, loomed up dark and ominous-looking in the fading light.

A barge was waiting at the landing-place, and in a few minutes we were on the island of Conderogan, which was, I thought, near a thousand feet from the place where we had embarked.

Broad steps, broken halfway up by a resting-place, conducted us to the brow of the island, where we passed two guards. We crossed a beautiful courtyard, ascended a short flight of steps and entered the palace, passing two more guards at the entrance.

We were now met by a high functionary of some sort, who gave Henry and myself each a magnificent bow and Mynine a look that was hard and curious. Then he said something to the captain, whereupon, instead of proceeding through the large passage before us, our guides turned short to the left and conducted us through several passages to a set of rooms.

These rooms looked out upon the lake and were sumptuously furnished. Arabesque curtains hung at the doorways and the windows—the latter had glass—and the carpet was the loveliest I had ever set eyes on. Here were men-servants and women-servants to wait upon us. Captain Sotom and Mr. High Functionary soon bowed themselves out—going, we thought, to Draconda.

Morgan was still sleeping, though not quietly. Now and again he groaned or talked. Knowing that sleep is the best thing in the world for a sick person, we did not move him from the litter, lest he might be awakened.

In ten or fifteen minutes, Captain Sotom returned with the information that Draconda wished to see us.

Accordingly, leaving our sleeping comrade, though not without misgivings, in the care of Draconda's servants, we—Henry, Mynine and myself—followed Sotom, we two Terrestrials carrying our Winchesters.

As we were leaving, St. Cloud cried out in tones of horror:

"Blanche! Blanche! Good God—you here!"

Mynine clung to Henry's left arm and evidently was very much frightened, and I confess that my heart was hitting on every cylinder.

What was this woman in whose presence we soon were to stand?

At length we were approaching an arched doorway, the curtains of which were slowly drawn aside by unseen hands. Just within the entrance, were two guards, who, as we drew near, raised their halberds (and vicious-looking weapons they were) in salute. Passing through, we found ourselves in a great hall, pretty well filled with people and flooded with soft light, sparkling from thousands of jewels.

Our ingress was from the left and near one end. At the other end of the great vaulted place, about one hundred and twenty-five feet away, was a dais, covered with red carpet; upon this dais, was a throne—and there sat Draconda!

Up toward the throne, we proceeded. All eyes in the room were upon us, except the queen's. I felt inexpressibly uncomfortable; Henry, however, appeared to be untroubled by the gaze of the many Venusians.

Near Draconda was our old friend Ta Antom. The queen was talking with an old man and examining what I took to be a sheet of paper; but the old Venusian evidently was more interested in us than in the talk of his queen—whose indifference, I thought, surely was assumed.

On we went, Draconda continuing her examination of the sheet.

And of a sudden, when we were very near, something shot through me that was like a pang. I was suddenly aware of a beauty that was so beautiful that it hurt.

Her head was turned a little to one side, and the thought of looking into her eyes sent the blood wildly coursing through my veins.

We stopped, Mynine falling on her knees before her dread queen, though I am sure that Henry would not have permitted this if he had not become oblivious to the very existence of Mynine.

Slowly Draconda raised her eyes, raised them until they looked straight into mine.

Then it was that I got the full force of her matchless beauty. Her beauty surged against me, wave upon wave, beauty such as I had never dreamed could be possessed by one of the earth, earthy. And yet, had I then and there been snatched out of her presence and asked to describe it, I could not have even told whether she was a blonde or a brunette.

For an instant only did her eyes look into mine. Over my whole person they leaped, resting for a moment on the rifle, and I saw a look of unutterable amazement rush into those glorious orbs, which of a sudden went to Henry Quainfan.

They widened, one hand clutched at the arm of her chair, the other closed on the sheet, sending a thousand wrinkles through it, and I saw her breast rise with a quick intake of breath and a pallor dash the blood from her face.

She sank back in the chair and stared at him.

Utter silence reigned.

She looked from one to the other of us, unutterable astoundment on every lovely lineament.

Inexpressibly amazed I was at her awful beauty—awful is the only adjective that really describes it—but soon this was not the only thing there was to be amazed at.

For slowly she came to her feet, slowly she rose to her full and imperial height, and, with one hand on the arm of the chair and the other, the left, pressed against her cheek, she said in a voice that was as soft and sweet as the soft music of falling waters:

"You—you are Tellurians? You are Americans?"

CHAPTER 33
THE MYSTERY

I looked at Henry Quainfan—to see a slight pallor on his sunburned face. The silence hung heavy. I waited for him to break it. His lips moved as though he were going to speak, but no sound issued from them.

It was Draconda's English, I thought, that had struck him speechless, had brought that pallor to his cheeks; but, as I was soon to learn, this was not so.

I turned my look back to the queen and waited a moment, thinking she might speak again, but she, too, remained silent.

Then I spoke, my voice shaking little, and this is what I said:

"How on earth, O Queen, did you come to this place?"

A beautiful light leaped into her eyes; she clapped her hands like a little girl.

"I was right, I was right!" she cried. "And yet it may not be: you are Americans, aren't you?"

"Americans," I told her. "But, in Heaven's name, how did you come from the earth to this world called Venus? We never dreamed that any one had made that journey before us."

She looked at me curiously, her brows contracting slightly; when she spoke, it was not to give answer to my question.

"Of course, I knew that you were Tellurians, but I was not sure that Americans stood before me."

That voice so sweet and silvery—of such have poets dreamed.

"But, O Draconda," I asked again, "how did you come to this planet?"

She gave me a puzzling smile.

"Why do you think I did?"

"Great Heaven!" I exclaimed.

She laughed a little.

"You think I am fooling—but how did you cross that awful abyss between Terra and the Planet of Love? Never had I dreamed such a thing possible."

I stared.

Here was a thing to puzzle and amaze: never had she dreamed it possible to make that terrible intermundane journey, and yet here *she* was! Why had she not given me answer? Why did our wondrous and mysterious Draconda utter such foolishness?

"Yes," she said, "how came you from Terra to this world that earth-men call Venus?"

"As you came, I fancy, O Draconda: in a—in a thing."

"A thing? I never saw a *thing* that could journey through the interplanetary deeps!"

"Well, O Queen, such it was that brought us here. Only Heaven knows what made it come, Heaven and my comrade," indicating Henry: "he made it."

"So," said Draconda, looking at Henry Quainfan I thought a little shyly. "And some disaster occurred, else you would not have come journeying down the river on a raft. Was it not so?"

Henry made no response—just stood there like a dummy. It was patent, too, that Draconda was agitated not a little.

"Yes, O Queen," I made answer. "After bringing us through all those millions of miles of void, the thing—it was called the *Hornet*—was destroyed by a celestial wanderer, a huge meteorite. Not a vestige of the *Hornet* remained. Then we made the raft and came down the river; and I suppose all that has occurred since our arrival in your land is known to you."

Draconda nodded.

"Couriers came daily, keeping me informed of everything. And well did you three fight at that temple. It is a wonder that you were not killed, for you had committed one of the most horrible crimes it is possible to commit here. Yes, it is indeed a marvel that you are here before me, and I shall say, though perhaps I should not, that there is not yet an end to the matter—though," she added a little quickly, "no harm will befall you if aught in my power can prevent it."

Her look went to Mynine.

"And this," said she, "is the girl you saved from the sacrificial knife?"

"This is she," I said.

Here Henry stooped and raised Mynine to her feet.

"Yes," said Draconda, giving Mynine a look that I did not like, "it were not well that she kneel. Forgive me," addressing Henry Quainfan; "forgive me my forgetfulness."

Again she gave Mynine that icy look.

"It seems," she observed, her eyes looking straight into Henry's, "that it is indeed the Planet of Love."

He stood silent. Forsooth, what could he have said to that?

"And your companion—is his condition serious?" Draconda asked after a short and somewhat awkward pause, addressing the words to me.

"He is indeed very ill," I made answer, "and sorely wounded. However, I do not think that he is in any imminent danger. The worst, I think, is over. He is sleeping now."

"I shall visit him," she said, "this night if he awakes; if not, tomorrow. By the way, what is your name?"

"Farnermain, Rider Farnermain, O Queen."

"Rider Farnermain," she repeated, with an inclination of the head.

Her look went to Henry Quainfan.

"And yours? Why do you stand so silent? You have not spoken once."

I thought there was a tremulous note in her voice as she spoke these words, but of that I was not sure.

"His name is Quainfan," I interposed, "Henry Quainfan. O Queen, he is dumb."

"Dumb!" exclaimed Draconda.

"Alas, 'tis so. Does he not look like a dummy?"

"It was the surprise, amazement, astoundment, O Draconda," he said.

She looked at me with inquiring eyes.

"He made me do all the talking, O Queen," I explained.

Draconda laughed musically and descended from the dais with a grace and imperial bearing that would have shamed the proudest woman on Terra.

"I can imagine how astonished you were," she said, advancing to Henry Quainfan with outstretched hands, "to hear English on the lips of a Cytherean. I am inexpressibly happy to meet you, Mr. Quainfan."

And she shook both his hands. Henry stammered something in reply, I don't know what. I never had seen any woman faze him at all, and here he was flurried indeed!

"Of course, you know my name," she said. "And please do not call me Queen. I like Draconda better—just Draconda."

"Miss Draconda?" Henry asked. "Or—or Mrs.?"

Observe, he was recovering.

"Miss," she answered, unable to repress the coquettish smile that crept about her dimpled mouth. "But do not call me Miss, please—just Draconda, O Quainfan."

Then the queen advanced to me with outstretched hands. As her fingers touched mine, my senses swayed and reeled in wild ecstasy, leaving me faint and atremble. Perhaps you will remember that I had doubted there was such a thing as love at first sight: and now I loved this Draconda, had loved her from that moment her eyes first looked into mine. Yes, I loved her, this woman so unutterably beautiful, beautiful as I had never dreamed a woman could be.

She was a brunette. Her hair, upon which rested a glittering ampyx richly studded with diamonds, was of raven blackness, the rich tresses having a tendency to beautiful curls and tangles; her eyes too were black, her complexion olive—eyes in which, it seemed to me, something cosmic slumbered and stirred, something that reminded me of the mystery of space and the Milky Way, of the twinkling of stars and the flaming of nebulae.

She wore no gems save those in the ampyx, one of which was a great red diamond—though I took it to be a ruby. Her dress was of a delicious cream color, cut low at the throat and short of sleeve. On her feet, which now and again peeped out from the silken folds, were sandals with fastenings of jeweled gold. Neither throat, arms nor hands bore ornament of any kind. There was no need to bedeck that matchless body of hers, as instinct with health as with dazzling loveliness.

Her figure was tall and slender and willowy. In her depthless eyes, and on and about her full lips, was a look the like of which I had never seen in all my life. It reminded one of sadness, and yet it was not an expression of sadness. If I were to say that it was one of deep experience, there would come, I believe, an idea of harshness or even cruelty perhaps; but there was neither harshness nor cruelty in the eyes of Draconda. It was, I fancy, an expression very like that in the orbs of Poe's Ligeia: "I have felt it in the ocean—in the falling of a meteor."

But I cannot describe it, I simply cannot; nor could any other man—even one with all the words of all languages at his command. Nor can I at all describe her terrific, her superhuman loveliness.

"But," I know you will say, "Jack in love is no judge of Jill's beauty."

So be it. But of this I am convinced: love itself could not magnify the loveliness of Draconda.

Her age I put at about twenty-five years, that is, using terrestrial years; employing Venusian years, her age would, of course, be forty.

I have made it plain that Mynine was a wonderfully beautiful woman; but Draconda put her quite into the shade. Of course, the queen had a slight advantage: though careful to protect her beauty from its ravages, Mynine had not come through the intense sunlight untouched, and she was travel-stained, to say nothing of those horrors she had gone through. But, even had she been her very best, Mynine could not have fared with noteworthy gain.

The queen and our charge made a sharp and lovely contrast—Mynine with her white skin, blue eyes, blue as the dome of heaven on a clear day, and her curling golden hair; Draconda with her olive complexion, hair of raven blackness and eyes as dark and lovely and mysterious as the starry deeps of heaven—eyes in which shone the stars of immortality and Paradise, those orbs that will shed their splendor undimmed when the stars are cold.

Suddenly came the memory of Henry Quainfan's dream woman: she, too, had black eyes, raven hair and complexion olive, and her beauty transcended that of the daughters of men.

Was there something in this picture of his, after all! Was this extraordinary being that woman of his dreams? The thought, the fear that 'twas so went to my brain like fire.

But—nonsense, utter nonsense! How could Draconda's picture have been stamped on his brain? Yes, how indeed? It was nonsense; it was worse than nonsense. If she were his dream woman, why had she been born on Venus and he on

Terra? But, confound it! she had not been born on Venus—what was the matter with me? She had been born on Terra—because she spoke English. And yet how could she be a Terrestrial when she had just said it never had occurred to her that a journey from the earth to Venus was possible? And, if she—ye gods, what a mixup!

Why had she not answered my question as to how she had come to this planet? Why had she told that palpable fib? On what idea had she reared that flimsy structure of absurdity?

All these thoughts came with the quickness of the lightning; indeed, they did not come in succession but all at once; and the result was that my brain became muddled—little wonder, forsooth!—and I could not think at all. Indeed, what light could have broken in had it been otherwise?

And, through my muddled brain, and through my veins, coursing like a flaming flood, rushed a frightful jealousy. For, after all, it seemed certain that Draconda was the woman of Henry's dreams—this woman whom I thus so strangely loved. And I hated him. Yes, I did; shame, shame! A few minutes before, I had never seen Draconda; and now I loved her. And my love, as suddenly as it had come, had engendered in my breast this hate for the kindest and truest friend any son of Adam has known.

Why does Love, sacred Love, thus make sinners of men? With no little joy, however, I remember that, even as the insensate hatred ran like fire through my veins, I cursed myself for that weakness which had permitted this monster to enter my heart; to find even momentary lodgment there.

Even now, as I write this, now when all is over and done, I burn with the shame of my weakness and that sin born thereof.

"Let us now leave this room," said Draconda, "for it is not meet that you stand, and you are travel-weary. See, that chair of mine is the only one in the room. Here everyone stands save myself; here even the high priest stands, who, in some ways, is stronger than I. And see how the people are staring! They are amazed—and little wonder—to see me talking thus with the dread men from the stars. And doubtless you are amazed as they."

"More than they can imagine," said Henry Quainfan.

"O Draconda," I said, becoming bold, "it is a mystery for which I can find no key—your statement that it had never occurred to you that the gap between the earth and this planet could be crossed by mortal men."

"Can you cut this Gordian knot, O Farnermain: how did you go to the earth?"

"Which means this: you were born on Venus."

"Of a surety I was—on this very island."

"O Draconda, why do you befool us like this?"

"Like what?" she queried sweetly.

"Pardon me, O Queen, but one born here on Venus, unless a Terrestrial had come, could not know English."

"Could not?" she exclaimed. "How do you know that? But, after all, it is no wonder that you think my words untrue. Have patience, O Farnermain, I pray you. All will be explained—or maybe you will see."

She looked at me whimsically.

"He has keen eyes who sees when he can't see."

"Which means that a lantern will not help a mole."

"My Farnermain," said the queen, laughing and shaking a finger at me, "why put a rope to the eye of the needle?

"However," she went on, "it is no wonder that you think I have said the thing which is not; but it is a fact that I was born on this planet, in this city, in this very palace of Conderogan, and that I never have seen or heard of a Terrestrial here before you. You, my Farnermain, have made the most amazing and mysterious journey ever made by mortal men, and doubtless you have glimpsed deep into the terrible and wondrous arcana of Creation, or 'tis like you would not be near to him who conquered the icy deeps of space, for knowledge calls to knowledge, even as ignorance sings in its darkness; but you have not unlocked all the mysteries, O Farnermain, else would you know how it comes that English falls from my lips, how I know Greek and Latin, Hebrew and what not. Verily, you are stupid!"

And she stamped her pretty sandaled foot lightly on the carpeted floor, smiling at me archly.

"Of a truth, you are stupid. But no, you are not. Forgive me. How could you know? And yet why can you not see? I have told you the fact: I am a—what do you call us Venus people? Cythereans, Venusians? What name do you use?"

"Usually Venusians."

"Well, my Farnermain, I am a Venusian, and no Terrestrial ever set foot on this planet before you three. Have patience, O Farnermain. Soon will the mystery be unlocked for you."

"Pardon me, O Draconda," I said humbly; and yet, for the life of me, I could not believe that she had spoken the truth, nor could I see why she should tell us a lie about the matter. "Pardon me, I pray you, O Draconda; but, to my poor intellect—"

"Nay, mention it not," she interrupted, smiling her quick and wondrous smile. "And now, if it be favored of you, my guests, we shall leave this room—but no, not yet; almost had I forgotten my sister."

"Does she too speak English?" Henry asked. "But, then, surely she does."

"No; not a word can she speak," was Draconda's amazing answer. "She does not even know what English is."

Draconda's sister was standing on one side of the throne, and near her, was our old friend The Wolf, whose face was as dark as Erebus.

The queen said something to the girl, who descended from the dais and came slowly toward us, like a timid deer. She had dark brown hair and eyes of blue, and was exceedingly beautiful. Her age I put at about eighteen.

"My sister," said the queen, taking the girl's hand, "my only sister—Nytes."

Draconda made the introduction as well as the language difficulty allowed, and very well did she make it under that difficulty. The fair Nytes said she would render a million thanks to the gods for this occasion of infinite felicity (though Draconda did not translate literally) and made a remarkable and beautiful genuflection; and Henry and myself, wishing to render back as much as we had received from the fair Venusian, kowtowed a magnificent salaam, which, I noted, caused the corners of Draconda's mouth to twitch with suppressed amusement.

No doubt we did it awkwardly, for, if one wishes to salaam well, he must salaam often.

"Is that the manner wherewith you now go through an introduction on the earth?" she asked. "Then of a surety, have many and mighty changes occurred in recent years—some of them, I fear, not for the better."

"Nothing is constant but change, O Draconda," I made grave answer, "as no doubt you have heard before."

She laughed a little. When she spoke, it was in a changed voice.

"There," she said, "is he who imprisoned you in that mountain tomb and, as it were, wounded your companion so sorely."

And I saw a troubled expression in her eyes as they rested, in a manner somewhat vacuous, on the handsome face of Ta Antom, who, like every other Venusian in the great hall, was the very picture of amazement.

Also, I had seen him give Henry Quainfan, and so had the queen, several looks in which shone unbridled malignancy.

"I had seen him," I told her. "I had seen and recognized Ta Antom. One does not easily forget old friends."

"Especially," Henry added, "friends so deeply interested in one's spiritual welfare, with so ardent a desire to raise one's soul above the sordid things of the earth."

Draconda smiled a little at this inimitable wit of ours, but she made no answer.

That troubled look had not left her eyes, which returned to the lowering face of The Wolf.

"And we have forgotten to thank you, O Draconda," I said, "for rescuing us from that tomb chamber. To you we owe it that we are not lying there in that mountain blackness. To you we owe our lives; and, if ever the time comes when we can repay the debt we owe you—"

"You owe me no debt," she interrupted me in a voice somewhat absent. "But perchance that time you have in mind will come sooner than—what am I saying? Do not, I pray you, talk of thanks to me, who am made inexpressibly happy by your coming. 'Tis I that thank God in heaven that you were saved!"

And she sent a shy glance in Henry's direction, a glance that made me wince and the blood hiss in my ears as a serpent hisses, that made The Wolf's dark face grow darker still and the lovely Mynine's visible hand clench so that the pretty knuckles became livid spots.

"So talk not of thanks to me, O Farnermain," the queen went on. "And now let us leave this room, so that we can have where to sit, to talk without having all these staring eyes upon us; and truly you have much to tell me."

"Not so much, I fancy, O Draconda, as you have to tell us. And why—oh, why—will you not unlock the mystery now?"

"Soon, my Farnermain," she answered in a musing, troubled manner. "Soon will the mystery, which troubles you so sorely, be made clear. And now let us leave this room—but no; first I must speak to the people. They too will want an explanation, but I shall not make it clear to them now. The time is not meet. Perchance I shall be able—"

There was a momentary pause.

"See that pursy man," she went on with a marked alteration of voice and manner, "near him of the noble countenance and the white beard: that man is the high priest, and, of a verity, he is a son of Satan."

I liked the appearance of the old man, who, as Draconda had said, was noble of countenance; but certainly I did not like the looks of that sleek-faced, snake-eyed high priest, whose name, we soon learned, was Sallysherib.

Our mysterious Draconda now addressed the people, speaking earnestly for two or three minutes. Then ensued a hot dialogue with Sallysherib, one of the most evil-looking men I ever have laid eyes on. All the Venusians listened greedily, as if in fear they might lose a syllable. Soon it became patent that the priest was getting the worst of it. The queen remained calm; but Sallysherib's face became suffused with choleric blood, and he choked and spluttered in his wrath and finally stood speechless.

And the end of the matter was that this sacerdotal son of Satan "begged" the queen's permission to leave the room, which readily was given, and then, with a vicious little bow, he turned and marched away, honoring Henry and myself with a look truly malignant as he was vanishing between the curtains, held aside for his spectacular exit.

Henry and I looked at each other significantly.

"Confound it," said I to myself, "that old cock had gone to sharpen his spurs, and, if our beautiful feathers don't fly, I miss my guess."

There was silence for a little space, during which Draconda stood plunged in thought.

"Let us go now," she said.

She addressed something to The Wolf, who, it was clear, was in no serene state of mind—the man giving an answer short and sullen.

Then this mysterious queen took Henry's left hand and my right, and, as unseen trumpets sounded, she led us from the great hall, followed by Princess Nytes, Mynine and that noble-looking old man.

Such was our meeting with Draconda.

And there was soon to occur, in another room in this palace, a meeting even more strange.

CHAPTER 34
ST. CLOUD AWAKES

We entered a richly-furnished room and took seat, Henry and I beside Draconda on a divan, the princess and Mynine on another and the old man in a big chair, which, though there were several servants in the room (soon dismissed by the queen), had been pushed forward by Nytes.

It was a pretty sight to see the princess perform this little act of kindness for the old man. She was on the threshold of life, in the first flush of womanly beauty, while he was white-haired and wrinkled, had one foot on the brink of the grave, as it were. He thanked her with a smile, then looked at us with wondering eyes.

The room was rich in furnishings, but everything bore the stamp, sumptuous though all things were, of a beautiful simplicity—a simplicity akin to the dress of Draconda. The room was lighted by little hanging lamps of silver, and the plain, somber beauty of the place seemed to soothe the eyes and the mind.

"Now we are alone," said Draconda, "and can talk. I thought we should be favored with the company of the high priest, whose name, by the way, is Sallysherib, and that of Ta Antom, which means The Wolf; but Ta Antom—there is no need to speak of Sallysherib—wished to be excused. He is not pleased with what—with the mystery of that which has occurred. It is just as well that they did not come—no, better. I am more at ease."

She was silent for a moment, as though in troubled, painful thought.

"Oh!" she cried, with a sudden movement, a curious look flashing over her face.

Then her low, musical laughter filled the room.

"How silly!" she exclaimed. "Pardon me, my Quainfan, my Farnermain, but I was thinking of something that— How happy it were if sometimes we could only raise a barrier against thought! But enough of this!

"I was going to tell you—"

She looked at me, a smile touching the corners of her mouth.

"Not yet, my Farnermain!" she laughed.

"But I was going to tell you—this is my old friend Mayto. He is a philosopher—the wisest man in all the land. But he does not give his wisdom to the world, because of the priests, of whom more anon."

"It seems," I observed, "that they wield a power truly dreadful."

"Dreadful? Alas, my Farnermain, you have caught a glimpse of it. But hear now the story of Mayto.

"Many years ago, he was seized and condemned to death by burning for the blasphemous teaching that Venus is a sphere and goes round the sun. That this world is a globe he proved by the rising of Alpha Lyrae as one goes northward, the sinking as one goes to the south. This phenomenon, too, enabled him to deduce a planetary circumference—which was remarkably near the true one. That Venus goes round the sun was not so easily proved, but he did it. Alas, though, Truth finds foes where she makes none.

"For the people thought him a madman, acclaimed the horrible condemnation of the sacerdotal supreme council as only ignorance can acclaim. Mayto received the horrible pronouncement with composure, flinched not at all.

"I had closely followed the trial—if trial it may be called, for Mayto was condemned to death or ever he was apprehended, and he knew it—and greatly wished to see this philosopher whose love for Truth raised him above the qualms of the flesh and the pain and destruction thereof.

"Therefore, the day before he was to be burned—for the matter was moving with despatch—he was brought before me, who then was very young: it was ten years since, terrestrial years, that is. Into this very room he was brought and stood there where you see him now. There he stood brave and defiant, asking no mercy from any one. He was a giant among Yahoos, a Newton among Pithecanthropi, and my heart went out toward him. There he stood naked to the waist, bare of foot, his hands tied behind him and his body, wasted by dungeon starvation, encircled by lash welts; and upon his head, a crown of great thorns had been pressed down tight, the blood from the thorn wounds trickling down his white hair and wasted cheeks.

"The sight cut me to the heart, and I resolved to save him—if the thing were possible. Of course, it was, or he would not be here now. Another time I shall tell you the whole of the story. Let it suffice now to say that the expedient I seized upon, and which might have cost me my own, saved Mayto's life. The revocation of the death sentence, however, had this proviso, to which I at first feared Mayto was not going to assent: he must maintain an absolute silence as to his blasphemous belief that Venus is round and goes round the sun, even as the moon goes round the earth. A fool had but to look to see that the sun moves, and, as for the earth and the moon, they are lamps, not worlds. Any but a fool could see that, too.

"And thus it was that I, who then had seen but three lustrums, incurred the enmity of Sallysherib, and there has been war between us to this day. There was a mystery about me that he could not fathom, and that mystery drew the people to me, even though he tried to make it appear that I was an emissary of Satan. Ever has he watched for something that would enable him to destroy me, but that something never came. As perhaps you have seen, the war between us is not likely soon to end. The end will come only when one or the other goes down."

There was a slight pause.

"A strange story, is it not? And, if nothing else, it proves that humanity is humanity no matter where you find it—on earth or Venus, on Mars perhaps, or worlds that encircle about Aldebaran or Vega."

She looked at me whimsically.

"Something seems not clear in your mind, my Farnermain."

"It is this, O Draconda: couldn't you have conquered by revealing—?"

Query that comprehended was in her eyes,

"The truth?"

"Just so."

She smiled bitterly.

"Have you not learned, my Farnermain, that, as Innocence herself sometimes has to wear a mask, so Truth must at times stay hidden or silent? Alas, in the world of consciousness, man's intellect is as a bat—a hideous, poisonous thing, hiding in caves and fearsome places, moving only in the twilight zone and the kingdom of darkness."

"Yes," said Henry Quainfan. "And he who carries a torch for others must himself walk in shadow."

"By the way," I asked, "does Mayto know how you learned English?"

Draconda laughed.

"No, my Farnermain; he doesn't even know what English is."

"He is a great man," Henry said. "Tell him, O Draconda, that I am honored to meet one so learned and brave."

The queen translated, when the old man arose and bowed to us, Henry and I stood and bowed with deep respect in turn.

"And now tell me things!" said Draconda. "Tell me about your discovery and the journey, O Quainfan—no, first the year. Judging from your dress and weapons, I should say that it is not, after all, far from the year nineteen hundred."

"How in the world," said I, amazed, "did you lose all count of the time?"

"I didn't," she told me. "And for a good reason: I never had it to lose!"

I was dumbfounded.

"Mystery follows mystery," said Henry Quainfan.

Draconda laughed a little.

"But what is the year?" she asked.

Henry told her.

"And the month?"

The month was given and the day of the month also.

"I could tell from your arms and your weapons that not many years had elapsed since—that the time was near the year nineteen hundred," she said; "but, before you came, I did not know whether it was the twentieth century, the fortieth—or the eightieth! And now tell me things."

"I think it is you who should tell us things, O Draconda," I said. "We are in utter darkness."

"No," she laughed; "you tell me. I am not cognizant of anything that has occurred on Terra since eighteen hundred and eighty-six. But, first, tell me of your journey and that marvelous thing in which you came, O Quainfan. It was called the *Hornet,* was it not? That was a funny name."

Henry and I looked at each other. Was it any wonder? What on earth were we to make of these things?

Draconda was twenty-five. She had just said so. She had been born on Venus, and yet her knowledge of things terrestrial did not go beyond the year eighteen hundred and eighty-six! Nonsense—gibberish—hocus-pocus!

Draconda broke the silence with a little silvery laugh, which rippled merrily round the room, and again asked Henry to tell her of our journey and the thing in which we had come. So he proceeded to give her a succinct account of the discovery, the *Hornet* and those unearthly days in space. She broke in with many exclamations and questions, and, when he had finished, told him he was the greatest man that had ever lived, whereupon he flushed like an abashed country swain.

"Now tell me of the terrestrial happenings," she said. "Of course, I mean the ones that have occurred since the year eighteen hundred and eighty-six; the others I know full well—some of them too well, perhaps."

So Henry went on to tell this mysterious woman what had happened on the earth since eighteen hundred and eighty-six.

I tried to think, but think I could not. My thoughts were all jumbled up. I found myself imagining the absurdest things. I sat bewildered, dumbfounded, thunderstruck. I often think of those first minutes with Draconda. Ever had I to assure myself in various ways that I was not dreaming it all. The strangeness of it, the unreality of that which was real—no wonder I am making a fool of myself—made my poor brain fairly spin.

Just think of it. Was it any wonder that my brain went round and round and round? Bear with me a moment. Here we had journeyed all the way from the earth, and on this planet called Venus, whose orbit is twenty-five millions of miles sunward of Terra, we had met a woman who spoke English. We were sitting beside her now. And she had said the possibility of coming from Terra to Venus never had entered her head; ergo, she had lied. That was incontestable, or else nothing ever was incontestable.

But why? Yes, why? However, there was no light forthcoming in that direction. All that was palpable was that this mysterious and wondrous being had said the thing which was not.

Also, what had happened on the earth since eighteen hundred and eighty-six was a blank to her; in other words, she was not cognizant of anything that had occurred on Terra for near thirty years. And she was only twenty-five! How in the world had she crossed those years between?

Furthermore, she had been born here on Venus, never had left Venus, and no Terrestrial ever had landed on Venus before us.

What did she think we were?

Also and furthermore, before our arrival, she had not known whether the time that separated the now from that year eighteen hundred and eighty-six was fifty years, a hundred, a thousand or a million years in extent:

Ye gods! What was I to make of these things?

"So!" exclaimed Draconda when Henry had finished. "So men see through solid steel and granite now, talk without wires, soar with the eagle and the condor, sport with the dolphins and dive to the haunts of the mermaid! And you, my Quainfan—you have unlocked the terrible mystery of the atom, seen the heat, as it were, of Nature's heart!"

"No, no," he said: "unlocked but one of its mysteries. And her heart, I fear, is not there."

"Ah, well," said Draconda, "you have blazoned your name big on the marble cliffs of time, my Quainfan, high above the names of Newton and Columbus.

"And thus science advances, and theology advances with her. And yet scientist and theologian—there they sit, glaring away at each other. Well, so it has always been, and so, I have no doubt, it will always be.

"Unfortunate it is that Science and Religion are so antagonistic to each other, for neither is wholly right, and where one has weakness the other has strength. One could not be without the other. Each owes to the other a debt, and each will not consider that debt—acknowledge it even.

"Science is iconoclastic; and Religion shows a weakness for which it is difficult to account, in view of her strength of ages, in believing that, because Science has, for instance, forced man to live on a ball instead of a pancake, her antagonist will one day destroy the anagogetical verity. That will never be destroyed by Science. Her domain does not include the spiritual, and, when she ponders on spiritual things and attempts to put them into a test-tube, then she is anything but scientific.

"Just what I've said a thousand times," I remarked, for Draconda had paused.

"And, in like manner," she went on, "Religion is anything but religious when she ponders on earthly, material things, attempts to make of them a balloon in which one must ride to reach heaven, or, if blasphemous enough to doubt its Divine manufacture, go down to damnation eternal."

She glanced at Henry Quainfan.

"Just what I've said a thousand times," he told her.

Draconda laughed a little.

"I thought it," she said. "However, Religion, if unrestrained by Science, who ever forces her to let the *material* alone, would fill the beautiful Universe with devils, ghosts and the shrieks of damned souls, would plunge the minds of men and women into darkness and the fear that surges in darkness; while, on the other hand, Science, if unrestrained by Religion, who ever forces her to let the *spiritual* alone, would send the glorious Cosmos crumbling to a heap of dead atoms.

"But my, how I have been talking! Now I listen. Tell me about literature—oh, did you bring any books?"

"We had five or six dozen," Henry said; "but, when the *Hornet*—"

"Oh, you lost them all!"

"No; we have three."

"Goody, goody!" exclaimed Draconda, clapping her hands in girlish fashion. "Let me see them! Quick! What are they? Hurry, hurry!"

"That we have two of them is due to the merest chance: his Bible Rider has with him always, but Goodness only knows how I happened to have, in one of my pockets, *The Deerslayer*—"

"Dear old Leather-Stocking!" exclaimed Draconda. "And the other?"

"A little volume of Poe."

"Not *Gordon Pym,* I hope."

"No: *The Murders in the Rue Morgue, The Gold Bug, Ligeia, The Fall of the House of Usher* and a few others. The best of Poe, you see."

"Yes; but I could easily wish it had been something else. Life isn't tombs and grave-worms—nor is that death, either.

> "'Tis not the whole of Life to live,
> Nor all of death to die.'

"Probably, though, my Quainfan, you think—or have thought—otherwise."

"How on earth, O Draconda, did you know that?"

"I didn't know it," the queen smiled; "I but thought it."

For a time she sat silent, turning the pages.

"What a contrast!" she said. "Where an antithesis more striking: Cooper and Poe! One like the sunlight streaming on forest and ocean; the either like the moon-gleams gloating o'er tombs: one clear-eyed, with the brown of the sun on his cheek; the other a companion to dragons and owls."

"Pretty hard on Poe," I thought, but all I said was:

"You love Cooper?"

"Adore him!" said Draconda.

She took up the Bible from her lap.

"Ah," she said, suddenly pausing in the turning of the leaves. "Listen:

"'Where wast thou when I laid the foundations of the earth? declare, if thou hast understanding.'"

Neither Henry nor I made response.

"Silent!" Draconda observed, with a whimsical smile.

"Your answer, O Queen," Henry said.

"No—even I cannot say," returned Draconda. "But this I do know, my Quainfan: *we were!* Yes, and even eternities before our sun his terrible march began!"[9]

Henry Quainfan said:

"In a certain sense, O Draconda, that is undoubtedly sober truth: what I mean is, not that I believe in the immortality of the individual soul (though it may be immortal) but in that of—what shall I say?—in the immortality of the Spirit of Life. As Lord Kelvin puts it:

"'I am ready to adopt, as an article of scientific faith, true through all space and through all time, that life proceeds from life, and from nothing but life.'"

"My Quainfan, my Quainfan!" said Draconda. "I don't mean that."

"I know it," he told her.

"You have left the highway," said she, "taken a footpath leading into shadows."

"Just so, Draconda: the shadows cast by the mountains called the Mystery of Life."

"But—" began the queen.

Came a sharp word or two from just without one of the doorways, a woman's voice in answer, then the clang of weapons on the marble floor.

A moment, and the lady had entered. She made obeisance to her queen and stood with bowed head till Draconda bade her speak.

The sick man from the stars was awake—with which intelligence Draconda acquainted us forthwith.

---

9. "Whence have we come, and whither do we go? . . . Since the traditional time of Adam the sun has led his planets through the wastes of space not less than 225,000,000,000 miles, or more than 2400 times the distance that separates him from the earth . . . Where was our little planet when it emerged out of the clouds of chaos? Where was the sun when his "thunder march" began?"—Garrett P. Serviss: *Curiosities of the Sky.*

CHAPTER 35
THE MEETING

"He is lying quiet," said Draconda, "though plainly surprised. Shall we go to him now? I would that I might bid him welcome, but that would not be expedient, what with the surprise it might give him to hear a Venusian speak English."

So we all arose and directed our steps toward the room in which we had left St. Cloud.

It was not until afterwards, by the way, that I thought of this curious fact to be writ on my brain in letters of fire:

Draconda had not asked, nor had we mentioned, our companion's name.

However, we found St. Cloud apparently asleep again, his face partly covered and *in shadow*.

I have often wondered what the anagnorisis would have been had his features been in the full light and wholly uncovered. Then the queen would have discovered the terrible truth from a distance, and, if he had not awakened from the light sleep or stupor in which he lay, she might have stolen out quietly so as not to disturb him, knowing—as surely she would have known—that the sight of her, what with his weakened mind and body, would inevitably prove fatal.

Of course, she might not have done this; she might have screamed just the same, and the same horrible thing might have happened. What is the use of wondering? We can only hope that it will never be seen again. Nor, indeed, do I think that, throughout all the ages of eternity itself, any mortal eye will behold what we saw in that room.

All was still when we entered. Could be heard only the soft rustling of the women's dresses and the faint sound of our feet as they sank into the deep nap. Once there came from without a distant and wailing cry, which I thought came from some aquatic bird on the lake. Mynine, the princess and the old philosopher came to a stop about three yards from the litter, the old man leaning on his cane; Draconda, Henry and myself advanced to Morgan's side. He had not stirred.

"It seems he had gone to sleep again," Draconda said in a whisper.

I nodded.

"Yes, it seems so," Henry whispered back.

Then Draconda took a step forward and, leaning over, looked at Morgan's face.

I was watching closely.

Suddenly I heard a sharp, painful intake of breath; over her features shot the strangest look—terrible, ghastly. She stood there, leaning over and staring for a few seconds, then of a sudden flung her body up and back as though struck at by a serpent, her face white as death, even the lips it seemed, and then there burst from her throat a scream that drove into my brain like a dagger.

"He!" she exclaimed, her voice a hoarse whisper.

I stepped toward her, for I feared she was going to fall.

"What is it?" I asked. "What—?"

"Why didn't I ask—oh, why didn't I ask his name?"

Then a little fiercely:

"Why didn't you—?"

Here speech was frozen on her lips; her eyes, which had never left Morgan's face for an instant, became wide and agleam with horror.

There was a sound from the litter.

I turned my look to St. Cloud, but, before it had reached him, there burst from his lips the most frightful, terror-filled scream I have ever heard in all my life.

He had raised himself up on one elbow and was staring at Draconda with eyes that seemed about to start from his head. Never have I seen on another face that unutterable terror which was stamped on his still and livid features. The face seemed to be crushed in, the eyes bulged out, by a terror and horror that were out of the earth.

His lips moved; no sound, though, issued from them. Again they moved; but still no sound. At the third attempt, he succeeded, and the words burst from his lips like a thunderclap:

"Blanche! Blanche!"

I started at that name, and a shiver ran through me.

Draconda drew herself up. This simple movement had an effect as swift as awful: St. Cloud's terror became a thing for which there is no utterance.

"Speak!" he shrieked. "Speak!"

Draconda said never a word.

She just stood there looking at him.

"Speak!" he shrieked again. "In God's name, Blanche—are you in the flesh?"

Than from Draconda's lips came these words, her voice hard and cold:

"Of course!"

Morgan shrieked horribly.

"Why—oh!" he screamed. "I saw you—with my own eyes I saw you—oh,—oh!"

His body jerked into a sitting position, the eyes flashing shut; then, uttering one short, frightful scream, which must have reached to every corner in the great palace, he fell back and was still.

For a little space, no one moved; then Henry went and leaned over Morgan.

"Dead," he said, straightening up.

He stood looking at Draconda.

She said nothing.

Silence fell—heavy, awful.

So this mysterious Draconda, whom I loved, was Blanche, the woman whom St. Cloud had in some way wronged on far-off Terra, who had stalked through his dreams, whose ghost had come and tortured him in the mountain tomb—but who was Blanche?

Henry had known St. Cloud for nearly ten years, and he knew nothing about Blanche. He had never heard of her on the earth, had never heard her name ere Morgan in slumber spoke it in that ruined city in which dwell the Ohams.

Of course, he was not conversant with St. Cloud's affairs; but, had this disastrous one with Draconda (whatever it was) occurred during that decade, he would, in all likelihood, have known of it. Henry had told me he was almost sure that Blanche had come into Morgan's life prior to their meeting. This, it is obvious, would make Blanche—or, rather, Draconda—at the most fifteen years of age when that unknown tragedy, a love tragedy perhaps, had occurred; wherefore, it seemed to me, there was something wrong here.

Not that I did much thinking. Indeed, I did not try. These things just came darting through my mind, that was all. What was the use of thinking? Mystery had succeeded mystery; and what was the use of thinking at all?

We should have to wait, wait till Draconda was minded to explain.

But who in the world was this mysterious woman, the mere sight of whom had killed in a manner so terrible our dark, handsome, mysterious Morgan St. Cloud? Who was she? How had she come from the earth to the Planet of Love? And why—oh, why—had she lied?

How long the silence lasted, I do not know, At last, however, Draconda spoke:

"It was unfortunate; it was awful. I would to Heaven I had asked your companion's name. Had I known he was Morgan St. Cloud, this awful thing would not have happened. He has changed much, yet I knew him the instant I looked closely. I shall explain later—not now. I must be alone. He is dead—slain by his own folly, his own sin."

She fell silent and seemed to ponder deeply, once glancing quickly at the face of the dead man.

The silence was broken by Henry Quainfan, who addressed himself to the queen.

"Why will you not explain, O Draconda? What, in the name of Heaven, does this mean? How did you come here? You knew this man on the earth?"

"Yes; I did," she answered.

"Why, Draconda," he said a little wildly, "do you spin these webs of gibberish? You have given us nonsense, utter nonsense. This meeting has proved it. Why, O Draconda, do you spin these webs of words more flimsy than the spider's web?"

"Those are bold words," she said softly, looking straight into his eyes. "No Venusian would dare speak like that to me."

He made a sudden wild gesture, then said humbly:

"I beg your forgiveness, O Draconda. But surely you knew what was in my mind. This meeting threw me into a frightful tumult—which perhaps you understand, O Draconda. But I am sorry; I beg your forgiveness."

Draconda forgave him with a look. As her eyes looked into his, I saw in them a mysterious softness that brought my heart into my throat.

"Do not mention it any more," she said. "And, indeed, I cannot blame you for doubting my word. But, here in the presence of this dead man, I cannot explain."

She now turned and addressed a few words to the princess and old Mayto. I saw Henry's look wander from her to the face of St. Cloud, then back to the queen.

"I am sorry," she said, turning to us, "but I must go now. I want to be alone. Here you will be safe from intrusion or snares—may entertain every feeling of security. And now I must thus unseemly bid you good-night."

"Good-night," we murmured as this mysterious and, in a way, awful woman, with a swift glance at the face of the dead man, turned to go.

She and the bewildered Nytes, followed by the equally-bewildered philosopher, walked slowly to the curtained doorway, where the queen stopped (whereupon the princess and old Mayto also came to a halt) and stood looking back at us.

"And yet," said Draconda in a low voice, looking at Henry Quainfan, "it hurts me sorely to know that you think my words false."

She paused, still looking at my companion. The curtains were held aside by two servants.

"Good-night," she concluded.

Then they went slowly through the doorway and were hid from view as the curtains fell back into their places behind them.

CHAPTER 36
ACCURSED

For a while, I gazed at the curtains, then turned my look to Henry, to see him staring at the face of the dead man.

A few moments, and our eyes met, questioning. He shook his head, muttering something that I could not catch.

Then suddenly he turned and signed to the Venusians to leave the room, which they did immediately, leaving us with Mynine and the thing that so short a time before had been Morgan St. Cloud.

Shortly afterwards, he explained to the girl, who had been watching him with a look steady and troubled, that we wished to be alone now. She hesitated a moment, looking at him in a strange, questioning manner, with eyes in which, it seemed to me, there were adumbrations of a terrible fear (I knew what she feared; it was that the queen might take her lover from her), and then she turned and slowly left the room, hesitating at the doorway and glancing at Henry with unchanged eyes. But he did not see, for he was again staring at the face of St. Cloud.

There was silence for a time, broken only by the beating of my heart.

Henry was the first to speak, his voice husky, curiously unnatural:

"In Heaven's name, Rider, what does this mean? Good God! what—?"

He left the sentence unfinished.

"We'll know—when Draconda is minded to explain."

He went to the litter and stood looking down on St. Cloud's face, a strange, hard expression on his own. At last he covered up those pallid, horror-stamped features, then, with a wild, and, I think, unconscious, gesture, began walking back and forth with nervous steps, at length coming to a stop beside me.

"Rider—" he began.

His eyes fixed themselves on vacancy.

"Yes?" I suggested.

There was no response.

It was patent that his mind was in a terrible turmoil. And why? Because the sight of Draconda had killed Morgan St. Cloud? I did not think so; no, I was sure there was something else.

I remembered certain words he had spoken to the queen, that peculiar softness I had seen in her eyes, the way in which she had addressed him when she was leaving, and other things. She had spoken, it seemed to me, as though there was some tacit understanding between them. And all this, of course, pointed to but one thing: That this mysterious queen was the woman of his dreams—though I could not, for the life of me, see how her picture could have been stamped on his brain.

Yet, even so, I feared that it was true—and I loved her. Strange—terribly, sweetly strange. But I loved her, and I do now.

And, of course, all this threw my own mind into a frightful turmoil. Jealousy went coursing through my veins like a molten flood. If Draconda was his "dream woman," there could be no hope for me; if she was, my life was blasted even now, for I knew that only Death could end that sweet, agonizing pain at my heart—and I knew not what Draconda was nor what she had been.

Love had come in its mysterious way, as swift and blinding as the lightning—in a manner I never had believed that love could come.

And, anyway, what hope could I have of winning this queen? Why, the thought itself was a madness.

I longed to know if Draconda was indeed his dream woman—and yet dreaded the knowing.

It was Henry who broke the silence.

"Rider!"

"Yes?"

"Maybe you'll think—it's a queer thing; but it's a fact."

"A fact—what?" I asked, with a sinking of the heart.

"It is she, Rider: Draconda is my picture woman, the woman of my dreams."

"Oh!" said I. "How wonderful!"

"Wonderful beyond words, Rider."

I said it was, or something to that effect.

And there was a silence.

So there it was! I had expected that, had steeled myself to keep back any sign of the effect it would have upon me. And I succeeded. At least, I am pretty sure that I did. I do not think Henry ever learned by word or sign that I loved his Draconda. And yet how can we be sure of these things?

Perhaps, though, Draconda herself knew.

Well, it had come, the expected had come, and my life was blasted, I was accursed. As he spoke those words, something came crashing down upon me, something that crushed with the weight of mountains, whose awful weight is crushing me still.

Often have I pondered on the exceeding strangeness of it all. A short time before—such a short time—I had never set eyes on this mysterious queen, and now I loved her, knew my life was blasted because she was Henry Quainfan's "dream woman"—the woman whose picture had been stamped on his mind, stamped in a manner which, I thought, would be forever beyond the understanding of the finite mind.

And to see her become his wife—well, I would be a man, though my heart would be broken: already it was broken. Yes, I would be a man. Though jealousy went through my veins like a flaming flood, filled my brain with spluttering and hissing lights, though I hated Henry, yes, actually hated him (and yet loved him, too), even so, I would be a man, would conquer all the weaknesses of the flesh-imprisoned spirit. Yes, I would hide all that was in my soul, that might be in the days to come, and I would fight side by side with him and her until they were happy or disaster overwhelmed us all; and, if the first came to pass, then I would go away. Yes, I decided upon this as I stood there. I would go away, so that I could not see Draconda any more—for that would be a torture unbearable.

It was I who broke the silence:

"It *is* wondrous, Henry, as wondrous as mysterious. And think of it—the chance of chances that brought you to her!"

And I reached out my hand and wrung his—yes, congratulated him there in the presence of the dead man.

CHAPTER 37
DEATH AGAIN

"But—" said Henry Quainfan.

"Well?"

"You think that Draconda—well, has a mind photograph of me?"

"It's possible."

"Of course, it is possible, Rider. But—has she?"

"You must ask the lady herself that question."

"From certain little things, though, Rider—"

He looked at me quizzically.

"Yes—I think so, too," I said.

"You do?" he asked quickly.

I nodded.

"You noticed?"

"Yes, I noticed."

"I never believed it possible, Rider. And life has changed, changed wondrously, in an undreamed-of manner, since we entered that hall—though what the end may be, who can guess that? Everything is different now. I see why things always hurt, why I didn't know what to do—except lose myself in work. Something hurt, and in work, and work only, I forgot. It was because I hadn't found Draconda!"

"Little wonder you hadn't found her!"

"But, Rider—this meeting!"

His jaws snapped shut, his eyes went to the litter, and his handsome face grew dark and lined.

"In Heaven's name," he broke out, "what was he to Draconda? She is a mysterious woman, and this meeting—it bespeaks something awful. I had just seen immortality for the first time—I saw it in her eyes—and then came this dreadful thing to fill my mind with black, writhing thoughts. Why didn't Draconda explain? And how on earth, Rider, is she going to straighten the thing out? Born on Venus—and then she had known Morgan on the earth!"

A terrible look came into the gray eyes, which turned again to that covered and lifeless form in the litter.

"It must have been something terrible, Rider."

"But—he lied! He said so himself. Good Lord, don't you remember what he said in the tomb, to Draconda's ghost—or, rather, to the ghost of Blanche?"

"I remember," said Henry. "Of course!"

"Well, don't be a fool!" I told him. "Don't let—remember Cambyses and Nitetis, Henry. More tragedies have been caused by black thoughts, fears and blunders, than by all the he and she devils that ever have lived."

"I remember. And *that* will not bring about any tragedy here—though tragedy there may be. And Mynine, Rider! How can I explain? The girl will never believe."

"Oh, well," I said, "there's not need of a lighted lantern until it's dark."

"Yes, but you can't light the lantern until you have it. However, let's go into this other room; it will be more cheerful in there, and Morgan can sleep just as well alone."

So we went into the room in question, where Henry took seat on a chair, myself on the bed. In a few minutes, I lay down. I closed my eyes and thought—thought—thought. Minute after minute passed, the minutes became hours, and still I lay there thinking—thinking.

How I wished that I could sleep, so that, for a time, all would be forgotten.

My imagination ran riot—became phantasmagoria that was a nightmare, a nightmare in which, ever and anon, would appear that mummy-like thing I had seen in a dream, that creature who had warned me never to set eyes on Queen Draconda.

Never once did Henry Quainfan break the silence; and, when I spoke, which was seldom, his response was monosyllabic. Whenever I looked, it was to see him sitting there staring into vacancy.

At length—it must have been in the last hours of darkness—I sank off to sleep. It was a troubled sleep, a nightmare indeed, and from it I was aroused, about two hours before midday, by a great crash, which brought me to my feet before I was even half awake. And, so overwrought were my nerves, as I sprang up I screamed and screamed yet again.

I was dreaming when that crash came, still was dreaming when I sprang up and screamed—the dream and the reality blended together, though at the time I did not know but what it all was a dream.

I would to Heaven it had been!

The sunlight was streaming in through the windows. In a strange, unearthly way, I saw a form madly struggling on the floor, in one of the far corners of the room. Even as my eyes fell upon it, it arose and instantaneously became two forms—one Henry Quainfan, the other The Wolf, locked in a struggle so savage that the men were like beasts.

I may as well, I suppose, set down here what had happened, what had brought about this terrible scene, to have so strange and terrible an end.

Of course, a woman was the cause of it, and that woman, as doubtless the reader has anticipated, was none other than the queen.

For Draconda loved Henry even as Henry loved Draconda, had a picture of him more vivid even than that one which Love had limned, with so sure a touch, on the canvas of his soul; but, like her lover from the earth, she had never believed her picture was that of a real mate, that he existed or ever had existed; and, so believing, she had (and here is the terrible thing) fallen in love, though in a troubled way, with Ta Antom.

Believing that the breaking of her betrothal to the powerful Venusian would, in all likelihood, be succeeded by something unpleasant in the extreme, even if she exercised all the diplomacy of which she was capable, the queen had planned to proceed with this unpleasant business as gently and judiciously as possible. But, when she met The Wolf this day, her plans were in some manner overthrown: she smashed the engagement then and there, whereupon The Wolf watched his chance and, sword in hand, crept into our room to make an end of the man who had taken his sweetheart from him.

But Henry, who had not fallen asleep once, heard Ta Antom stealing up behind him. Springing to his feet, he saved himself from what surely would have been a fatal thrust, though he received a wound in the left arm, near the shoulder, that rendered that limb utterly useless. He succeeded in gripping his antagonist's sword arm, and now his strength stood him in good stead indeed. He managed to throw his enemy, and the two, falling upon a chair and smashing it to pieces, crashed to the door; and the crash of their falling aroused me.

The Venusian was a powerful man, but, in a struggle with strength as the decisive factor, Henry, I am sure, easily could have come out the victor. Ta Antom, however, had taken him by surprise, had two arms to his one—to say nothing of the weapon.

The instant I became wide awake and grasped the perilous position of my companion, I jerked out a revolver (I had, since our rescue from the tomb, worn St. Cloud's cartridge-belt, with its pendent weapon, as well as my own, and had lain down without taking them off), but, so swift were the gyrating movements of friend and foe, I hesitated to fire, for fear of hitting Henry, from whose wound was gushing a crimson stream.

I started toward them; but, at that very instant, a white-robed female figure, sword in hand, looking like a specter against the dark background of wall, came rushing into the room.

Some fluffy stuff that the woman wore had flown up over that side of her face which was toward me, completely hiding the features and enhancing not a little that terrible spectral quality of the figure.

With a little cry, she darted toward the men, and, with another cry, short and fiercely wild, she drove her weapon into the Venusian's body—drove it clean to the hilt.

As the stricken man, with two feet or so of the blade protruding from his back, pitched to the floor on his face with a groan, that gauzy stuff slowly fell from the countenance of the being who made the fatal thrust, revealing to my astonished eyes the lovely face of the queen.

CHAPTER 38
THE BLOW FALLS

I made an exclamation and stood aghast.

Draconda gave way to no feminine weakness. Though pallid of face, cadaverous even, and trembling a little, she was calm—her calmness somehow striking me with horror.

She gave the fallen man a swift look, then hurried to Henry Quainfan, who was leaning weakly against the wall. From his wound a fountain of blood was gushing forth. He was so covered with gore that I feared he had received at least a half dozen wounds.

I looked at the stricken man, writhing there in mortal agony. Draconda, too, turned her eyes to her victim—to her quondam lover, who so short a time before had held her in his arms, aflame with her velvety embrace and her kisses.

With a groan, one hand gripping the hilt of the sword, he rolled over on one side that he might see her better and curse her with his eyes; then suddenly he rolled back and in a moment had expired.

Some men and women, among whom I saw Mynine, who was pushing her way through them, had appeared in the doorway through which the queen had entered on her swift mission of death—taking in the bloody scene with wide eyes.

Draconda turned and gave a sharp command, whereupon one of the men vanished on the instant.

Without her queen's permission, Mynine came boldly into the room and hurried toward her beloved, her lovely eyes swimming in tears. She made a hurried obeisance to Draconda, and the next moment was beside Henry—the dark eyes of the queen, for a moment, fixed on her in a look that had something simply terrible in it.

Henry, we soon learned, had received but one wound, but that certainly was one of an alarming nature. I feared, as I looked, that he would never use that arm again.

"A tourniquet, my Farnermain!" said Draconda.

"I doubt—"

"Do not doubt," also said a little sharply, "but fetch me one of those curtain-cords! Something, anything to stop the flow! The physician should be here in a moment, but, in the meantime—"

I was already hurrying back with one of the cords, slashed off with my hunting-knife, and in a few moments the tourniquet was in place.

Mynine, her bloody fingers atremble, had started to help with this instrument of torture, but the queen had spoken sharply to her, whereupon the girl had sullenly desisted.

We checked the flow, but stop it we could not.

Henry was sitting on the bed; finally he lay down.

"Winged me, all right," he smiled.

"That man!" exclaimed Draconda. "Why doesn't he come?"

Scarcely had she spoken, however, when her Æsculapius entered—one of the skinniest, ugliest men I ever have set eyes on, and as cool as an icicle. A skillful man, however, was our Dr. Quixote—who, by the way, was a priest also; all physicians are here. Remembering Sallysherib, I felt a little uneasy on that score, even though I assured myself that Draconda knew what she was about.

But my fears were groundless: Draconda had no stauncher friend (even though he was a purple-robe) than this doc of the sorrowful figure.

In a few minutes he had stanched the flow and was dressing the wound. This latter done, the soiled bed-clothes were removed and new ones put in their place.

Not long afterwards, Dr. Quixote left us.

Draconda was sitting on the bed, her eyes on Henry's face, while Mynine, silent and motionless, stood watching the twain with an expression that cut me to the very heart.

Of a sudden a new thought struck the queen. Her eyes rested for a moment on The Wolf, then she arose, and, going to that doorway through which she had entered, she spoke a few words, whereupon some men came in and bore away the body of her whilom lover.

She stood watching the melancholy little group till it had vanished with its lifeless burden, and then, turning to me, she said:

"I never dreamed that Atropos would commission me to sever the thread of that life. The Moerae are more cruel than kind. They will not let us wander for long on the flowery ways of our hearts' desire. They drive us forth to the brambled and jagged ways of our hearts' loathing—ways which we must tread or surely we shall perish and upon which mayhap we shall perish in the treading.

"But," and she sighed, "what is the use of talking thus? What is is, my Farnermain, and the ears of the Fates are deaf to our prayers and our wailing."

"The Fates obey, Draconda."

She looked at me quickly.

"'Tis so, my Farnermain. And sometimes 'tis we who command them."

"So it seems. But my poor intellect has no plummet to sound those deeps in the Ocean of Being."

"But the golden dawns, the sunsets of glory and the storms that sweep over it—why, my Farnermain, what Columbus, unless indeed he be mad, thinks the black sea abysms more wondrous than the beauties and the mystery through which he is sailing?"

"Yet, in fancy, he wanders down into coral halls and the awful abysms below them."

"In fancy—yes, my Farnermain. And, in fancy—at times, indeed in truth—we can wander through the coral palaces and the terrible sea caves of Fate."

Now came the most surprising thing, in its way, that I have seen in all my life. There, in the presence of the golden-haired woman who loved him so well, to say nothing of my own—why did Henry Quainfan tell Draconda there? I fancy, however, that Henry could not answer that question himself.

For, after pondering for a moment, Draconda suddenly turned, went back and seated herself in a chair which she had drawn up to the bedside—her left hand resting on the bed-clothes, near Henry's right.

It must have been accidental; at any rate, his hand touched the queen's, whereupon his eyes opened and his fingers closed over hers. Draconda started, and I could see her atremble—trembling as she had not done at the slaying of Ta Antom.

I, too, trembled, and something rose up in my throat that threatened to suffocate me.

I wanted to go away, but something seemed to hold me in that spot.

He drew her to him, drew her close and whispered in her ear. Yes, with Morgan St. Cloud lying in the next room a corpse, with Mynine standing there so near him—thus did Henry Quainfan tell his love to this mysterious queen.

As he whispered, I saw her face light up until her beauty shone us if through a spiritual radiance—through a halo that rendered visible on that face of ineffable loveliness a glory not of the earth, one that would shine on in its beauty when the sun and the stars are dark.

Her lips were slightly parted, her breast, on which the dress was cut low, rising and falling tumultuously.

When Henry had done whispering, Draconda bent her head until her cheek touched his; though I could not see her lips, I knew that she was whispering back—

words than which sweeter never fell on human ear. Suddenly she raised her head, kissed him softly but passionately on the lips. Then it was that I heard something like a sob, and yet not a sob at all, and which broke from the lips of Mynine.

I turned and looked at the girl. She was white, white as a sheet. Her hands had clenched so tight, as I afterwards learned, the pink nails had broken through the soft white flesh. Her lips were slightly parted, discovering her snow-white teeth of pearl. And upon her quivering features was stamped the most awful suffering I have ever seen on a woman's face.

I have not attempted to describe, have left to the reader's imagination the effect this strange love scene had upon me. I felt that I was suffering in a degree beyond which no man's agony of heart ever had gone; but, so great was that suffering upon this poor woman's face, even in my own I was cut to the soul by the sight of it.

We had saved her from death, and now something had come perhaps as black and awful. There was no telling what this stricken woman might do.

Draconda, too, heard that sound. She arose, flushed and trembling. As the blue eyes met the dark, there was something in those cerulean depths that made the orbs actually hideous.

I took the stricken woman by the arm and tried to lead her away.

But Mynine would not budge.

CHAPTER 39
MYNINE GOES

"So," said Draconda, as though speaking to herself, "it has come—so soon."

I turned my look to Henry Quainfan; his eyes wore on Mynine, misty with tears.

Rather to my surprise, it was to me the queen addressed herself.

"Caught in the winds of Fate, my Farnermain!" she said. "And every moment whirls us into new troubles."

I nodded, though it was my opinion that Fate had been assisted somewhat in this matter.

The queen said:

"I understand—that is, this girl told me, this morning, that she is betrothed to—to my Quainfan here."

"It seems it is so, O Draconda. As for the customs of this land—well, how can I know of them?"

"True, true. How could you know? How could my Quainfan know? In this land, then, the prerogative of love-making is the woman's, and the woman's only; if the man accepts her advances, embraces or kisses her, then they are engaged; furthermore, strange though this may seem, the engagement can be broken only by the woman—except, that is, in certain cases."

She looked at me interrogatively; however, I stood silent.

By the goddess Melpomene, why select me as expositor?

"That the girl spoke the truth," the queen went on, "I believe. But—well, you see he loves me."

She blushed like the pale dawn.

"Yes," I nodded.

"Mynine did speak the truth," came Henry's voice, weak and troubled. "But I never loved her."

A curious look—probably one of bepuzzlement and passion commingled—shot across Draconda's features and lingered there.

"It seems," she said, "that there has been a strange, a terrible mistake."

"A terrible mistake, indeed," I told her.

"I do not understand. However, if Henry were a Venusian—but my Quainfan is not, and so the law can not apply.

"But," with a sudden alteration of voice, turning toward her lover, "this is very unpleasant, you are weak and wounded, and so I shall dismiss the girl, and the matter can be explained to her later."

"No," said he. "Now that it has come, let it be explained here. But—I know that Mynine will never believe me."

Draconda listened intently, holding her sweetheart's hand, the while Mynine stood like a statue.

"Mynine," said the queen, when Henry had finished, "explanation has been made and I regret exceedingly that it had to be given in a tongue that thou canst not understand, for perchance thou wilt think I use my office of translator to color the explanation. But I pray thee, my Mynine, do not think that, for that thing I will not do.

"This man whom thou lovest—my Mynine, the Lord Quainfan never did love thee. A great mistake hath been made, a strange mistake, and it hurteth him sorely. Hear now, my Mynine: knowing that thou didst love him, and believing that there was no escape from that tomb wherein ye had been imprisoned by the Lord Ta Antom, that all of you would surely perish in the awful blackness, and wishing to fill thy last earthly hours with that sweet which he knew the belief that thou want loved would bring to thee—"

Here Mynine's face grew deathly pale, her body rigid as stone; only, the lips quivered, quivered so pitifully that I turned my eyes away.

"Because of this, my Mynine," the queen went on, a perceptible change in her tones, "the Lord Quainfan made believe that he did love thee. After the rescue, he could have told thee that he did not love, but he could have made no explanation; wherefore did he remain silent, continue to make believe that thou wast loved. That was why he did not tell thee the truth, my Mynine."

The girl made no response.

After looking at her queen for a space, with eyes somewhat vacant and yet very hard, she turned her blue orbs to the man who was the innocent cause of her tragedy; and, as they looked into his, her eyes did not change at all: they were somewhat vacant and very hard.

"Tell her, Draconda, that I am very sorry," Henry said, "and that I hope we will be friends always."

Draconda translated forthwith, but Mynine made not the slightest response.

Draconda's face showed her displeasure, and I saw that the poor girl noted this. Henry held out his hand to her; after glancing at her mysterious and dread queen, Mynine extended her own—the shudder that came when his hand touched hers telling more forcibly than any words could have done the awful revulsion that had come over the girl.

The blow had fallen; all her wondrous love had been metamorphosed into a frightful hate—how frightful we soon were to learn.

"After all, my Mynine," said Draconda, "there is a sweet cup beside the one that is so bitter: the Lord Quainfan and his companions did save thee from the sacrificial knife and flames."

And then it was that Mynine spoke:

"I would, O Queen, that he had been too late!"

There were no tears in her eyes now; her voice, though, was like that of a weeping woman.

Draconda went to the girl, placed a hand gently on her shoulder. At the touch, however, Mynine quivered like a leaf in the wind; hastily the queen removed her hand, looking at me with hurt eyes.

"I am very, very sorry, my Mynine," she said, "and I will do for thee whatsoever is in my power to do. Tell me, I pray thee, what thou wouldst have. And I hope, deep in my heart, that thou wilt not harbor black thoughts against me, my Mynine."

"I pray thee, O Queen, that I may depart hence. I pray thee to accept my poor thanks for thy proffered kindness, O Queen; but my life is like a tree blasted by the fire of heaven now, and I would go hence."

"But whither wilt thou go?"

"Nay—I know not, O Queen. Only do I know that I would be gone."

"Bethink thee well," said Draconda: "Here thou wilt have all that thou mayest desire; if thou go hence, I believe, then thou shalt surely die."

"Perchance, my Queen. But, pardon me, O Draconda, here I could not have aught that I desire—here I should have only pain and such an ache in the heart that death itself would be sweet. So I pray, O Queen, that I may go hence. And I thank thee for thy proffered kindness to one so unworthy—which my heart will always treasure."

"Well, do whatsoever thou wilt," said Draconda. "But I say unto thee, my Mynine, that I think thou art a fool. And—well, I did not mean in this very palace of Conderogan, if thou wouldst not so desire."

"May I go hence, O Queen?"

"Yes; thou mayest go. I have said that thou mayest do whatsoever thou wilt. But I say unto thee again, my Mynine: I think thou art a fool and that, if thou go hence, then surely shalt thou die."

Mynine made obeisance to her queen, courtesied to me; then, without even the most fleeting glance at Henry Quainfan (who had fallen asleep) the girl went, her face toward the dread Draconda until she had passed through the doorway.

I wondered if I would ever see her again, and I confess that I was a little bit afraid of Mynine.

CHAPTER 40
TO SALLYSHERIB

"Only fancy!"

So I told myself.

The queen's words, however, showed that it was not a fancy lightly to be dismissed:

"I should fear that girl, my Farnermain—were her position one of power."

"Are you sure, O Draconda, that you have nothing at all to fear?"

She laughed a little.

"Nothing! What can she do? In all likelihood, she shall be slain by the priests. I tell you, my Farnermain, I believe she is walking straight to her doom."

"But is there not perhaps some——?"

"My Farnermain, she can do nothing," Draconda interrupted lightly.

"I hope so," said I.

"Have no fear," she said, smiling.

But Draconda was mistaken.

For—as we learned some time afterwards, of course—Mynine went straight to the high priest, Sallysherib, and made such an impression on that pious gentleman that he decided she would be a good auxiliary in the prosecution of his scheme to overthrow the queen's power, destroy her and men from the stars.

And, as the issue proved, Sallysherib did not overvalue his fair confederate; indeed, how could even that son of iniquity have known the truth?

"I feel very sorry for that girl," the queen said after a pause. "It was a cruel blow, cruel indeed. What says Anac—do you know Greek, my Farnermain?"

"I have studied it."

She then quoted in the original the following lines of Anacreon's, though her Greek was not like that which I had studied:

> "Yes—loving is a painful thrill,
> And not to love more painful still;
> But oh, it is the worst of pain,
> To love and not be loved again!"

"I fancy, O Draconda, that Anacreon knew his subject."

"And to love and not be loved again sometimes causes terrible disaster, my Farnermain. However, we have nothing to fear from that girl. As I said, in all likelihood she shall be slain by the priests—mayhap before you sun enters the gates of twilight."

She went to the sleeping man and kissed him tenderly on the forehead. Then she sat down softly on the bed, putting her hand on his, a rapt, angelic look on her lovely features.

For a little time, she sat watching his face, apparently oblivious to my very existence, then looked up and blushed a little.

"My Farnermain, did he tell you? I mean about the picture, his love picture of me."

I nodded.

"Did you ever hear of anything more strange and wonderful? And I have a picture of him, too, my Farnermain. And we have met at last, after all these years—after so many ages."

"Ages?" I exclaimed.

"Even so."

"What do you mean, O Draconda?"

"That it has been a long, long time, my Farnermain. But at last we have found each other. And I am so glad."

She certainly looked it. She was a queen, the ruler of a mighty empire; and the great ones bowed down before her—and a loving woman watching her beloved as he slept.

Suddenly Princess Nytes entered, pale of face and excited. She came alone. She courtesied to me, who arose and bowed in return, and then hurried to Draconda. They held talk in low tones; several times I caught the name Ta Antom.

This woman of mystery had just killed a man—and there she sat on the bed, talking quietly, her hand on Henry Quainfan's, while the man whom, until a few hours since, she had loved was lying dead in some other room in the palace.

Of course, however, at that time I did not know that Draconda had loved Ta Antom.

And there was Morgan St. Cloud. The thought of those dead men filled me with horror.

And she took it so coolly. This somehow contributed to the horror that I felt. I wondered if she had killed any one before. Perhaps, indeed, she had slain many persons. After all, what manner of woman was this Queen Draconda of Loom? Cleopatra-like? But I soon dismissed that dark thought. For something told me that this mysterious queen, who I wished soon would issue from that mystery which enshrouded her, was a woman noble and pure.

Of course, it was obvious that Draconda and Henry Quainfan had lived and loved in some other world. But what world? And where? For thus only could be explained their love pictures of each other. This other world, no doubt, was a Paradise; and from this Paradise all human beings had been banished because of some transgression, which doubtless must be expiated in some way during this life of the flesh.

Thus we have an explanation of those wonderful and elusive feelings and visions that are aroused in the human soul at times, especially by music and more especially and powerfully by love. Some one has said that music tells us of things that we never have seen and never shall see; but I do not believe that now.

For I believe that music arouses memories of that other world, a world that was—or, rather, is—a Paradise. These memories aroused by music and love are so faint and mysterious that we do not recognize them as memories, that is all. The predominant thing in them, as everyone knows, is their wondrous and elusive beauty; never is there anything sordid in them; never can they be aroused by things sordid or terrible; and what does this prove (or indicate, if you please) if not that these visions are visions of Paradise?

It is scarcely necessary, by the way, to suggest how this belief affects our conception of love.

As has been said, I believe that for some transgression (and a terrible one it must have been) human beings have been banished to this life of the flesh and that in this life they must make themselves fit to enter again into their Paradise home, perhaps, indeed, living many lives, and on many spheres, before the day of their redemption comes; and I believe that their redemption must be won—as, indeed, every redemption must be—through goodly deed and through love.

But to return.

At length Draconda said:

"I have told Nytes all. And I must go now, my Farnermain, as there are some important matters waiting. And probably more important ones forthcoming."

She looked at me curiously for a few moments.

"My Farnermain," she began, "would you mind—?"

"I would be glad, O Draconda."

"One of your revolvers," she said.

"Great heavens!" I exclaimed. "Is it like that?"

She nodded.

"Probably worse."

I began unbuckling one of the belts—not thinking that it was St. Cloud's.

"You came well-armed," Draconda observed.

"Yes. And yet not so well either, One of these—this one was Morgan's."

Her brows drew together.

"*Yours,* please, my Farnermain," she said.

Accordingly I removed the other belt, and in a few moments it was enzoning Draconda's waist.

"I shall keep it concealed—so," she said.

"It seems, O Draconda, that Trouble came with us, and in terrible guise."

"My Farnermain," she smiled, "don't be myopic!"

She bent and softly kissed Henry on the forehead, then turned to go; but, as she turned, her eyes fell on the blood-stained place of the struggle and the resultant tragedy, and she stopped.

"Those stains must be removed at once," she said. "I forgot them."

Then she and the princess quitted the room.

In a few minutes, a couple of men entered and began to remove the blood stains and the other marks of the struggle.

And, as I watched them working, noiseless almost as shadows, some freak of memory brought these words of Southey's to mind:

"Thou hast been busy, Death, this day, and yet
But half thy work is done!"

CHAPTER 41
ANOTHER MYSTERY

Darkness lay upon the palace of Conderogan when Henry Quainfan awoke.

"How late, Rider?" he asked.

"Dark about two hours. How's the fin?"

"Darned sore. So I fell asleep? Kind of—well, effeminate, eh? But—what happened?"

"Mynine went."

"Where?"

I shrugged my shoulders.

"Don't know."

"They'll probably kill her!" he exclaimed.

"That's what Draconda told her; but the girl wouldn't listen to reason."

Henry groaned in wretchedness of spirit.

"What a brute I've been, Rider!" he burst out. "Mynine believes that I lied—lied and acted like a mongrel. And how can you blame her for thinking that very thing?"

"Forget that," I told him, "How—?"

"You know well enough, Rider, that I never can forget it—that my manhood lies besmirched."

"You've hitched your fancy to a kite," I said—though full well did I know that he never could forget.

He was sitting on the edge of the bed now, bracing himself up with his right arm.

"Deucedly weak, Rider," said he. "Must have lost a deal of blood, or spirit, or something. However, to return to Mynine: you know, I should—"

"Stop it! Or, if you must indulge in reproach, let it be against the lady that deserves it."

"Who's that?" he demanded. "Not Draconda, certainly. And Mynine, poor girl—"

"I don't mean Draconda or Mynine: I mean Fate."

"Poor Fate!" he murmured. "What crimes they commit in your name!"

He sat staring at the carpet, his head sinking forward.

"I'll sound the alarm," said I, "for something to eat."

"No. I want nothing—only a drink of water. You know, my head feels like a collapsed balloon."

In a few minutes, he lay down and, rather to my surprise, was soon asleep once more.

In the meantime, I had seen much of Queen Draconda and had had much talk with her, which had enhanced the mystery of this extraordinary woman and revealed her marvelous intellectual possessions and powers. Her mathesis was, without exaggeration, simply amazing. Never had I dreamed that intellectual acquisitions so diverse or so gigantic could be found in one so young.

Also—and this puzzled me in a way of which I could give no adequate conception—there was a certain *maturity* in her thoughts, a cynicism even, that surprised me in a way as vague as it was disturbing. I thought I was prepared for anything, quite beyond surprise now; but, when I remarked on this cynical quality, it led to something that amazed me exceedingly, as I think it will the reader also.

"So you do not understand this cynicism, as you call it, my Farnermain?"

"No; it strikes me as strange that one so young should find that bitterness in the cup."

"Young!" she exclaimed.

And she laughed a little mysterious laugh.

"We become cynical, my Farnermain," she went on, "when many years and the bitter experience of many years are ours. And, indeed, what is cynicism but a name for an unpleasant kind of truth?"

"I do not understand, O Draconda: what can many years have to do with *your* cynicism?"

"Many years have done it, my Farnermain," she smiled, "many years and experiences many and terrible. I know this sounds absurd to you; but it is a solemn fact. Now, how many years do you think I have seen? I mean, of course, terrestrial years, not Venusian."

"Twenty-five."

Again that mysterious smile.

"You said so, O Draconda!"

She shook her head.

"No, my Farnermain; I did not say solemn fact. Now, how many years do—"

"What?" I cried.

"I did not say that, my Farnermain," she laughed.

Good heavens, there was another one!

"You said that you had seen but three lustrums when Mayto was brought before you condemned," said I, not a little bewildered, "and that ten years, ten terrestrial years, have passed since then. That surely makes twenty-five years—unless, indeed, you meant Venusian lustrums, which would make you even younger. But surely you meant terrestrial ones."

She nodded.

"I meant terrestrial lustra."

"But, good heavens, O Draconda, twenty-five years are not many years!"

She laughed softly, her laughter the music of falling waters.

The princess was watching us intently, a plaintive look on her lovely face.

"Of a surety twenty-five years are not many years," said the queen. "But I have seen more, many more. In all likelihood, this will seem an utter absurdity to you, my Farnermain, but I have seen—"

"Good heavens, O Draconda," I broke in, "what—?"

And there I stopped, and I stared.

"My Farnermain," she laughed, "I have seen five times twenty-five years! One hundred and twenty-five years have I seen! Think you not, my Farnermain, that *that* is many years?"

"I should say it is!"

She leaned back, laughing, and looked at me whimsically. Good heavens, there it was again! A hundred and twenty-five years old! And she was in the first flush of mature beauty! Two lustra since, she was fifteen years of age, and now she was one hundred and twenty-five! Ye gods and starfishes! That certainly was going some! Perhaps she had used a round number for convenience and was even a little older. One hundred and twenty-five years of age! And ten years before, she was but fifteen!

Draconda, who was hugely enjoying my mystification, broke the silence, saying:

"Well, my Farnermain, who do stare as though there was something unearthly before your eyes—well, my Farnermain, what do you think?"

"Nothing," said I, "nothing at all, O Draconda. I have discarded that function as useless."

She laughed a little.

"Do you think that I am a fibber?" she teased.

"O Draconda," I exclaimed, "why do you fool me thus? How in the name of Reason can you, who are in the first full bloom of womanhood's flower, be one hundred and twenty-five years of age? It is absurd—utter nonsense—moonshine in daylight. Why do you befool me thus, O Draconda?"

"Pardon me, my Farnermain," she said sweetly, "but I did not say that I am one hundred and twenty-five years of age."

"What?" I cried.

She laughed.

"I did not say that I am one hundred and twenty-five years of age."

"Good heavens," said I, "what did you say then?"

"I did not say that, my Farnermain: I am but twenty-five—twenty-five terrestrial years, forty Venusian."

I was amazed, astounded. Draconda looked at me roguishly from under her lowered lashes for a little space, then burst into sudden and rippling laughter.

"You looked so funny!" she said.

"Funny? Is it any wonder that I looked funny? Your age is one hundred and twenty-five years, and yet you are only twenty-five years old! About as rational, that, as the old belief that the Universe was created in six days and yet in an instant of time."

"And how do you know, my Farnermain," said she, "that six days are any longer than an instant of time? Infinity of time and space there must be. Nothing can annihilate either time or space. Indeed, are they not one and the same? In order to annihilate them, nothing would have to be created, and nothing simply cannot be. For, on the instant of creation, it would be *something*, would it not? What think you, my Farnermain?"

"That that, O Draconda, is a mystery unsolvable."

"And," she went on, "since time is infinite, how can one part of it be any greater than any other part or less than the whole?"

"It cannot be," said I, "if time is infinite; and then those old priests were right. But that is only an assumption; in the nature of things, it cannot be anything else. How can time be infinite? If it is, then the Almighty is not, and it is unutterably absurd, O Draconda, to think that God is finite. How could the Infinite create another infinity? The moment it came into being, God would lose His infinity, and, of course, the created *infinity* would be finite, for it would not be Omnipotence, and, in order to be infinite, it would have to be everything. If the Infinity created another infinity, then all infinity would be destroyed, and it is absurd to suppose for an instant that infinity can be annihilated."

Draconda laughed.

"Then how, my Farnermain—and watch your words—can God create a finite? And remember, if He can't, then He is not all-powerful."

"O Draconda, why ask the unanswerable?"

"No answer, my Farnermain!" she smiled, uplifting a finger.

"Of course not: one cannot answer the unanswerable."

"But," said she, "if the Almighty were to create a finite, He too would be finite, for He would not be that created finite, and if the Almighty were not, how could He be infinite? Either infinity or its antithesis must be. Both cannot. There is no such thing as finite, my Farnermain: only infinity is. And what have you to say against that?"

"Preposterous!" I cried.

Again the silver of her laughter.

"From your own words, my Farnermain, I have asked it! But—let us not pursue the matter farther now. To return. I shall stop with the statement that I have seen one hundred and twenty-five years and yet am but twenty-five years of age—for, it seems, that will give you enough to think about for some time."

"I should say it will!"

"Do you think that I am fibbing?"

"That you are fooling, O Draconda."

"My Farnermain," she said with a tone of seriousness that had not been in her voice, though her eyes and lips remained smiling, "I am not befooling you—really I am not! What I have said is the truth, the whole truth and nothing but the truth: I was born in this very city of Loom, in this very Palace of Conderogan, and that was twenty-five years ago, and so I am but twenty-five years of age! How could I be any older? Now—"

"But—" I struck in.

"Oh, you big goose," she laughed, "stop butting and do some thinking!"

"What's the use?" I wailed. "What's the use of even trying to think?"

"My Farnermain," she said seriously, "can you not see how what I have uttered can be divested of its seeming absurdity? For I assure you it is no more than that."

I shook my head.

"Won't you explain, O Draconda?"

"In due season," she smiled. "I must go now. And I pray you to ponder on the *absurdities* that I have uttered, to seek the key that will unlock the mystery. I tell you, the human mind is one of the blindest of all things created, what with its prison walls of the flesh.

"You, my Farnermain, put all your faith in those beliefs and thought processes that the wise ones have declared infallible, and thus you do not see (who should long ago have seen) and think that the darkness which is in your own brain is gibberish uttered by me.

"Your mind, my Farnermain, is like an eagle with its wings weighted down—though it is not your fault at all. But strive to cast off those weights, my Farnermain, which are but the blunders of divers flesh-entombed souls, and thus let your mind soar up to the wonder heights, even as the free-pinioned eagle soars."

But I shook my head, feeling certain that it would be futile to try to discover in her gibberish anything save gibberish.

"Well, I must go now," she said, smiling at my mystification.

Then, with the princess, she quitted the room, saying with a little laugh as she vanished:

"Think hard, O Farnermain."

For a little space, I stared at the curtains through which this extraordinary creature had vanished, then began to walk back and forth, my feet falling noiselessly on the rich carpet.

Think! I did think, but I could not make out anything rational.

She was born on Venus, had passed all her life on Venus, and yet she had known Morgan St. Cloud on the earth! She had seen one hundred and twenty-five years, and yet she was but twenty-five years of age!

That, to use a phrase of Natty Bumppo's, certainly was a "nonplusser."

CHAPTER 42
DRACONDA EXPLAINS

The next day St. Cloud was borne to his sepulcher—rock-hewn, in that mountain range whence we had first seen Conderogan. Shortly afterward, however, the desecrating body of our unfortunate companion (at the instigation of Sallysherib) was taken from its vault, and the place of his sepulcher is now unknown—probably, I have always thought, the blue waters of the Uava.

The great sun was setting when Henry and I stepped ashore at Conderogan, flooding sky, earth and water with a beauty that Turner himself never even dreamed.

At length (darkness had now fallen) we issued from our chambers and directed our steps toward that apartment into which Draconda had conducted us on our arrival—and from which we had gone to witness that awful meeting with St. Cloud.

As we drew near, we heard Draconda singing, accompanying her song on a guitar-like instrument. The words were in Greek, their burden:

> "Sorrow, sing a hymn for me
> That shall only joyful be."

We paused, waited till the last golden note had died away. As we moved forward, came the clang of steel as the guards grounded their weapons, and a word or two to announce our coming. Each guard stretched forth a hand, grasped his curtain and drew it, and in a moment we were in the queen's presence.

The princess was there, and old Mayto.

Draconda's eyes lingered on her lover.

"You are fatigued, my Henry," she observed, with some solicitude. "I said you ought not go."

"'Tis nothing, Draconda," he returned. "And this remains: no matter what his evil, yet Morgan, was our companion in hours, in days, in an adventure never to be forgotten; and memory and comradeship called me to his tomb."

The queen was silent for a space. She had laid aside her guitar. Her chin was resting on her palm, her brows slightly drawn together, and her eyes fixed on Henry Quainfan's face in a look of curious intensity.

"Let the dead past bury its dead," said Draconda.

A little silence.

"It seems," Henry returned, somewhat irrelevantly I thought at first, "that Poe had a legion of Truth marching under his awful banner:

> "'And the angels, all pallid and wan,
>   Uprising, unveiling, affirm
> That the play is the tragedy, "Man,"
>   And its Hero the Conqueror Worm.'"

The dark eyes of Draconda seemed to smile mournfully—and yet, strangely enough, they seemed to remain unchanged.

"Yet he had another banner," she said, "one radiant, iridescent, ineffable. How do you explain the legion marching under the banner of Love? that sweetest, perhaps, of all love poems?—

> "'And neither the angels in heaven above,
>   Nor the demons down under the sea,
> Can ever dissever my soul from the soul
>   Of the beautiful Annabel Lee.'"

"What's the explanation, my Henry? Dreams— only dreams? And those rainbow glimpses of things cosmic and spiritual in *The Power of Words* and *The Colloquy of Monos and Una*? The explanation, my Henry? Only dreams?"

"That *was* my explanation, Draconda."

"And now?"

"Now I do not know," he said.

She smiled wanly, with a curious spiritual sadness.

"'Twas thus you explained your picture of me," she said, "and alas, I my soul vision of you—even I, who should have known!"

He looked at her inquiringly.

"How so, Draconda?"

There was a swift change: she suddenly drew herself erect, the thought shadows vanishing from her eyes and features.

"'*Come!*'" she said in a thrilling voice, "'*we will leave to the left the loud harmony of the Pleiades, and swoop outward from the throne into the starry meadows beyond Orion, where, for pansies and violets, and heart's-ease, are the beds of the triplicate and triple-tinted suns.*'"

"I follow," said Henry Quainfan.

Her lips severed for speech, then suddenly broke into one of her wondrous smiles as she sent a roguish glance in my direction, a glance that seemed to say:

"Now, my Farnermain, you get yours!"

At any rate, I did!

Explain? Draconda did explain. At the beginning, I felt confident, in spite of her air of certitude, that she could neither undo nor cut this Gordian knot which her tongue had tied. But she did. And her anacalypsis brought a sharp realization of the curious impedimenta under which our flesh-enshrouded spirits march along toward the terrible-wondrous Gates of Destiny.

Science, who has destroyed so many of our cherished superstitions (and, I fear, some things that were not superstitions), would destroy, too, the belief in anything *supernatural;* and thus, under the influence of her materialistic teaching (more or less unconsciously, that is), we often pronounce the unexplicable an hallucination or a hocus-pocus—and think we have delivered a crushing refutation.

Now, it is scarcely necessary to remark, I am not, and never have been, scientific. On the other hand, though, I have never been a believer in those phenomena, noumena and so on that must be called either hallucinations or things supernatural—in other words, I simply regarded such things as hallucinations and let it go at that.

And so, in spite of all the amazing things we had heard or seen, I had not entertained the idea that there might be something supernatural about this mysterious Draconda.

"Of course, it is obvious," she said, after a meditative pause, "that I have been on the earth; indeed, I said so. And yet, when I told you I was born on this planet, in this very palace of Conderogan, and that I never had dreamed that that awful interplanetary abysm could be crossed by mortal men (and, of course, I meant women too) I spoke the truth—paradoxical, absurd though it may seem to you.

> "'There are more things in heaven and earth, Horatio,
> Than are dreamt of in your philosophy.'"

Here she paused, looking at us whimsically. Henry and I, however, merely gave each other a bepuzzled glance—said nothing.

"Yes, my Henry and my Farnermain," nodding her head prettily, "when I said that, I gave the truth. And yet—"

Again she paused.

"And yet?" I suggested.

"And yet," Draconda told us, "I did not say I never had dreamed that that terrible intermundane gap could be crossed by men!"

"What!" I exclaimed.

There was another one!

She laughed.

"You are making it worse and worse, Draconda," said Henry Quainfan. "Instead of explaining the matter, you are enhancing our bewilderment."

Draconda smiled at him with whimsical, love-touched eyes.

Suddenly she turned her look to me.

"Well, my Farnermain," she queried sweetly, "what think you?"

"In Heaven's name, Draconda, what did you say if it was not that?"

"Well, Farnermain the Myopic," she laughed musically, "you tell me what I said. Bethink you well."

I spent perhaps a minute in careful recollection but could not find anything that changed the matter in the least, and then I spoke:

"You said, O Draconda, you never had dreamed that the gap between Terra and Venus could be crossed by men."

"You are sure?" she asked.

"Sure!" I returned.

"You are in error, my Farnermain," she smiled. "I did not say that."

I stared at her dumbfounded.

"My Farnermain, you should pay more attention. And you too, Henry. But perhaps you know. What was it I said?"

"I do not know, Draconda. I thought it was what Rider said. But I am not sure. I must have let some little thing escape—an adjective or something like that. I think you are bewildering us with a play on words. What I am beginning to think, Draconda, is this: There must be something supernatural about you."

"At last!" she exclaimed. "Of course, though, that is only one of those many words under which man hides his ignorance."

"Just so," Henry nodded.

"And yet," after a brief pause, "you have not the key that will unlock the mystery?"

Henry Quainfan shook his head.

"I said *mortal* men," Draconda explained.

"Oh!" exclaimed Henry.

"Plain, my Farnermain?" she queried.

"As two and two make twenty-two."

"I thought so," she smiled.

"O Draconda," I asked, "aren't mortal men men?"

She laughed.

"Of a surety they are men. How could they not be men?"

"And yet you said—"

Here I broke off speaking, for a sudden thought had come to me—a thought that seemed to explain everything. And yet it had come before, but I had dismissed it without a second thought.

"I see!" cried Henry Quainfan. "I see it all now!"

"So do I," I said; "at any rate, I think I do. It seems—no, it must be. You came, O Draconda, not as a mortal woman but in the spirit. In other words—though the thing seems incredible—you lived on the earth, died there and were born again on Venus; and, in some way, the memory of your terrestrial life was not blotted out—or, rather, the memory of your terrestrial lives."

"Wonderful, wonderful!" she cried, clapping her hands.

"Then that is it?" I said.

"Of a surety it is."

"Why didn't I think of that before?" said Henry Quainfan. "I am sorry, Draconda, that I thought—"

"Hush," she said. "Hush."

Just think of it—here we were talking with a woman who had been dead!

And this certainly was not her first reincarnation, for it left one hundred terrestrial years to be accounted for, and that century undoubtedly had not been lived in a single life.

In all likelihood, she had known two or three, or more, lives on the earth. Perhaps she had lived in the time of Helen of Troy. Mayhap she had seen Helen—indeed, had been Helen. And perhaps she had lived in the time of Moses, of Cleopatra, of Christ—had seen the Savior bleeding on Calvary. She had, mayhap, lived in the time of Cheops, or wandered on the banks of the Nile in that far time when the first of the pharaohs was. Perchance she had been a prehistoric woman—a troglodyte of the Pleistocene.

Well, for that matter, so perhaps had I!

"Then," Henry Quainfan said, "when Morgan exclaimed, 'I saw you—with my own eyes I saw you—' he meant that he had seen you interred."

"I suppose so," Draconda nodded. "That must have been what he meant, for I know nothing of what happened after death. I then was in a dreamless sleep, was nothing, as it were, and in the black profundity of nothing—and, when I awoke, I was here, on the glorious planet Ishtar."

"You lived in Babylonia?" Henry said.

Draconda nodded.

"Of course," she went on, "I had no means of discovering how long I had been sleeping. Why, or how, my slumbering spirit left the earth and came through those icy deeps of space to the Planet of Love, I, of course, do not know. Nor can I ever know—at least while the flesh imprisons me in, or that darkness is which comes when the spirit leaves the flesh. Perhaps, though, on a day it will be known, for I do believe that we shall some time live in Paradise world (to use that phrase for want of a better one) and there mayhap we shall see those things now involved in the profundity of darkness and mystery.

"From that Paradise, or spirit, world—where nothing sordid is—I believe we have been banished for a time, undoubtedly because of some sin committed; and I believe that memories of that old home linger in our souls, though very few regard them as such—memories aroused by grand scenery, music and love. And, when the day of our redemption comes, then perchance we shall learn (or remember) that for which we were banished to the flesh and the gross things thereof and that blackness which men call death.

"How full must the starry spaces be of ghosts—not the ghosts that dwell in superstitious minds but the slumbering souls of humans! And how glorious must be their long-lost home, that home in which some day they will dwell again!"

She fell silent—that strange expression I have spoken of now strong on her features. It was there always, even when she smiled her quick and wondrous smile, though at such times it did but lurk in the background, as it were.

A hundred and twenty-five years of life! What she must have gone through in that century and a quarter! What deep acquaintance she must have made with passion and sorrow—what terrible memories must haunt her hours!

"You know," said Draconda, "in myths and things mystical much truth lies hidden. But long ages, misunderstanding, ignorance and what not have done their work only too well. For instance, there is that strange mystery of the Pleiades: why has this group of stars, in many lands, from the Euphrates to the Andes, and during the course of long ages, exercised so powerful a mystical and religious influence over the fancies and hearts of mankind? Indeed, that influence has been felt even in the halls of Science: for what was it, if not this very thing, that led Maedler to assign to Alcyone the magnitude and glory of the Central Sun?

>"'Canst thou bind the sweet influence of Pleiades, or loose the bands of Orion?'

"But—what I had in mind is the sacred number seven. Who, now, can unlock the mystery of that?"

"And who," queried Henry Quainfan, "the mystery of the number four—the mystic number among the Indians of America?"

"Not I," said Draconda. "But to return."

>"'Moreover the light of the moon shall be as the light of the sun, and the light of the sun shall be sevenfold, as the light of seven days, in the day that the Lord bindeth up the breach of his people, and healeth the stroke of their wound.'

"Now, there are seven days in the week, the wonders of the ancient world were seven, Rome was built on seven hills, the Apocalypse is a book of sevens, there were seven wise men, seven champions of Christendom, seven stars in the Pleiades—"

"But, in reality," observed Henry, "as photography has shown, there are over *two thousand!*"

"And the Egyptians," Draconda returned quickly, "called the Pleiades *chooa*—which means *thousands!* How, my Henry, do you explain that?"

He glanced in my direction.

"Our old friend Nisroch again, Rider," he smiled.

"Just so," Draconda said. "And how did those men of old time know that the planet Saturn is ringed?"

"Did they really know it, Draconda?"

"Yes."

"Then Proctor was right: they had telescopes!"

"And why not?" she smiled. "For remember that, after the light and science of the ancient world—after the glory that was Greece and the grandeur that was Rome—came the ignorance and terror of the Dark Ages: and that was not the first time the light of intellect and imagination was quenched in impenetrable darkness and mystery.

"Old, old is the world, old or ever the great ice sheets (another unfathomable enigma to the scientists of earth) came creeping southward. Yes, old the world, and countless the prehistoric Ninevehs and Babylons engulfed in the sands of the ages.

"But that mystic seven: What significance it may have, I shall not presume to say, but my lives on the planet earth were just seven—the first in some prehistoric age (ere Sirius had fled across to the western border of the Galaxy), the last in the nineteenth century in the city of New York, where I met Morgan St. Cloud."

Henry Quainfan made an exclamation.

"Sirius on the eastern border of the Milky Way!"

"Just so," Draconda nodded. "There can be no shadow of uncertainty about it, for in that land, as in Egypt and elsewhere, Sirius (and the Pleiades) was worshipped—great temples built in his honor. Yes, thousands of years ago it was when I first saw his silvery beams—how many thousand, who can say?"

"Who indeed?" echoed Henry Quainfan. "The star's proper motion, though, shows that sixty thousand years have passed since it shone on the eastern border of the Galaxy!"

Draconda smiled a little.

"I rather antedated Adam, didn't I?"

"Slightly," he nodded.

"And this," said the queen, "brings us to an instance of that truth I have spoken of hidden in myths, for the Chaldeans had a story founded on this very journey of Sirius across the Galactic belt—with which story, as given by Al-Sufi, you are doubtless familiar."

"Yes," Henry nodded, "Canopus murdered his wife, Rigel, and fled away to the southward to escape the vengeance of the pursuing Al-abu—Sirius, his sister."[10]

"But, Draconda: that land where you first saw the Dog Star and the light of the sun?"

Draconda shook her head.

"I do not know. From the height of the pole-star there—Alpha Cephei—the place was twenty degrees or so from the equator: more than that I cannot say."

"Yucatan or Mexico, perhaps," I suggested.

"No," she smiled; "our style of architecture, for one thing, was different."

"By the way, Draconda," Henry queried, "in any of these lives, were you married?"

The dimples rushed into her cheeks.

"Strange to say, my Henry," she laughed, "not once! But—"

"Yes?" said he.

"I was in love—well, more than once."

"With Morgan St. Cloud?" he asked bluntly.

Draconda's dark eyes met his with a curious half-smiling, half-mournful expression.

"Yes," she said. "But mark this: in all my loves, from that of the girl Draconda (for Draconda was my name then, and I fancy before that, even) who so long ago beheld the blazing glory that is Sirius to the love of Draconda the Venusian for Ta Antom—"

"Great Heaven," he broke in, "did you love that man?"

"I did, my Henry. But listen: in all those loves of mine, my heart was sad and

---

10. "Possibly the Arabian story may be based on a tradition of Sirius having been seen on the opposite side of the Milky Way by the men of the Stone Age."—*Gore Astronomical Essays*, page 22.

troubled; that was because I had not found you, my dream one, dearest of men. For I thought that you were only—*an ideal!*

"And in this, alas, how many women are Dracondas!"

"Ah!" I exclaimed, for (as they say) a great light had burst upon me.

"But," I added, "unlike you, O Draconda, they have no visions—yes, visions, but no pictures of those who come to them—for they come as shadows in dreams."

"Just so," she nodded; "only visions and memories, dim and uncertain, dusky as those moonbeams which, to the temples of lost Atlantis, struggle down through the gloom of the sea."

She was silent for a while, a curious, dreamy expression in her eyes.

"Of the seven Dracondas," she went on suddenly, "who yet were one and the same being; of that Draconda of the prehistoric age; of that girl who knew the Euphrates before, and she who knew it after, the walls of Babylon rose on high—of these Dracondas, and all the others, I shall tell you, and fully, some other time. No, not today.

"But there is one of whom I should tell you know—Morgan St. Cloud.

"The story, though, shall be brief—as the terrible always should be.

"I was then that Blanche of whom you heard him speak; only a girl, and he came—a man to catch any woman's fancy, handsome and charming and debonair. And not only that: the intellectual attainments of Morgan St. Cloud heralded (so I thought, and so, indeed, I still think) a conspicuous, if not commanding, position in certain branches of the sciences and of discovery. But there was another Morgan St. Cloud, one as yet unknown to me—that Morgan St. Cloud who gained the ascendancy, blasted a life which should have been one verdant with achievement, happiness and fame.

"By a curious coincidence, among those studies in which he was deeply interested at the time of our meeting was Assyriology—"

"Strange!" was my involuntary ejaculation.

Draconda turned her eyes upon me with a curious expression in their somber depths.

"How so, my Farnermain?" she asked.

"Once, and only once," I made answer, "I appealed to him for guidance through some dark Babylonian labyrinth of myth, theology and science: never shall I forget that look which rushed across his face when I lay the book before him and pointed out the puzzling passage—that sudden, impetuous, *insensate* way in which he thrust the volume from him across the table. On the instant, however, he collected himself and asked pardon—explained that, when it came to any of the phases of Assyriology, his knowledge was virtually nil."

The queen smiled wanly.

"It was, in fact, my Farnermain, profound!"

"Then why his profession of ignorance?"

"Alas, my Farnermain, who can tell in what strange way Guilt may strike whom she has in bondage?"

"I have spoken of Morgan St. Cloud's interest in Assyriology as a coincidence. And so it was. For at that very time I was deeply occupied in preparing myself for as thorough an exposition of that science as possible to one who had seen the very hand of the sculptor at work on the monuments. How scholars would have stared and rubbed their eyes! For, with all due respect to our Rawlinsons and Grotefends—with their Sumerian theories, homophonies, polyphonies, poly-idiographies, and so on—despite all their admirable, their great achievements, Assyriology yet bears a closer resemblance to that melancholy ruin called Birs Nimrud than to the wondrous Euriminanki (known to the Hebrews as the Tower of Babel) which, in that spot now so deserted and silent, aspired to the very glories of heaven.

"That Morgan St. Cloud was astonished, astounded, easily can be imagined. But I did not reach forth to him the key to the mystery.

"However, let me hasten to the end.

"As I have told you, I loved Morgan St. Cloud—I was even betrothed to him. Fortunately, however, his other self was revealed; there is no occasion to dwell on particulars; suffice it to say that the iridescent veil was rent asunder and I saw the terrible truth.

"However, not a little to my surprise, he showed no resentment—was as charming and devoted, at our now infrequent meetings, as ever he had been in our happiest hours. Had it not been for my experience in life (which experience I may call one deep and troubled) my heart doubtless would have been softened toward him. But, even as it was, I never dreamed of that thing which he had in mind.

"The opportunity for which he was biding his time soon presented itself— at an informal archery meet. It so chanced (and yet it was not chance after all) that we at length found ourselves, he and I, alone beneath the great and gnarled branches of the oaks. And there it was that he did the deed.

"I had stooped for one of my arrows. Why it was I do not know; but, in some way—that which man in ignorance calls the sixth sense—I suddenly became aware of danger, terrible, impending. I looked up, and screamed. For there was Morgan St. Cloud with his arrow to the head and my heart the target.

"He was momentarily disconcerted. But, with a terrible exclamation, he loosed, and the bolt struck me full in the throat, flinging me to the turf in the agonies of death.

"Then he began calling wildly for help. An utter blackness blotted things out. When it cleared away (for a few moments only) I found myself in my mother's arms; heard, as the numbness of death stole over my senses, the voice of Morgan St. Cloud, in grief-stricken tones, explaining how—*his arrow had glanced from one of the tree-trunks and, thus deflected, struck me down!*"

CHAPTER 43
WAR

The day following, disturbing intelligence reached the queen: his pontifical highness, Sallysherib (whom we had not seen since our arrival at Conderogan), had left for the city of Secamnos, about ninety miles north of Loom and on the farther side of a beautiful, though shaggy, range of mountains.

"I expected something of the kind," said Draconda.

"And the meaning?" queried Henry Quainfan.

"Trouble," she returned, "war perhaps, for in all likelihood he is plotting an insurrection. That he is plotting something I know: what, the near future will tell us."

"But isn't there anything you could do to forestall his plot, whatever that may be?"

"Nothing. Nothing can I do to Sallysherib. His arms are the most terrible of weapons; they are invisible, strike like a bolt from the blue. Well, I also have my arms and my friends—friends even in the temple of Sallysherib, perhaps."

"Why not risk it?" I suggested.

"Risk what, my Farnermain?"

"Why, seize Mr. Sally, and explain things afterward."

She smiled a little.

"You forget, my Farnermain: you are on Loom; and, if you knew—if I were to do that—no, I cannot do that. It is simply out of the question."

"I was thinking—" began Henry Quainfan.

Draconda looked at him inquiringly.

"Yes?" she suggested.

"Since the queen, any member of the royal house, I believe you said, can be married by no one but Sallysherib himself, then we can't be wedded unless—"

"He comes back," said Draconda.

"But if he doesn't?"

"Then there will be war—war!"

"In that case, Draconda—well, can you find a way out of the difficulty?"

"Nay—alas, no!" sighed the queen. "If Sallysherib does not return, we shall be married—if we win."

"And if we don't?"

"Then we shall die unwedded," said Draconda.

Followed a few days of troubled expectancy on our part (and in all likelihood Draconda's) but nothing happened—that is, until the fifth day after the intelligence that Sallysherib had hied himself northward reached the queen.

Doubtless the Venusians sensed the first gusts of that impending storm, but to eyes such as Henry Quainfan's and my own, the waters of life about us lay enshadowed or asparkle in their wonted hues and placidity.

"You know," said Henry, "I was just thinking (and the thought is one to appall) of the infinite interdependence of events."

"Anan?" said I rather languidly, for I confess that wasn't what I was thinking about.

"The infinite interdependence of events, Mr. Bumppo," he repeated sweetly.

"In other words—?"

"In other words, even the minutest event, the most insignificant of acts sends its pulsations, so to speak, to the remotest star."

"Great Zeus!" I exclaimed, sitting up and staring at him. "Say, come down to earth."

"There you go, Rider! 'Down to earth!' There it is, the whole miserable story, in a nutshell. That's just what the matter is: man keeps his nose down to earth—like a pig. Yes, 'tis so—like a grunting porker. He has grunted and rooted the earth long enough: 'tis time he looked overhead."

"Not if it's to see what, right now, you are seeing!"

I made a sudden sweep with my hand.

"There! Watch, and you'll see Sirius rock in his orbit!"

He smiled a little at this conceit of mine.

"Hopeless, Rider; hopeless. All the same what I have said is physical truth. Why, there is your favorite, Poe:

"'You are,' he says, 'well aware that, as no thought can perish, so no act is without infinite result.'"

"Fine!" I exclaimed. "That is, in the way that Poe meant it—not as an expression of physical fact."

"He never wrote lines more true, Rider. Listen:

"'We moved our hands, for example, when we were dwellers on the earth, and, in so doing, we gave vibration to the atmosphere which engirdled it. This vibration was indefinitely extended, till it gave impulse to every particle of the earth's air, which thenceforth, *and for ever,* was actuated by the one movement of the hand.'"

"Superfine!" I told him. "You'll be introducing me to the Lady Ligeia next!"

"Well, then, if you won't believe either Poe or myself, possibly you'll believe one of the soundest thinkers and mathematicians of the age:

"'In fact, if we consider the matter attentively, we see that there cannot be a single atom throughout space which could have attained its present exact position and state, had the history of any part of the universe, however insignificant, been otherwise than it has actually been, in even the minutest degree.'

"Again:

"'But in reality it is only because our conceptions are finite that we thus look forward to an end even as we seek to trace events back to a beginning.'

"And yet again:

"'If a grain of sand contains in its state, figure, and position, the picture of the universe as it is, and the whole history of the universe throughout the infinite past—and who can doubt that this is so?—it contains with equal completeness the history of the universe throughout the infinite future. No other view is compatible with the assumption of the Almighty's infinite wisdom, and no assumption which limits the wisdom of God is compatible with our belief that He is supreme in the universe.'"

"This is all very profound and, in its way, interesting," said I; "but here is the point: what is it all about?"

"It came to me, Rider, as I sat thinking of the awful things we may see here, for Draconda, though she does not dilate on the subject, greatly fears, I know, terrible turmoil and the horrors of war. I was thinking of that, running back along the series of episodes and events which led up to the present momentous situation—back to that insignificant, *accidental* beginning. For, as you know, it was an accident (that is, what we in our ignorance call such) which led me on to the great discovery.

"But why stop at that so-called beginning? Why not go on—back, through a million-million ramifications of thought, passion and matter, to *the* beginning, if ever there was one!—back to, and beyond, certain atoms in that nebulous cloud from which the sun and his planets, and ourselves, evolved?"

"Come back to earth!" said I. "Yes, sir, to earth. For, if Mars tramples the Loomians underfoot, you won't have to go back, for the cause of his wrath, to any atoms, or configuration of atoms, in the fire-mist of La Place. You won't have to go beyond a certain conglomeration of atoms right here on this planet— a conglomeration two-legged and bald-headed."

"Sallysherib."

"Sallysherib—yes. And Mynine too, may Beelzebub bless her soul!"

"Don't be too hard on poor Mynine, Rider. After all, now, what has she done—except go to Sallysherib?"

"Great heavens, isn't that enough! She hasn't started yet: you mark my word on that. Just forget your atoms, your nebulas, your infinite interdependence of events, and all the rest of it, and keep a sharp lookout in Mynine's direction. Unless I am greatly mistaken, you'll not have long to wait."

Nor did he.

For on the very day following, as Nytes was returning to Conderogan from the gardens of Ulinis, a mob headed by Mynine attacked the little party, killing or wounding every one save Nytes, who was taken captive.

Instantly the mob vanished; and, though every effort was made to apprehend the perpetrators of the dastardly deed, no trace of the princess or her captors was discovered.

CHAPTER 44
WE SEE NYTES

Seven days after the capture of the princess, an army of insurrectionists attacked the little city of Noto, just this side of the aforementioned mountain range, which is called the Secamnos. The insurrectionists were repulsed after fierce fighting; the commander was for departing. This was Mynine's opportunity: she opposed the commander, won the army to her and at its head, as fearless as a lioness, attacked and captured Noto, putting every man, woman and child to the sword. The city she destroyed with fire.

Draconda hurried troops to the place, and Mynine, after destroying several towns and laying waste the country, took her little army up the range, coming to bay in the Untes Pass.

When he had received a reinforcement, the queen's general, whose name was Soto, attacked the enemy, but he was repulsed, and with fearful losses, Soto himself being amongst the slain.

Then occurred the battle of Tyno. Had Fortune favored the queen's army, the insurrection would have been crushed then and there. And—terrible thought!—the army of the queen would have been victorious had we been five minutes or so later in arriving at that cursed temple of Teenemtos.

On hearing that a great battle was imminent, Mynine left the Untes (though her army held the place) and hurried toward the spot of the impending struggle.

When she reached the field of battle, the insurrectionists were in full and disastrous flight. But Mynine's remarkable military genius turned this defeat into a victory—turned what would have been for the queen a crushing triumph into an awful rout. Draconda's army was all but annihilated.

This sudden victory placed Mynine—a mere slip of a girl—generalissima of the insurrectionist armies.

She did not pause but wheeled about and struck straight for Reetam, a walled city about twenty miles to the north of Tyno: this place she captured, putting every man, woman and child to the sword.

And now I come to Tigras—the queen's brother. This prince, eight years (Venusian) younger than Draconda, commanded an army on the northwestern borders of Loom, whether he had advanced against those semibarbarous and ferocious tribesmen of the North. Tigras had inflicted terrible punishment upon these Venusian Scythians (who, like their ancient fellows of the earth, use human skulls for drinking-bowls) and was moving southward when met by the emissaries of Sallysherib. The prince saw accession to the throne dangling before his eyes—and went over to the enemy. This apostasy of Tigras was a severe blow to Draconda, for it took a large and veteran force over to the rapidly-growing host of Sallysherib—for, of course, though out of the turmoil himself, his was the mind directing this terrible drama of struggle, blood and destruction.

On meeting her, the prince fell a victim to Mynine's charms, remaining callous to the terrible treatment accorded his captive sister, who suffered before his very eyes.

Retribution, however, soon came, following a drunken fight over Mynine. Tigras was struck down by the dagger of one of the high priests—the assassin being literally torn to pieces by the enraged soldiers.

"Word has just been received," said Draconda one day, "that Mynine is gathering her forces preparatory to crossing the Secamnos, by the Untes Pass. We shall have about eighty thousand men, I believe, while, according to the reports of my spies, Mynine and Sallysherib have nearly one hundred and sixty thousand. What accessions are to follow, that we shall learn soon enough."

She smiled a little at that glance which I sent in Henry's direction.

"But it takes more than mere numbers to win a battle," Draconda went on lightly. "Remember Marathan and Cannae, Issus and Arbela, and all the others.

"Now, about twenty-five miles from the pass as the eagle flies, there is—I'll show you the spot on the map. I know it well. This is the valley of Long, and see: at this place, where the flanking hills approach most nearly, my army will give battle to the invaders. Fifty thousand men are in that place even now. There, my Henry and Farnermain—there will my warriors conquer Mynine's proud host."

"You forget something, O Draconda," I observed.

She looked at me interrogatively.

"What, my Farnermain?" she said in that whimsical way which I found so charming.

"This: there will Draconda *or Mynine* conquer."

She laughed.

"As I said, it takes more than warriors to win a battle, my Farnermain. Fear not. There you will see another Cannae."

"Very likely," said I to myself. "But who is Hannibal and who Varro?"

Shortly after this, we started for that place in the valley of Long which Draconda had chosen. As the bee flies, the spot is almost forty-five miles from the city of Loom; by the road, it is some fifteen miles farther.

The journey, which lay almost due north, was made on horseback, the queen riding astride: no Loomian equestrienne rides sidewise. Mayto, the old philosopher (not a little to my surprise), was one of the party.

The day following, about two o'clock, we were met by general Angto himself, and, as the great sun was setting, going down in a sky that was dripping with blood, we reached the place where, ere long, the great hosts would meet, and where were pitched seventy thousand men. Ten thousand more were to arrive on the day following.

And those seventy thousand warriors greeted Draconda with a rolling shout of

"Ningtos a ta leenam!"

Which means, "Victory to the queen!"

The valley was here cultivated and quite treeless, while the hills on either side, very steep and broken, were clothed in dense forest. On the left wing of the army was the River Thayno, which, at this point, laves the base of the western hills. It is here a deep and noble stream, with an average width of about two hundred and fifty feet.

The next day, the expected ten thousand arrived.

Three days later, Draconda's scouts reported that Mynine's vast army was beginning the descent of the Secamnos. According to the reports that had been coming in, her host outnumbered Draconda's almost three to one.

I took cheer in remembering Marathon, Arbela, and all the others.

Draconda was commander-in-chief, something no queen before her ever had been.

A day passed uneventfully, and on the second, just as the sun reached the meridian, Mynine's great army came swarming into view, coming to a stop, in full battle panoply and array, when a mile or so lay between the opposing hosts.

Draconda's army was drawn up for battle. But Mynine did not attack, and the queen, what with her numerical inferiority, was going to stand strictly on the defensive.

All was tranquil in the valley when the shades of night gathered over the fateful place.

It was a little after the noon of night when I lay down, but it was a long time ere sleep came to me. And the night I saw again that mummylike woman of my dreams.

I had ascended a lofty hill; through an opening in the dense forest, I was surveying Mynine's great host. Twilight was deepening to darkness. I was all alone; but suddenly I felt an unseen presence, and in a moment saw standing there directly before me a ghostly form—that white-robed, veiled creature who had warned me never to set eyes on Draconda.

"So you have seen me at last, O man! Again I come to warn you. You took not heed of my warning never to set eyes upon the queen, and the curse fell. Ha, ha! And the curse fell. And tomorrow destruction falls upon Draconda. Another Cannae—ha, ha! Another Cannae indeed! But for you, O man (that is, if you will avail yourself of it), there lies a way of escape—"

"Away!" I cried. "Away—"

And here I was awakened by Henry, his hand gently shaking my shoulder.

The sun had just appeared. Bright and brighter became his beams, flashing on weapon and armor. Higher and higher swung the great, glorious orb—in whose sway the great worlds are as peppercorns. And there we watched and waited.

Draconda rode through the ranks, giving words of encouragement, and the warriors cheered their wondrous and mysterious queen until, as the saying has it, the ground shook.

Just after mounting, in one of those moments of carelessness that come to us at times, I dropped my Winchester, and the weapon, striking a rock, was so badly damaged that it was no longer a rifle, though not irreparable. Henry had left his rifle in Loom, as he could not yet use his left arm. He had his revolvers, however, and Draconda—who wore a close-fitting coat of golden mail, a golden helmet and jeweled-hilted sword—had my cartridge-belt, with its pendent weapon, enzoning her waist. As for myself, I had St. Cloud's revolver.

About nine o'clock, Mynine's vast army began to move down toward us, Mynine, with her glittering staff, riding a little in advance.

When something less than a half mile from the foremost of the queen's warriors, she and her army halted—and then an awful thing happened.

Scarcely had she stopped when I perceived a woman, naked to the waist, being dragged forward by two human brutes.

"Nytes!" cried Draconda, who had been looking through Henry's glasses.

From the ranks of the enemy arose a rolling shout, in which I caught the princess' name, and an awful murmur ran along the serried lines of our legions.

Nytes' hands were bound before her; the girl was blindfolded.

The queen had turned ghastly pale.

The two men who had led the princess forward of a sudden drew back. Mynine rode a little distance in front of Nytes, who was facing us, and wheeled her horse round. Then she rode straight toward the captive with back-drawn sword.

Suddenly her weapon sent a great flash of silver across the plain, and the next instant she delivered the stroke, severing the princess' head.

CHAPTER 45
THE END OF IT ALL

A low, awful cry broke from the lips of Draconda; a deep murmur ran along her waiting legions, while from the ranks of the enemy, came a shout like the pealing of thunder.

"Here they come!" I cried.

Draconda straightened up with a sob, shook herself as if throwing off a palpable something, then suddenly gave her attention to the pressing matters of the moment, the pallor on her cheek alone attesting the effect of that brutal murder.

She had drawn her army up in the form (roughly) of a half moon, the convex side toward the enemy—like Hannibal's at Cannae. Her left wing, as I have said, was protected by the river. The right, I have forgotten to say, was protected by a strip of rugged, rocky and bush-covered ground, which would render a successful flank attack very difficult indeed. However, it was believed, before Mynine formed her army for battle, that no such attack would be made, and when ready to move her host down upon us, that belief became a certitude.

In the front ranks of the center, Draconda had placed her weakest infantry. Behind, and on either side, were her veteran foot-soldiers. The line of infantry reached from the rugged rocky ground just spoken of to the river, and in front, at the horns of the crescent, was posted the cavalry, which, by the way, was wonderfully efficient.

Draconda, Henry, a number of generals and myself, with the queen's bodyguard, had taken station behind the center.

The whole of Mynine's terrible army was coming to the attack. It was in a wedge-like shape and in mass formation. Half her cavalry—which outnumbered our own almost two to one—was on either wing at the rear. Mynine, I may remark, was not leading the attack in person.

On across the plain, with echoing cheers and shouts, came those thousands upon thousands of warriors, and I must say that it was a grandly terrible sight.

Suddenly their cheering and shouting was drowned in a deafening roar from Draconda's warriors, a deafening and rolling shout of—

"Victory to the queen!"

On they came, the ground quivering from the mighty tread, and then suddenly, with an awful roar and clash, the warriors met.

The queen did not try to stop that awful charge. By her orders, the infantry in the center retreated: it was the business of those veterans in the rear to prevent the enemy from breaking through the lines.

Back we were pressed, and back and back, and ever more swiftly. And at last, the warriors in front suddenly were flung about us as one could fling a bunch of bees with a flirt of the hand, and in an instant we were enveloped by friend and foe, in inextricable confusion and struggling like fiends incarnate.

Pandemonium reigned. The cries of the combatants, the shrieks of the wounded and the dying, and the clashing of arms and shields—it all was indescribable, deafening, horrible.

I soon emptied my revolver, and I took unholy delight in the belief that I got a man with every one of the bullets. I had no opportunity of reloading the weapon. My horse went down. I had lost my revolver. Somehow, though, I managed to get hold of a sword. I succeeded in running a man through who was coming at me, though it was owing to luck and not to any skill of my own that I emerged the victor.

The next instant, I saw Draconda's horse plunge madly and disappear. The enemy were trying their best to kill the queen. She, too, had emptied her revolver.

Henry Quainfan shot a man who was in the act of cutting her down with his sword—killing the warrior with his last bullet. I saw one of her guard leap in front of her, pushing her back as he did so, and receive a stroke aimed at the queen: the sword struck the man on the right shoulder and clove down through armor, flesh and bone to the heart. Before the warrior who wielded the sword could free his weapon, the queen drove her own blade through his body and clean to the hilt, avenging the death of her guardsman. Even as she ran the man through, I saw her lover's horse go down, and then I lost sight of them both.

For two burly fellows were flinging themselves upon me. From one side a sword came leaping out and transfixed one of them. Somehow, with the blade of my weapon, I saved myself from the blow of the other, but the next instant he struck me a terrible blow with his shield, driving me sidewise and to my knees. Back leaped the steel to run me through; but Draconda's sword shot into view, and the man went down with a crash of shield and armor.

All this time we had been carried steadily back. All had lost our revolvers. As I struggled to my feet, I drove my sword through a man who was coming at the queen. Her warriors seemed to be increasing about us now. On the other side of Draconda, was Henry Quainfan; I saw that his face was bloody, that he was wielding a sword—and then of a sudden I saw no more.

Down I went plunging through myriads of stinging and spluttering lights; about me sounded a great clashing and shouting, as if hell was spewing forth all its fiends—then suddenly I plunged into the utter blackness of oblivion.

When consciousness returned, I found Henry Quainfan bending over me and Draconda's cool hand on my forehead.

"How's everything?" I asked.

"Fine," said Henry. "And you, Rider?"

"Then it worked!" I cried. "It worked!"

"Yes, my Farnermain," nodded the queen. "And I am so glad to see you yourself again. At first I thought you were dead—but it was only a blow, not a wound."

"And the battle?" I asked. "Tell me. And let me see."

"Wait a little," admonished Draconda. "Wait till you have recovered somewhat. And the battle is another Cannae, my Farnermain—another Cannae, indeed! And Mynine herself is a captive. But is there aught I can do for you, my Farnermain?"

"Thanks, O Draconda, but soon I shall be quite myself again."

Henry, I soon noticed, had received a slight scalp wound; somehow his left arm had escaped hurt in that awful melee.

I was still weak and dazed, but strength was coming swiftly back and to my mind clarity of thought and perception.

We were on a high knoll, whence could be got a good view of the field. I mounted to the summit and surveyed the bloody field of battle.

"See!" exclaimed Draconda, her face flushed and her wondrous eyes shining like stars. "See, my Farnermain! It is indeed another Cannae! The enemy is surrounded. Mynine's warriors are being cut down by thousands, like the grass before the sickle."

I turned away and covered my eyes with my hand.

"I am glad, Draconda," I said, "and yet I sicken at the sight."

"Yes," returned the queen, laying a hand on my shoulder. "But it must be. What a monster, after all, is man—when banished to this terrible land of the flesh!"

It was indeed another Cannae. A little while after I received that terrible blow, Draconda's warriors succeeded in staying the advance of Mynine's host. The queen's army was again in the form of a half moon, but this time was the *concave* side against the enemy. As Mynine's army pressed forward, the queen's right wing faced to the left, using its flank as a pivot, and the left wing swung about to the right. The cavalry engaged Mynine's horse, and the foot fell upon her flanks. General Angto soon routed the horse on her right flank, and he then dashed over to her left, by a brilliant coup capturing Mynine herself as he did so, and put the cavalry there to flight. Then, swinging his men out into a long line, he came thundering down on the rear of the infantry.

Mynine's horse rallied and came bravely to the attack, but it was again routed, half of it being destroyed; and Draconda was bothered no more by Mynine's cavalry.

Of course, Mynine's vast army was now completely surrounded. When Angto came thundering down on the rear, its fate was sealed. It did not have the ghost of a show now. The rest was massacre. It was a slaughter, a butcher, a horror unutterable, a hell on earth. The blood ran into that river in streams. I saw it. It coursed down the banks of that river in streams.

For Mynine's warriors were packed together so closely that they could not use their weapons—went down indeed like the grass before the sickle.

And for seven long hours that butchering went on. When all was over, one hundred and twenty thousand insurrectionists lay dead or wounded on that awful field, and twenty thousand were prisoners. Draconda's loss was very small—a little over twelve thousand men, dead and wounded.

The body of poor Nytes was found—headless, crushed and hoof-mangled.

The sun was shining brightly when the battle began, but the clouds increased in number and volume; and, about noon, the sun, which for some time had been shining but fitfully, went out altogether, sending a heavy gloom down upon the awful field. Then a wind sprang up and slowly grew stronger, at last sweeping across the field in sudden and wrathful gusts. The sky threatened rain. And, as the end was drawing near, the heavens in the west parted of a sudden, and, for several minutes only, the sun sent yellow and bloody rays down upon the terrible place, when it disappeared to shine no more that day.

At length Draconda gave an order that Mynine be brought before her.

Henry gave me a troubled look, but he said nothing either to Draconda or to me.

In a few minutes, the captive was standing before the queen, who was mounted.

Mynine had not received even so much as a scratch. She wore a coat of golden mail, and upon her head was a stephane, studded with precious stones.

She courtesied to the queen with a smile on her pale lips, when she stood erect and looked fixedly into Draconda's eyes. She was very pale, but she did not tremble at all; at any rate, I could not detect the least tremor in the slender frame—which housed that terrible thing of her called a soul, that thing which had brought down upon this Venusian nation so much turmoil, sorrow, blood and destruction.

"So, my Mynine," said Draconda in her softest tones, "we meet again, and it is I that have the honor of holding *thee* captive. Perchance thou didst anger the gods, my Mynine. And now tell me this: what hast thou to say?"

Mynine said never a word, though her wide blue eyes spoke volumes.

The wind was sweeping across the plain in a stronger gust than common, and, as Draconda spoke the last words, the first drops of that rain which the dark skies had long portended came driving down, stinging like hailstones.

Draconda drew her sword.

"Now shalt thou die, my Mynine," she said evenly. "I shall slay thee now, even as thou didst slay my sister."

Mynine laughed.

"So be it, O queen. You win. Perchance, though, in some other world, we shall meet again."

"Mayhap, my Mynine. And mayhap we have met before."

"Good heavens, Draconda!" cried Henry Quainfan, standing aghast, "what are you going to do—kill her?"

"Kill her," was the quiet response. "Kill her, even as she killed my Nytes—smite off her head to the earth."

He gave an exclamation of horror.

"Vengeance, Draconda—"

"I am going to kill me that woman," she interrupted him, a steely ring in her tones. "Just now I am Themis. What! Would you, if in my place, set her free, strew her pathway with roses?"

"Not that. But—"

"Justice is justice," she interrupted again: "it matters not whose the hand that delivers the stroke."

She ordered Mynine blindfolded and her hands tied behind her. This was done speedily and in utter silence.

Henry begged Draconda not to do this thing, and to his entreaties my own were added; but the queen was not to be moved an inch in her determination.

"If you kill her, Draconda," exclaimed Henry Quainfan at last, pale with anger and helplessness, "then I'll go away! For I won't—no, I won't marry a murderess!"

"A murderess!" echoed Draconda, looking at her lover curiously. "Don't be foolish, my Henry. Remember that just now I am Themis."

Suddenly a hard, steely light—one that for an instant was actually terrible—shot into the queen's dark eyes.

"This girl believes, my Henry, that you loved her—really and truly loved her—until you saw me. And, after all, what woman really knows the heart of her lover? Yes, perhaps memory stings—and you have good reason to ask it!"

He stood silent.

"However, I am going to kill that woman. And you will not take me to wife if I do?"

Still he did not speak.

Draconda laughed.

At a sign from her, the men drew back from Mynine, who was standing straight and still. Not the slightest tremor was perceptible, though her cheeks were as pale as Death's own. A curious smile, though—one that often rises before my eyes and lingers there—hovered about her lips.

Draconda raised her weapon, rode toward Mynine and smote off Mynine's head, which rolled over twice or thrice, opened and shut its blue eyes several times, then stared straight at Henry Quainfan through the driving rain.

The queen wheeled her horse round and in a moment had dismounted before her lover. She said nothing, just looked at him. And he stepped to her, put his right arm around her and drew her close. And, clinging to him tightly, she cried a little.

And here I may well bring this narrative to a close. The day before Mynine's great army met destruction, his pontifical highness was killed by a priest in a drunken fight: this occurred in Secamnos, and shows that, though delighting in intrigue and turmoil, Sallysherib took good care to keep his sacred person distant from the scene of action. Peace followed the great battle. Draconda was able to abolish human sacrifices and many other things of that order—the reform being facilitated by the cruel oppression the people long had endured from the hands of the priests. However, the gravest problem in Loom today is, in all likelihood, this one of the sacerdotal caste. Draconda and Henry Quainfan (who is the king now and called King Henry) are going to direct all possible energy toward the final dissolution of its pernicious influence.

Henry has just begun work on a wireless apparatus (though, of course, he is sadly hampered) with which he hopes to speak the earth. He is sure it is possible to enter into communication with our mother planet and is jubilant over the thought of it.

So this story of Draconda will be read by Terrestrials after all! What a surprise Mr. Homer L. Wood will receive when Henry Quainfan's voice comes to him from out the void!

Neither Draconda nor Henry has seen a page of the record, I withholding it for reasons that will be sufficiently obvious. Of course, that part of it, and the many notes necessary for its complete understanding by the Venusians will not be transmitted—at any rate, I suppose Henry will not transmit that part of the text and those many notes.

In a few moments, the last word of this history will have been penned. And I am going away now—with a single companion, whose name is Reem Gomar.

Though the good things of life are accessible to him, yet he is going away with me—to what, we can only dream.

The great sun is just setting: I wonder in what far places Gomar and I shall see it go down in the west. Of course, neither Draconda nor Henry knows that we are going—we only know.

I have been writing for a long time now, and my hand is tired, and my mind is tired, and so I shall say good-bye. Perhaps—who knows?—many years lie before me and one day I shall even take up my pen to write another history of marvelous things and happenings.

Until then, farewell.

CHAPTER 46
BY THE HAND OF HIS COMRADE

Here Rider Farnermain's manuscript ends. Of course, Henry Quainfan succeeded in making an apparatus with which he could send electromagnetic waves to our earth—else your eye never would have lighted on this story of Draconda.

The first message was received by me (Homer L. Wood) on the tenth day of May at about a quarter past nine in the evening; and I succeeded, with the instrument that Mr. Quainfan gave me shortly before his mysterious disappearance (and which Mr. Farnermain forgot to mention), in soon getting an answer to him. Then came explanations, which I need not give her, and almost immediately was begun the transmission of the marvelous history—now all ready to be given to the world; the most extraordinary true narrative, I believe, ever penned by mortal hand.

"I have omitted," says Mr. Quainfan, "certain lines in which Rider speaks of me in unmerited terms, though, of course, this was not done without his permission. Otherwise certainly I should not have done so. Even as it is, some passages make me to blush like the rose of Sharon. In other respects, however, Rider's narrative (save, of course, that part of the text, and those many notes, written for the benefit of the Venusians) has been transmitted to you just as written. Nothing pertaining to Draconda has been omitted, though Rider extended to her the favor of making any deletion that might be desired; however, not even a comma was struck from the record by her hand.

"Often do we, Draconda and I, sit in the stillness of the night (in which no moon ever shines) and gaze with indescribable feelings at those two stars, the one much larger than the other, that we know so well—the earth and the moon.

When they are in opposition, and for some time before and after, the disk of the earth is distinctly visible, and Terra is then a lovely object indeed in our Venusian skies. Mercury too blazes out nobly, now evening star, now star of morn. But, oh, how I long for the silvery light of the moon!

"And how interesting now will be the beautiful star Hesperus and Lucifer to eyes on the earth, now when it is known that this shining world, too, is the abode of men and women; that here also, in this far-distant world, which in its remoteness seems but a shining point, are love and hate, laughter and tears, ecstasy, death and sorrow—that great brooding shrouded thing that men, under various names, know as the Mystery of Being.

"As for Rider, not a single word has ever come to us from him or about him. Every day I hope that the long silence will be broken, and never a messenger arrives but the hope rises in my heart that at last word has come to me, but it is only to sink again into those troubled depths whence it comes.

"Does he see those two stars upon which we so often gaze, or has darkness closed his eyelids in that sleep which men call death?

"Only time can answer, and perhaps even from it no answer ever will come.

"But I still hope: some time, if he is still living and goes not down to death, he will send word to me—some time will come to me again. Yes, surely there will come a day when he will long to see me as I do him and grasp his hand in mine once more.

"Peradventure, though, he will circle the planet ere he comes to us again.

"And now, to all who have known us, to every man, woman and child on the whole earth, Draconda and I send our best greetings and best wishes—send them silently throbbing across that terrible, unfathomable abyss which I shall never cross again."

So now the curtain descends, the drama is done.

And, as the great discoverer and his wondrous queen sit in the stillness of the night and gaze at those two stars that are Terra and Selene, so do I sit and gaze away at that lovely orb which now hangs in our western sky at eve like some glorious jewel; and thousands of pictures come and go in my eyes, and I wonder if Rider Farnermain still lives somewhere in that shining vastness which is to us but a point of light—if ever again his voice, as it were, will wing its swift and silent way across that everchanging, bottomless abyss that lies between.

The Voices from the Cliff

This is a damnable and fearful fact.
—The Headsman.

1. What I Heard at the Club

Peabody suddenly sat up in his chair and drove one hand, clenched, into the palm of the other.

"Science!" he ejaculated. "For heaven's sake, spare us that! Science—the star hypothesis-patcher, the A Number One, the dyed-in-the-wool, the blown-in-the-bottle, the peerless, the inimitable guessologist!"

"Come again, George!" the doctor smiled.

"Well, it's so. Leave her there to explain her dust and cobwebs and her heaps of bones. That is where she belongs. But when you send for the dusty old girl to adjudicate in matters pertaining to the psychic, to things as high above these gross senses and lives of ours as the rainbow is above a frog in his puddle—oh, gosh! Why, you might just as well send a mole to judge the beauty of the Venus of Melos."

"And again, George," said the doctor. "Oxford isn't here, and so you can make up for lost time."

"Well," said Peabody, "what show have I got against *him*? All the same—and I'm glad I can give a loud blare on my trumpet at this point—I think with my own mind. And do you know what Locke says about that?"

"What does Locke say? I thought that you were going to say Blavatsky."

"Well," Peabody exclaimed, "I'm not going to shout with Aristotle that there are cattle in Phrygia that can wiggle their horns like ears; that the salamander can live in fire; that the little busy bee, when the wind is high, carries along a stone—for the same reason that a ship goes out in ballast! Oh, ain't science wonderful, though? Nor am I going to accept Kepler's belief (some more science) that the earth is an animal, the tides caused by the monster's respiration!"

"Keep on, sweet expounder!"

"No; I'll come back to Locke. Here is what Locke says: that 'we may as rationally hope to see with other men's eyes, as to know by other men's understandings.'"

"Very true," nodded the doctor, "but about as much to the point, I fancy, as Newton's 'Fishes looke one way with one eye, ye other way with ye other.'"

"Is that so?"

"And," the doctor continued, "that reminds me of Locke's American aborigine seeking information on architectural matters. Do you know what he was told?"

"I wonder."

"That a pillar is a thing supported by a basis and a basis is something that supports a pillar."

"Science in a nutshell!" exclaimed Peabody.

"Not so. It wasn't science that gave Poor Lo that beautiful answer. Only the mystic, the occult, the psychic could have done that."

"Heaven help us!" Peabody said. "Science and Oxford certainly have got you fellows hypnotized—that is, all of you except" (with a glance in my direction) "Hudson here."

"Speaking of Oxford," I observed, "that reminds me: I haven't seen him since my return, or even heard his name spoken until now. What's his latest?"

There was the briefest silence. I was puzzled by that curious, barely perceptible change of expression which came to the different faces. I said "barely perceptible," but, in one or two instances, there was a significant lift of the eyebrows and that faint, indescribable (terrible) smile which speaks more plainly than can any words.

"Gone," Peabody said.

"Gone! Where?" I asked him. "It was time, though, for Oxford to take a vacation."

Peabody glanced at Dr. Thompson.

"Hardly a vacation, Hudson," he said, returning his look to me, "though he may call it that himself. After all, Guy Oxford is—er—well, rather eccentric, you know, and, what makes the matter worse, scientifically eccentric. He would be a puzzle, I imagine, even to his closest friend—that is, if there was such a gentleman, which there isn't. Probably you yourself, Hudson, come the nearest to that; and yet I fancy he never admitted even you to anything having the semblance of real intimacy."

"No. He is something of a recluse, certainly. But his investigations, you know—the requisite intense mental application!"

"All the more reason," returned Peabody, "why he should relax at times and be human. And all those cold-blooded, materialistic ideas of his! 'Tis enough to freeze the heart and the soul of a man. Why, if an angel were to come down from heaven, Guy Oxford would merely glance around and say that the movie people were somewhere on the job!"

"And so," said I, "he has gone: but where to?"

"To Timbuctoo, or Shanghai, or somewhere; and *on a windjammer!*"

"What!" I exclaimed.

"Just so, Hudson: on a schooner, a yawl, a barkentine, a brig, a catamaran, or whatever they call the *Shadow* in their confounded nautical lingo."

He turned to Donohue.

"What is she, Cap?"

"Bark," returned Donohue, who was somewhat of a yachtsman, "bound for Sydney."

"Great Neptune!" said I. "What put that kind of a voyage into his head. Sea-dogs and Guy Oxford! It seems, somehow—well, incongruous, you know."

"Incongruous—yes, rather."

"Still," I told him, "I don't understand."

"You see," explained Peabody, "it was Miss Maitland—or, rather, Mrs. Dirk."

"And Mrs. Dirk is who?"

"And who," put in Donohue, "would have imagined that one so unemotional as Oxford—about as romantic, apparently, as the Sphinx or an iceberg—would have been hit so hard?"

"Simply smashed him," said the doctor. "I never expected anything like that from Oxford."

"And what," Donohue queried, "do you really think of that queer business out there at Alta Vista?"

Alta Vista, I well knew, was the old summer home—grandly picturesque with its wild sea setting—of the Maitlands; or, rather, of Clara Maitland (now Mrs. Dirk) for of that proud and once numerous family she was (had been, I soon learned) the sole surviving member.

"And this Dirk?" I queried, forgetting for the moment Donohue's remark. "Who is the fellow, anyway? Anything like his name?"

"One of these gay young birds—of good connections but penniless and yet somehow a high-sailer," returned Peabody. "Heaven only knows why such things happen; but Dirk caught the girl's fancy, she gave Oxford the mitten, and in a few days (all too few indeed!) she was Mrs. Dirk—and not so happy, it was soon whispered, as a bride should be."

"And ere long," said the doctor, "lay stiff and cold in death."

He turned to me.

"Found, a crushed and gory thing, on the stones and seaweed of the beach."

"What was it—murder?"

"Murder," nodded the doctor. "It happened on the night of Wednesday last—at that pretty place called Cupid's Tryst."

"But," interposed Donohue, "what should take a woman to *that* place all alone in the hours of darkness?"

"I wonder," returned the doctor, "how many have asked that very question. However, there she was—either alone or with the murderer."

He turned his look back to me as he reverted to the story:

"The body was found in the twilight of dawn by a beachcomber—crushed and mangled on the stones below. The cliff, you will remember, in that place drops down sheer for two hundred feet or more. They say every bone in her body is broken. In the Cupid's Tryst were found plain signs of a violent struggle, but neither an examination of the place nor the autopsy has shown whether the victim met her death in that spot or whether she was hurled alive over the edge."

"Where," I asked, "was the husband that night?"

"At home—so he says. Oh, Dirk has a good story. And yet—is it so good a story after all?"

"Well, it works," put in Peabody: "coroner, coroner's jury, sheriff, deputy sheriffs, and detectives—all seem to think the man as innocent as a lamb."

Doctor Thompson nodded.

"It is one of those cases," said he, "which makes you think ugly things—but where is your proof? And a man is innocent, you know, until you prove him to be guilty."

"As for proofs, there, for instance, is that penknife," said Peabody.

"Dirk explained that," returned the doctor. "You see, Hudson, the only thing found at the scene of the struggle was a penknife—Dirk's own."

"That looks bad."

"The explanation, however, is very simple: his wife borrowed it and forgot to return it to him."

"And another is the quarrel," Peabody said.

"No proof. Points an accusing finger at the man, it would seem, but that is all: it proves nothing. Dirk readily admitted that quarrel, did not seek in any way to minimize the fact that it had been a violent one—and over money."

"How could he?" queried Peabody. "Two of the servants heard it."

"His disgraceful speech and conduct, however," added the doctor, "brush aside, as it were, that accusing finger."

"How is that?" I exclaimed.

"Why, the bereaved husband, almost prostrated (according to these sob-reporters), keeps crying:

"'Oh, if I could only have told Clara how sorry I was!'"

"Then," demanded Peabody, a little vehemently, I thought, "why didn't he go and tell her? Instead, what does the man do? He goes to his room (so he tells us), sleeps sweetly (so he says) until awakened in the morning to learn that his wife, who (so he would have us believe) he thought was all this time in her room, is a crushed and gory corpse."

There was a brief pause.

"You see, Hudson," remarked the doctor, "the case does present some sinister features."

"Probably," I suggested, "if Guy Oxford were here—"

Peabody and the doctor smiled a little.

"Rather out of his line, don't you think?" the doctor queried.

"He solved the Bradshaw mystery," I reminded him, "and that when all those crack detectives had ignominiously failed."

"He did. But that was a coldly scientific proposition, Hudson—a mystery insoluble to any man save one with Guy Oxford's deep and peculiar scientific attainments. But this—well, this is different."

"Quite so," concurred Peabody.

"No, Hudson," he added; "for my part, I am glad that the man who lost is out there at sea. He doesn't know."

2. Statement of James X. Hendryx, First Mate of the *Shadow*

I think it well to set down, while memory of it is still vivid, an account of this strange business. That something terrible happened is clear. But where? And, in heaven's name, how did Mr. Oxford, standing there on the deck of the *Shadow*, by the weather mizzen-shrouds—in God's name, I say, how was that sudden, awful intelligence borne to him there?

The Voices from the Cliff

For I was present, within a few yards of the man, and I heard nothing, absolutely nothing—save, that is, the soft sighing of the wind and the eternal wash of the sea. 'Tis true, the man at the wheel thinks he heard voices *in the air,* as he describes it—low, indistinct, terrible, ghostly. In fact, he thinks that he heard spirits. But, for my part, I dismiss that helmsman's testimony (if I may call it that) without a moment's hesitation. For I was there myself, saw ten times as much as he did, heard from Mr. Oxford's own lips what the helmsman never did; and I can swear that (save for Oxford's and my own) there were no voices—from the air or from lips, ghostly or otherwise.

That an intelligence, however, was actually borne to him, that there was nothing of delusion about it, I am convinced as fully as that I am this moment aboard the *Shadow.* For, brief though our acquaintance, nevertheless I know Mr. Oxford is too coolly scientific, too profoundly (terribly even) materialistic to permit superstition or fantasy to enter as a possible explanation of the matter.

No, the key to this mystery is *material!* But what is that key?

Now for the facts in the case.

It was the first watch of the night—one of those still, starry nights that are so beautiful. There was a steady, gentle breeze from the direction of the land, some eighty miles distant now, and we were going large. To be precise, the wind was from the east, our course was southwest by west.

Though unusually laconic of speech and subject to queer spells of abstraction and moody silence, yet, pleasantly to my surprise, I found Mr. Oxford a charming conversationist when once started—eloquent, truly poetical, if I may use that much-abused word, when deeply stirred by his subject.

In this instance, talk turned to the stars, and, though always profoundly moved to speculation by those mysterious lights set in the firmament, never had I heard, or imagined, till now the true poetry of the heavens.

I honestly believe that he knows the name of every lucid star in the sky. Also, as an instance of the man's wonderful memory, I learned that he has in his head the mantissa—to seven places!—of every single number from 1 to 10,000.

It was now that he drew my attention to a curious thing. Pointing out the stars Mu and Nu Andromedæ (the constellation was well up in the eastern heavens) he said that, if my look were fixed on either of those points, preferably Nu, I would see, a few degrees distant and a mere elusive patch of light, the glorious Andromeda Nebula.

"Then," said Mr. Oxford, "turn your look to the nebula itself—and see it vanish."

I fixed my eye on Nu, and there, sure enough, was that fairylike wisp of light—one of the most beautiful (as the telescope has shown), stupendous and mysterious objects in the whole expanse of the heavens.

Then, following his suggestion, I looked directly at the nebula itself, and lo, it had vanished!

I had never heard of this curious freak of optics, though I had long since noticed that the Pleiades (immersed in a nebulous mass) have a flocculent appearance if the eye is not turned directly upon the group.

As we stood there talking of these things, the moon rose, blotting out the smaller stars and hiding the great nebula with her yellow beams.

Not long after this, five bells struck, when suddenly Mr. Oxford lapsed into one of those fits of profound abstraction so common with him. And so I left him standing there, silent and with an air somehow curiously forlorn, by the weather mizzen-rigging.

As I have said, the wind, though blowing gently, was steady. At the time it had freshened somewhat, so that the maincourse had filled till the canvas had the semblance of a great concave mirror. I thought nothing of the matter at the time, and even now, when it comes to the explanation, I am as utterly as I am literally at sea. Why I so particularly mention the *Shadow's* mainsail will in a moment be sufficiently obvious.

For now I come to the mystery itself.

I was pacing back and forth and thinking; but of a sudden, as my eyes chanced to fall upon Mr. Oxford, I was fetched up short on the deck.

At the same instant, an exclamation of commingled awe and terror burst from the man at the helm.

"My God, sir!" he cried in a sort of whisper. "Did you hear *that?*"

I did not answer for a moment or two, for my look was fixed on Mr. Oxford, and it is no wonder that I was utterly mystified and not a little astonished at what I saw. In fact, it was as if something uncanny had crept aboard the *Shadow*.

As has been said, Mr. Oxford had fallen into profound abstraction, by the weather mizzen-shrouds: he was still there—but what an inexplicable, terrible change had suddenly come over the man!

Even from where I stood, the ghastliness of his face was startling—producing a sense of horror for which I am at a loss to find any adequate expression. The eyes, fixed (it seemed) on something in the air near the helmsman—whose own features showed pale in the rays of the binnacle lamp—were wide and staring, as if their owner had been caught in some petrifying spell. The attitude was that of one listening intently, fearful lest the slightest movement break or destroy some dreadful message.

"What is it?" I demanded of the man at the wheel.

A face upon which horror pitifully struggled was turned toward me.

"I don't know, sir!" he whispered. "So help me, God!—*voices! And in the air!*"

I cannot swear that I am myself entirely free from that cursed thing superstition, but thereupon I turned away from the man with an exclamation of disgust. I was just in time to see Mr. Oxford grasping one of the stays with his right hand, a curious quality of uncertainty in the movement; his face was covered with the left, and I thought that a groan was borne across the deck and away to leeward.

I lost no time in placing myself at his side.

"Mr. Oxford," I exclaimed, laying a hand on his arm, "what is it?"

He made as if to fling off my touch, then suddenly stood erect and very still.

"You caught it?" he queried.

"I heard nothing—saw nothing," I told him. "'Tis all a mystery to me."

"'Tis over now," he said, and his eyes became vacant—terrible.

"You speak in riddles, man! What has happened?"

"Murder!" said Mr. Oxford. "Foul murder!"

And then he covered his face with his hand again, muttering something, in which I caught only "Cupid's Tryst" and a woman's name—"Clara."

"Murder?" I exclaimed.

"Murder," said Mr. Oxford.

"Great Heaven, where?"

He uncovered his face and raised his eyes up to the big mainsail. Involuntarily mine followed. God knows I didn't expect to see anything, though, I fancy, I should not have been surprised or astonished if I had. However, nothing was visible there in the moonlight—save the vast spread of canvas itself.

The voice beside me brought my look back to the man's face. His gaze was still aloft, as if held there by some baleful charm.

"There has been no change there," said he, "and all is silent. It is all over now."

"All over?" I queried, scarcely knowing what to think or say. "What on earth, Mr. Oxford, do you mean?"

"That she is dead now."

A silence fell.

Suddenly he gripped my arm.

"Is it possible for me to return to land?"

I shook my head, wondering if, after all, the man had not completely lost his reason.

'Tis my conviction now, however, that no man ever was more sane than Mr. Oxford was at that moment.

"One of these boats—" he suggested.

"Why, 'tis eighty miles to land!"

"Though no sailor," he persisted, "yet I believe that I could make it."

"It is simply impossible!" I told him.

And there, rather to my surprise, Mr. Oxford permitted the matter to drop.

At the earliest opportunity, I questioned that helmsman closely, but all I received was the absurd asseveration that there had been voices *in the air.*

That the man truly believes this, I do not question at all; neither do I hesitate for one moment to dismiss the statement as the sheerest of nonsense—utterly unworthy the consideration of any mind save one sunk in the deepest abyss of credulity and superstition.

Voices in the air! And the *Shadow* distant eighty miles from the land!

However—a face, drawn, ghastly in the moonlight, haunts my vision, and over and over again I ask myself: What did happen there on the *Shadow's* deck last night?

3. "Solved!"

Certain matters necessitated a journey on the day following that night at the club, to the little town of Klepton, far up in the mountains. The road is, for the most part, an excellent one, and so I drove there in the auto. Arrived at Klepton—encircled by its jagged mountain ramparts—I found a further journey (on horseback) imperative. This was up to the Ruby mine, where I passed the night and the day and night following. News does not reach this place until "tomorrow," and so it chanced that I did not know that Guy Oxford had returned.

For the *Shadow* spoke a schooner—the *Sardis,* from Honolulu—and the result was that the bark hove to, a weather boat was lowered, and Guy Oxford was rowed over to the stranger. The schooner filled away, close-hauled (for the wind still held from the east) and the chief actor in that strange scene on the moonlit deck of the *Shadow* was on his way to the place of the tragedy.

It was about midafternoon when, tired and dusty, I drove into the city. Suddenly, through the rumble and clangor, came the shrill shout of a newsboy:

"Paypee here! Here Paypee! Great mystery solved!"

There in the big headlines was of all names—Oxford's!

Another moment, and the car was alongside the curb and I was reaching for a copy.

Oh, what was I to make of the story!

For, notwithstanding the allowance made for inevitable reportorial embellishment, what I read was so amazing as almost to challenge belief.

That morning, Guy Oxford, Sheriff Williamson, Deputy Sheriff Maxwell and Pierce, the well-known feature-writer of the *Daily Bulletin* (I wondered how Pierce had come to be one of that party) had gone out to Alta Vista, their car arriving there a few minutes past 10, just as Dirk was backing his own machine out of the garage.

There was a scowl as his eye fell upon Guy Oxford, but on the instant the man was dissembling.

"This is indeed a surprise, Mr. Oxford," was his somewhat sardonic exclamation. "I thought you were well out at sea."

"I was," returned Oxford, his black eyes fixed upon the other. "But fortunately, Mr. Dirk—in what manner fortunately you soon shall learn—I was only some eighty miles from land *on the night of Wednesday, the fifteenth.*"

"Only eighty miles," echoed Dirk, a little stiffly. "I'm afraid I don't understand you."

"You shall in good season," Oxford told him. "And ninety from Alta Vista. Fortunately, too, we met the *Sardis*. Fortunately, also, my position of third mate was merely nominal, for the *Shadow* is not allowed to carry passengers. So I changed ships, and here I am."

"I see," said Dirk.

"I'm afraid, Mr. Dirk, that you don't. But you shall, and soon at that."

"You speak in riddles," replied Dirk after a momentary pause.

He turned to the others.

"Will you come in, gentlemen?" he said.

The sheriff looked at the scientist.

"If you please, Mr. Dirk," said Oxford, "we shall, instead, visit Cupid's Tryst."

Dirk was silent for a moment, then:

"I don't know why you have come, gentlemen, for I have told all that I know. I can't see why you wish to drag me out to that cursed spot again, the very name of which is a horror now—"

"The first true words, those last, that you have uttered!" Guy Oxford told him.

"This is a most unusual—this is a most unwarranted proceeding, it seems to me, gentlemen!" said Dirk, ignoring the dark import of Oxford's words. "But, of course, I shall go with you. If I can in any way help to solve this awful mystery, help to bring this dastardly brute to justice—"

He was silent for a space and was actually seen to shed tears, dabbling at his eyes with a handkerchief bordered with black.

Pierce has given us some remarkable work in the columns of the *Daily Bulletin,* but here, I believe, we have this brilliant journalist's *magnum opus*—his description of what followed there at Cupid's Tryst. His grasp of the psychology of the scene is well-nigh uncanny. Of Oxford's cruel, subtle vivisection (so to speak) of Dirk's guilty soul, Pierce remarks that it was as dramatic, as awful a thing as it is possible to conceive. His remark, however, is supererogatory: every one knows *that* as he reads.

Guy Oxford proceeded slowly—unrolling, as it were, the deed like a scroll before the eyes of the murderer and the astonished trio. He put Dirk's soul on the rack, watching his victim with the stony placidity of the Sphinx. He mentioned the very hour. He described certain details of the tragedy—never once, however, mentioning the murderer by name. He repeated words uttered that night—words that, it seemed, only Death (and the murderer himself) could have known. He was proceeding to the dénouement when a wild, inarticulate cry—a cry that was neither beast nor human—broke from Dirk. The next instant he was seen springing with the mad fury of a tiger at Oxford. But Williamson and Maxwell were watching; they seized the man and dragged him back.

Then Dirk broke down completely and confessed the deed.

"I don't know why I did it!" he wailed. "I was mad at that moment!"

"Over money!" said Guy Oxford. "It was for that you killed her. Your madness, I fancy, didn't blot that will from your brain."

"Will?" cried Dirk.

"Will," Oxford told him. "I suppose you deny knowledge of that?"

"No. But I didn't know to whom—"

"Tell that to the jury!" ejaculated Oxford with unutterable disgust and loathing.

"You fiend!" cried the murderer, "where were you?"

"On the *Shadow.*"

"You, you," cried Dirk, "—are you human?"

4. The Maincourse

"But," said I, "in the name of all that's inconceivable, how did you solve it?"

We were sitting in his den—that room which has seen so many problems solved.

Guy Oxford looked at me quizzically, his dark brows contracted.

"I never solved it," said he; "I knew it all the time."

"Never solved it!"

"Not at all, Hudson. There I was, some eighty miles out, ninety from Alta Vista, and I *knew*—so there was nothing to solve."

"Then there must have been something supernatural somewhere."

"Supernatural!" he ejaculated, giving a swift gesture of impatience. "Banish all that, Hudson. There are forces mysterious, elusive, some of them terrible—how terrible they may be man is just beginning to imagine—but there is no supernatural. No, banish that thought."

"Then," I persisted, "what the generality of mankind, in ignorance, would call supernatural."

"Not at all. No more supernatural than the senses of the blind man: on entering a strange room, the sound of his first footfall gives him the room's dimensions and even the character of its furniture."

"I didn't know that. However, I can see no connection between the acute senses of one deprived of sight and—the confession of Dirk."

"You could," said Oxford, "had you given to natural philosophy one tenth of the time that you have devoted to the mystic and occult. If one would know the wonders of this world, he should seek for them in the daylight, not go stumbling about in the dark."

"It is then," I reminded him, "that the stars are seen."

"The same old Hudson!" he smiled. "However, as I said, I didn't solve the mystery. It was owing to the sheerest chance, to a remarkable, to a most remarkable, fortuitous combination of circumstances that I knew.

"It is scarcely necessary to remind you, Hudson, that the laws of reflection and refraction are the same for sound as for light."

"I think I have heard or read that somewhere."

"As in the case of light," Guy Oxford continued, "the angle of incidence and that of reflection are coincident; the intensity of sound (as with gravitation also) varies inversely as the square of the distance; it can be concentrated by a lens, say a bag of India rubber or collodion distended by carbonic acid gas to the form of a double-convex lens or by a concave surface—"

"What on earth," I exclaimed, "has all this got to do with the explanation!"

He gazed at me for a moment in silence.

"To make a physicist out of you, Hudson, is, I perceive, impossible—utterly so. However, you will remember that acoustic phenomenon known as the *Ear of Dionysius.*"

I nodded.

"I do not understand the allusion, though. But go on."

"Also, you know the principle on which whispering-galleries are constructed—how a person standing at one of the focal points can carry on a conversation with a person in the other, though the words will be inaudible to a person at any point between."

"I know that. But—"

"Well, I knew that, too—that and other things. And that was why I knew that those voices which I heard there on the *Shadow* were real—that, incredible though it may seem, I actually heard Dirk's curses and Clara's cries of fear and mortal agony. That was the difference between myself and that embodiment of ignorance and superstition, the man at the wheel. He believed that the supernatural had come aboard the *Shadow.*"

"Still I cannot conceive how—good Lord!" I burst out; "do you really mean to tell me that the voices carried clear out there to the *Shadow?*"

He nodded.

"That you, ninety miles distant at sea, heard that struggle on the cliff?"

"Yes," said Guy Oxford.

For some seconds, I could only stare at him in speechless astonishment.

"How can such a thing be possible? I never dreamed that sounds like those could carry so far."

"Farther—much farther. But, of course, at that distance, such sounds *cannot be heard.*"

"And yet you heard them?"

"And yet I heard them," said Guy Oxford.

"Great Heaven! What next?"

"The proper reflector, however," he went on, "can concentrate the inaudible sound and render it audible."

"Render it audible?"

"Yes; just as the speculum of a reflecting-telescope concentrates the rays from an invisible star, brings them to a focus and thus makes it possible for the observer to see the invisible."

"But where was such a reflector there at sea?"

"The *Shadow's* big maincourse, or mainsail, filled to concavity by the breeze!"

I made an exclamation and for some moments sat there staring at him.

"There is one thing, though, that I don't understand."

"And what is that, Hudson?"

"The mate did not hear those voices from the cliff."

"He would have heard them had he been where I was, or beside the helmsman, at the proper moment. Remember, the big maincourse brought the sounds to a focus; it did not broadcast them."

"What a sensation," I cried, "there will be when this is made known! There never has been anything like this!"

"In that you are mistaken, Hudson," Guy Oxford told me. "As for the sensational part of it, science will not be astonished, though even she may be a little surprised. For there is that instance, well known to her physicists, of the sound of bells on land, at São Salvador, Brazil, being rendered audible one hundred miles out at sea by a ship's big mainsail—pressed by the breeze as the *Shadow's* was, into the form of a great concave reflector."

The Voice of Bills

"I am safe! Safe!" he repeated. "Nobody knows that Bills was here. Nothing went wrong. Not a sign, not a clue remains. Ha, ha! Why don't these crime bunglers do things like me?"

The day had been bright and sunny, but, as the man, a mattock and a shovel on his shoulder, issued from the shadows of the dense spruce forest, the sun slipped behind heavy clouds and the wilderness landscape suddenly turned dark and sinister.

But Slickmer did not notice this. For him, the sun still rode high and bright in the sky. His heart was glad; his soul sang and shouted for very joy. For it was done. Yes, at last, after all his dreaming, all his planning and scheming, the deed was done. At last he had killed Bills, as years before he had sworn he would some day do. And not a sign, not the faintest clue remained. Oh, he had seen to that! The deed was a thing to be proud of.

He could have killed Bills long, long ago—only he would take no chances. There must be no mistake, nothing to raise a finger of suspicion against him. No bungler, he!

It had taken a long time, but this day had seen it done. No one knew that Bills had come to this lonely cabin far up on the middle fork of the Snoqualmie. Oh, he, Slickmer, had been very careful as to that! No one ever would know of what had happened there in the depths of the dark spruce forest; no one ever would know that in a certain spot where long damp mosses grew and vine-maples made a tangle roundabout—no one ever would dream that in that spot a man had been done to death and buried there beneath the long green mosses.

For how could anyone ever know? Not a clue remained. These bunglers in crime! The poor boobs, why didn't they do it as carefully as he had done?

He stopped there in the field, and, while the surrounding forest grew more somber and forbidding of aspect, and the clouds massed thicker and blacker overhead, he went over every action of his that had led up to the crime.

The man laughed suddenly aloud. Safe? His plan had worked without a single hitch. There was nothing for the sharpest-eyed Sherlock Holmes of them all to see.

Then he studied with his mind's eye the crime itself. Safe? Yes, those bunglers should be as crafty and careful as himself. Nothing had been forgotten. How cool he had been all the time! He had overlooked nothing. Nothing had gone amiss. Not a single clue remained. Only the dark trees had seen; and trees, like dead men, could tell no tales.

Slickmer chuckled to himself as he saw again, as vivid as he had seen it in the flesh, that sudden puzzled look on Bills' face when, on their breaking from the tangle of vine-maple and stepping out into that little mossy spot, he, Slickmer, had said: "Well, Bills, this is the place. Not a bad one to spend eternity in, eh?"

Bills had eyed him keenly, questioningly, for a few moments, then Bills had said: "Slickmer, what do you mean? That look of yours—"

Bills had not been able to finish that.

"I mean, Bills, that you had better say your prayers and prepare to go on a long journey. You'll never leave this spot alive—or dead either, for I am going to bury you here, Bills. It's nice and cool here, which will be a good thing to remember—for you are going to be hot enough. Yes, it is nice and cool, Bills. See how the water drips from the moss at times."

"My God, man!" Bills had exclaimed. "Surely you can't mean this, Slickmer!"

"I am not joking, Bills. I have been waiting for this moment for years, planning it, dreaming about it waking and sleeping."

At this point Slickmer had drawn his big blue revolver from his pocket.

"I have waited long, Bills, for I wasn't going to take any chance. I wasn't going to be caught, for then all my vengeance would be wormwood and gall. See how cool I am! That is because I have planned it all out so carefully, and it all is going as I planned it. I have waited long, Bills, but I ain't going to lose no time now that I have you here."

How Bills had pleaded! How Bills had tried to explain!

"My God, Slickmer, I didn't know you believed this. I knew that you hated me, that there had been misunderstandings. But I never dreamed that you had got things twisted in this hellish fashion. If I had done *it*, Slickmer, God knows I couldn't blame you for this thing you are going to do. But, as there is a heaven above us, Slickmer, I am innocent!"

"That's what they all say," had been Slickmer's answer. "I am going to give you just four minutes, Bills," he had added, glancing at his watch.

"My God, Slickmer! I tell you that I am innocent! I tell you—"

But he had cut Bills short. This had been the only thing in all the terrible scene that had threatened Slickmer's sang-froid—this impassioned protestation of innocence on Bills' part.

After that Bills had stood very straight and very silent for some moments.

Then: "You may kill the flesh, Slickmer, you may splatter this green moss with my brains; but you can't kill the soul."

Slickmer's only answer to this had been a smile.

"You believe, Slickmer, that dead men yet live?"

"Of course. But dead men never can touch the living. Else there would be no crime here on earth. But this that I am about to do is not a crime. You know that, Bills. It is vengeance."

"'Vengeance is mine,' saith the Lord."

"And mine," Slickmer had answered.

"So be it then," Bills had said quietly. "You may kill me and bury me here, but my spirit will be with you."

He, Slickmer, had laughed at this. Foolish Bills—trying to save himself with spooky threats!

"I'll be with you, Slickmer," Bills had continued. "You'll hear from me, and when you are least expecting it. You'll hear my voice in the night—perhaps when the wind whispers and moans. I'll dog your footsteps when the moon shines and sends long shadows. Before I am done with you, Slickmer, you will pray God on your knees to bury your bones here beneath mine!"

"You have just two minutes left, Bills," had been Slickmer's imperturbable answer.

A pallor had touched Bills' face, but other sign of fear he had given none. Yes, Bills had been a brave man. He, Slickmer, had to say that much for Bills.

And then suddenly the doomed man had sprung. Ah, crafty Bills! He had thought, because at that moment Slickmer's eyes had been on the watch, that Slickmer would not see.

The next instant Bills had pitched to the ground with a bullet through his lungs. Slickmer had fired again and yet again, and then he had placed the revolver close up to Bills' head and pressed the trigger for the fourth time, splattering the green moss with Bills' gore and brains.

"Ha, ha!" Slickmer had half shouted. "Haunt away now, Bills, and be welcome! Go ahead and speak now—when the wind whispers and moans and the moon sends its long shadows!"

Then Slickmer had fetched the mattock and the shovel (brought to the spot the day before and hidden in the bushes), dug the grave and rolled Bills into it.

The hole refilled, he had carefully proceeded to obliterate every trace of the sepulture. He had worked long at this, using moss and leaves and sticks, and his work done, he had found himself almost wishing that someone would issue from the vine-maple tangle and step forth onto the very grave itself, so that he, Slickmer, might gloat over his work—the skill with which he had covered up every vestige of the dark, bloody secret hidden there.

Yes, if those bunglers would only be as careful as he had been. Why didn't they hide every—?

What was that?

Slickmer started, whirled so quickly in the direction of the cabin that the shovel and the mattock slid from his shoulder.

Surely a sound had come from his cabin. But all he could hear now was the roaring of the wind in the trees.

Great drops of rain began to fall; the sky was turning dark like ink.

Slickmer slung his grave tools back to his shoulder and moved on toward the cabin.

"Yes," he muttered, "I must just have imagined that I heard something."

As for those bunglers, now, why didn't they hide every sign, cover up every movement, every clue—as he had done? Yes, why didn't they—?

Slickmer stopped short in his tracks, staring at the cabin as though he expected to see the spirit of Bills come forth from its shadows.

That sound had come again.

But the next moment Slickmer laughed and started on.

"Easy, old man!" said he. "You are getting the jumps already. The next thing you know you'll be hearing the voice of Bills. Ha, ha! In the wind. Yes, he's going to haunt me when the wind whispers and moans and the moon sends its long shadows!"

This struck Slickmer as very funny. He chuckled, shaking his head in appreciation.

The next instant, however, he was again fetched up. The rain began to fall with great violence, the wind to roar in the trees like a lion gone mad; but the man stood there as if unconscious of rain and turmoil, his eyes fixed on his cabin.

This rude pile of logs partly concealed the woodshed, in the obscurity of which Slickmer saw a form take shape. That form seated itself; another appeared beside it. Then the rain swept in a sheety flood, and Slickmer could see no more.

He was moving swiftly forward, however, muttering a curse at that momentary weakness. For he had let foolish thoughts of Bills get into his head.

"Huh," said Slickmer, "I wonder who's here."

He strode round the cabin. Three young fellows were there in the woodshed.

"Sports!" was Slickmer's observation.

They nodded a greeting, and Slickmer, as he stepped into the shelter, growled: "Howdeedo."

He began to feel fiercely angry, and a lump began to rise in his throat. Where had these confounded fellows come from, anyway? How long had they been here in the hills? Damn their souls, had they seen anything?

"I hope," one of the young men observed, looking at Slickmer a little curiously, "that we are not intruding. But the storm broke as we were coming by, and we stepped in here for shelter."

"Oh, not a bit," returned Slickmer, "not a bit of it. Make yourself at home. She's a wild one now, but she's only a thunderstorm and will soon blow over. Look at that flash! Probably in half an hour, though, there won't be half a dozen clouds in the sky."

Came a pause, when the young man, whom Slickmer had heard addressed as Rufus, said: "Any deer up this way?"

"Oh, a few," Slickmer grunted.

He knew where there were more than a few deer, but he wasn't going to tell these city dudes that.

"When," Slickmer asked suddenly, "did you arrive?"

"Got here—at the place where we are camping, that is—about 2 o'clock. Our camp is there at the bend below. If it wasn't raining so hard, you could see our fire through the trees."

Slickmer felt as though a load had been lifted from his heart. Two o'clock! Thank God, they couldn't know a thing! What a fool he was to let fears grip him like this!

"I suppose," Rufus remarked, "that you don't have many visitors up here."

Slickmer seemed to eye him a little sharply.

"No! Visitors to this cabin are rare birds. You are the first human beings I have seen for more than a month—since I was down last to North Bend."

"Well, isn't that strange now!" the young man exclaimed.

Slickmer's eyes seemed to snap at him.

"Strange? What is there so strange about that, son?"

"Oh, nothing; nothing at all, really. Only it struck me as—well, somewhat odd that a man hadn't seen another for a month, for more than a whole month."

"You seem," said Slickmer, "to be quite interested in my visitors—that is, supposing I have any."

"Not a bit, not a bit," returned the hunter, showing some uneasiness. "Only I thought that a man who went off without even closing his door must not have many callers. That was all."

"Not shut? That is strange!" Slickmer exclaimed.

He flung a sudden curse at his own head, for he had let foolish thoughts of Bills come into it again.

"Was *that* door open?"

"It was."

"Strange! Because I know that I shut it."

"Well," returned Rufus, "it was open when we came—about five minutes ago. I shut it myself, for the wind was slamming it back and forth."

"So that was what I heard?"

"I suppose so; it made quite a sound when it struck."

"And to think," said Slickmer to himself with colossal disgust, "that I let that give me spooky thoughts!"

And then a thought came that was anything but spooky—a thought that brought his heart leaping into his throat and a chill through his breast.

Not a single human being had visited his cabin for over a year. Such a contingency had had no place in his plans. There still remained behind those logs damning proof of Bills' presence there.

"Have you," he said abruptly, though he endeavored with all his might to make his question seem casual, "been in the cabin?"

"Of course not," Rufus told him.

"Of course not," one of the others echoed.

"I was just wondering," said Slickmer. "No harm done if you had. That cabin, boys, has no secrets to hide."

At this the trio looked at Slickmer, as he thought, a little queerly, but nobody said anything.

"I wonder if they did go in. Are they lying to me? Why be so emphatic about it if they didn't?"

But what was the matter with him? When he had wreaked his vengeance on Bills, he had been singularly cool. Why was he so nervous now? Why, in whatever direction he turned, did he see suspicion about to raise a finger and point it at him?

"Easy, old man!" Slickmer admonished himself. "All's safe, you know. Even if they did go into the cabin and see certain things that are there, it wouldn't mean anything to *them*, would it? Certainly not. For how could they know that those things had belonged to one Bills?

"Don't be foolish, old man," Slickmer continued. "Don't get jumpy, you poor fool, or you'll give the whole thing away yourself. You must be as cool now—now when all's done and everything's safe—as you were when you took Bills over there and killed him. All *is* safe, you know—even though you do get foolish scares. So don't get jumpy. Not a single clue remains to enable any man to—"

"By George," Rufus broke in upon his thoughts, "you must have got a bad cut!"

Had Slickmer suddenly found a sizzling bomb at his feet, the shock scarcely could have been more terrible. He succeeded very well, however (at least so he believed) in hiding this. A cut—blood! Good God, had be brought in some of the telltale blood of Bills?

"A cut?" queried Slickmer. "Now what made you think that, son?"

"Why, look at that mattock handle!"

Slickmer looked and saw a great smear of gore there just where the handle entered the mattock. He cursed savagely to himself. To think that he had overlooked that! Had he overlooked anything else—anything there in that mossy spot where he had buried Bills? He would go back and see the very first thing in the morning. No! He would go back this very day—just as soon as he could get rid of these cursed meddlers.

"Oh, yes," said Slickmer to Rufus. "I remember now. I thought the rain had washed that off."

The young man was silent for a moment.

"Damn him!" thought Slickmer. "What is he looking at me that way for? What's in his cursed head now, anyway?"

"You weren't out in the rain long enough," Rufus observed. "And besides, that part was underneath as you carried the mattock on your shoulder."

"Of course. How stupid of me! As for the cut, though, it was a bad one—I mean, that is, that it bled rather freely."

Slickmer touched his left arm just below the elbow.

"Right there," he said. "But it doesn't amount to much. Really I had forgotten all about it.

"See," he added. "She's clearing up now. Probably the evening will be as calm and fine as one could wish."

"Probably," nodded Rufus, his look abstracted.

Slickmer swore to himself as he watched him covertly.

"What's he thinking about, anyway?"

Rufus arose and glanced up at the brightening sky, then roundabout.

"Clearing up fast," said he. "There," pointing downstream, "is Jim's fire blazing away as bright as though there had been no rain at all."

"Four of you?" observed Slickmer.

"Four of us," Rufus told him.

"Well," said Slickmer when, five minutes or so afterward, the hunters were on the point of quitting him, "drop over sometime—any time. You'll always find me here of an evening, and we'll have a game of cards or something."

From one of the cabin windows, he watched the three young fellows until they disappeared down the forest trail. Then, with a muttered oath, he turned and became suddenly active.

He must visit the scene of the crime to see if he had overlooked anything there—as he had overlooked that blood on the mattock handle. He had no time to lose, for the dark autumn afternoon was already drawing toward a close. But there were two things that he must do before he went: he must gather up and hide (on his return he would burn them, every one) all the things that had belonged to Bills, and he must remove that blood, every spot of it, from the mattock handle. True, he had explained that. He had explained that very cleverly, hadn't he? The stain must be destroyed, however, perfectly innocuous though it was.

He worked with haste, yet so carefully—oh, so carefully! Nothing would be overlooked this time.

And nothing was.

Within ten minutes of the time that the three hunters had disappeared, Slickmer had started on his way to the scene of the murder.

He had nearly reached the place before he noticed how dark the forest was now. This realization came to him with a force like that of a sudden, unexpected shock. He stopped and gazed about into the deepening gloom with a fear at which he hurled fierce curses.

"Buck up, you fool!" he said vehemently. "Are you going to be scared by shadows?"

He pressed forward through the wet undergrowth; but thoughts were crowding into his mind so dark and terrible that an indescribable fear—a thing of horror—gripped him as though with the talons of the Fiend. In broad daylight, with the sun glowing warmly on the dank green moss, he could laugh at Bills' spooky threats; but now, with evening closing in and gloom pervading the depths of the thick spruce forest, he could not have forced even sardonic mirth to his lips had his immortal soul itself been the forfeit else to fiends and goblins damned.

A cold sweat oozed from his forehead, trickled down his cheeks. Why hadn't he waited till morning? Yet Slickmer, though he paused once or twice, would not turn back. He would brazen this thing out; then he would never have to visit the hellish spot again.

When he broke through the vine-maple tangle and on to the grave of Bills, the man was trembling like a leaf in the wind. Nameless terrors ringed him around, seemed to grin and gibber at him and glide this way and that in the darkness. Sounds were all about him—only the water, shaken from the branches of the great trees by the wind, striking on the leaves; only the brushing of limbs, the low moaning of a tree rubbing against another. But, had these sounds come from the depths of hell itself, the effect upon Slickmer could not have been more terrible.

Bills had said he would haunt him. Could a dead man, after all, torture a man still clothed in the flesh? No, no! God would not permit a thing like that! But—supposing it was so—would Bills wait until the moon cast long shadows?

Slickmer turned to flee but with a mighty effort stayed his steps. He must see the thing through now—once and for all. But, as he looked, he cursed in wild, insensate anger. The place was already damnably dark. Why hadn't he noticed that the day was so nearly done? Why hadn't he waited until the morrow?

But, now that he was at the grave of Bills, he must make sure. It seemed to be growing darker every moment; he had not a single second to lose.

His examination of the place, however, revealed nothing. There was, in fact, nothing there to discover. This part of his work Slickmer had indeed done well.

"But," thought he, "what if the darkness does hide some clue?"

He struck a match. The wind was growling in the tree-tops, but here in the depths of the woods there was but the softest movement of the air. He held the match and scrutinized roundabout until the flame burnt thumb and finger. The gloom that followed made Slickmer exclaim aloud. The next instant a noise was heard close at hand, sending new terrors through the man. It was only a branch stirring in a sudden gust, but to the mind of Slickmer it brought a thousand horrors.

A long and loud moan suddenly filled the forest. It was nothing but the sound made by that tree rubbing against its neighbor; but Slickmer cried out in the extremity of fear and terror, turned and fled from the spot.

On entering his clearing, he felt a sudden relief. A feeling of confidence, of security, came to him. It was still quite light here in the open space. Above the mountains there beyond the river, a bright yellow streak glowed beneath the clouds.

"You poor fool!" said Slickmer. "That must have been nothing more than the tree rubbing against the other in the wind!"

But, though he had left the dark forest with its grisly horrors behind him, it was a broken, soul-torn man that moved across the little meadow toward his cabin. What his guilty conscience, his jumpy nerves (so firm when he had killed Bills and buried him) and his foolish fears and suspicions had begun, that his visit to the grave of Bills had completed.

He built a fire in the rusty old cook-stove, and in the fireplace another, which ere the lapse of many minutes had consumed to ashes the last vestige of the last article that had belonged to Bills.

Not a clue remained now—only Slickmer could not be sure of that. Indeed, the uncertainties and fears that came crowding into his mind were as terrible as ever. In such a pass did he find himself when at last he stood safe—absolutely safe. There was not a thing in the world now to discover his crime to any man.

But vain were all his efforts to make himself believe that it was really so. Always the thought would follow: "But if—?"

He needed something to brace his nerves—those nerves that had been so steady when he had killed Bills.

He went to the table and took up a jug there. The jug was empty. He knew that it was empty. That very morning he and Bills had drunk the last of the moonshine it had contained. Yet Slickmer shook the vessel to make sure. There was no sound of liquid—as he had known there would be none. Yet he removed the cork and inverted the jug to make certitude certain. A few drops of the vile stuff fell onto the table; Slickmer slammed the jug down on the boards with an oath.

If he only had a glass of hootch! But there was the coffee. That would have to do the trick. He brewed a full pot and drank cup after cup of the smoking black liquid.

"This means insomnia, perhaps, but I've got to have a bracer, or I'll go off my head."

For a long time he sat in black thought and gloomy revery. What an hour of triumph was this! But, then, he suffered himself to become a prey to foolish thoughts and more foolish fears and fancies. He was acting like a weakling instead of like the man that he was—that he-man who had killed Bills.

"Like a damned female!" said Slickmer.

But in the morning he would be all right. Yes, in the morning his shaken, quivering nerves would be firm once more.

He came back to his immediate surroundings with a start. The cabin (there was but a single room) was growing dark. In the fireplace, only two coals were to be seen, glowing at him like baleful eyes. The flame of his kerosene lamp was sinking low; already the chimney was growing black with its smoke. Night had fallen.

Slickmer exclaimed aloud, then muttered savagely for that he had heard fear in his voice.

He lighted the lantern and took the extinguished lamp, the wick of it smoking vilely, out on to the back porch.

Not the faintest breath stirred the air—though Slickmer did not notice this. But he did note the heavy stillness that brooded over the place, broken only by the low and mournful wash of the river. Through rents in the cloud curtain, patches of clear sky were to be seen, blue and star-dusted. The darkness, therefore, though dense, was not pitchy. But Slickmer shrank from it as though from the blackness of the Pit.

"Steady, old man!" said Slickmer. "Don't get spooky jumps, you know."

From a box nailed to the log wall, he took a jug, its capacity about two gallons.

"Hell," said Slickmer, shaking the vessel, "almost empty!"

There was sufficient oil, however, to fill the lamp nearly to overflowing, and Slickmer gave a sigh of relief. He would have light, anyway! He shot a look over his shoulder, then snatched up the lamp and fairly bolted indoors.

He had forgotten to return the jug to its box cupboard; he had even forgotten to replace the cork.

The lamp trimmed and lighted, he rekindled a blaze in the fireplace. Light! That was what he needed—light to steady his nerves. And there was enough wood in the cabin to keep a fire going till daybreak. He was glad of that—that he would not have to make a trip out to the woodshed.

It was 10 o'clock when he went to bed—the fire and the lamp burning high and bright. Heavy clothes curtained the windows.

"So that," said Slickmer, "those cursed campers won't get curious."

If he could only get to sleep! He would be a new man on waking. But minute followed minute, an hour passed, and still he could not sleep. It was that coffee. Yes, that was what it was. It was that coffee that was keeping him awake.

How still everything was! Not a breath of wind. If it would only stay like that—at least until he could get to sleep.

He looked at his watch, and he groaned. It was half past 11. The moon would be rising above the mountains now and casting long shadows. The night before, he and Bills had seen it come up a little after 10, and so it would be shining now—unless clouds hid it.

"If I only knew! But, old woman and coward that I am, I'm afraid to get up and look. Thank God, though, there is no wind!"

What was that? Slickmer groaned again. It was the wind at last.

And, as he lay there in his warm bed, he shivered as though the covers were icy.

He listened in clammy fear. Ten minutes passed, and then a twisted smile moved Slickmer's ashy face. What a fool he had been to listen for Bills' voice just because the wind was blowing—what a fool to even think of Bills' threat! Ah, crafty Bills! But his spooky bravado hadn't saved him.

The next instant Slickmer stiffened and thrust a hand to his mouth to stifle a cry. A low sobbing, moaning sound was mingling with the rushing of the wind, then suddenly ceased.

Slickmer's eyes rolled wildly in a face as livid as that of a cadaver. He pressed his hand to his mouth until blood broke from the lips.

A long wait succeeded, when the moaning and sobbing came again. This time there could be no mistake: it *was* Bills, and he wad right there at the door. That scratching noise—that was Bills trying to get in!

If the wind would only blow harder—a devastating hurricane—anything to drown the voice of Bills. The wind did come harder, but Bills only raised his voice the louder—scratched harder at the door as he tried to gain an entrance.

How long the man lay there shivering and listening while that sobbing and moaning rose and fell and died away only to rise and fall again, he never knew. Fear held him stretched in his bed of terror, but a greater fear drove him from it. He crossed over to the lamp, trembling from head to foot, and turned up the flame until it began to pour forth smoke and soot and he had to lower it again. He threw wood into the fireplace, then began to dress in feverish haste. For he couldn't stay here. Bills would drive him mad—why, Bills might get in at any moment!

But, when he stood ready to go, Slickmer groaned and sank, a quivering heap, upon a chair. How could he leave the cabin when Bills was there outside?

But how could he stay? Morning, if he did, would find him a madman. And, besides, Bills might get in at any moment.

Probably if he begged Bills to go away . . . Yes, that was his only hope. But no! Why hadn't he thought of that before? *That* was his only hope. While Bills was trying to get in at the back door, he, Slickmer, could steal out the front and make his escape to the camp of the hunters. He had cursed their presence, but how glad he was now that they were here! For surely Bills would not follow him right into their camp.

He began to open the door—guardedly, so guardedly! The least sound would betray him. Light went streaming out through the crack; but Bills, there in the rear, could not see that. Fifteen minutes, and Slickmer had the door opened six inches. Twenty, and the space was nearly wide enough to admit his body.

The moon was shining above the mountains with a cold and baleful fire, casting long shadows across the clearing—almost to the very door of the cabin.

There! Another inch, and he could slip through.

A sudden sound, however, jerked Slickmer round, at that very instant when the moon went out in darkness. It was only a piece of wood falling in the fireplace, but it cost Slickmer his hold on the door. As it swung violently open in the wind, a harsh grating sound came from the rusty hinges and rose to a shrill shriek.

A piercing scream, one of mortal agony and terror, followed. Then silence. Even the voice of Bills had ceased.

That scream reached the ears of Rufus. He raised himself up in his hard bed and listened. Nothing was heard, however, save the low growl of the wind in the trees and the voice of the river tumbling along on its eternal way to the sea.

"I wonder—" thought Rufus.

He wondered for a while, then got up and piled fresh wood on the fire. And still he wondered.

A chill wind was blowing, coming in strong, sudden gusts. Clouds were traveling swiftly southward. In one of the patches of clear sky, the young hunter saw the beautiful Pleiades twinkling down at him; then suddenly a fierce pale light broke through the forest, and, turning, Rufus saw, there behind the black, swaying trees, the broad gibbous moon shining with leprous fire.

Scarcely had he turned when the sound came again. And this time there could be no uncertainty: it was a scream.

Rufus quickly turned and entered the tent, seized his rifle and shook one of the sleepers by the shoulder.

"Whazza matter? Whazza matter now?"

"I don't know, Tom. Something queer going on. You needn't wake the others, though."

Rufus stepped out again—stood with his look fixed in the direction of Slickmer's cabin.

"Queer bird, that mountaineer," was Rufus' thought. "Darned suspicious, now that I think of it! Blood on mattock! I had forgotten about that, but—"

There! What was that, visible for a fleeting moment in a pool of moonlight? A wild, inarticulate cry, one of fear and horror unutterable followed; and a moment afterward—just as Tom thrust his pale visage out of the tent—a man broke from the trail, half leaped, half stumbled across the little open space and sank, a quivering, chattering heap, by the fire.

It was Slickmer.

"Good God, man!" cried Rufus. "What's happened to you?"

"Bills came! I killed him—buried him and covered up the spot so that no man could tell! He told me he would haunt me if I killed him. But I laughed. My God, I only laughed! He said he would come in the wind and when the moon casts long shadows."

Rufus stared at Slickmer in detestation and horror and yet not without a trace of pity in his look.

"So," said he, "that was his blood on the mattock?"

"His!" moaned the murderer. "I confess all. I'll show you his grave tomorrow, and you can dig Bills up and see for yourselves that I tell no lie."

"Take us there now!"

"Oh, Lord!" burst from Tom.

"No, no!" Slickmer half shrieked. "Not now! Tomorrow, tomorrow—that is, if the sun shines bright."

"So the man you murdered paid you a visit?"

Slickmer moaned.

"He has been there for hours—I don't know for how long. I kept waiting—fighting the thing, hoping he would go away. But he wouldn't go. He still kept muttering and moaning and sobbing and scratching."

"Scratching?" said Rufus.

"Yes—scratching to get in. And at last I knew that there was only one thing to do to get him to go away—or at least be quiet. Maybe he told me. I don't know—my nerves are in shreds. But I knew there was only one thing on earth that would make him quit haunting me. And that was to confess! And, now that I have done it, don't you think," wailed Slickmer, "that Bills will leave me alone?"

"Did you see him?"

"No, no! What he did was worse than if he had shown himself. But I heard him. He said he would come when the wind blows and that he would dog me when the moon casts long shadows."

"When the wind blows," repeated Rufus.

Then to Slickmer: "Do you hear Bills now?"

"No, no! Not now. For I have confessed. Surely he will leave me alone now."

"And yet," said Rufus to himself, "the wind still blows."

Their voices had aroused the two others; and, when they came out, Slickmer asked them if they thought Bills would still haunt him now when he had confessed everything.

"Something queer about this," said Rufus in an aside to Tom. "I'm going to see what I can see over there at that cabin—I mean what I can hear."

"Tonight?"

"Tonight—right away."

"Can't you wait till morning?"

"What for? No! Coming along, Tom?"

"Ye-es—that is—certainly—if you are so determined to go. I don't think you ought to go over there alone. There's no telling what—"

Rufus made a sign, and Jim joined them.

"We're going over to the cabin to investigate," Rufus told him. "Keep an eye on that bird, Jim. Not that I think he's dangerous. On the contrary, I think he's a very harmless killer now. But it won't do any harm to keep an eye on the man."

Rufus had turned before the last word was spoken. Tom, after some hesitation, followed in his footsteps. A moment, and they had disappeared in the forest.

Just as the two stepped into Slickmer's clearing, the leprous moon slid behind a cloud and the wild landscape was involved in sudden darkness. The cabin rose, a black splotch; from the front doorway strong light was streaming out.

"Why—er—now why," said Tom, "can't we wait till morning?"

"No!"

"Confound it," Tom exclaimed in a husky whisper, "there isn't anything there. That bird is clean off his head. He just imagined he heard Bills."

"I don't think it was just imagination. A guilty conscience needs no accuser; but there is more than a guilty conscience in this."

"Aw, Rufus, you can't see anything now. Wait till morning."

"The moon will come again. And, besides, it isn't pitch-dark. Supposing we can't see, we can still hear, can't we?"

The other groaned.

Rufus was moving forward—a dark, vague shadow—straight toward the cabin. Tom followed.

Twenty feet or so from the door, the two hunters halted. The clouds had parted before the moon, and its fire was glimmering down pale and dreadful as light on tombstones.

"I don't hear a sound," whispered Tom, his voice trembling. "We might just as well go back."

"Wait!"

Rufus was waiting for the wind. Tom had not noticed that the air was still as death.

Then abruptly the stillness was broken. The sound was low at first, but it steadily grew stronger—a low moaning and sobbing sound that seemed to curdle the blood in Tom's veins and heart. It rose, fell, rose higher than before; then it abruptly ceased, as though borne away on the wind.

"My God, what was that?"

"Bills!" said Rufus.

"No wonder," came from Tom's chattering teeth, "that that murderer is a wreck! Let's go back!"

But Rufus was going forward. He stepped on to the porch and stood, a dark figure, in the light of the doorway.

Again that blood-curdling sound was heard. Tom's face, in moon shadow, was like the visage of a corpse.

He was on the point of turning and dashing from that place of disembodied horror when Rufus suddenly turned and said:

"Didn't come from inside. Must be around at the back."

"For God's sake, Rufus, where are you going?"

"To find Bills."

The next instant Rufus had vanished around a corner of the hut.

A long wait followed—or a wait that was long to Tom. He grasped his rifle fiercely, holding it in readiness for instant use. But what could it avail? A bullet couldn't save him from this Thing.

The sound came again, more terrible than before; then utter silence.

A space, and Tom's voice was heard, rising in trembling and whispered accents: "Rufus! Rufus! Come back!"

A laugh was the answer.

"Come around here!" Rufus cried. "Come here and look at this!"

Tom went, not, however, without many a fearful glance cast to right and to left.

He found Rufus standing in the shadow of the house, by the porch. Though the spot was in gloom, objects there were to be distinguished without much difficulty.

"There's the ghost!" Rufus laughed.

And he pointed to Slickmer's kerosene jug!

"What are you talking about?" exclaimed the other.

"That's Bills! When we took shelter there in the woodshed, that jug wasn't here; it was up in that box that serves as a cupboard."

"I didn't notice."

"Well, I did," Rufus told him. "And the explanation must be this: he took down that jug to fill his lamp and forgot to put it back—he even forgot to put the cork in it again!"

"What on earth are you talking about?"

"Oh, Lord!" Rufus exclaimed. "Don't you see it? Look here! When the wind comes strong, the air—thanks to the way it eddies here or something—is forced in and out of that jug and makes the low moaning and sobbing sound that—"

"Ha, ha!" cried Tom. "Isn't that rich, though?"

"Yes," said Rufus to himself, "it's ha-ha now, but a moment ago it was spook-spook!"

"But that scratching he spoke of?"

"That rope hanging there by the door," Rufus told him. "It has a ring at the end, and that ring scratches back and forth when the wind blows."

"Ha, ha! You know, Rufus," said Tom, "I thought we would find it was something like this!"

In Amundsen's Tent

"Inside the tent, in a little bag, I left a letter, addressed to R. M. the King, giving information of what he [sic] had accomplished. . . . Besides this letter, I wrote a short epistle to Captain Scott, who, I assumed, would be the first to find the tent."

Captain Amundsen: The South Pole.

"We have just arrived at this tent, 2 miles from our camp, therefore about 1½ miles from the pole. In the tent we find a record of five Norwegians having been here, as follows:

> Roald Amundsen
> Olav Olavson Bjaaland
> Hilmer Hanssen
> Sverre H. Hassel
> Oscar Wisting
> 16 Dec. 1911.

"Left a note to say I had visited the tent with companions."

Captain Scott: His Last Journal.

"Travelers," says Richard A. Proctor, "are sometimes said to tell marvelous stories; but it is a noteworthy fact that, in nine cases out of ten, the marvelous stories of travelers have been confirmed."

Certainly no traveler ever set down a more marvelous story than that of Robert Drumgold. This record I am at last giving to the world, with my humble apologies to the spirit of the hapless explorer for withholding it so long. But the truth is that Eastman, Dahlstrom and I thought it the work of a mind deranged; little wonder, forsooth, if his mind had given way, what with the fearful sufferings which he had gone through and the horror of that fate which was closing in upon him.

What was it, that *thing* (if thing it was) which came to him, the sole survivor of the party which had reached the Southern Pole, thrust itself into the tent and, issuing, left but the severed head of Drumgold there?

Our explanation at the time, and until recently, was that Drumgold had been set upon by his dogs and devoured. Why, though, the flesh had not been stripped from the head was to us an utter mystery. But that was only one of many things that were utter mysteries.

But now we know—or feel certain—that this explanation was as far from the truth as that desolate, ice-mantled spot where he met his end is from the smiling, flower-spangled regions of the tropics.

Yes, we thought that the mind of poor Robert Drumgold had given way, that the horror in Amundsen's tent and that thing which came to Drumgold there in his own—we thought all was madness only. Hence our suppression of this part of the Drumgold manuscript. We feared that the publication of so extraordinary a record might cast a cloud of doubt upon the real achievements of the Sutherland expedition.

But of late our ideas and beliefs have undergone a change that is nothing less than a metamorphosis. This metamorphosis, it is scarcely necessary to say, was due to the startling discoveries made in the region of the Southern Pole by the late Captain Stanley Livingstone, as confirmed and extended by the expedition conducted by Darwin Frontenac. Captain Livingstone, we now learn, kept his real discovery, what with the doubts and derision which met him on his return to the world, a secret from every living soul but two—Darwin Frontenac and Bond McQuestion. It is but now, on the return of Frontenac, that we learn how truly wonderful and amazing were those discoveries made by the ill-starred captain. And yet, despite the success of the Frontenac expedition, it must be admitted that the mystery down there in the Antarctic is enhanced rather than dissipated. Darwin Frontenac and his companions saw much; but we know that there are things and beings down there that they did not see. The Antarctic—or, rather, part of it—has thus suddenly become the most interesting and certainly the most fearful place upon this interesting and fearful globe of ours.

So another marvelous story told—or, rather, only partly told—by a traveler has been confirmed. And here are Eastman and I preparing to go once more to the Antarctic to confirm, as we hope, another story—one eery and fearful as any ever conceived by any romanticist.

And to think that it was ourselves, Eastman, Dahlstrom and I, who made the discovery! Yes, it was we who entered the tent, found there the head of Robert

Drumgold and the pages whereon he had scrawled his story of mystery and horror. To think that we stood there, in the very spot where it had been, and thought the story but as the baseless fabric of some madman's vision!

How vividly it all rises before me again—the white expanse, glaring, blinding in the untempered light of the Antarctic sun; the dogs straining in the harness, the cases on the sleds long and black like coffins; our sudden halt as Eastman fetched up in his tracks, pointed and said, "Hello! What's that?"

A half-mile or so off to the left, some object broke the blinding white of the plain.

"*Nunatak,* I suppose," was my answer.

"Looks to me like a cairn or a tent," Dahlstrom said.

"How on earth," I queried, "could a tent have got down here in 87° 30□ south? We are far from the route of either Amundsen or Scott."

"H'm," said Eastman, shoving his amber-colored glasses up onto his forehead that he might get a better look, "I wonder. Jupiter Ammon, Nels," he added, glancing at Dahlstrom, "I believe that you are right."

"It certainly," Dahlstrom nodded, "looks like a cairn or a tent to me. I don't think it's a *nunatak.*"

"Well," said I, "it would not be difficult to put it to the proof."

"And that, my hearties," exclaimed Eastman, "is just what we'll do! We'll soon see what it is—whether it is a cairn, a tent, or only a *nunatak.*"

The next moment we were in motion, heading straight for that mysterious object there in the midst of the eternal desolation of snow and ice.

"Look there!" Eastman, who was leading the way, suddenly shouted. "See that? It *is* a tent!"

A few moments, and I saw that it was indeed so. But who had pitched it there? What were we to find within it?

I could never describe those thoughts and feelings which were ours as we approached that spot. The snow lay piled about the tent to a depth of four feet or more. Near by a splintered ski protruded from the surface—and that was all.

And the stillness! The air, at the moment, was without the slightest movement. No sound but those made by our movements, and those of the dogs, and our own breathing, broke that awful silence of death.

"Poor devils!" said Eastman at last. "One thing, they certainly pitched their tent well."

The tent was supported by a single pole, set in the middle. To this pole three guy-lines were fastened, one of them as taut as the day its stake had been driven into the surface. But this was not all, a half-dozen lines, or more, were attached to the sides of the tent. There it stood, and had stood for we knew not how long, bidding defiance to the fierce winds of that terrible region.

Dahlstrom and I got each a spade and began to remove the snow. The entrance we found unfastened but completely blocked by a couple of provision-cases (empty) and a piece of canvas.

"How on earth," I exclaimed, "did those things get into that position?"

"The wind," said Dahlstrom. "And, if the entrance had not been blocked, there wouldn't have been any tent here now; the wind would have split and destroyed it long ago."

"H'm," mused Eastman. "The wind did it, Nels—blocked the place like that? I wonder."

The next moment we had cleared the entrance. I thrust my head through the opening. Strangely enough, very little snow had drifted in. The tent was of a dark green color, a circumstance which rendered the light within somewhat weird and ghastly—or perhaps my imagination contributed not a little to that effect.

"What do you see, Bill?" asked Eastman. "What's inside?"

My answer was a cry, and the next instant I had sprung back from the entrance.

"What is it, Bill?" Eastman exclaimed. "Great heaven, what is it, man?"

"A head!" I told him.

"A head?"

"A human head!"

He and Dahlstrom stooped and peered in.

"What is the meaning of this?" Eastman cried. "A severed human head!"

Dahlstrom dashed a mittened hand across his eyes.

"Are we dreaming?" he exclaimed.

"'Tis no dream, Nels," returned our leader. "I wish to heaven it was. A head! A human head!"

"Is there nothing more?" I asked.

"Nothing. No body, not even a stripped bone—only that severed head. Could the dogs—?"

"Yes?" queried Dahlstrom.

"Could the dogs have done this?"

"Dogs!" Dahlstrom said. "This is not the work of dogs."

We entered and stood looking down upon that grisly remnant of mortality.

In Amundsen's Tent 269

"It wasn't dogs," said Dahlstrom.

"Not dogs?" Eastman queried. "What other explanation is there? Except this—cannibalism."

Cannibalism! A shudder went through my heart. I may as well say at once, however, that our discovery of a good supply of pemmican and biscuit on the sled, at that moment completely hidden by the snow, was to show us that that fearful explanation was not the true one. The dogs! That was it, that was the explanation—even though what the victim himself had set down told us a very different story. Yes, the explorer had been set upon by his dogs and devoured. But there were things that militated against that theory. Why had the animals left that head—in the frozen eyes (they were blue eyes) and upon the frozen features of which was a look of horror that sends a shudder through my very soul even now? Why, the head did not have even the mark of a single fang, though it appeared to have been *chewed* from the trunk. Dahlstrom, however, was of the opinion that it had been *hacked* off.

And there, in the man's story, in the story of Robert Drumgold, we found another mystery—a mystery as insoluble (if it was true) as the presence here of his severed head. There the story was, scrawled in lead-pencil across the pages of his journal. But what were we to make of a record—the concluding pages of it, that is—so strange and so dreadful?

But enough of this, of what we thought and of what we wondered. The journal itself lies before me, and I now proceed to set down the story of Robert Drumgold in his own words. Not a word, not a comma shall be deleted, inserted or changed.

Let it begin with his entry for January the 3rd, at the end of which day the little party was only fifteen miles (geographical) from the Pole.

Here it is:

Jan. 3.—Lat. of our camp 89° 45☐ 10☐. Only fifteen miles more, and the Pole is ours—unless Amundsen or Scott has beaten us to it, or both. But it will be ours just the same, even though the glory of discovery is found to be another's. What shall we find there?

All are in fine spirits. Even the dogs seem to know that this is the consummation of some great achievement. And a thing that is a mystery to us is the interest they have shown this day in the region before us. Did we halt, there they were gazing and gazing straight south and sometimes sniffing and sniffing. What does it mean?

Yes, in fine spirits all—dogs as well as we three men. Everything is auspicious. The weather for the last three days has been simply glorious. Not once, in this time, has the temperature been below minus 5. As I write this, the thermometer shows one degree above. The blue of the sky is like that of which painters dream, and, in that blue, tower cloud-formations, violet-tinged in the shadows, that are beautiful beyond all description. If it were possible to forget the fact that nothing stands between ourselves and a horrible death save the meager supply of food on the sleds, one could think he was in some fairyland—a glorious fairyland of white and blue and violet.

A fairyland? Why has that thought so often occurred to me? Why have I so often likened this desolate, terrible region to fairyland? Terrible? Yes, to human beings it is terrible—frightful beyond all words. But, though so unutterably terrible to men, it may not be so in reality. After all, are all things, even of this earth of ours, to say nothing of the universe, made for man—this being (a godlike spirit in the body of a quasi-ape) who, set in the midst of wonders, leers and slavers in madness and hate and wallows in the muck of a thousand lusts? May there not be other beings—yes, even on this very earth of ours—more wonderful—yes, and more terrible too—than he?

Heaven knows, more than once, in this desolation of snow and ice, have I seemed to feel their presence in the air about us—nameless entities, disembodied, *watching* things.

Little wonder, forsooth, that I have again and again thought of these strange words of one of America's greatest scientists, Alexander Winchell:

"Nor is incorporated rational existence conditioned on warm blood, nor on any temperature which does not change the forms of matter of which the organism may be composed. There may be intelligences corporealized after some concept not involving the processes of ingestion, assimilation and reproduction. Such bodies would not require daily food and warmth. They might be lost in the abysses of the ocean, or laid up on a stormy cliff through the tempests of an arctic winter, or plunged in a volcano for a hundred years, and yet retain consciousness and thought."

All this Winchell tells us is conceivable, and he adds:

"Bodies are merely the local fitting of intelligence to particular modifications of universal matter and force."

And these entities, nameless things whose presence I seem to feel at times—are they benignant beings or things more fearful than even the madness of the human brain ever has fashioned?

But, then, I must stop this. If Sutherland or Travers were to read what I have set down here, he, *they* would think that I was losing my senses or would declare me already insane. And yet, as there is a heaven above us, it seems that I do actually believe that this frightful place knows the presence of beings other than ourselves and our dogs—things which we cannot see but which are watching us.

Enough of this.

Only fifteen miles from the Pole. Now for a sleep and on to our goal in the morning. Morning! There is no morning here, but day unending. The sun now rides as high at midnight as he does at midday. Of course, there is a change in his altitude, but it is so slight as to be imperceptible without an instrument.

But the Pole! Tomorrow the Pole! What will we find there? Only an unbroken expanse of white, or—?

Jan. 4.—The mystery and horror of this day—oh, how could I ever set that down? Sometimes, so fearful were those hours through which we have just passed, I even find myself wondering if it wasn't all only a dream. A dream! I would to heaven that it had been but a dream! As for the end—there, there, I must keep such thoughts out of my head.

Got under way at an early hour. Weather more wondrous than ever. Sky an azure that would have sent a painter into ecstasies. Cloud-formations indescribably beautiful and grand. The going, however, was pretty difficult. The place a great plain stretching away with a monotonous uniformity of surface as far as the eye could reach. A plain never trod by human foot before? At length, when our dead reckoning showed that we were drawing near to the Pole, we had the answer to that. Then it was that the keen eyes of Travers detected some object rising above the blinding white of the snow.

On the instant Sutherland had thrust his amber glasses up onto his forehead and had his binoculars to his eyes.

"Cairn!" he exclaimed, and his voice sounded hollow and very strange. "A cairn or a—*tent*. Boys, they have beaten us to the Pole!"

He handed the glasses to Travers and leaned, as though a sudden weariness had settled upon him, against the provision-cases on his sled.

"Forestalled!" said he. "Forestalled!"

I felt very sorry for our brave leader in those, his moments of terrible disappointment, but for the life of me I did not know what to say. And so I said nothing.

At that moment a cloud concealed the sun, and the place where we stood was suddenly involved in a gloom that was deep and awful. So sudden and pronounced, indeed, was the change that we gazed about us with curious and wondering looks. Far off to the right and to the left, the plain blazed white and blinding. Soon, however, the last gleam of sunshine had vanished from off it. I raised my look up to the heavens. Here and there edges of cloud were touched as though with the light of wrathful golden fire. Even then, however, that light was fading. A few minutes, and the last angry gleam of the sun had vanished. The gloom seemed to deepen about us every moment. A curious haze was concealing the blue expanse of the sky overhead. There was not the slightest movement in the gloomy and weird atmosphere. The silence was heavy, awful, the silence of the abode of utter desolation and of death.

"What on earth are we in for now?" said Travers.

Sutherland moved from his sled and stood gazing about into the eery gloom.

"Queer change, this!" said he. "It would have delighted the heart of Doré."

"It means a blizzard, most likely," I observed. "Hadn't we better make camp before it strikes us? No telling what a blizzard may be like in this awful spot."

"Blizzard?" said Sutherland. "I don't think it means a blizzard, Bob. No telling, though. Mighty queer change, certainly. And how different the place looks now, in this strange gloom! It is surely weird and terrible—that is, it certainly *looks* weird and terrible."

He turned his look to Travers.

"Well, Bill," he asked, "what did you make of it?"

He waved a hand in the direction of that mysterious object the sight of which had so suddenly brought us to a halt. I say in the direction of the object, for the thing itself was no longer to be seen.

"I believe it is a tent," Travers told him.

"Well," said our leader, "we can soon find out what it is—cairn or tent, for one or the other it must certainly be."

The next instant the heavy, awful silence was broken by the sharp crack of his whip.

"Mush on, you poor brutes!" he cried. "On we go to see what is over there. Here we are at the South Pole. Let us see who has beaten us to it."

But the dogs didn't want to go on, which did not surprise me at all, because, for some time now, they had been showing signs of some strange, inexplicable uneasiness. What had got into the creatures, anyway? For a time we puzzled over it; then we *knew,* though the explanation was still an utter mystery to us. They were *afraid.* Afraid? An inadequate word, indeed. It was fear, stark, terrible, that had entered the poor brutes. But whence had come this inexplicable fear? That also we soon knew. The thing they feared, whatever it was, was in that very direction in which we were headed!

A cairn, a tent? What did this thing mean?

"What on earth is the matter with the critters?" exclaimed Travers. "Can it be that—?"

"It's for us to find out what it means," said Sutherland.

Again we got in motion. The place was still involved in that strange, weird gloom. The silence was still that awful silence of desolation and of death.

Slowly but steadily we moved forward, urging on the reluctant, fearful animals with our whips.

At last Sutherland, who was leading, cried out that he saw it. He halted, peering forward into the gloom, and we urged our teams up alongside his.

"It must be a tent," he said.

And a tent we found it to be—a small one supported by a single bamboo and well guyed in all directions. Made of drab-colored gabardine. To the top of the tent-pole another had been lashed. From this, motionless in the still air, hung the remains of a small Norwegian flag and, underneath it, a pennant. with the word "Fram" upon it. Amundsen's tent!

What should we find inside it? And what was the meaning of that—*the strange way it bulged out on one side?*

The entrance was securely laced. The tent, it was certain, had been here for a year, all through the long Antarctic night; and yet, to our astonishment, but little snow was piled up about it, and most of this was drift. The explanation of this must, I suppose, be that, before the air currents have reached the Pole, almost all the snow has been deposited from them.

For some minutes we just stood there, and many, and some of them dreadful enough, were the thoughts that came and went. Through the long Antarctic night! What strange things this tent could tell us had it been vouchsafed the power of words! But strange things it might tell us, nevertheless. For what was that inside, making the tent bulge out in so unaccountable a manner? I moved forward to feel of it there with my mittened hand, but, for some reason that I cannot explain, I of a sudden drew back. At that instant one of the dogs whined—the sound so strange and the terror of the animal so unmistakable that I shuddered and felt a chill pass through my heart. Others of the dogs began to whine in that mysterious manner, and all shrank back cowering from the tent.

"What does it mean?" said Travers, his voice sunk almost to a whisper. "Look at them. It is as though they are imploring us to—*keep away.*"

"To keep away," echoed Sutherland, his look leaving the dogs and fixing itself once more on the tent.

"Their senses," said Travers, "are keener than ours. They already know what we can't know until we see it."

"See it!" Sutherland exclaimed. "I wonder. Boys, what are we going to see when we look into that tent? Poor fellows! They reached the Pole. But did they ever leave it? Are we going to find them in there dead?"

"Dead?" said Travers with a sudden start. "The dogs would never act that way if 'twas only a corpse inside. And, besides, if that theory was true, wouldn't the sleds be here to tell the story? Yet look around. The level uniformity of the place shows that no sled lies buried here."

"That is true," said our leader. "What *can* it mean? What *could* make the tent bulge out like that? Well, here is the mystery before us, and all we have to do is unlace the entrance and look inside to solve it."

He stepped to the entrance, followed by Travers and me, and began to unlace it. At that instant an icy current of air struck the place and the pennant above our heads flapped with a dull and ominous sound. One of the dogs, too, thrust his muzzle skyward, and a deep and long-drawn howl, sad, terrible as that of a lost soul, arose. And whilst the mournful, savage sound yet filled the air, a strange thing happened:

Through a sudden rent in that gloomy curtain of cloud, the sun sent a golden, awful light down upon the spot where we stood. It was but a shaft of light, only three or four hundred feet wide, though miles in length, and there we stood in the very middle of it, the plain on each side involved in that weird gloom, now denser and more eery than ever in contrast to that sword of golden fire which thus so suddenly had been flung down across the snow.

"Queer place this!" said Travers. "Just like a beam lying across a stage in a theater."

Travers' simile was a most apposite one, more so than he perhaps ever dreamed himself. That place *was* a stage, our light the wrathful fire of the Antarctic sun, ourselves the actors in a scene stranger than any ever beheld in the mimic world.

For some moments, so strange was it all, we stood there looking about us in wonder and perhaps each one of us in not a little secret awe.

"Queer place, all right!" said Sutherland. "But—"

He laughed a hollow, sardonic laugh. Up above, the pennant flapped and flapped again, the sound of it hollow and ghostly. Again rose the long-drawn, mournful, fiercely sad howl of the wolf-dog.

"But," added our leader, "we don't want to be imagining things, you know."

"Of course not," said Travers.

"Of course not," I echoed.

A little space, and the entrance was open and Sutherland had thrust head and shoulders through it.

I don't know how long it was that he stood there like that. Perhaps it was only a few seconds, but to Travers and me it seemed rather long.

"What is it?" Travers exclaimed at last. "What do you see?"

The answer was a scream—oh, the horror of that sound I can never forget!—and Sutherland came staggering back and, I believe, would have fallen had we not sprung and caught him.

"What is it?" cried Travers. "In God's name, Sutherland, what did you see?"

Sutherland beat the side of his head with his hand, and his look was wild and horrible.

"What is it?" I exclaimed. "*What* did you see in there?"

"I can't tell you—I can't! Oh, oh, I wish that I had never seen it! Don't look! Boys, don't look into that tent—unless you are prepared to welcome madness, or worse."

"What gibberish is this?" Travers demanded, gazing at our leader in utter astonishment. "Come, come, man! Buck up. Get a grip on yourself. Let's have an end to this nonsense. Why should the sight of a dead man, or dead men, affect you in this mad fashion?"

"*Dead* men?"

Sutherland laughed, the sound wild, maniacal.

"Dead men? If 'twas only that! Is this the South Pole? Is this the earth, or are we in a nightmare on some other planet?"

"For heaven's sake," cried Travers, "come out of it! What's got into you? Don't let your nerves go like this."

"A dead man?" queried our leader, peering into the face of Travers. "You think I saw a dead man? I wish it was only a dead man. Thank God, you two didn't look!"

On the instant Travers had turned.

"Well," said he, "I *am going* to look!"

But Sutherland cried out, screamed, sprang after him and tried to drag him back.

"It would mean horror and perhaps madness!" cried Sutherland. "Look at me. Do you want to be like me?"

"No!" Travers returned. "But I am going to see what is in that tent."

He struggled to break free, but Sutherland clung to him in a frenzy of madness.

"Help me, Bob!" Sutherland cried. "Hold him back, or we'll all go insane."

But I did not help him to hold Travers back, for, of course, 'twas my belief that Sutherland himself was insane. Nor did Sutherland hold Travers. With a sudden wrench, Travers was free. The next instant he had thrust head and shoulders through the entrance of the tent.

Sutherland groaned and watched him with eyes full of unutterable horror.

I moved toward the entrance, but Sutherland flung himself at me with such violence that I was sent over into the snow. I sprang to my feet full of anger and amazement.

"What the hell," I cried, "is the matter with you, anyway? Have you gone crazy?"

The answer was a groan, horrible beyond all words of man, but that sound did not come from Sutherland. I turned. Travers was staggering away from the entrance, a hand pressed over his face, sounds that I could never describe breaking from deep in his throat. Sutherland, as the man came staggering up to him, thrust forth an arm and touched Travers lightly on the shoulder. The effect was instantaneous and frightful. Travers sprang aside as though a serpent had struck at him, screamed and screamed yet again.

"There, there!" said Sutherland gently. "I told you not to do it. I tried to make you understand, but—but you thought that I was mad."

"It can't belong to this earth!" moaned Travers.

"No," said Sutherland. "That horror was never born on this planet of ours. And the inhabitants of earth, though they do not know it, can thank God Almighty for that."

"But it is *here!*" Travers exclaimed. "How did it come to this awful place? And where did it come from?"

"Well," consoled Sutherland, "it is dead—it must be dead."

"Dead? How do we know that it is dead? And don't forget this: it didn't come here alone!"

Sutherland started. At that moment the sunlight vanished, and everything was once more involved in gloom.

"What do you mean?" Sutherland asked. "Not alone? How do you know that it did not come alone?"

"Why, it is there *inside* the tent; but the entrance was laced—from the *outside!*"

"Fool, fool that I am!" cried Sutherland a little fiercely. "Why didn't I think of that? Not alone! Of course it was not alone!"

He gazed about into the gloom, and I knew the nameless fear and horror that chilled him to the very heart, for they chilled me to my own.

Of a sudden arose again that mournful, savage howl of the wolf-dog. We three men started as though 'twas the voice of some ghoul from hell's most dreadful corner.

"Shut up, you brute!" gritted Travers. "Shut up, or I'll brain you!"

Whether it was Travers' threat or not, I do not know; but that howl sank, ceased almost on the instant. Again the silence of desolation and of death lay upon the spot. But above the tent the pennant stirred and rustled, the sound of it, I thought, like the slithering of some repulsive serpent.

"What did you see in there?" I asked them.

"Bob—Bob," said Sutherland, "don't ask us that."

"The thing itself," said I, turning, "can't be any worse than this mystery and nightmare of imagination."

But the two of them threw themselves before me and barred my way. "No!" said Sutherland firmly. "You must not look into that tent, Bob. You must not see that—that—I don't know what to call it. Trust us; believe us, Bob! 'Tis for your sake that we say that you must not do it. We, Travers and I, can never be the same men again—the brains, the *souls* of us can never be what they were before we saw *that!*"

"Very well," I acquiesced. "I can't help saying, though, that the whole thing seems to me like the dream of a madman."

"That," said Sutherland, "is a small matter indeed. Insane? Believe that it is the dream of a madman. Believe that we are insane. Believe that you are insane yourself. Believe anything that you like. Only *don't look!*"

"Very well," I told them. "I won't look. I give in. You two have made a coward of me."

"A coward?" said Sutherland. "Don't talk nonsense, Bob. There are some things that a man should never know; there are some things that a man should never see; that horror there in Amundsen's tent is—*both!*"

"But you said that it is dead."

Travers groaned. Sutherland laughed a little wildly.

"Trust us," said the latter; "believe us, Bob. 'Tis for your sake, not for our own. For that is too late now. We have seen it, and you have not."

For some minutes we stood there by that tent, in that weird gloom, then turned to leave the cursed spot. I said that undoubtedly Amundsen had left some records inside, that possibly Scott too had reached the Pole, and visited the tent, and that we ought to secure any such mementos. Sutherland and Travers nodded, but each declared that he would not put his head through that entrance again for all the wealth of Ormus and of Ind—or words to that effect. We must, they said, get away from the awful place—get back to the world of men with our fearful message.

"You won't tell me what you saw," I said, "and yet you want to get back so that you can tell it to the world."

"We aren't going to tell the world what we *saw*," answered Sutherland. "In the first place, we couldn't, and, in the second place, if we could, not a living soul would believe us. But we can *warn* people, for that thing in there did not come alone. Where is the other one—or the others?"

"Dead, too, let us hope!" I exclaimed.

"Amen!" said Sutherland. "But maybe, as Bill says, it isn't dead. Probably—"

Sutherland paused, and a wild, indescribable look came into his eyes.

"Maybe it—*can't die!*"

"Probably," said I nonchalantly, yet with secret disgust and with poignant sorrow.

What was the use? What good would it do to try to reason with a couple of madmen? Yes, we must get away from this spot, or they would have me insane, too. And the long road back? Could we ever make it now? And what *had* they seen? What unimaginable horror was there behind that thin wall of gabardine? Well, whatever it was, it was real. Of that I could not entertain the slightest doubt. Real? Real enough to wreck, virtually instantaneously, the strong brains of two strong men. But—but were my poor companions really mad, after all?

"Or maybe," Sutherland was saying, "the other one, or the others, went back to Venus or Mars or Sirius or Algol, or hell itself, or wherever they came from, to get more of their kind. If that is so, heaven have pity on poor humanity! And, if it or they are still here on this earth, then sooner or later—it may be a dozen years, it may be a century—but sooner or later the world will know it, know it to its woe and to its horror. For they, if living, or if gone for others, will come again."

"I was thinking—" began Travers, his eyes fixed on the tent.

"Yes?" Sutherland queried.

"That," Travers told him, "it might be a good plan to empty the rifle into that thing. Maybe it isn't dead; maybe it can't die—maybe it only *changes*. Probably it is just hibernating, so to speak."

"If so," I laughed, "it will probably hibernate till doomsday."

But neither one of my companions laughed.

"Or," said Travers "it may be a demon, a ghost *materialized*. I can't say incarnated."

"A ghost materialized!" I exclaimed. "Well, may not every man or woman be just that? Heaven knows, many a one acts like a demon or a fiend incarnate."

"They may be," nodded Sutherland. "But that hypothesis doesn't help us any here."

"I may help things some," said Travers, starting toward his sled.

A moment or two, and he had got out the rifle.

"I thought," said he, "that nothing could ever take me back to that entrance. But the hope that I may—"

Sutherland groaned.

"It isn't earthly, Bill," he said hoarsely. "It's a nightmare. I think we had better go now."

Travers was going—straight toward the tent.

"Come back, Bill!" groaned Sutherland. "Come back! Let us go while we can."

But Travers did not come back. Slowly he moved forward, rifle thrust out before him, finger on the trigger. He reached the tent, hesitated a moment, then thrust the rifle-barrel through. As fast as he could work trigger and lever, he emptied the weapon into the tent—into that horror inside it.

He whirled and came back as though in fear the tent was about to spew forth behind him all the legions of foulest hell.

What was that? The blood seemed to freeze in my veins and heart as there arose from out the tent a sound—a sound low and throbbing—a sound that no man ever had heard on this earth—one that I hope no man will ever hear again.

A panic, a madness seized upon us, upon men and dogs alike, and away we fled from that cursed place.

The sound ceased. But again we heard it. It was more fearful, more unearthly, soul-maddening, hellish than before.

"Look!" cried Sutherland. "Oh, my God, *look at that!*"

The tent was barely visible now. A moment or two, and the curtain of gloom would conceal it. At first I could not imagine what had made Southerland cry out like that. Then I saw it, in that very moment before the gloom hid it from view. The tent was *moving!* It swayed, jerked like some shapeless monster in the throes of death, like some nameless thing seen in the horror of nightmare or limned on the brain of utter madness itself.

And that is what happened there; that is what we saw. I have set it down at some length and to the best of my ability under the truly awful circumstances in which I am placed. In these hastily scrawled pages is recorded an experience that, I believe, is not surpassed by the wildest to be found in the pages of the most imaginative romanticist. Whether the record is destined ever to reach the world, ever to be scanned by the eye of another—only the future can answer that.

I will try to hope for the best. I cannot blink the fact, however, that things are pretty bad for us. It is not only this sinister, nameless mystery from which we are fleeing—though heaven knows that is horrible enough—but it is the *minds* of my companions. And, added to that, is the fear for my own. But there, I must get myself in hand. After all, as Sutherland said, I didn't see it. I must not give way. We must somehow get our story to the world, though we may have for our reward only the mockery of the world's unbelief, its scoffing—the world, against which is now moving, gathering, a menace more dreadful than any that ever moved in the fevered brain of any prophet of woe and blood and disaster.

We are a dozen miles or so from the Pole now. In that mad dash away from that tent of horror, lost our bearings and for a time, I fear, went panicky. The strange, eery gloom denser than ever. Then came a fall of fine snow-crystals, which rendered things worse than ever. Just when about to give up in despair, we chanced upon one of our beacons. This gave us our bearings, and we pressed on to this spot.

Travers has just thrust his head into the tent to tell us that he is sure he saw something moving off in the gloom. Something moving! This must be looked into.

[If Robert Drumgold could only have left as full a record of those days which followed as he had of that fearful 4th of January! No man can ever know what the three explorers went through in their struggle to escape that doom from which there was no escape—a doom the mystery and horror of which perhaps surpass in gruesomeness what the most dreadful Gothic imagination ever conceived in its utterest abandonment to delirium and madness.]

Jan. 5.—Travers *had* seen something, for we, the three of us, saw it again today. Was it that horror, that thing not of this earth, which they saw in Amundsen's tent? We don't know what it is. All we know is that it is something *moves.* God have pity on us all—and on every man and woman and child on this earth of ours if this thing is what we fear!

6th.—Made 25 mi. today—20 yesterday. Did not see it today. *But heard it!* Seemed near—once, in fact, as though right over our heads. But that must have been imagination. Effect on dogs most terrible. Poor brutes! It is as horrible to them as it is to us. Sometimes I think even more. Why is it following us?

7th.—Two of dogs gone this morning. One or another of us on guard all "night." Nothing seen, not a sound heard, yet the animals have vanished. Did they desert us? We say that is what happened, but each man of us knows that none of us believes it. Made 18 mi. Fear that Travers *is* going mad.

8th.—Travers gone! He took the watch last night at 12, relieving Sutherland. That was the last seen of Travers—the last that we shall ever see. No tracks—not a sign in the snow. Travers, poor Travers, gone! Who will be the next?

Jan. 9.—*Saw it again!* Why does it let us see it like this—sometimes? Is it that horror in Amundsen's tent? Sutherland declares that it is not—that it is something even more hellish. But then S. is mad now—mad—mad—mad. If I wasn't sane, I could think that it all was only imagination. *But I saw it!*

Jan. 11.—Think it is the 11th but not sure. I can no longer be sure of anything—save that I am alone and that it is watching me. Don't know how I know, for I cannot see it. But I do know—it is watching me. It is always watching. And sometime it will come and get me—as it got Travers and Sutherland and half of the dogs.

Yes, today must be the 11th. For it was yesterday—surely it was only yesterday—that it took Sutherland. I didn't see it take him, for a fog had come up, and Sutherland—he would go on in the fog—was so slow in following that the vapor hid him from view. At last when he didn't come, I went back. But S. was gone—man, dogs, sled, everything was gone. Poor Sutherland! But then he was mad. Probably that was why it took him. Has it spared me because I am yet sane? S. had the rifle. Always he clung to that rifle—as though a bullet could save him from what we saw! My only weapon is an ax. But what good is an ax?

Jan. 13.—Maybe it is the 14th. I don't know. What does it matter? Saw it *three* times today. Each time it was closer. Dogs still whining about tent. There—that horrible, hellish sound again. Dogs still now. That sound again. But I dare not look out. The ax.

Hours later. Can't write any more.

Silence. Voices—I seem to hear voices. But that sound again.

Coming nearer. At entrance now—now—

The Isle of the Fairy Morgana

What fairies haunt this ground?
—Shakespeare: *Cymbeline*.

1. The Meeting

Desolate and lone it rises there in the midst of one of the loneliest reaches in all the lonely Sea of Bering. Flang Island it is called, this mass of rock, black, rent, smashed and jagged—the summit, perhaps, of a mountain range sunk beneath the waters in some lost age of the earth. It is barely a half-mile in length, its greatest width is but half of that, the highest point only about two hundred feet above the sea.

Flang Island (soon to be a place of tragedy, the scene of what is perhaps the strangest dénouement to murder on record) lies very near the fifty-fifth parallel of north latitude. The time was the beginning of July; to be precise, the date was the 2nd. At this season (unless the sky be overcast) darkness never settles upon that black and desolate place—the abode of a few seals and fewer sea-birds. The sun, his declination 23° north, does not set till near 9 o'clock; at midnight he is only twelve degrees below the (northern) horizon, so that there is no darkness but twilight only; and at half-past 3 he once more has emerged from out the wastes of ocean. How great the contrast at the opposite season! For, at the winter solstice, the sun does not rise till 8:30, to attain at midday an altitude of only a dozen degrees, and at half-past 3 he disappears. A strange place, forsooth, for any fairy to choose for a place of habitation—this dark and savage, this storm-beaten isle in the midst of the dark and tempestuous subarctic sea. A fairy's, though, it was, this Island of Flang. That, however, the lone watcher there on the summit was doomed never to know. But Cuthbert Griswold was to know it, know it soon and to his sorrow—that this was the Isle of the Fairy Morgana.

The little *Gorgon*, a twenty-five-foot sloop, was actually passing Flang when Griswold saw him. The sloop was sailing on a northeast course before a very gentle breeze from the south. At the time Cuthbert Griswold (the only soul on board, except a half-grown wolf-dog) made the discovery, the eastern extremity of the island was on his port beam, distant perhaps a little less than a half-mile. This part of the island rises sheer to a height of fifty feet or so, and there, on the very edge of that rock wall, was the figure of a man, clear-cut against the blue of the sky and signaling frantically. Even as Griswold saw him, the voice of the castaway came across the water, the sound faint as that soft wash of the sea against the sides of the *Gorgon*. On the instant the wolf-dog raised himself up from his warm bed and thrust his savage visage above the cockpit coaming, his look fixed upon Flang.

"A man, Pluto," said Griswold. "See him there? But what on earth is a man doing in this accursed place? Well, I have been on that island myself a couple of times, and perhaps people, had any seen me there, would have wondered the same thing. And look at that, Pluto: he is signaling to us like a man gone mad. If he's a castaway, little wonder, for a dozen years might pass, and never a sail lift above the horizon of this bit of ocean. We'll run down into the bay and see what it means."

Griswold put his helm over, and the little vessel glided off in a direction at right angles to the course on which she had been standing, slowly drawing in, as she advanced, toward the rocks, along which the surf broke with a sound like the low growl, so Griswold thought, of some savage beast.

A little space—the *Gorgon* was then about midway the isle—the sails were lowered and the gasoline engine was started. Slowly the little craft moved in toward the broken wall, passed in behind three rocks which thrust up out of the sea like monstrous black tusks and was heading into a passage, two hundred feet or so in width, that some convulsion of nature had riven into the island.

For a little distance the great fissure (which comes very near making of Flang two islets) ran slantingly. Then came a sharp turn to port, a gentle one to starboard, and the *Gorgon* was gliding out into a little oval-shaped basin, rock-walled and as placid as a mill-pond. On the left the rocks rose up sheer from the water's edge and to a height of one hundred feet. The other side was broken and smashed; in one place there was a bit of beach. Off went the engine, and, when he was abreast of this spot, Griswold let his anchor go in three fathoms water, it being low tide at the time.

"Hello!" he sang out to the figure, haggard and wobegone, that had just appeared on the ribbon of beach. "How the devil did you get here?"

"*Mother Goose,*" was the answer.

Griswold stared.

"Mother Goose? Do you mean that the old girl brought you here on her broomstick?"

A wan smile flitted across the face of the castaway.

"Trading schooner," he explained. "She was smashed on those rocks at the western end of the island. Every soul was lost but me."

"When was that?" Griswold asked.

"In that storm—on the 27th. The captain thought that he was well to the eastward of this island. The schooner caved in like an empty barrel smashed against a stone. Never saw so much as a single plank afterward. Don't know how it happened, but I found myself flung up into a cleft in the wall, and somehow I managed to crawl to a place of safety."

"But found," said Griswold, "that you hadn't landed in Eden."

"In hell," returned the castaway. "I knew that years might pass and no ship ever sight this cursed island—or sight me on it. But I knew that I could not live for years—perhaps not even for months. I'm nearly starved. Tried to get a seal but couldn't make it."

"Well," Griswold told him, "there is no dearth of *muckymuck* in the *Gorgon's* lazaret, and you can make up for lost time."

Griswold, as he spoke, was launching his little dingey—dinkey, he called it.

"I thought," the castaway said, "that you would never see me."

"Lucky thing for you that I did! And 'tis horrible to think that I might have passed by and left you here to your fate. But—well, you're safe now. No use worrying about what might have been, you know."

Safe? Little did either man dream of that revelation which a few short minutes were to bring. In that moment in which Griswold had sighted him there on the rock wall, signaling so frantically—in that very moment the castaway (though neither man dreamed it) had received the doom of death.

For this man, as Cuthbert Griswold was soon to learn, was Ferdinand Chantrell.

2. "You!"

"All alone?" queried the castaway as Griswold stepped into the little skiff.

"All alone, save for Pluto there. On my way from Antatu to Tamahnowis."

"I should think that you'd want a bigger boat and a crew of one at least."

Griswold laughed.

"Some folks," said he, "think that I'm crazy to be Christopher-Columbusing about in a craft like the *Gorgon;* but I've been half-way around the world in that little tub. Maybe some day I'll circumnavigate the globe in it just to show them that I'm not dippy."

Griswold was now moving toward the beach. The sloop was only fifty or sixty feet out.

"You seemed," said the other, "to know this place."

"Oh, yes. I have been here before, more than once. Queer place, this."

The next moment the bow rumbled up the strand and the little craft became stationary. Cuthbert Griswold arose and thrust forth a hand.

"Welcome, stranger," said he. "The little *Gorgon* isn't just what you'd call a palatial yacht, but I fancy that you'll find her better than these naked rocks of Flang. You are welcome to the best that she has to offer."

"You have saved my life!" exclaimed the other, wringing Griswold's hand—which was soon to send a bullet crashing into the speaker's heart. "And I am not a man that forgets. My name is Chantrell—Ferdinand Chantrell."

Griswold gave a low cry and dropped the other's hand as though it had been a deadly serpent.

"*You!*"

"What—what—?" faltered the castaway, recoiling from that fearful visage which was thrust toward him.

"You!" Griswold cried. "At last—you!"

"What—what are you talking about?"

"So you don't know *me?*"

"I don't. I never saw you before."

"I know that. But you ought to know who I am."

"*Who* are you?"

Griswold laughed—the sound sardonic, horrible. Pluto, the wolf-dog, out there on the *Gorgon,* was watching; but (as regards things like this meeting and what followed) wolf-dogs, like dead men, can tell no tales. But (what Griswold never dreamed) fairies can. And this was the Isle of the Fairy Morgans.

"Who am I?" Griswold said. "Can't you guess?"

"No."

"Well, well! He can't guess. Handsome Ferdy Chantrell, that devil with the ladies—so he can't guess who I am! Well, well! But why should I be surprised at that? For, of course, I am not the only one who has a score to settle with Handsome Ferdy, and he's wondering which one it can be. Of course! I might have known that. *She* wasn't the only one."

"She!" exclaimed Ferdinand Chantrell. "Whom do you mean?"

"See there, you hovering angels!" cried Griswold. "He admits it. He doesn't know whom I mean. If there had been only one, he wouldn't be puzzled the least; he would know who I am."

"Can't you tell me?"

"Yes!" half screamed Griswold. "I can tell you, all right! Her name was Amanda!"

Chantrell recoiled a step, and his haggard face went pale as ashes.

"You—you!"

"Yes! It is I—I! It is Cuthbert Griswold!"

"I thought that you were dead."

Griswold laughed.

"So that's your explanation? And, I suppose, that isn't the only thing that you thought. But you see that I am not dead, that I am very much alive. And at last I've got you—got you right where I want you. There is no one here to see, and Flang will hold its secret well. Why, it couldn't have been better if I had had the ordering of it all myself. It is almost too good to be true!"

Chantrell's look became hard, defiant.

"What do you mean?"

"What do I mean? That I am going to kill you," Griswold told him, "kill you and feed you to the fishes. Before I am done with you, Handsome Ferdy, you will wish that you had gone down with that schooner—wish to God that you had never been born."

"So you are going to murder me?"

"Call it what you like. No!" Griswold cried, whipping out a revolver. "Don't edge an inch nearer, or I'll drill you through this very instant. I intend to let you live a while, but that, of course, is contingent upon your good behavior."

"I am indeed grateful," said Chantrell, bowing with mock gravity.

Cuthbert Griswold stared, and then he laughed.

"You don't know what you are grateful for!"

"You!" exclaimed the other. "You! Millions of men—this island in the sea—and it had to be *you* that came!"

"Well, Handsome Ferdy, they say that truth is stranger than any fiction, you know. And who can guess what Nemesis may do? Handsome Ferdy! Well, well, and at last he stands before me. You know, I often wondered what you were like. What did Amanda see so wonderful in you, anyway? Well, well."

And he eyed Chantrell down and up and from this side and from that as though the man belonged to some strange species.

"Handsome Ferdy! How do you lady-killers do it, anyway? I can't say that I am a bit the wiser now that you stand here before me, even though I see that the name was not wholly unmerited. Oh, I can see that Handsome Ferdy is one of those guys that women go crazy over. But why do they do it? And I thought that my Amanda was far, far above any such weakness as that. Why did she fall for you? Well, well! She might have done the decent thing, though: she, the both of you, might have waited until she had divorced poor me. But no, while I was gone, slaving away for her, you had to steal her."

"Steal her!"

Chantrell laughed—a laugh that cut Griswold to the very heart.

"Steal her? No man has to *steal* a woman from the likes of you! As for a divorce, you know that she was afraid—afraid that you would murder her, as you threatened her more than once that you would. If ever fear, stark fear, had a woman's heart in its grip, it had Amanda's. No use trying any camouflage with me, Griswold. I know."

"I suppose so. What a lot you know! But Fate has given you into my hands to wreak my vengeance upon you. *Thou shalt not covet thy neighbor's wife.* You have had your hour of triumph. Now I shall have mine."

"So be it, then."

"You'll sing a very different tune before I am done with you, Handsome Ferdy. You'll curse the very hour that you were born into this world."

Ferdinand Chantrell laughed.

"You poor fool! Curse the hour I was born when I have known the heaven of a noble woman's love?"

"Bosh!" cut in Griswold, gnashing his teeth.

"Of course it is bosh to a warped, niggard soul such as yours. Love! You don't know what love is. You never can know."

"I should have had you to lesson me! But you are mine, mine at last, and you'll rue the day that you set eyes on Amanda!"

"Never!" cried Chantrell, his dark eyes flashing with a light that, to Griswold, for an instant, seemed to belong to some world more wonderful and mysterious than this. "She was mine—mine, *mine!* though I had her for one short year only. Rue the day? Nothing that you can do could make me do that. Rue the day that I saw Amanda? If I had a thousand thousand lives, and you a thousand thousand fiends to torture each one in a thousand thousand ways for a hundred thousand thousand years—if that were so, yet I would glory in my love for Amanda!"

"Gosh!" said Griswold. "They ought to have called you Ferdy the Hyperbolical."

For some moments, in silence, he gazed at Ferdinand Chantrell, then he said:

"But, poetics aside, was she, is she so very dear to you, though now she is—?"

"An angel," Chantrell exclaimed, "in heaven!"

"A skull and some bones," Griswold said, "unless, that is, she is a few ashes in an urn."

Chantrell stood silent. A strange change was coming over the face and mien of Griswold. He thrust the weapon into his pocket and smiled at the other in a mysterious manner.

"So you thought that I meant it?" he laughed. "Well, well!"

"What are you talking about?"

"That bit of play-acting of mine," Cuthbert Griswold told him. "So you thought that I meant it, Ferdy? Just a little joke, and—"

"Joke!"

"A bit of melodramatics, Ferdy," smiled Griswold. "So you thought that I was going to kill you? Forget all that. Amanda—a skull and a few bones now or a handful of ashes—is nothing to me, the memory of her even less than that. The world is full of fools, but there is not a bigger fool in it than the man or woman who would keep husband or wife when the heart of that husband or wife belongs to another. Of course, if you love the one who is going—as I loved Amanda—the loss is a bitter one. But it is in such moments that a man proves himself either a philosopher or a fool. If a fool, he is going to kill the lover or kill them both. If a philosopher, he says, 'Since she no longer cares for me and wants another, let her go,' and he consoles himself with the thought that she isn't the only fish in this puddle that men call life.

"As for the threats that you mentioned—well, I admit them, though they were largely melodramatics, Ferdy, as witness to the fact that, when the test came, I proved myself a philosopher. For do not think that I didn't follow you because I couldn't find you. I repeat, I was a philosopher. It was a bitter hour, but I said, 'Let her go, and may she find with him the happiness that she failed to find with me.' Yes, Ferdy, it was a cruel stroke; but that is what I said. And I would say it again."

"I am glad," said Chantrell after some hesitation, "that you look at it in so sensible a manner."

"The only thing, Ferdy, I wish that she had done the sensible, the decent thing—that she had waited and got a divorce. But I, with my cursed melodramatics—always was that way, Ferdy—am to blame for that, I suppose, and I hope that she'll forgive me for it. Well, it is done, and it cannot be mended. Peace to her soul."

Ferdinand Chantrell made no response. He was regarding the other in a searching, wondering manner. What was he to make of this strange business? Had Griswold's fearful threat, after all, been nothing but melodramatics? Or was this some fiendish cunning of a man fiendish and half mad?

"But come," said Griswold, turning. "Step into the tub, and we'll go out to the *Gorgon,* and I'll get you something to eat. Deuce of a way to treat a man who is half famished—telling him that you are going to murder him and feed him to the fishes! But sometimes, you know, Ferdy, a fellow must have his little joke."

"Joke! If all your jokes are of that grisly species, I hope that you'll never spring another on me."

"Ha, ha!" said Griswold, shoving off. "I fooled you that time. Admit it, Ferdy: you thought that I really meant it—meant to kill you."

"You certainly had a bloodthirsty, horrible look in your eye."

"Ha, ha!" barked Griswold.

"But why," Chantrell asked, "did you do it?"

"Just my idea of a little joke, Ferdy. Just a bit of melodramatics, as I said. Always was a weakness of mine. It has got me into a scrape more than once, but I could never resist it when the chance offered. I have been told a good many times that I missed my true vocation when I did not become an actor."

"If," said his victim, "all your acting could have been as real as that of a few minutes ago, you certainly did."

"I suppose so, Ferdy. But here's the *Gorgon,* and have you a feed in a jiffy."

Joke? Griswold grinned and chuckled to himself. A joke? It was a joke indeed. An actor? If that infernal fool only knew the truth! But he didn't. *That* was what made it a joke. Ferdy thought that he was going to live; that his, Griswold's, fearful threat had been nothing but melodramatics; thought that he, Griswold, was—a philosopher! Yes, Ferdy thought that he was going to be taken back to the world of men (and women) in the *Gorgon!* Ha, ha! That was delectable. Ferdy had visions of safety—undoubtedly of other Amandas. That would add to the bitterness of the cup when he drained it—perhaps in an hour, probably in two hours. Griswold didn't know yet; all he knew was that he was going to kill Handsome Ferdy, kill him here on this desolate and forbidding Island of Flang.

And how beautifully everything had befallen! No one would ever know what had happened to the schooner. No one would ever know that Ferdy Chantrell had even set foot on the island. And no living soul would ever know that he himself, Cuthbert Griswold, had met Chantrell there and killed him. Not a soul was there to see, not a sign would remain, and the Island of Flang could never tell.

"A joke!" thought the schemer. "Ha, ha! He is yet to learn what a grim joke it really is!"

Never once, however, did the thought flicker athwart the dark brain of Cuthbert Griswold that he himself might learn that, too.

3. The Murder

They stood upon the very summit of the isle—Griswold, Chantrell and the wolf-dog, Pluto.

"Queer place, this Flang," said Griswold.

"Yes," thought the other, "but no more queer than you are yourself. Now, why did we come up to this summit? Maybe my imagination is playing me tricks; but I'll be mighty glad when I am once more back in the world of men."

A covert watch upon Cuthbert Griswold as he stood there would have enhanced those vague and sinister misgivings that the victim tried, but in vain, to banish. This visit to the summit of Flang had been no mere whim on Griswold's part. He had come with a definite object in view. This would be one murder that would never out. Though alone with his victim on an uninhabited isle in the midst of a deserted sea, he would take no chances, would make sure that the sea *was* deserted. One could never tell. Ships had a strange way of suddenly appearing in the most unlikely places and at the most unlikely times.

Slowly, covertly his eye made the circuit of the distant horizon. Not a spot visible anywhere. The sea was deserted indeed. And he was alone with his victim, alone with Handsome Ferdy—who soon would be a thing the very antithesis of handsome, a thing from which an Amanda would recoil in horror. Alone, alone! Ha, ha, he had now made sure that the secret could never out. Why did he wait? The wolf-dog, the dark rocks —they could never tell.

"But not here," said Griswold. "I am going to fling him into the sea, feed him to the fishes. Why should I drag him over there when he can walk to the spot himself?"

"I wonder," Chantrell said, "how far it is out to that skyline."

"About sixteen nautical miles," Griswold told him, "nineteen statute; we are at a height of just about two hundred feet."

"Only nineteen miles? I thought it was much farther than that."

"Oh, no. At a height of fifty feet, one can see out only nine miles, statute; one hundred feet, thirteen miles; three hundred feet, twenty-three; four hundred, only twenty-six miles; and so on."

"I didn't know that. But how still," said Chantrell, gazing curiously about him, "it has become! I wasn't aware of the change until this moment. There is but the softest movement of the air now."

"'Tis true," Griswold nodded, turning his head as though listening. "I didn't notice myself how marked the change was."

"And," added the other, "it seems warmer up here."

"It does. Probably that is because the breeze, gentle though it was, has fallen."

A thermometer at sea-level and another here at the summit would have shown a difference of more than 15°, Fahrenheit. Not that Griswold, had he known it, would have given this fact a second thought. Nor did he once think that something might be hidden there beyond that distant skyline. Nor would he have given *that* more than a second thought had he known it.

Already the Fairy Morgana was waving her wand—she whose magic was to bring the secret of Griswold and the man himself to wrack and utter ruin.

"Well," Griswold said suddenly, "let's go down, Ferdy."

His victim arose with alacrity.

"But," Griswold added, "not to the *Gorgon* just yet. Let's go over there," waving a hand toward the eastern extremity of the island.

The other made no response, and they made their way down in silence, the wolf-dog following, savage of visage and almost as noiseless as some gliding shadow.

Suddenly—they were then drawing near the edge of the rock wall, here some fifty feet in height—Griswold jerked out his revolver.

"Watch me," he said, his look upon a passing gull, "plug that fellow."

"What," Chantrell asked, "do you want to shoot the poor devil for?"

"Sport, Ferdy, sport. And just to see if my eye and hand are in trim. I used to be considered a crack shot with a revolver, Ferdy. But no," said Griswold, turning until the weapon was bearing directly upon the other, "why should I send a bullet into the bird? It never harmed me."

"Look out!" cried Chantrell. "Turn that thing the other way!"

He stepped quickly to one side, but the weapon followed him.

"Watch what you're doing! That thing's pointed right at me!"

"At you?" queried Griswold with simulated surprise. "I'm glad you told me, Ferdy. You see, I was thinking of something else."

The victim made another swift movement, but it was only to find, as before, that the weapon was still bearing upon him.

Then of a sudden Ferdinand Chantrell understood, and he stood very straight and still, looking squarely into the terrible, fiendish eyes of Griswold.

"Ha, ha!" said Griswold, his voice harsh and quivering with passion. "You see the joke now, Handsome Ferdy! You thought that I didn't mean it. You thought that I was acting when I wasn't and that I wasn't when I was. Ha, ha! If you have a prayer to make, Handsome Ferdy, be about it quick, for I am going to kill you as I said I would, and as I said I wouldn't—kill you and feed you to the fishes and the slimy things. You'll never steal another Amanda."

"You beast! You insane, cowardly beast!"

Griswold's answer was a taunting laugh.

Of a sudden the eyes of the victim moved, and the next instant they had fixed themselves, it seemed, on some object directly behind Griswold.

"Look!" cried Ferdinand Chantrell, pointing. *"Look at that!"*

But Griswold chuckled and shook his head knowingly.

"Don't think that you can play that old trick on me!" he said. "Don't you ever think, Handsome Ferdy, that I'm going to look behind me. You are too close for one thing, and there isn't anything to see there, anyway."

"But there is something—*in the sky!*"

"In the sky! Ferdy, Ferdy! This puerile nonsense will never save you. No! Don't move another inch! Well, then, take *that* and *that!*"

Chantrell went staggering and collapsed upon his face, two bullets in his chest. With a heavy groan, he rolled over onto his back, his look upon the twisted, grinning face of Griswold.

"Not dead yet?" Griswold said. "Then take another. But no. I'll give you time, all the time you'll want, perhaps, to think over your sins and of what you will look like when the fishes are making of your handsome face a death's-head. Ah, you wince at that thought, Handsome Ferdy! You had your hour of triumph, and now I have mine. Glare away! If looks were daggers, my heart would be cut throbbing from my chest. But no look or word of yours can hurt me now. Probably, however, *this* will give you something else to think about."

He raised the revolver, took deliberate aim and sent a shattering bullet into Chantrell's right knee-cap. Again he fired, the bullet this time burying itself in the joint, right between the bones. Chantrell screamed.

Cuthbert Griswold looked down upon his victim and laughed in triumph and gloating.

"I told you!" he cried. "Now you are paying for those stolen kisses. You scream. What do you think of the price, eh? I told you that, before I was done with you, you would rue the day that you set eyes on Amanda."

"For God's sake," cried Chantrell, "kill me—*kill* me! If you are a man and not a fiend, send a bullet into my heart and end it!"

"Not yet, Handsome Ferdy. But here is one for your other knee-joint."

As the last word left his lips, Griswold fired. Chantrell did not scream this time, but his fingers dug at the rock until the flesh broke.

"Ha, ha! Were her kisses worth the price that you are paying, Handsome Ferdy? And I wonder if you know how sweet is this, the hour of my triumph. And it is all the sweeter because I shall never be called to account for it. Flang will keep its secret well, Ferdy."

Again he raised the weapon and, firing twice, smashed the left knee of his victim. Then he sent shattering bullets into Chantrell's elbows and wrists.

"Fainted at last," Griswold laughed. "A bullet into the heart and end it all! Well, here it is, Ferdy—now when you can not feel the mercy of it."

And so at last it was ended. There on the black rock lay the lifeless body of Ferdinand Chantrell—who had known the glory of a noble woman's love and the horror of a husband's vengeance. There it lay, a thing horrible to look upon but not so horrible, in blood and death, as the thing that stood and looked down upon it.

The wolf-dog crept forward and sniffed blood and corpse, then slunk back as though a sudden fear had entered the savage heart of it.

"Even Pluto!" Griswold said aloud. "Yes, even a wolf-dog slinks from the blood that warmed the false heart of him."

How long he stood there by the corpse, Griswold himself never knew—*though another did.* At last, however, he thrust the revolver into his pocket, seized the body, dragged it to the edge and sent it over into the sea.

For some moments—he did not know how long it was, *but one watching did*—he crouched there at the edge. The water was shallow there below, and he could make out the body of Chantrell, indistinct, blurred. At times it moved, for all the world like a thing endowed with life, but that was caused by the movements of the water itself.

Of a sudden these words of Chantrell flashed through Griswold's brain:

"But there is something—*in the sky!*"

Ha, ha! Ferdy had thought that he would fall for that old, old trick. Ferdy had thought that he would turn to look and that Ferdy could leap upon him. But he, Griswold, had been no such fool as that. *Something behind you!* That, whether spoken or looked, had brought many a man to grief; but it had not brought him. But—in the sky? Why had Ferdy said that it was in the sky?

Cuthbert Griswold arose and turned his look in the direction in which Chantrell had pointed.

What was that? There, there—*in the sky!* A dim, fading, hideous *face,* its look fixed upon him! *A face!*

Griswold dashed a hand across his eyes. A face? He laughed aloud. There was nothing there! His eyes, his brain had tricked him. A face, a face dim and fading and hideous and in the distant sky there above the sea! He would be seeing spirits next, fairies and goblins. What a strange weakness of nerves and brain! He had never dreamed that he would go like that. Such things were for women. But it would not happen again. A face—and in the sky! Again Griswold laughed aloud. A momentary weakness. Yes, nothing more—only the weakness of a moment. But he was himself now—was Cuthbert Griswold, he of the steady nerves and the sober brain. This, too, his hour of triumph! And Flang would keep his secret well!

4. Guy Oxford

"Well, Pluto," said Griswold as he made his way back toward the *Gorgon,* "it's a little after 12; fine breeze, too, springing up now; but we won't get under way until the morning. Yes, we'll stay, *tillicum*—if for no other reason, just to show the spirit of Handsome Ferdy that we are not afraid to linger near his sepulcher. His spirit! Ha, ha! I wonder where the spirit of Ferdy is right now, Pluto."

And so it was, some hours later, that they found him there. Ships, Cuthbert Griswold had told himself, have a strange way of suddenly appearing in the most unlikely places and at most unlikely times. And there was the schooner *Queen Mab,* three-masted, white and beautiful, come to Flang, though Griswold did not know, what with the rock wall that shut off the view, until her little launch came putting in through the fissure. Of the six occupants of the launch, which came up alongside the sloop, two at once held the look and thoughts of Griswold. The first he knew at a glance to be a ship's officer—the *Queen Mab's* skipper, as he soon learned, Captain Spar. But it was the other man who really held Griswold's look. This individual was tall, lean to emaciation and with the blackest eyes that

Cuthbert Griswold had ever seen in a human head, his look so impassive that Griswold wondered if a smile had ever touched a single lineament of that lean, swarthy visage of his. Cuthbert Griswold had not the slightest idea who or what this man was, but he distinctly felt, though he could not have told why, that the being before him was one amongst a million. And, in spite of himself, the murderer felt a chill pass through his heart when he learned that this man was the noted scientist and (at times) criminologist, Guy Oxford.

The next instant, however, he inwardly flung a savage curse at this weakness of his. Afraid? Why should he be afraid because this was Guy Oxford? True, the man had solved many a mystery that other investigators, the best to be had, had given up as insoluble; the powers of which this man sometimes showed himself the master seemed well-nigh uncanny; but, bah, what had he, Cuthbert Griswold, to fear from the presence, mysterious though that presence was, of Guy Oxford here on the Island of Flang? Mysterious! But why should there be anything mysterious about it? He was letting his imagination run riot. The *Queen Mab* and Guy Oxford would have come whether he, Griswold, had ever set foot on the island or not. It had just happened, that was all. But *why* had they come to Flang?

And then another fear, a fear sudden and terrible, went through the heart of the murderer. The blood! The blood there in that spot in which he had killed Chantrell! If he had only known, he would have removed that. But he had never dreamed. And the body too! But, then, one would have to look closely to see it; and why should anyone do that? The blood—but what on earth was the matter with him, anyway? For he could explain that. Explain it easily. Yes, *that* would be his explanation. What a fool to let such a fear get him! But would it work? Of course it would work—unless this cursed Guy Oxford were to place some of Chantrell's blood under the microscope. But why should Guy Oxford ever do that?

But the *Queen Mab*. Why had the *Queen Mab* come here to Flang?

"This is indeed a surprise, Mr. Oxford," said Cuthbert Griswold, "meeting you here in this God-forsaken sea, on this Island of Flang."

"The cruise of the *Queen Mab*," returned Oxford, "is a purely scientific one, and scientists, you know, sometimes visit strange places."

"Yes, yes; of course! Too bad, though," Griswold smiled, "that we haven't a mystery here for you to solve. But there is no mystery here."

"No, Mr. Griswold; there is no mystery here——to be solved."

Griswold chuckled to himself. Another joke, and wasn't it a good one, too?

No mystery here. Ha, ha, if Guy Oxford only knew! Wasn't it a joke, though? Too bad he couldn't share it with them! It was a joke indeed. For Guy Oxford, as the murderer was soon to learn, *did* know.

"However," Griswold added, "if you had been here about noon, you would have seen murder done."

What a strange look was that which the captain flashed at Oxford! Strange, too, was that expression which, for a fleeting moment, Griswold saw in those strange black eyes of the scientist.

"Oh, don't misunderstand me, gentlemen!" Griswold laughed. "The victim was Buck, a wolf-dog, father to Pluto here. Went mad, and I had to kill the poor brute."

"Where," Captain Spar asked rather quickly, "did that happen?"

"Over there," replied Griswold, waving a hand, "at the eastern end of the island."

"I should like," Oxford said, "to visit that spot."

"*That* spot?"

The other nodded.

"Of course," said Griswold. "At once?"

"At once. Will you guide us to it?"

"With pleasure," Cuthbert Griswold told him with an inward shiver. "But—but why, Mr. Oxford, are you so interested in that spot? There is nothing there but blood."

"What did you do with the body?"

"Ah, I see; you are interested in rabies, as well as in all those scientific subjects—and in crime."

"I am interested," the scientist answered, "in everything."

"Of course, of course. As for the body, unfortunately I cast it into the sea. Poor Buck! I hated to kill the noble creature; but, when they go mad, there is nothing else that you can do."

"Of course," said Oxford. "But—well, Mr. Griswold, I am anxious to see that spot, anyway."

"Yes, yes; of course."

Still Griswold made no movement to conduct the other to it. The blood, that cursed telltale blood! Why had he mentioned it? But there. He had done the wise thing. Of course he had. They would, in all likelihood, have chanced upon the spot. And the blood was not telltale—unless examined under a microscope. And, now that he had mentioned it—mentioned it in so nonchalant a manner—

there would be no suspicion, no examination under a microscope. So why was he hesitating? He must not hesitate a moment longer. That was the worst thing that he could do.

A few minutes, therefore, and they had reached the scene of the tragedy—the murderer himself, Oxford, Captain Spar and two sailors. Though he evinced not the slightest hesitation, the slightest uneasiness, yet a horrible fear had Griswold in its grip. It was as though this dark, mysterious Oxford *knew* something. Why had he been so anxious to come to this spot? Why, on the arriving there, had he motioned for the others to keep back, and why was he examining the place so keenly? And there! Look at that! He was thrusting a finger of his right hand right into a mass of the coagulated blood—the coagulated blood of Ferdinand Chantrell!

Griswold did not see Oxford's signal, but of a sudden he discovered that the others had come up to him, up to Griswold, that is—that Captain Spar stood at his right side, those two husky sailors at his left.

"Hum!" said Oxford, raising his look from his finger and fixing it upon the eyes of Cuthbert Griswold. "You say that this is the blood of a dog?"

"Yes, yes! Of course it was a dog! The blood of Buck!"

"Imaginary dogs," said the scientist, "don't have any blood at all."

"Why, why do you think, Mr. Oxford, that, that—?"

"I don't think," the other interrupted; "I know: this is not the blood of any canine; it is the blood of a human being, the blood of a man!"

"A man?"

Griswold barked out a sardonic laugh.

"I confess," he said, "that I don't see your little joke. There was no man here, only poor Buck."

"There was no dog here," Oxford told him, "save Pluto there. The victim was a man."

"Ha, ha!" said Griswold. "I must say, though, that you have a queer idea of humor, Mr. Oxford. Your humor is a little too grisly for me—even though your victim is only an imaginary one."

"Come, Griswold! You might as well make a clean breast of it. Why did you kill him and in a manner so brutal?"

"As I told you, because he went mad; and there was nothing brutal about it. Poor Buck! He was a noble creature."

Then a strange thing happened: Guy Oxford laughed. And that laugh sent a chill through and through the heart of the murderer.

"You—you fiend!" Griswold cried.

"Why a fiend?" Oxford queried sweetly.

"Well, you look like one, and you laugh like one, too."

"I do? Gently there, Griswold!" Oxford exclaimed softly. "I would suggest that you keep your hand away from that revolver. Better get that weapon, Captain. No telling what he may try to do when he learns the truth."

Griswold's right hand made a sudden movement toward the piece, but the hand of Captain Spar was swifter, and thus, in a flash, Griswold found himself disarmed.

He laughed defiantly.

"Say, what's the idea? Is this the Island of—?"

"'Tis the Island of the Fay."

"The fay?" Griswold ejaculated. "What fay?"

"For the present," Guy Oxford answered, "she shall be nameless."

"So there is a fairy here?" And Griswold laughed harshly. "A fairy on Flang? Ha, ha! Why not Circe, Mr. Scientist, and make a good job of it?"

"My fairy," Guy Oxford told him, "did better than even Circe herself could have done."

"Oh, gosh!" Cuthbert Griswold exclaimed. "I suppose I'll be hearing about gnomes and spooks and goblins next. So Flang is the Island of the Fay? I thought, from the way you fellows are acting, that it was a movie studio in Hollywood. But what's the meaning of all this hocus-pocus and flubdub, anyway? What's the meaning of this grisly mummery—putting your finger into that gore and pretending you can see that it is human blood? No, you *see* more than that; you can even tell the sex of this imaginary victim that in reality was Buck. The victim, you say, was a man. Might it not have been a woman, or a baby, or—or a fairy?"

"It might, but it wasn't. And that isn't the only thing that I saw."

"On that bloody finger of yours?" Griswold asked.

Guy Oxford raised his hand and eyed the finger more closely than before.

"Do you want me to tell you?" he asked after some moments of silence.

"Of course. Tell me everything."

"It was not a dog," Guy Oxford said, "that you killed in this spot, Griswold. It was a man, and you murdered him in cold blood, in a manner most brutal and revolting. You felled him with two bullets in, in—"

Oxford eyed his finger very keenly.

"Yes, in the chest. Then you proceeded to torture him by smashing—at any rate, I believe that the bullets smashed them—his knee-joints, his elbows and his wrists."

A fierce, inhuman cry burst from Griswold.

"Shall I tell you more?" Guy Oxford queried. "Shall I tell you that you dragged the body over there to the edge and tumbled it off into the sea?"

"You—you cunning fiend!" Griswold cried. "You cunning, cursed fiend! Where were you hiding?"

"Then you confess the deed?"

"Why should I deny it any longer when you— oh, you cunning devil!—when you know everything? You fiend, oh, you crafty fiend! Yes, I confess it. Go over there to the edge and you can see his body."

"We'll do that presently, and we'll recover the body if that is possible. So you admit that you killed him?"

"Yes, I killed Handsome Ferdy—Handsome Ferdy Chantrell. And I would kill him again. Do you hear that? I would kill him again. I glory in the deed! I wish that I had him here so I could torture him once more! I would make a better job of it the second time. But you—you!"

Griswold glanced about a little wildly.

"Where were you hiding? There was no sail in sight. I went up to the very summit and made sure of that before I killed him. This, I thought, was one murder that would never out. But you—you saw it all."

"Yes," said Guy Oxford; "I saw it all."

"But where was your *Queen Mab* then? In God's name, where were you?"

Oxford turned and waved a hand to the southward.

"The *Queen Mab* was down there, distant something over thirty-five miles, statute, and so below the horizon to one standing on the very summit of this island."

"And you? Where were you hiding, and how had you got here on Flang?"

"I wasn't hiding," Guy Oxford told him. "And I wasn't here. I was on board the *Queen Mab,* and the vessel herself, as I have said, even the very tips of her masts, was hidden from here."

"Do you expect me to believe that? Why not give over this flubdub, Oxford? You were *here,* or you could not have *seen.* But you were seen! And I thought that it was only a trick of Ferdy's! Yes, you were seen, and I—I never dreamed it."

"You mean when he pointed—just before he made to spring at you and you shot him?"

"Yes," said Griswold. "But how could it have been you? He said that you— he said *it* was in the sky!"

Guy Oxford looked at Captain Spar, and Griswold saw a smile in those black (and to the murderer terrible) eyes of his.

"Up in the sky!" Guy Oxford said. "We were! Yes, we were in two places at once, though, of course, we didn't know that until I saw Chantrell point."

"What on earth are you talking about?"

"About our being on the *Queen Mab's* deck and yet up in the sky. You should have turned, Griswold, turned and seen us there. Then, perhaps, your hour of triumph would not have proved your hour of disaster and ruin. And a fairy—Griswold, 'twas a fairy that did it all! I told you this is the Island of the Fay."

5. The Fairy Morgana

"A fairy?" Cuthbert Griswold exclaimed. "Do you expect me to believe such bosh? You a scientist and talking about fairies!"

"Your scientist," Oxford returned, "is the true believer in fairies—only he doesn't call them that, unless he happens to be in a poetic mood."

"You and all your fairies and your hocus-pocus and your flubdub be damned!" Griswold cried. "What I want to know is this: where were you hiding, and how had you got here? Handsome Ferdy no more dreamed than I did myself that another man was on this island, on this—ha, ha, this Island of the Fay."

"I told you that I wasn't here, that I was on board the *Queen Mab*. But I had an excellent little telescope. Oh, not one of your spy-glasses but an astronomical, fitted, of course, with a terrestrial eyepiece, so that the image is upright."

"But you were thirty-five miles away! A line drawn from the very summit of Flang—and I was one hundred and fifty feet below that—to the very tip of the *Queen Mab's* mainmast would be intercepted by the ocean. Can you, with this wonderful telescope of yours, see around curves?"

"No. But you forget my fairy! No telescope can enable a man to see what is on the other side of a hill; but my fairy has shown men that more than once. Do you want an instance? Here you are:

"Between Ramsgate, England, and Dover Castle, a hill intervenes—or did when this happened. Above this hill—to an observer at Ramsgate—only the turrets of the castle were visible. Yet Dr. Vince and a companion, on the 2nd of August, 1806, saw the whole castle itself. And not only did they see the whole of it, but the castle seemed to be *on their side* of the hill! Oh, she's a wonderful fairy, Griswold."

The murderer groaned.

"Then," continued Guy Oxford, "there were the horsemen seen on Sonterfell, a hill in Scotland, in the year 1744. These figures, performing various military evolutions, were visible for over two hours, until darkness concealed them. Yet there was no man there where those troopers were moving; but a body of rebels were going through their exercises *on the other side of the fell!*

"There is the well-known Specter of the Brocken, too. Our fairy again, Griswold. And she visits the Lake of Killarney, also. Men moving along the shore of that romantic sheet often appear to be walking (or riding) out on the very lake itself—a phenomenon that doubtless explains the legend of O'Donoghue.

> "'And spirits, from all the lake's deep bowers,
> Glide o'er the blue waves scattering flowers,
> Around my love and thee.'

"And we have a record of her visit in 1595 to desolate Nova Zembla, where, ending the long arctic night, she brought the sun to some shipwrecked Dutch sailors sixteen days before that on which he should have appeared according to calculation. The sun was more than four degrees below the horizon at the time; but our fairy waved her wand, and there he was shining in the sky.

"On Sunday, December the 17th, 1826, she was in the vicinity of Poitiers, and before three thousand worshipers (and just as one of the divines was speaking of that emblem of the Christian faith seen in the heavens by Constantine and his army) a cross suddenly took form in the sky—a great cross 'of a bright silver color, tinged with red.' A miracle, said the devout, while, according to the scientist, a magnified image of a cross which had been placed near the church had been 'cast on the concave surface of some atmospheric mirror.'

"In 1822, in the polar sea, she revealed her presence to Captain Scoresby by limning in the sky an inverted image of his father's ship, the *Fame,* which was almost as far from his own vessel as the *Queen Mab* was distant from Flang. In 1839 she was with Wilkes off Cape Horn. A favorite spot of hers is the Strait of Messina, so often transformed by our fairy's magic into a catoptric theater. There, for centuries, with her spectral witchery, she amazed and awed the ignorant and set at naught the explanations of the wise.[1]

"I think, Griswold," Oxford concluded, "that you know the name of my fairy now."

---

1. "The complexity of these phenomena [looming and mirage] is enormous, nor, except in most general terms, have they been adequately explained."—Hastings.

The murderer nodded and groaned aloud in bitterness of soul.

"The Fay Morgana!"

"The Fay Morgana," said Guy Oxford.

"I was so careful," Griswold cried, "so sure; this was one vengeance that would never out; and then, by a cursed mirage, to be brought to this!"

"There were two images of the isle," said Guy Oxford, "the lower inverted, the upper erect. Undoubtedly they were greatly magnified, certainly they appeared to be no farther off than five or six miles. Everything was extraordinarily distinct, so that, with telescopic aid, I saw you and your victim almost as plainly as though I had been here close at hand, instead of thirty-five miles away. In all likelihood, too, the image, or images, of the *Queen Mab* (seen by Chantrell) were as remarkable as those of the island itself."

"And I thought," exclaimed Griswold bitterly, "that Flang would keep the secret well, the secret that in reality never was a secret at all, what with that cursed looming—that cursed Fairy Morgana, to use your poetical term. But the blood? Why did you put your finger into that blood?"

"I suppose I ought to be somewhat ashamed of that mummery," said Guy Oxford; "but I did it so that my perfect knowledge of the crime might be to you all the greater mystery. Revelation of the truth at that moment would have been premature.

"And, besides," he added, "you didn't believe in fairies then."

`Bibliography

Draconda. Weird Tales 2, No. 4 (November 1923): 3–17, 84; 3, No. 1 (January 1924): 43 55; 3, No. 2 (February 1924): 53–65; 3, No. 3 (March 1924): 59–72; 3, No. 4 (April 1924): 57–67, 84; 4, No. 2 (May/June/July 1924): 41–49.

"In Amundsen's Tent." *Weird Tales* 11, No. 1 (January 1928): 72–84.

"The Isle of the Fairy Morgana." *Weird Tales* 11, No. 2 (February 1928): 237–52.

"The Voice of Bills." *Weird Tales* 8, No. 4 (October 1926): 449–61.

"The Voices in the Cliff." *Weird Tales* 5, No. 5 (May 1925): 225–34.

Printed in Dunstable, United Kingdom

66207538R00171